When Winter Comes

When Winter Comes

V.A. SHANNON

KENSINGTON BOOKS are published by

Kensington Publishing Corp.
119 West 40th Street
New York, NY 10018

All Kensington titles, imprints, and distributed lines are available at special quantity discounts for bulk purchases for sales promotion, premiums, fund-raising, educational, or institutional use.

Special book excerpts or customized printings can also be created to fit specific needs. For details, write or phone the office of the Kensington Sales Manager: Kensington Publishing Corp., 119 West 40th Street, New York, NY 10018. Attn. Sales Department. Phone: 1-800-221-2647.

eISBN-13: 978-1-4967-1651-4
eISBN-10: 1-4967-1651-5
First Kensington Electronic Edition: November 2018

ISBN-13: 978-1-4967-1650-7
ISBN-10: 1-4967-1650-7
First Kensington Trade Paperback Printing: November 2018

10 9 8 7 6 5 4 3 2 1

Printed in the United States of America

Prologue

December 1859

Christmas Eve. Our parlor is decorated in readiness for the holiday. Twisted along the mantelshelf is a long skein of ivy and in the hearth below a fire of fragrant cedar logs blazes up. The golden-skinned winter apples that sit in a blue dish at my elbow mingle their scent with the spicy fragrance of the little evergreen tree over in the corner of the room. Jacob dug it up yesterday, and has planted it in a wooden pail.

Beneath its branches the children have set out their shoes in a neat row, three sets of them filled with flowers, in the certain expectation that St. Nicholas will come in the night and exchange the flowers for gingerbread and oranges. Even Meggie, who at twelve—nearly thirteen—considers herself vastly grown up, and who knows that the gingerbread boys I made yesterday in our kitchen are the same gingerbread boys that will make their way into those shoes, and that jovial Saint Nick is really just her gray-beard old pa, has shined up her good leather boots in readiness.

After the girls had finally gone to their beds, chattering and laughing and declaring that they would stay awake and creep downstairs at midnight to catch Saint Nick at his work, Jacob and I set to and decorated the tree so that it would be a surprise in the morning. Clipped to every branch is a tin holder with a candle waiting to be lit, and a little carved animal hanging from a string—pigs and horses, ducks and rabbits and bears. There are angels, too, and stars and hearts. Jacob has whittled these in the evenings, using scraps of wood left over from his work. My husband is a craftsman, making chairs and cupboards and tables that sell in Sacramento and Yuba, and even as far away as some of the fine shops in the big towns on the coast.

This is my life, now. The Christmas tree and the evergreens on the hearth. The three little pairs of shoes, with their oranges and gingerbread. The gifts sent from Jacob's family back in the Old Country waiting to be unwrapped and exclaimed over after breakfast in the morning; and, across the room, Jacob asleep in his big chair, his hands folded across his chest, which rises and falls with the slow rumble of his breathing.

On the table before me is my journal, given to me by my husband this very evening. I cannot say it is a welcome gift, though it is a beautiful thing, bound in green leather with a little silver lock. There is a matching key on a silver chain that Jacob put round my neck, and a kiss with it.

But truly, what is there to write? The purpose of a journal is to write down the events of the day, and for the past thirteen years every day has passed the same, and I guess I have been content it should be so; caring for my family, with nothing out of the ordinary to fill the pages. But I must show some signs of appreciating this kind thought. So I have set myself down with my pen and the blotter, a smile on my face and great reluctance in my heart, to record the events of this day.

I write by candlelight and the light of the fire, so a long finger of black shadow follows my pen as it scratches across the clean white paper. Behind it comes a sad trail of crossings out and blots, for my penmanship leaves much to be desired. Around the room, shadows jump and startle, as the fire shifts and settles. A last tongue of flame suddenly snatches up an overlooked morsel of kindling. It flares up, bright and alive, before dying away, finally, to red embers. The red embers fall in upon themselves, and give up their heat at last, and crumble into gray ash. Outside the wind is rising. It moans, and rattles the windowpanes. And with it comes the snow.

1

There was a special service in church this morning, which was filled to bursting.

Preacher Holden—well now, there is a storyteller. He can tell a Bible story like no one else I ever heard. His tales always seem to start somewhere in the middle, like a traveler who's been set down smack in the middle of a wood. Off he sets on his journey, sometimes looking ahead and sometimes over his shoulder. Soon enough this thing reminds him of that, and that thing recalls another, and Preacher Holden wanders round the highways and byways of his story until, by some mystery known only to him, he arrives back where he began.

His services are well attended, and not just out of a sense of duty, or a fear of being judged wanting by our neighbors. It's because one minute we're thinking how hard the benches are and what we'll be eating for our dinners, and the next, we're right along with Jonah, trapped in that whale's stomach and feeling miserable as all get-out. At the same time we're feeling sorry for the whale with that great undigested lump inside him, hammering and kicking at his insides and wailing to be set free.

If it's the feast for the prodigal son, our mouths water for the smell of the hot butter and cinnamon in Mrs. Jackson's apple turnovers that she's so famous for; or we'll find ourselves sitting beside the happy couple at Cana and quietly wishing for something a bit stronger than water to toast them in.

When he comes to the end of the story, Preacher Holden lets us sit for a minute and digest his words. Then we come to realize that along the way he's managed to set traps for the unwary, adding in sly comments that point to those of us who've sinned somewhat and need a little gentle reminding of it. And he always ends up with a few home truths that catch out those of us that have let our minds wander away.

He had plenty of those today, for it is during his story that the snow begins falling on the other side of the big arched window that we subscribed for last spring. Snow on Christmas Eve! The children are wriggling in their seats, desperate to get outside, and even the older folks who should know better are nudging their neighbors, jerking their heads toward the windows with their eyebrows raised and smiling themselves silly, as if they'd never seen snow before.

Perhaps some of them hadn't, for it almost never snows here. We have a few days of pretty heavy rain through December and January, but other than that, even when it's cold enough to want the fires lit from breakfast onward and an extra quilt or two on the beds, most days give us blue skies and sun. The grass stays green and the crops are good and lush year-round, and the animals fare well.

Our own animals do better than most, for I feed them with a generous hand. They don't amount to much, a few chickens and a goat or two. We don't have cows. I don't like to hear their lowing, a sad and lonely noise to my way of thinking. The rooster crowing, good and loud, and the hens squawking over which has the choicest bit of potato peeling or the last shuck of corn, that's a noise I like to hear.

I wonder if Jacob thought to shut them safely into the henhouse when the snow started up. Once the thought has entered my head I cannot shift it, and I stop listening to the Bible story and think about the snow instead.

Preacher Holden announces the last hymn. It's one of my favorites, "Lord, We Thank Thee for This Day." Bustling up the aisle toward the little upright pianoforte comes Mrs. Holden—his mother, not his wife, for Preacher Holden is a single young man of but eight-and-twenty. He is exceeding handsome, with dark flashing eyes and brown hair curling over his starched white collar, so attendance at his church might not be just on account of his storytelling skills. But he has his eye on Betsey Mueller, a pretty girl of eighteen or so. With three much older sisters all long since married and families of their own, I guess Betsey's arrival was a surprise to her ma, who must have thought herself long since free of the burden of child-rearing. I know the family well. Betsey's father, Heinrich, owns the lumberyard along with my husband, and Heinrich and Jacob were young men together in Germany before they set out to adventure to the New World and pitched up here in California.

Mrs. Holden is a widow, and on the lookout for husband number three, or so they say. She's in an outfit I've not seen before. It's a sober enough shade of blue, in keeping with Preacher Holden's views on appropriate dress for women, but even so, as she rustles past me I hear the distinctive sound of a silk taffeta petticoat. There's a hint of lace at her wrists, too, and some startling green and yellow feathers in her bonnet. She seats herself at the key-

board with a girlish shake of her head that sets her curls dancing—curls that have surely seen the benefit of blacking lotion as well as the curl papers—and a single yellow feather detaches itself from the bonnet and goes floating up into the air.

My close friend Minnie Arbuthnot raises her eyebrows at me from across the aisle. Her mouth twitches, and despite my increasing fears for my poor chickens, mine does the same. Respectable wives and mothers we might be, but when we are together we can't help laughing over any silly thing, just as much as the foolish girls in the schoolroom. I bite my lips together, my shoulders shaking, and look down at the floor until I can control myself.

I've left seven-year-old Hannah and six-year-old Clara at home with Jacob, who has a head cold and needs to stay in the warm. But I have my Meggie to one side of me, and we raise to our feet along with the rest, opening our hymnals. On the other side of me is old Peabody, the owner of the town mercantile, as close with a smile as he is with a cent. He only comes to church as the chance to get warm for nothing. But even Mr. Peabody can't sit when all else are standing, so with a great show of suffering he pulls himself to his feet, disclosing the fact that he has been sitting upon a newspaper. It's one of the local scandal sheets that spreads speculation and tittle-tattle, not a respectable sort of periodical at all.

Mrs. Holden strikes up the opening chords of the hymn. I open my mouth and take a deep breath, ready to sing. Mr. Peabody's newspaper slithers to the floor and my eyes follow it, and I suddenly make sense of the upside-down print of the headline. My mouth stays open but not a sound comes out.

We come out of church to find that the snow has stopped, with the paths and tree branches frosted as thick as a white layer cake. Folks are saying how it looks a right pretty pic-

ture, and asking one another if they think it'll stay put for a day or two more. But I have no need to squint up at the flat white sky above us to know that a big storm is on the way. I can smell it and taste it in the air.

I take a firm hold of Meggie's hand, and we set off along the path that will lead us around the back of the church and out of the town. I move at such a pace that the poor child has to fairly run to keep up with me, nodding and smiling at my neighbors as I go and hoping I look sociable enough, but with no desire to stop and pass the time of day. Our headlong flight is checked, though. Preacher Holden emerges from the crowd with his mother on his arm, and I am bidden by good manners to stop in my tracks and bid them Season's Greetings.

In his hand he carries old Peabody's paper. He sees me looking at it and gives a half laugh.

"I see you have noticed—I'm afraid I had reason to reprimand Mr. Peabody for bringing this vulgar gossip-sheet into the Lord's House." He clears his throat. "But I reckon that if anyone is deserving of being in the Lord's presence this day, it is this fine gentleman."

He holds the paper up, to display what had snagged my attention in church: the likeness of a weak-faced man with wispy fine hair, and the headline.

DIED. In Sonoma County, Mr. HENRY EDDY, age 43, late of Mass., a pioneer of 1846, and well known as the heroic rescuer of the "Donner party."

With an effort, I wrench my eyes away from the paper and bring them back to Preacher Holden's face. There is an avid look in his eyes that no amount of piety can conceal. I know what his next words will be before he even opens his mouth.

"And as for that other wretched fellow who accompa-

nied him on his journey—Keseberg—well, he is in sore need of our prayers, that much is certain."

I can make no answer. I mutter something foolish about the snow; then I pick up my skirts and fairly run out of the churchyard, Meggie at my heels, and Preacher and Mrs. Holden openmouthed behind me.

2

I have always believed that I would meet Mr. Eddy again. It would be a day like any other; a blowy day in spring maybe, or the high heat of midsummer. I would be walking along the street in my print frock and bonnet, on my way to the mercantile perhaps, or taking the air with my husband and children on a Sunday afternoon.

And Mr. Eddy would be there.

He would walk toward me, and as he passed by he would look at me something quizzical. His stride might falter some, thinking that perhaps he knew me. He'd tip his hat. He might smile a little. But then he would look again.

In that moment, sick horror would go sliding across his face, and oh! I would fall upon Mr. Eddy! My nails out to claw at his face and my fists ready to knock his teeth down his throat!

My poor husband would have to pull me away in shame, with all the townsfolk watching. Mr. Eddy would turn tail and flee. But no matter how fast he might go flying down the street, my words would go screaming along behind him, "Liar! LIAR! LIAR!"

It is what I have been waiting for, all these years. But I have been cheated. He has died a hero, and been written in the newspapers so; and his lies will live on, immortalized.

Dear God, there is no justice in the world!

If I cannot tell Mr. Eddy what I think of him to his face, then I must use my pen to cut through the twisty tangle of lies that he planted and that have grown up these long years to conceal the truth. Now they will fall away and the straight facts of the matter show through at long last. How I knew Mr. Eddy, and Mr. Keseberg, too; and how Mr. Eddy, carpenter, coffin maker, betrayed us both at the last.

Mr. Eddy's death is not the beginning of my story. It is where my story ends. But with the ending comes the beginning, and my story starts back in Cincinnati, when I was but fifteen. Yes. I may as well start there as anywhere.

My parents were both born in Cincinnati, when it was nothing more than a handful of little farms, with a population of maybe thirty families. It never was a peaceful place. Even then it was known for lawlessness, with the farmers turning their corn crop into moonshine and selling it to the soldiers stationed at Fort Washington. In no more than thirty years, this little hamlet changed beyond recognition, and by the time I was born it was become a city, grown fat on the proceeds of slaughter.

Great herds of pigs, a hundred strong or more, were whipped hourly through the unpaved streets, leaving a thick, stinking trail behind them, and their desperate squealing chorus from the slaughterhouses was in our ears from dawn until dusk. Grindhouses turned teeth, snouts, tusks, tails, and gristle into fertilizer, to be shipped to the South for use on the great cotton plantations. And in every other street in our part of the city were the render-houses where they boiled down the pig fat. Some of this went to the army to grease their bullet casings, and some to the cotton mills of the North to lubricate the spinning and weaving machines. What was left went to the other factories in the city, and the creeks and streams that fed into the mighty Ohio River foamed with the foul-smelling run-off from the dyers, tanners, candle-makers, soapmakers, and the rest. The sky and the streets alike were clotted with the smoking stench from the factory chimneys, a ripe, greasy fog that clung to everything it touched; and the black smoke of the steamers churning their way up and down the river all the live-long day contributed to the choking miasma that filled our lungs and stung our eyes.

Cincinnati was a rich city, with money streaming in just as fast as the hog meat was shipped out. For the factory owners living in their grand mansions in the leafy airiness of Auburn Hill, I daresay it was a splendid life. But my life was not. For the life I was born into was a hard one, and a brutal one.

I had two brothers a couple of years younger than me, and then a whole parcel of snot-nosed, grizzling little sisters. With them and Ma and Pa, there were ten of us in two rooms. We dealt with one another with a cruel, low cunning, using fists and teeth without a second thought, if it meant a rag to sleep under for the night or some scrap of food.

We lived close by the river, in the stench and filth of fish heads and pig muck and rotting vegetables and with the scutter and mess of immigrants all piled in on top of one another, with virtually no sanitation and no common language. Most of the men worked the wharves, loading and unloading the great steamboats. They spent their nights in the alehouse, and were always with an eye to the main chance, wanting to make as much cash as they could by doing as little work as possible. Most of the women made a living selling themselves in some alleyway. My parents were the same, with thievery and whoring their trades when they were sober enough. I was no different. Other girls my age were apprenticed out as milliners, or worked from dawn to midnight in the factories, but I had mastered the easier art of coin-from-pocket at an early age. And now it seemed it was time for the whoring.

Late one night in early spring, Pa staggered home with a man who stank of the drink, and had a sly, sideways look to him. He was dressed real sharp, with a fancy hat and waistcoat. I reckon he was a passenger on one of the steamboats come ashore for a night of low roistering, and had fallen in with my pa on his way.

Pa shouted me downstairs, and told me that now I was grown enough, I could earn my keep. He sent me into the privy outhouse, no more than a rotting shack that we shared with half a dozen other families, with this man. He was drunk, right enough, but it didn't stop him being lustful. As soon as he had shut the door behind us, he was fumbling in his pants with one hand and grabbing at my hair with the other, forcing me to my knees.

I knelt in front of him, shaking all over. I was right sickened to do it, and too afraid not to. This moment's hesitation was enough to make him land me a sharp crack across the ear. That decided me; I leapt to my feet and gave him an almighty shove. He staggered back, and lost his balance, catching his head on the wooden door where a big nail stuck out hung with scraps of paper, and then he fell down in a heap across the privy.

I pressed myself back against the wall, fearful for what I had done. I thought that any minute he would rise to his feet and land me one before carrying on what he had started. Worse, he'd tell Pa. I didn't want to think what Pa would do to me. It wouldn't be just his fists, it would be his buckle-belt at least. My back was already crisscrossed with scars; the last time he'd thrashed me it had been days before I could stir from my bed. But the man didn't move, not a twitch. After a while I reached out my foot and kicked at his leg.

"Mister. Hey, Mister. Wake up."

There was no reply, not even a groan or a sigh. His eyes were half-open, gazing milky up at the roof, and a little trickle of blood slid across his forehead. I stood there, staring down at him, dreading the thought of Pa coming to see what we were about. And then I had the sudden thought that perhaps he was dead. If so, Pa's buckle-belt was the least of my worries.

A great rush of fear made me spring away from the door. Without a second's thought I set to rummage through the man's clothing to see what he had about him. In his pants pocket I found some coin, and in his waistcoat pocket a silver watch on a heavy chain. Then I legged out of there as fast as I could run, out of the privy outhouse, out of our street, and out into the maze of alleyways that led down to the river.

It was getting on toward dawn, and a cold gray mist was rolling in off the water. Most of the night's revelers were gone, so the streets were as quiet as ever they got. There was a drunkard spewing up his guts in a doorway, and two women passed me, one with an eye that was beginning to black up and blood on her bodice, her friend holding her up as she wept her way along the street. Other than that I saw no one, and no one spoke to me. I ran as fast as I could through the narrow alleyways that led to the water's edge.

One of my shoes was losing its sole, and at every step it flapped and caught, causing me once to fall and gash my hand. I kicked it off, and its broke-down fellow, too, and ran faster, stumbling on the uneven ground in my bare feet. My breath was coming in great ragged gasps, and I thought that any minute the hangman's hand would reach out and grab me.

Eventually I could run no more, and stopped to catch my breath. I was out on the wharves by now, among the warehouses that lined the waterfront. There were some wooden crates piled up, and I found a space between them and crept inside.

Here I stayed for a while, trying to quiet my heaving gasps for air, and listening fearfully for the sounds of pursuit. All was quiet but for the heavy slap of the water against the sides of the ships, and the slow creak of their timbers, and the rats scuttling in the shadows beside me.

After a while I grew a little calmer, and tried to think what to do next. I supposed I'd run away from home, quite without meaning to. Where I would go, I had no idea. I had never thought about leaving Cincinnati, it had never crossed my mind that I could. But indeed, there was a great leaving of the place, especially by the Germans.

The Germans had been among the first to arrive and settle in the area, and I guess in the early days they were as accepted as any other. But as time wore on, feelings began to build against them. The German wharfmen worked cheaper and harder than the rest, and went home to their families at the end of the day, which caused great ill feeling among the men lingering in the alehouses. And their wives were neat and clean, scrubbing their doorsteps down and planting up their little gardens, which riled the slovenly women of our neighborhood.

This resentment was not confined to the river folk, but ran high in all parts of the town, the rich as well as the poor. The Germans had a great love of music and theater and gaiety of all kinds, and thought nothing of indulging themselves with these treats on a Sunday; and as well, a goodly number of them were Catholics. All in all, the pious folk of Cincinnati came to consider them unsuitable inhabitants of a God-fearing city.

The more that feelings grew against them, the more they were forced to live among their own kind. This meant that as more and more new Germans settled in, so the town became more divided, the Germans in one part, and everyone else in another. Laws were passed to keep them from some types of employment, and soon moves were afoot to drive them all out, if possible, for it was feared that they would come to overtake the place entirely. So, just as fast as new folk rolled in off the boats, clutching their baskets of sausage and black bread close to them and looking bewildered about them and not a word of English to be heard, so others rolled out in their wagons.

I am sure that the same was true in many of the towns in the East. It was the foreigners, Germans and Irish the most, who made up the main part of the wagon trains heading west, inspired by the tales of great forests ripe for the felling and with good hunting, rich meadows stretching to the horizon, with herds of wild horses running free, and anyone's for the taking. There was talk of slow-moving rivers and fast-running streams, clean air and cloudless blue skies and the chance for every person, young or old, rich or poor, to make something better of themselves. It was no wonder that so many folks scratched together their few possessions and set off in pursuit of this dream, eager to escape the nightmare of the squalid struggle for survival in the backstreet slums.

It struck me now, that this was just the time of year when the wagons departed on the trail to the West. Their gathering point was some meadowland on the outskirts of the city, where they made ready to start on the first part of their journey to Independence, Missouri, a journey of some five hundred miles.

I had heard tell that in Independence the wagons collected in their hundreds, the little trickles of travelers from every town in the East joining together to form a great river that swept across the plains toward Oregon and California. I longed to see this great sight, for even with only a dozen or so wagons departing from Cincinnati, during the first week of spring our little stretch of meadow turned into a bustling marketplace.

Stalls set up with dried goods for purchase, peas and beans and rice, and there were drapers with silks and calicos, and wool merchants with bales of cloth, and trinket stalls with beads and other gewgaws that could be traded with the Indians on the way, or the Mexicos on arrival in California. The tallower was there with candles and lanterns and axle grease in buckets, and the cooper, to make or mend barrels. There would be a blacksmith sharpening knives and shoeing horses, cursing and yelling in the heat of his forge, and the clang of the hammers and the sparks flying up; and drovers with beeves and cows and mules for sale, all bellowing and braying and neighing. And there were cages filled with chickens, the hens clucking and squawking and the roosters crowing fit to burst, and dogs reputed to be fine ratters, and cats said to be great mousers.

Over all, a preacher yelling like enough to raise the dead in one corner, and the medicine man in another, offering Dr. Cooper's Tonic and Mrs. Madison's Liniment, guaranteed to mend everything from a fever to a broken leg. He made good money, for most women bought a bottle or two of his cure-all. No woman wanted to birth a baby on the journey, and it was well known that if you took a spoonful or so the early morning grips that showed a baby was started would disappear, and the baby with them.

It was a sight to see the wagons arriving day by day. They'd have their teams of heavy beeves pulling, with another yoke or two roped behind, and maybe a goat or a milk cow and a calf or two. The women in their caps and bonnets would be helped down from their high seats in front and they would go from stall to stall, fingering the goods and bartering, and their teamsters would load their purchases into the wagons. There would be some down-at-heel folks, looking to work their passage, and a few single men up on their glossy horses, intending to join with a train. These men would strut about with their fingers stuck in their waistcoats, stiff new-leather gun belts with shiny-handled guns in the holsters slung casually over their hips and cigarillos perched in the corners of their mouths, talking in loud voices of their plans for getting rich in California, at the same time pulling their hats low on their foreheads, to hide their assessing glances at the plump matrons and the pretty daughters.

It was possible to join a wagon train, even if you had no horse or wagon of your own. They went at walking pace, and if you could find someone to take on your belongings for a fee you could walk the trail with them. I felt in my pocket, and pulled out the coins I had taken. There were some dimes and quarters, and five silver dollars, too. I had never seen so much money in my life before. I had no belongings, but I had the fee right enough.

I poked my head cautiously out of my little hidey-hole, and looked to left and right. There was no one to see me.

I got to my feet, and set off, my legs shaking beneath me. I had decided. I would leave Cincinnati for good, and make the journey to the West.

3

It was a long walk out of the city. By the time I arrived at the meadow, near to fainting with hunger, the sun was well up, and all in fine swing with five or six wagons already arrived.

The air smelled of new bread and hot fat, making my mouth water and my stomach ache. Close to me a man was selling doughballs, four for a dime, hot from the pan and sprinkled with sugar. Being hungry was nothing new, but for the first time in my whole life, I could buy anything I wanted. And now I thought of my little brothers. I imagined saying to them, "Choose what you want, and eat as much as you like!" and their faces lighting up at the notion. I turned my money over and over in my pocket and my fingers knocked against the silver pocket watch.

I had all but forgot the watch, and how I had come by it. No one could prove where I got the coin from but a silver pocket watch was a different matter, and I thought I was a fool to have took it. I looked around me real quick and sharp. There was no one looking toward me in any particular manner. Casual as could be, I sauntered across the grass to where I had spied a ragged little lad, who I half knew. As I went, I took off my neckerchief, and folded the pocket watch into it, and held it in one hand, with a dime in the other.

When I reached the lad, I held out the dime and asked him if he wanted it. He nodded, yes, of course, and reached out to grab it, but I was quicker than he, and held it out of reach.

"You know my brothers, don't you? You know where I live?"

He nodded.

"You take this"—I handed him the little package—"and give it to my ma. Just my ma, mind!—not my pa, you understand?"

He nodded again.

"And then you come back here, and I will give you this dime, and another one as well."

Maybe he'd deliver the watch safe, and maybe he wouldn't. Ma could hock it in the pawnshop and buy some food for the little ones, or she might use it for drink, I didn't know. But at least, I thought, I had done my best.

He seized the parcel and sped away, excited at his task and the promise of a reward. I felt bad for a minute, for of course I was never going to give him one dime, let alone two. I used that dime to buy myself a bagful of those doughballs, and they tasted just as good as I thought they would.

After I had eaten, I went to the pump and washed my fingers and wiped over my face as best I could with the dampened hem of my skirt. Then I straightened my back and set off to the first wagon to ask if they would take me with them. I was refused there, and then at all the others, the women taking but one look at me with my rattail hair and my bare feet and my hand-me-down clothes from my mother. Gaudy bits of things they were, and I reckon they thought me no more than a harlot, come to tout for business.

At last I turned away, much cast down, and leaned against a fence post, watching as two more wagons came up and stopped by the others.

The first was pulled by a team of six beeves. Walking along of the team, with the guide rope in one hand and a long whip in the other, was a tall, broad-shouldered man.

The sun was full overhead now, but it was not that warm. Even so he wore no coat—I could see it heaped, careless-like, on the wagon seat. His pants and waist-coat were in some dull stuff, but his shirt was blue as the sky above. Abandoned along with his coat was his hat, and his hair—cut shorter than was the fashion, and just curling over his ears—was the milky color of the butterweed flowers that grew in the grass along the foot of the fence posts, where the ground wasn't too kicked up by the animals and wagon wheels.

I stared at him, I could not help myself.

After a moment, as if he felt my eyes on him, he turned his head.

His gaze locked onto mine. His eyes were the self-same shade of blue as his shirt and the sky. He smiled straight at me and I smiled back. I could not help it—I thought I knew him. Then someone spoke to him from inside the wagon, and he turned away.

The second, smaller wagon was pulled by a couple of mules with another yoke of beeves roped up to walk be-hind. Up on the driving board was an older man, the reins in his hands and a small clay pipe clamped be-tween his lips. He pulled to a halt, and climbed down with some difficulty. Throwing the reins over the fence post, and nodding at me as he did so, he went to join his fellow.

Between them they unhitched one of the beeves; I

could see it had cast a shoe. The elderly man led it away in the direction of the blacksmith, and the first man went round the back of the first wagon and helped down a woman green about the face, who sat down heavy on the ground, faint and sweating. He swung down a little girl, with pretty fair hair in little braids looped up with ribbons, and dropped a kiss on her forehead, then left them and went across to the ale stall.

They were Germans, I could tell from the few words they exchanged, and you couldn't grow up where I did without learning something of their speech. I looked away from them, too tied up in my own thoughts of what I was to do to take much notice, but after a little while I began to feel sorry for the little girl. She was crying for the privy, and pulling at her ma, but the poor woman was heaving with sickness and in no fit state to look to her. I had seen Ma so, when a baby was started, and knew it was a bad way to be in.

With a sigh, I pushed myself upright and stepped over to them, and offered to help with the child. The woman was so beyond anything that she was grateful for this small kindness. I took the little girl's hand and asked her name: Ada Keseberg.

I walked her to a quiet spot away from the crowds and helped her do her business. Then I fetched one of the tin cups hanging on a nail at the side of the wagon, and took the little girl with me again. We were only to go to the pump for a cup of water, but of course the little girl wanted to see the sights. There was a juggler doing tricks with colored balls, and we passed someone selling puppies from a box and had to stop and pet them.

When we finally returned with the cup of water it was to find the elderly teamster hitching up the new-shod animal. The little girl's pa—Mr. Keseberg—was in a right taking, shouting round him, "Ada! ADA!" and berating his wife for her foolishness in letting the child go with a stranger. He seized the child from me, grabbed the water from my hand and gave it to his wife, and dismissed me with a curt nod. I guess his temper had wiped the smile off his face.

The teamster winked at me as he climbed back onto his driving seat and set to work with his pipe and tinder box. The woman, still green in the face, was assisted back into the wagon, and Ada lifted in after her. Then the bugle blast sounded, to warn the wagoners to be ready to move out. The beeves leaned into their traces with a snort and a grunt, and the wagons began to move off.

I seized the moment, and set off to walk alongside, calling across the beeves' broad backs, "Sir, oh sir, take me with you! I have money, I can pay for my passage! And I could help with your little girl—Ada." He turned his head, and looked me up and down.

The woman poked her head out of the canvas. She only leaned out to sick up, but she caught the end of this exchange.

"Oh, Louis! Let her come, I beg of you! She can help with Ada, and I—" But at that, she was seized again with the sickness and could not speak for retching.

Perhaps he had not heard his wife. He did not answer her at all, but looked me up and down with an assessing stare. I smiled and nodded at him, and held out my hand. The five silver dollars winked and sparkled in the sun. He jerked his head behind him.

"You can ride along with my teamster—for now." That was all he said to me. The wagon passed on, and the second wagon come up. I reached up my hand, and the teamster reached down and took it. I scrambled up onto the seat beside him. And off we went, heading for our new lives in California.

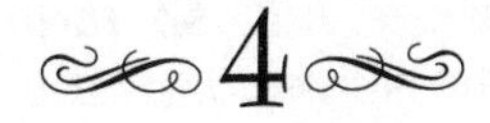

It is close to midnight. I lay down my pen, and stretch my cramped fingers, and yawn; I should awaken Jacob, and get us to bed.

Jacob stirs. The periodical that lies abandoned across his chest, The California Journal of Useful Sciences, *falls to the floor, open at a drawing of a house. Some scraps of paper come with it, scribbled over with notes and measurements. I go and gather them up neatly, and place them on the table beside me with a sigh. Jacob's business is prospering, and he is well established in our community and feels that we should live somewhere that reflects that fact. So he has purchased a parcel of land some way out of town with a view to the lake, and is intent on building us a grand house with a wraparound porch with steps up, and a turret with a window set in, and bits of carved whatnot all over; what the periodical describes as a Gingerbread Trim.*

It is a fine dream, and I understand it, but it is not one that I share. Even though our little house is modest and the girls sleep in one room, it is the house Jacob built for us when we married. I have lived here happy enough these past thirteen years and would for another thirteen, if the decision was mine to make.

The house faces southwest, giving us the afternoon sun in the parlor and the morning sun in the kitchen. It is on the side of a gentle hill, so that our yard out front slopes away from the house and down to the dusty track that leads into town. On the other side of the track, pastureland stretches into the far distance, with feathery clumps of grasses rippling in the wind, and pools of violets at the feet of tall lilies, and the little fire-bright-red cardinal flowers. Everywhere are golden-yellow poppies that shine like butter in the sun. A more beautiful sight it is hard to imagine.

With three children and a hungry husband to provide for, my yard is mostly given over to neat rows of vegetables. Even so, I can't help but have some flowers of my own, and one corner is given over to roses. Jacob fetches these home for me from Mr. Smith's botanical warehouse in Sacramento, when he goes there on business.

Their names are written on labels attached to the stems, and I wonder who chooses them, and where the plants have come from, but Jacob doesn't know, and never thinks to ask Mr. Smith, so they remain a mystery to me. I have one called Jaune Desprez, which has the loveliest fragrance, and is a color I cannot describe, not orange or yellow nor yet pink but something in between them all. I think of it as the color of a silk gown, though why that should be I do not know. I have the old white Cherokee rose, which everyone knows, and one of the very palest pink, called Duchesse de Gramont. Jacob tells me that "duchesse" means a grand lady. I long to know who she was, that grand lady, and why a rose should be named after her, but I guess I never will.

A garden is a sociable place. I'll be out there of an afternoon when school is over, pulling some beans or fixing up the tomato plants, and a neighbor will stop to pass the time of day. Some of my pupils will go by; a couple of the older girls whispering together and giggling, calling out a greeting, "Hello, Miz Klein!"

They are invariably followed by a couple of slouching boys with their hands in their pockets and their hats tipped to the backs of their heads, who mutter my name and then flush red to their ear tips. They are on their way to the other side of town, where our little trickle of a creek widens out into a shallow pool with sandy sides. Here the boys will have a sly, spluttering attempt at their pa's tobacco, while the girls make eyes at them, and cool their feet in the water.

It's unusual for a married woman, especially one with children, to be a schoolteacher; but in our new State of California, where there are ten men looking for wives for every girl who wants to be one, single schoolteachers are as rare as hen's teeth. We all pray for an ugly one to arrive in the town, in the hope that she might stay in the school for more than a few months, but they come and they go, even the ugliest being up and married and moving on before you know it.

A year or two previous I lost all patience at the town meeting, when yet again there was general grumbling and complaining, with no one able to find a solution to the unusual problem of young, unmarried women arriving in our town and energetic young single men wanting to marry them. Quite before I knew it, I'd stood up and said, "Well, I'm intending to stay put, so I'll do it and make a good job of it, too."

The school board is three men. They looked pretty startled at a woman jumping to her feet and speaking out. They whispered among themselves for a while, then asked Jacob for his opinion. He said it was fine by him, and so it was decided: I could run the school for now, until they could find someone more suitable.

Jacob comes from a family where learning is taken to be a necessity, not a luxury. Perhaps he is proud of me, in his quiet way. All he said to me, with a half smile playing round his lips, was that if I was to be pursuing such an illustrious career then I would need some help. And this is how we come to employ Martha. She lives in town with her mother, and walks out to us each morning and then home again in the evening escorted by her young man, Simon Cooke, who works in the blacksmithery.

Martha is a blessing to me. Many women of my acquaintance seem to be content with the endless round of cleaning and mending, but I cannot find it in my heart to love such tasks. I like cooking well enough and trying out new dishes, and Jacob seems to enjoy them; that is, he eats all that I put in front of him, and makes no comment, though I think sometimes there is something of a suspicious pucker round his lips.

I have no wish to change my life. But I can see that eventually a proper schoolmistress will arrive, with a recommendation from a college back East and qualifications I don't possess. I will stop being Miz Klein, schoolteacher, and be returned to being plain old Mrs. Jacob Klein, wife and mother. Martha will be let go, for I will have time enough and to spare for the cooking and washing and the rest. And we will move away from the town and out to the lake and into Jacob's fine new house.

Then every day will pass the same. The children will be off to their schooling and Jacob in his workshop over at the lumberyard. And I'll be sat alone and quiet on that fine wraparound porch, gazing out over the lake with just my own thoughts for company.

To think on it gives me a hard, bad feeling in the pit of my stomach. I don't tell my husband that, though.

5

That first morning when we left Cincinnati I felt grand, sitting up on the wagon seat like a fine lady, looking all around me with a great grin on my face to see the folks cheering as the wagons pulled out. I quite forgot that I was a fugitive from justice; for that little while the thought of arriving in California and doing something splendid with my life—though what that was I couldn't say—overtook all else, and I felt vastly superior to those folks I was leaving behind me.

After leaving the meadow our way lay through farmland. At first I thought it very pretty. Here was the clear blue sky stretching overhead, and to each side of us, fields of freshly turned black earth. In places they would be cut through by a creek. By the creek would be a cluster of cabins, and some little children in pinafores would come running out to wave at us; or a couple of mules or horses pulling a ploughshare, with the farmer walking behind, his dog scuffing along at his heels and turning to bark at our wagons. But after an hour or so of this, my head began to ache. And soon I began to feel quite peculiar.

I was used to clatter and noise and folks everywhere, but now it was so very quiet; nothing to hear but the creak of the carts and the slow clop of the animal hooves, and some muffled conversation floating back to me here and there from the other wagons.

I had spent all my life with closed-in streets and great tall buildings all around me and hardly no sky at all, but now the sky was everywhere I looked. I couldn't get away from it, and there was too much land and it was too flat. I began to think it was tilting this way and that, and I clutched hold of the wagon seat, in fear that I would slide off and go rolling across those fields with nothing to stop me until I fell right off the edge, into the sea or the sky, and was lost.

So far the teamster and I had rode along in silence, but I sensed him looking at me. Now he reached into his pocket and fetched out a wrapper with some candy in it. He handed a piece to me, and took a piece himself and popped it into his mouth.

"Goot. Is goot? Candy."

Feeling foolish to have been scared, I smiled at him, and felt a little better.

"What is name?"

I told him my name, and asked him about himself, and how he came to be here. I tried him in German and he understood some, and I tried him in English, and he understood some of that as well, but he wasn't either.

He told me his name, Lukas Benoit Hardkoop—"a good old name," he said. He came from a country called Belgium, and had a daughter there and grandchildren. When he reached California he was getting on a ship and going home, and couldn't wait to see them again.

I indicated the wagon ahead of us. Little Ada was leaning out of the back and waving at us, and I guess her ma was resting.

"I thought they were your family."

He shook his head. "The Kesebergs? *Ach,* no. I look

for work, driving wagon, but all say to me, too old, too old! But this man listens to his own head only!" He laughed, and shifted his candy to the other side of his mouth.

"Is my dream, to see California. And then home. Old man by fireside." He acted out the idea of an old man, huddled in a blanket and holding out his trembling hands to the fire, and then straightened up and laughed again, and I laughed, too.

He had the sort of weather-beaten face and faraway eyes of the sailors I had seen on the wharfside sometimes; men with itchy feet and a thirst for travel. Something about him reminded me of my pa—when I was younger, and he was with the India trade, and traveled the world on the sailing ships. Before he gave it up, and took to the drink.

Another couple of wagons came up behind us as the day wore on. By the time we reached our first stopping place, a trading post by a large pond, we were seven or eight families, with a handful of teamsters and outriders up on their horses.

Mr. Hardkoop pulled the wagon over. I climbed down, glad to stretch my legs, and wondering what I should do next. I didn't have to wonder long. Mrs. Keseberg came across to me, seeming something recovered from the sickness, with a tight little smile on her face.

She looked me up and down with her head tipped to one side, a tiny frown creasing between her brows. Her smile vanished away, and she turned down the corners of her mouth. She looked the very picture of sympathetic kindness.

"My goodness," she said. "I hadn't quite realized . . . well, we must do something about your clothes. And your hair. Oh, dear. We will do something about that, too." She had a girlish whisper of a voice, as sweet as could be, but it was something at odds with the glint in her eye.

With that, she set Mr. Hardkoop to heat up a kettle of water over the cooking fire, and sent me into the privy out back of the trading post. The hot water was handed in through the door, and with it a lump of rough green soap, and she bade me strip off my clothes and wash myself all over.

My clothes disappeared—I discovered them, after, burning on the fire—and Mrs. Keseberg found me a linsey gown to wear. The dress was too short, for she was a tiny slip of a woman and I was taller than her by several inches. It was an ugly color, too, a drab brownish-yellow, something faded in places from the sun, and I put it on right unwilling.

I had no shoes on my feet. Mrs. Keseberg took me into the trading post, and found me some boots. They were old and the laces gone, replaced by strings, but still had enough wear in them, or so she said. They didn't fit right and had to be padded out with some sheets of paper.

I thought my humiliation could get no worse, at the sight of my feet in these ugly boots, but I was wrong. For when we came out of the trading post, Mr. Hardkoop was waiting for me, a stool set out for me to sit on, and scissors and his razor in his hand. I stopped dead at the sight.

"I do not wish to have my hair cut off!"

"No, I am sure you do not! But you have the lice in your hair, my dear, and I will not allow you in the wagons until it is gone." Mrs. Keseberg's smile was quite vanished away. I took one look at her face and knew there was no arguing with her.

Most of the other folks pretended not to see as Mr. Hardkoop set to, busying themselves with their cooking pots and fetching water from the creek and seeing to their animals. But of course, the little children thought nothing of gathering round me and watching this fine show, laughing and pointing, and cheering each time a lock of my hair fell to the ground. When the long lengths of it were cut off, Mr. Hardkoop took his razor, and shaved the rest, so that my head was as naked as that of a newborn babe.

When it was done, Mrs. Keseberg set me to peeling vegetables, and with pure hatred in my heart for her, I set to work.

Through all this, Mr. Keseberg had kept his face from me and his back turned. But when our dinner was over, and Mrs. Keseberg had climbed back into the wagon to put Ada to bed, and I was at the creek washing out the cooking pots, he walked up to me quiet-like, and said, "I saw this in the trading post. I thought you might like it to cover your head, while your hair grows out." And he dropped a pretty pink kerchief into my hand, and walked away before I could thank him.

Through March, through April, and into May, we made our slow way from Ohio to Missouri. Every day followed the same routine. We rose at first light and Mr. Hardkoop made up the campfire. While he and Mr. Keseberg looked to the animals and Mrs. Keseberg looked to Ada, I was set to make the breakfast: bacon and biscuits, and coffee.

Oh, that coffee! Making it was a misery for me, and drinking it was a misery for everyone else.

Coffee was the mainstay of our diet and every wagon carried a great store of beans. It was said to be good to settle a bellyache and the very thing for a sick headache and to give energy for traveling. But even just the smell of the beans made Mrs. Keseberg heave and retch, and she stayed as far away from the cooking fire as she could. She was most put out to discover that I hardly knew how to even boil up a can of water, and Mr. Hardkoop was set to show me the mysteries of the coffeepot.

I would take a scoop of beans from the sack, and then tie the sack tight again, for the fields to each side of us were swarming with mice and at every stop along the way we would find a couple sneaked into the wagon and nibbling at the sacks of flour and sugar. These beans would be set into a pan over the fire, and it was my task to sit and stir them for thirty minutes at a time, so that they would roast but not burn. Woe betide me if my attention was caught by something else and I forgot the task at hand, but forget I did. I cannot tell how many times I burned those beans, too taken up by listening to conversations that did not concern me, or being distracted by the sight of a rabbit, or even just nodding my head with tiredness.

When the beans were evenly roasted, they were put into a bowl and pounded into a coarse powder. This was tipped into the coffeepot, which had been set over the fire to heat, and the coffeepot moved to the side to stay warm but not boil. I could not get the hang of it. I forgot to set the water to heat, and tipped the powder into cold water, or I forgot to move the coffeepot to the side, so water and powder boiled up and over into the fire. My coffee was stone cold, or bitter; too weak one day and too strong the next. I came to hate the sight of the beans and the coffeepot as well.

My only comfort was that Mrs. Keseberg knew nothing of these disasters, looking to the menfolk to tell her if it was good coffee or not. Mr. Hardkoop and Mr. Keseberg drank down what was given them with nothing more than a twist to their lips, and not a word to her of the filthy brew that they were consuming with such gallantry.

The process was too time-consuming to repeat night and morning, so what was left in the pot at night was warmed through again in the morning, with plenty of milk added and a good heaping spoonful or two of sugar. This should have been easy enough, but what with looking to the bacon and worrying about the biscuit batter, my last great disaster was to heap up the pot with salt instead of sugar.

Mr. Hardkoop took a great mouthful and then jumped to his feet and sped across to the wagon to fetch a dipperful of water, which he drank down in a very great hurry. Mrs. Keseberg was sitting up on the wagon seat with a cup of water and a bit of dried cracker, which was all she could keep down. When he had finished coughing, he said to her that he enjoyed cooking. Why not let him do it, and perhaps it would be a better use of my time if I were to see to Ada in the mornings.

Mr. Keseberg's mouth twitched, and he said, "Yes, my dear, I think this is an excellent idea. You are so very indisposed in the mornings and I cannot bear to see you work so hard."

At that, he and Mr. Hardkoop disappeared off together round the back of the wagon, where I could hear them both laughing fit to burst, and Mrs. Keseberg looked after them with a puzzled frown on her face.

So it was settled. Instead of making coffee I was to take Ada to the creek to wash her hands and face, and to brush her hair and dress her. I think all were happy with this arrangement, and by watching and helping Mr. Hardkoop here and there I eventually mastered the art of making good coffee, and many other dishes as well.

Once the cooking pots were cleared away, we set off along the trail once more. We'd have a short stop at noon, to give the animals a rest and a chance to graze a little at the side of the road, and we'd eat something cold and leftover from breakfast or the previous night's supper. The best part of the day was in the middle of the afternoon, when we finally drew into camp, anticipating a good hot meal and the chance to rest. The animals would be roped loosely together and turned out to pasture and the men made repairs to the wagons if they were required, and the women got the fires lit and the cooking pots set over. We ate well, for the farmland gave way to woodlands and then forest, and all around were birds and animals for the taking. Once supper was over and the cooking pots cleared away, folks would go visiting with their friends, and talk over the events of the day.

Most of our Cincinnati party were Germans, some of them already acquainted with the Kesebergs. These included a fine gentleman named Mr. Wolfinger and his wife, Dorisse, who were newly married. She spoke hardly a word of English and he not much more, and he was elderly and ugly and rich, and she was young and pretty. She was done up very fine with white lace gloves for everyday and gold earrings with red jewels in, which caught the light when she turned her head.

I looked at these with a right greedy eye, thinking how much they would earn me in the pawnshop.

That little thought of home twisted inside me, and I put it away from me and tried to think of something else. I did not wish to wonder if Ma missed me any, or even thought of me at all.

Most evenings after supper the Wolfingers came to visit with us, and Mrs. Wolfinger and Mrs. Keseberg would sit together with their mending or some knitting. Mr. Wolfinger made himself comfortable by our fire alongside Mr. Hardkoop and Mr. Keseberg, and they would be joined by two of the single men riding along on their horses: Mr. Spitzer, who was very close about his past life, and his companion Mr. Reinhardt. The men would smoke their pipes and talk over their plans for what they would do in California, and the women would add in their comments, and there would be some laughter here and there.

I would wash the cooking pots and clean out the wagon, all in silence, wishing that someone would invite me to sit by the fire and join in the conversation. But no one ever did.

With so many brothers and sisters, I had never lacked for company, albeit of the arguing and fighting kind; indeed, it had mostly been the dream of my life growing up to have no company at all. It seemed, now, that my wish was granted, but as the old folks say, "Watch out for your wishes," and it was true for me. I had wished to be alone, but I had never understood what it was to be lonely.

Mr. Hardkoop was kind enough, but he seemed content with his own thoughts, and spent a deal of time reading and paying no mind to me at all. Ada prattled on, but it was not what I would call a conversation. The person who spoke to me the most was Mrs. Keseberg, and I could not get the measure of her. She had a way of looking at me when I spoke to her—sort of thoughtful like, half-smiling and with a little tip of the head to one side—that made me stumble over my words, and feel like I was all elbows and knees. In front of other folks she was pure honey sweetness but she had a right sharp tongue on her to give me an order when other folks were not around.

No one else in our little train spoke to me at all. Why should they? I hardly crossed paths with another soul, spending all my time at our wagons, painfully aware of my shaved head and my poor appearance. And the folks in the other wagons were the same folks that had turned me away only a few weeks ago in Cincinnati. They didn't like the look of me then, and their opinions had changed not a jot.

I overheard Mrs. Wolfinger remark on it to Mrs. Keseberg, surprised to find me traveling with them. Mrs. Keseberg laughed, clearly embarrassed, and made some comment that it was a moment of weakness on her part and she had come to regret it pretty quick. She said that I was a shining example of something she called "dumb insolence." I didn't know what it meant, but had a pretty good idea it was something unpleasant.

Then she said that she had felt pity for me, and it was her weakness to try and help unfortunates.

"I ask only for a little gratitude from the girl," she added, "but I guess I will wait a long time for it. But she is good with the child, I will grant that, and Ada seems mighty attached to her."

I allowed myself a little gleam of pleasure at this, but her next words startled me plenty.

"Mr. Keseberg thinks most highly of her. Though I fail to see why."

I didn't have time to reflect on the matter. Mrs. Wolfinger made some other quiet remark that I did not hear, but I heard Mrs. Keseberg's reply—the honey vanished away in an instant, and vinegar took its place.

"My goodness me! How can you say such a thing? Do you think I would take that sort of girl into my wagon? And, jesting or not, I thank you to mind your remarks about my husband!"

6

At the beginning of May we crossed into Missouri. Here were no forests or woods, for the land to each side of us was plantations, acre after acre of land spreading to the horizon, and dozens of folks sowing seeds for hemp or tobacco. They paid us no mind, being too engrossed in their work or just too used to the sight of wagon after wagon passing along the trail. Or maybe just not allowed to look away from their task—for these laborers were black, and Missouri was a slaver state. I saw a white man pass by the nearest row, with a whip held in his hand, and shivered at the sight of it.

In the middle of one afternoon we finally arrived in Independence, and pulled into a field that must have been ten times the size of our Cincinnati meadow. There were too many wagons to count—row upon row of them as far as the eye could see—and folks working all around them, making repairs, leading off horses to be shod, or oiling the canvas covers for waterproofing.

Mrs. Keseberg appeared out of the back of the wagon in a fresh skirt and blouse, wearing a straw bonnet with a ribbon round it. She told me to mind Ada, and make her dinner for her and to put her to bed, for after they had strolled around the town, she and Mr. Keseberg were going to eat their dinners in one of the eating houses.

Off they set, Mrs. Keseberg with her arm linked through that of her husband. I stared after them in openmouthed outrage.

I had supposed I should go, too, and see the sights!—and I wanted to, more than anything!—but here I was, left to sit in a field with their child while they went gallivanting about and enjoying themselves!

I could not be still, and stamped backward and forward with my fists clenched. My thoughts whirled round in my head in a fury. What were these people to me? Circumstance—well, maybe my pa—had forced me to set out on my journey whether I wanted to or no, and the Kesebergs were simply what fate had thrown my way.

I said to myself, "I owe them nothing! I will not stay with them another minute to be treated so shameful! I will find someone else to take me along the route to California, and see how they like that! And Mrs. Keseberg can look after her own child, and make her own coffee! And carry her own pots down to the creek and wash them, too!"

I imagined the Kesebergs coming back to the wagon and finding me gone, and thought how it would serve them right. And I laughed out loud at the thought of the surprised look on their faces. This pleasant thought calmed me some. My thoughts stopped whirling round and settled themselves into a plan, and I turned my attention to Ada.

There was some leftover corn bread from breakfast, and I soaked it in a bit of milk and drizzled a little molasses over it and she ate that, with a slice of cold meat. I settled her to sleep and drew the wagon cover closed, and went round to where Mr. Hardkoop was sat leaning against one of the wagon wheels, his pipe in his mouth and a book in his hand, reading.

I said, as casual as I could, would he mind Ada while I walked about a little to stretch my legs and see some of the other wagons. He nodded, hardly looking up from his book.

I strolled away, humming a little tune and as casual as you like. Then, when I was sure he could not see, I changed direction, and ran out of the field and into the town.

Independence was just as thrilling as I had expected. It was busier by far than I could have imagined and as unlike Cincinnati as could be. There were no factories throwing smoke into the sky, and no river filled with ships, no grand brick houses and no rich folks driving along in carriages, and no avenues of shops selling fancy goods. Instead, the whole town was a ramshackle muddle of wooden buildings that seemed to have sprung up just where they liked, all given over to provisioning the wagon trains. Every other building was a dry goods store, and in even the smallest gap between buildings there would be a wagon pulled up selling eggs or cheeses, or heaped with garden produce.

I had to keep my wits about me as I made my way along. There were no boardwalks, and such a quantity of folks everywhere that I was in constant danger of being pushed into the roadway, to fall under a horse's hooves or be knocked down by one of the carts that rattled past in every direction. There were saloons and eating houses, and boardinghouses, too. I thought I could find employment here. I could clean, and by now I could cook some, and I thought it would be a fine thing to earn my own money to spend at the end of each week. But even as I thought it, I realized that this would never happen. For every other face around me was a black one, and of course in Missouri the black folks worked for free.

It was growing dark, and by now I had walked quite

some distance. My legs ached, and I was hungry. I hoisted myself up onto a hitching rail, and sat there, swinging my legs back and forth, while I considered what to do next.

In front of me was a group of men standing outside a saloon. They had been made merry by the drink, laughing at some joke and paying no mind to what was happening around them. They would have coin in their pockets, I knew that. It would be the work of a minute to knock against one of them, and walk on with a handful of coin to show for it. A few weeks ago I would have done it in a heartbeat. But now I found I could not.

"I have money of my own," I thought, pretty pleased with myself. "I will find a room for the night in one of these boardinghouses, and order myself a fine supper—with someone else doing the cooking!—then in the morning I will decide what to do next. I might even go back to Cincinnati."

That tiny thought was all it took. I was decided. I had seen Independence, which had been my wish, and now the thought of home pulled at me something fierce. Ma needed me, and I smiled at the thought of telling my brothers what a fine adventure I'd had.

I jumped down off the hitching rail, and walked across the street to a house I had seen that had a notice in the front window, ROOMS AVAILABLE. I banged on the door, and as I did so I put my hand in my pocket to take out my money—and found only empty air.

I had tied my silver dollars in a scrap of cloth for safekeeping and tucked them away in a corner of the wagon. All fired up with temper, I had quite forgot about them. They were still there, back in the wagon and not in my pocket at all.

It was full dark by now. I was in a strange town where I knew no one, with no bed for the night, and no money. I had passed the sheriff's office with posters tacked up outside with descriptions of those wanted for robbery and murder and the rest. With a sickening rush of fear, it occurred to me that maybe my own name was on one of those posters.

What a fool I was! How could I have forgot my reasons for being here? I could not go home, no matter how much I might want to. The Kesebergs were my salvation, their wagons my only place of refuge, and I had thrown my salvation away for no more reason than having my nose put out of joint.

Mrs. Keseberg was pretty sharp with me, but it was only words, and I was stupid to let myself be so cut up about them. I remembered how Mr. Hardkoop had shared his candy with me, and thought how Ada clutched hold of my hand and giggled when I swung her round and round. And I thought again of Mr. Keseberg dropping the pink kerchief into my hand, and how I had wondered why he did it, if it was for pity, or if he chose the color deliberate, thinking it would be pretty on me. He had never told on me about the coffee, but had give that great shout of laughter instead, and I remembered how blue his eyes were when he looked at me. Pulling the pink kerchief off my head I clutched it to me, twisting it round and round between my fingers for comfort.

I began to run this way and that, looking for the route back to the wagon field. All the buildings looked the same. I turned left and then right and then back on myself, getting more and more frightened as I plunged between the crowds of folks, all laughing and chattering.

What if I never found my way back at all? What if the wagons had pulled out already, and they had not waited for me? What would I do? Where would I go?

I rounded a corner, and ran slap into Mr. Keseberg. He gave a shout of surprise, and dropped the packages he was carrying and caught me in his arms. A little black lad was following him, pulling a cart loaded up with provisions, and Mrs. Keseberg was there as well.

"Good gracious! Whatever are you doing here? You

were told to stay with Ada! Where is she? And cover your head, for heaven's sake."

Her words were as sharp as ever. But I gave a little skip from one foot to the other with the relief of hearing them, sharp or not.

"Mr. Hardkoop is minding Ada. I came to find you. To see if you needed any help."

"How thoughtful of you!" Mr. Keseberg's words were nothing out of the ordinary, and his tone was dry. There was no reason for my cheeks to flame, but they did. I felt as if he could see right into my head, and know how foolish I had been. My blush spread and spread, and the more I wished it away, the worse it got.

He handed me some parcels to carry. When his fingers touched mine, I jumped. I scuttled away to walk behind them, looking at the way Mrs. Keseberg had her hand tucked into the crook of his arm.

My pa's attentions to my ma had been with fists and slaps only, and I'd never had any lad back home be sweet on me, or me, him. I knew what I was—a plain girl with a sharp tongue. When I was younger I'd maybe wished myself different, so that some lad would wink his eye at me, or catch ahold of my hand as I passed him in the street. But as I grew older I'd come to see that a wink one year was a black eye the next, and a hand-hold now would be a fist in the future; sweet-heart one time was broken-heart another. Now though, looking at the set of Mr. Keseberg's shoulders as he guided his wife through the busy street, I could not help but think that it would be nice to have someone take such care of me. I imagined the day when a handsome gentleman—in my imagination someone very like Mr. Keseberg, tall and strong—seeing me as quite the young lady, would offer me his arm.

So caught up was I in wondering what it would feel like to have a man's arm round my waist to see me across the road, that I didn't notice that the little black lad pulling the cart had stopped to tie his bootlace. I walked straight into the cart, banging my shins and letting out a yelp of pain. The Kesebergs didn't notice, but the lad, and a couple more who were lounging against a wall and saw me do it, let out a great roar of laughter, pointing at me and smacking their knees with their hands in a frenzy of mirth. I hobbled furiously onward, hating the lad, the cart—and myself, for being such a fool—in equal measure.

If only I had gone round to the back of our wagon and put my hand into the little hidey-hole I had found, and taken out my five dollars and put them into my pocket. If only I had lost my footing and stumbled against some man outside the saloon, and righted myself with a fluttering smile and a fistful of coin. I would have found someone to take me back to Cincinnati, to take my chances with the hangman's noose or my pa's fists. I would have been better to have done so; and if I had known what lay before me, I would have done it, too.

7

School starts back today, and right glad I am of it. Meggie will turn thirteen in a month, and since Christmas week my sweet child seems to have turned into a most unpleasant girl, considering herself an expert in all matters and fluttering her eyelashes at her pa to get her own way. She treats me as a mix of servant and simpleton with a toss of the head and a way of sighing at anything I say that makes my hand itch to give her a good slap, though this is something I would never do.

I know she is just acting her age. It will do no good to take issue with every silly thing she comes up with. All the same I have spent a considerable amount of time out in the yard this last week, rehearsing the smart retorts I would like to make to her in a below-the-breath mutter, and pulling the weeds—and any unfortunate vegetable that happens to get in my way—with considerable vigor.

We have some new pupils in school. The two McGillivray boys, eleven-year-old Matty and his eight-year-old brother, Thomas, turned up this morning barefoot and possessing no lunch pails. Mrs. McGillivray and these two, a babe in arms and another expected, or so I surmise upon sight of her, arrived in town a day or so since, with nothing more to their name than a cart and a spindle-shanked mule to pull it.

Mr. McGillivray and the older boys are away working a claim up in the hills, making a little bit of a living from washing gold out of the streams. I guess the family sold up all they had in the East, in the belief that they would strike rich in the West. Like so many, they have been sadly disappointed. The great days of the gold rush are well behind us now, and those who struck lucky have moved on, leaving this broken-down trail of beggars and speculators in their wake.

The rainy weather at the beginning of the week has given way to sun, with a bright, high sky full of little scudding clouds driven onward by a brisk breeze. At this time of year it's a bitter wind, blowing down off the mountains, and at dinnertime, when the rest of the children are rushing about outside in a game of tag, I keep the two McGillivray boys indoors. I set them by the stove over in the corner and give them what I had thought to eat myself, some cheese and an apple, and a couple of slices of sourdough, and they eat up a storm.

While they are eating, I open my copy of School and Family Geography *and turn to Mr. Young's map of the United States. Our lesson after lunch is to be geography. With my finger I find Cincinnati, and then I trace the journey I made, across the whole great Continent of America.*

When we left Independence, it was as part of a wagon train so vast that, from the departure of the first wagon to the departure of the last, it was nearly a week before we were all back on the trail. With close to five hundred wagons to manage, the train was divided into smaller companies, each headed up by a wagon master.

Our little band of German folks was absorbed into a company of close on ninety wagons, led by a Colonel

Russell. What with the families and the teamsters and the single men riding out on horses, we were something like three hundred people traveling together; at the rear of us, half that number again of cattle.

And now our journey took on a new character altogether. For beyond Independence, all was virgin land. Some adventurous spirit might have opened up a trading post here and there, but for the most part the land was as it had been since time began.

To start with, our route lay through ancient forest, where the trees reached so far above our heads that we traveled in a hushed, cool twilight. But eventually the forest grew less, and gave way to woodland filled with birdsong. And here I had my first chance at friendship; but a poor show of myself I made.

One particular morning Mrs. Keseberg was riding up on the wagon seat with her knitting, talking to her husband as he walked alongside, the beeves' guiding rope held loosely in his hands.

I was walking a little way behind, holding Ada by the hand, when running past us came Elitha and Leanna Donner with their little sisters.

Elitha and Leanna's father, Mr. George Donner, had married again after their mother died. Mrs. Tamsen Donner was a quiet, plain sort of woman. She had been a schoolteacher back East before her marriage, and intended to set up a school of her own when she reached California. Between them they had three more neat little girls, brown-haired and rosy-cheeked and as like to one another as peas in the pod.

Along with the George Donners was his brother, Mr. Jacob Donner, his wife and their children, a very great number of them indeed. The two men were in their sixties, something elderly to be traveling the pioneer trail, but ruddy-faced and hearty enough, and the two families were all good friends together, as unlike my own family as could be.

As the girls came running past, Leanna shouted to me, "Come with us!—we are going to pick bluebells!"

I could not have said what a bluebell was, but it sounded a lovely thing to be doing. I looked to Mrs. Keseberg, should I take Ada, and she nodded, yes.

I seized Ada by the hand, and we ran into the woods behind the rest. At first the trees blocked my view, but then suddenly before me was a river of flowers winding away through the tree trunks and into the distance.

Leanna and Elitha were running hither and thither, snatching up the flowers and filling their skirts, with the little ones tumbling about and laughing. I hesitated. Part of me longed to join them. But I found I could not, for the scene before me was so beautiful that I was struck silent and still.

The new leaves on the trees fluttered a soft lemon green color where the breeze caught them, and thin fingers of butter-gold sun reached down between the trees. Where the light caught the flowers, they shone a glorious purple blue, and where they pooled in the shadow of the tree trunks, they were a soft, silvery gray.

In Cincinnati we had poor scraps of girls on the street corners selling wilting violets for pennies, and there were shops selling flowers tied into stiff nosegays for rich folks. But I had never seen flowers growing wild like this. I had never even known that such beauty could exist. I knelt down in them, and plunged my hands into their damp coolness. I breathed in their delicious fragrance. Somewhere nearby a bird gave out a chuckling note or two, before embarking on a full-throated trill of song. Then came an answering melody from an unseen companion, far in the distance.

Leanna came running over to me. She had a smear of dirt on her cheek, and her sap-sticky hands were filled with drooping flowers. "Aren't they lovely? Did you ever see anything so pretty? We have flowers in the woods at home, but not so nice as this!"

Pure rage boiled up inside me. To have lived somewhere as beautiful as this? And to take it so much for granted!

"Look what you've done!" Thick jealousy clotted in my throat. "Why pick the flowers? For what? You should have let them be, for you have killed them!"

In a fury I grabbed at her and shook her as hard as I could. The stems fell to the ground, and I kicked at the poor little heap of wilting flowers and stamped them to a mush.

I caught a sight of Leanna's shocked face, and then looked beyond her to where Elitha had burst into tears. I snatched up Ada by the hand, and turned and ran back to the wagon.

Next afternoon when we made camp, I was sitting on the wagon step peeling potatoes when Elitha came up, leading her little sister Georgia by the hand. Georgia was of an age with Ada, and now Elitha asked Mrs. Keseberg if Ada could come to play with the other little girls. Ada and Georgia joined hands, giggling, and jumped about together. Mrs. Keseberg said she might, and then Elitha said that her mother had asked if I might go across as well.

I said I didn't want to go, and of course this was enough for Mrs. Keseberg to say that I should, and she would hear no different, and that Elitha must be sure and tell her mother that Mrs. Keseberg was obligated to her for her kindness.

Elitha and I walked across to the Donner wagons in silence. It struck me she was something afraid of me for the way I had carried on in the bluebell wood—spoiling Leanna's pleasure in the flowers and making her cry.

I knew that Mrs. Donner was going to give me a telling-off for it. I set my mouth, and said to myself that I didn't care. She could tell me off all she liked, but I would just stare at her, and hum a tune inside my head and not hear her. But that was not what she wanted at all. Instead, she welcomed me with a cookie, and then asked me to step into one of the wagons with her, for she had something to show me.

I could not help but look around me with great interest. All the while that we had been traveling, Mrs. Donner had been teaching school, and this was her school wagon, and I had been mighty curious to see inside it. It had a particular smell: not dusty, but something like linen dried in the sun and perhaps the smell of fresh turned-over earth as well. It was filled with boxes of books, and I stared at them, wondering what the writing on the covers said. By me was a basket of slates, slate pencils tied to them with string. My fingers itched to take up a pencil and see what it would be like to trace something on the slate.

Mrs. Donner showed me a place to sit on a trunk, and sat next to me with a folder of papers in her hand.

"My girls told me how much you loved the sight of the flowers in the woods," she said, quite as if I had been right nice to them, which I surely hadn't.

"I thought you might like to see my sketches. People back in the East are so interested in the adventure we pioneers are undertaking that they long to know more. Some of our fellow travelers are keeping journals, but I prefer to make drawings of all the flowers that we see on our journey. When we reach California I shall have them bound into a book for publication. What do you think?"

She pulled out the first sketch. It was a little group of yellow violets, like the ones that grew at the sides of the creeks we had passed along the way. They were so real I thought I could have gathered them up and held them to my nose to smell their scent. There were pictures of all types of grasses, and bees and butterflies with them, like as if they could fly right off the page and round our heads. And here was a page full of those bluebells, so delicate drawn that I longed to take that page and keep it for myself.

As if she could read my thoughts, Mrs. Donner took out another sheet of paper.

"This is another sketch I did that I didn't like so much. Look how my hand shook, and how I couldn't get the blue color quite right. If you can forgive my poor skills, my dear, I should be very honored if you would accept it as a gift from me."

I looked from the paper to her face, thinking it to be a trick of some sort. Every time I held that paper I would think of my cruel words to Leanna. I guess Mrs. Donner knew it, too. But I wanted the paper, and I knew that I deserved the lesson.

8

After another week's traveling, we arrived at the Big Blue River, one of the major landmarks on our journey. I expected the Big Blue to be something like the Ohio: gray and oily-looking, and so wide that we would hardly see the other bank. But it was not more than a hundred yards across, though it was deep. It was the season of the spring gales. Swelled by days of rain, the river was risen and spilling out over its banks, and the water went rushing by us, swirling sticks and logs and even whole tree trunks with it. With it came the bodies of animals that I guess had ventured too close to the water's edge and had been caught in the torrent. We could not cross it until the waters died down some, and so we had a very welcome holiday.

One morning Mrs. Donner came across to our wagon and visited awhile. Mrs. Keseberg was doing some darning and she laid it aside.

Mrs. Donner accepted a cup of coffee, which I poured from the coffeepot. Then she said that she had noticed I was not coming to lessons with the others, and she wondered why.

Mrs. Keseberg was something taken aback. Although I was of an age with the older Donner girls, still in their girlish pinafores and bonnets, I don't suppose Mrs. Keseberg thought of me as a child at all, and she certainly did not think of herself as my mother, or as having any responsibility for my education. And indeed, it had never occurred to her that I had no learning on me—though I could forgive her that, for I had a quick wit, and she would have no reason to think I could not even write my own name.

Mrs. Keseberg said all this, and plenty more besides, quite as if I was not there at all. Mrs. Donner looked a mite embarrassed, and looked over to me once or twice with an apologetic little smile. Eventually she addressed me direct.

"When we are traveling, we only have time for an hour's class or so in the afternoon. But it seems that we will be staying here for a few days. The older girls have asked if they could have drawing lessons. I thought this might be something that would interest you."

She smiled straight at me, but I glared at her, for the more they had discussed me, the angrier I had become.

I longed to join in Mrs. Donner's school. I would pass by with a pail of water, and the little ones would be learning a counting song, and I would catch a few words and find myself humming them below my breath. I would be collecting undergarments from the bushes near the creek, and the older girls would be taking turns at reading aloud, a Bible story or such, and I would get caught up in the story and linger for a while, folding and unfolding the washing. But one day one of them had noticed me, and pointed me out to the others. They had all begun to giggle, and I had scrambled away, my arms full of washing and my cheeks flaming.

After that I had gathered up the washing as quick as could be, and walked back a different route, telling myself that I had no need of book learning. I had managed just fine on my wits all these years with no help from anyone else.

Pa was cruel when the drink was in him, and my ma too beat down by life to do right by any of us, but in my heart I wanted to believe that they would have seen to some learning for us all, if they had the chance to do it. I was shamed by my family, but thought it no business of anyone else how we had fared. And come what may, I had no intention of sitting in class with those stuck-up giggling girls and admitting that I knew nothing of letters, and had never even held a slate in my hand.

I should have been grateful to Mrs. Donner but I was not. I jumped up and said I had no reason to attend school and I would thank her, and Mrs. Keseberg as well, to keep their pointy noses out of my business! And I stamped off over to the creek, trembling with rage.

Mrs. Keseberg reported this conversation to her husband, expecting him to be as mad as she, at Mrs. Donner's presumption and my rudeness. And he took me to task over it—but not in the way I expected.

He waited until that evening, when Mrs. Keseberg was in the wagon, settling Ada to sleep, and then he asked me to walk out with him awhile.

We walked away from the camp and up the slope a little. It wasn't full dark, and the first few stars were beginning to show in the sky.

There was a little outcrop of rocks, and he sat down, and patted the rock next to him. I sat beside him chewing on my fingernail, with a sick feeling in my stomach, wondering what he would say to me.

"I am angry with you." This was the first thing he said, and my heart sank like a stone to hear these words. "Do you know why?"

I shook my head, no.

"It is because you do not realize how lucky you are. You have been born in America, the land of opportunity, and are traveling to a new place, California, where anything is possible. You can make your own life in California, and you have a good brain to do it. But a good brain needs a good education.

"I cannot make you learn. But we have been traveling together now for some weeks, and I hope that you count me as your friend."

He said the last with a straight look at me. I stared straight back—I could not look away. After a moment he leaned closer, and reached his hand toward me. My heart thumped in my chest. There was the wild cry of something in the distance. A prairie dog, or some such.

"Moth." Mr. Keseberg showed me what he had picked from my shoulder. It was a great gray and brown moth, with a speckle of dust across its wings. I looked down and scuffed my foot in the earth for a minute or two, until I could raise my head again and meet his eyes.

"Well . . . if you do"—he turned his gaze away from me, looking out over the sea of grass that surrounded us, rippling in the breeze with a gentle shushing sound—"if you do think of me as a friend, I hope you will listen to what I say. I would be proud of you, if you were brave enough to go and apologize to Mrs. Donner, and take the help she is offering you. With some schooling, you could do anything you liked when we get to California, and make a good life for yourself.

"Tell me: What *would* you like to do, when our journey is ended?"

What I wanted, more than anything, was to stay with him. Not for love—indeed, I told myself that such thoughts on my part were pure and simple foolishness, for he was a married man and a deal older than I. No—it was for another reason entirely.

That first smile between us, when it seemed to me that we knew each other somehow, was never repeated. I had come to wonder if I had imagined it. He spoke to me right curt, and for the first few weeks of our journey

I thought him unpleasant and standoffish. Many others in our company felt the same. It was clear he had no patience with the gossip and idle chitchat that made up the greater part of our entertainment along the route. But I couldn't forget his little act of kindness, in buying me the kerchief to cover my head; and despite what others might say of him, Mr. Keseberg had friends enough, close friends, indeed, among our band of German folks. So he confused me, and I had begun to study him. And my first understanding of him came from listening to his conversation with his friends, round our fireside of an evening.

All spoke of their dreams, and what they wished to do with their lives once they reached California. Some folks thought of little more than to buy land and grow crops enough to sustain them. Others had ideas to open stores or run cattle. But Mr. Keseberg had an ambition like nothing I had heard before, and I listened to his speech as greedily as I listened to the fairy stories he told the children.

He had grown up in a place called Westphalia, known for its wine, and now he wished to grow grapes in California, and make wine that would be sent all over the world. And his words made me long to stand, myself, in the sunshine among those grapevines, which I imagined to be something like beanstalks, thrusting up into the sky and growing across the land as far as the eye could see.

Mr. Keseberg said that in some countries the grapes were put into great vats when they were picked, and a fiddler played while folks danced on the grapes with their naked feet to make the juice flow. I thought for certain sure he was jesting, but if it was true, well, I longed to see that, as well, and dance on those grapes myself, with the soft squelch and ooze of their juices between my naked toes.

I wanted to stand in the great cold cellars filled with

barrels up to the ceiling, and see the wine come gushing out of those barrels, pouring endlessly into row upon row of slender green glass bottles, and to pack the bottles into boxes, and watch those boxes being loaded onto the ships that would take them to all those distant lands I had heard him speak of. And maybe one day, I would travel on one of those ships myself, and go to the other side of the world, barefoot on the deck, with the salt wind blowing through my clothes and the sea spray tangling my hair, and hear the great whales singing to each other in the iceberg seas, and watch dolphins diving through the green waves in the warm oceans.

It was the most ridiculous of notions, and I knew it, of course. I would never speak a word of it to him or anyone else; but when Mr. Keseberg spoke of his dream it was with such passion that he seemed hardly older than I was myself.

He presented one face to his friends, and another to the rest of our company. I had concluded that he was no more than shy. He hid this shyness behind a cloak of indifference, and fended folks off with clever words and a sarcastic turn of phrase which made them feel foolish. He was, as folks say, his own worst enemy. Somehow I found this strangely comforting, for I had come to think the same could be said of me.

Of course, I could not say any of this. Instead, I told him I would go and speak to Mrs. Donner and say I was sorry.

He smiled a little, and said, "Good. I am very glad to hear it." Then he put his arm around me, and hugged me, briefly. His waistcoat was of some prickly material that scratched my ear, and he smelled of tobacco and the bay rum oil that he used on his hair.

Next afternoon I went along to school, unwilling enough. It was an agony to me, even worse than I thought. Great lump of a girl as I was, I was put to sit with the little children and spent my time scowling through my alphabet, knowing less than little Frances Donner, half my age. Mrs. Donner was kind, and patient with me, though little thanks she got, but Elitha and Leanna sat well away from me, and my face burned with shame each time I passed them by.

The thing that made me stick at it was the thought of Mr. Keseberg, and the promise I had made him. And as well, from time to time I would glance up from my slate, where I was tracing my letters with such care, and I would catch a sight of Virginia Reed over on the other side of the class, chewing on the end of her braid while she frowned over her sums. And I thought to have a second attempt at making a friend, and Virginia Reed was the person I set on to be it.

Virginia was the eldest of the four Reed children—a pretty girl about the same age as me. And the Reeds were fine folks for sure.

Mr. Reed considered himself mighty important, and made sure everyone else thought it too, and his wife the same. They had a number of teamsters traveling with them—surely more than they needed, even with three wagons and a great head of cattle to look to—and two household servants, a simple-witted fellow called Baylis Williams, and his sister Eliza, the Reeds' cook.

There were pamphlets printed up for those intending to travel to the West, giving good advice about how to prepare for the journey. It was to travel fast, investing in good beeves and plenty of them; and travel light, with just the bare essentials—tools to maintain the wagon, a change or two of clothes, and as much food as you could find room for. But it seemed that the Reeds thought this advice to be aimed at others and not for them, for Mr. Reed had commissioned a special traveling wagon for the journey, twice as big as everyone else's, and kitted out like a house on wheels. This marvelous contraption even had a cooking stove built in, and each day, Eliza

Williams prepared a hot dinner for the family, while the wagons were still rolling along the trail.

We would stop at noontime and set ourselves down at the side of the trail with our dipperful of water to drink and a bit of corn bread and an apple and cold bacon left over from breakfast to eat. And there would be the Reeds, eating at a table that was kept folded up in the wagon, with a cloth laid over and their servants setting out pies and roasted meats.

It was a source of amazement to all, and the subject of great hilarity round our fireside of an evening. Mr. Spitzer would ask Mrs. Keseberg when the silver candelabra would be brought out, and Mr. Reinhardt would demand a glass of port wine to go with his cigar, and suggest that Mrs. Wolfinger might honor the company with an air on the pianoforte.

Despite the jests aimed toward the Reeds, Mrs. Keseberg could not help but be impressed by them. From the start she had set out to strike up a friendship with Mrs. Reed, and would find any excuse to send me with a message, and drill me in what I was to say.

"Excuse me, Mrs. Reed, my mistress asks if you would care to visit with her this afternoon, as she has a new recipe for apple cake and would be interested in your opinion of it," or, "Excuse me, Mrs. Reed, my mistress is looking for a darning needle and wonders if you have one to lend for an hour or so." But Mrs. Keseberg's overtures of friendship were turned away every time with not even a pretense of courtesy.

All the weeks that I had been going back and forth between the two wagons, Virginia and I had spoke a word here and there as our paths crossed. And I'd seen how Virginia and a couple of the other girls would walk together, whispering and giggling, and after supper sometimes they would go and watch the boys playing ball.

Now I thought of a plan.

"This time tomorrow I will be part of Virginia's group.

And I will go walking with them when school is out, and head over to watch the boys play ball, too!" I couldn't wait.

That evening I didn't manage to choke down even a mouthful of food. When the pots were cleaned up and put away I marched over to the Reeds' wagon, where Virginia was sitting with her ma, with my words ready in my mouth and my feet shivering in their ugly boots.

Mrs. Reed looked up as I approached.

"What is it, girl? Your mistress doesn't have another message for me, surely?" She said this in a voice that spoke more of her feelings about Mrs. Keseberg than her words alone could manage.

"No," I stammered. "I only wanted to—I wish to speak with Virginia—I wish to ask about my schoolwork—so I thought Virginia might like to walk with me some—" And I looked at Mrs. Reed right anxious, well aware of Virginia staring at me in openmouthed surprise.

"Well!" said Mrs. Reed, equally astonished, and staring me up and down. "You may wish all you like, miss! But *my* wish is that my daughter should not associate with the likes of you!" And with no more thought than if I was a dog, she ordered me away from their wagon and forbid Virginia to speak to me. I flushed up to the very roots of my hair with the mortification of it, and turned and ran back to our wagon.

I guess Virginia was glad enough to take her ma's words right to heart. Next afternoon, when I went with unwilling footsteps along to the school wagon, Virginia was talking in a low voice with a couple of the other girls. As I walked past she pinched her nose with her fingers and said, "Phew, Cincinnati girl, what a piggy stink," and the girls with her laughed right out loud in my face.

From that time on she made out she could not see me when I was standing right before her, and that she could not understand me when I spoke. It was a mean trick, and it made me mad, but I wouldn't give her the satisfaction of knowing she'd hurt me. I stuck my nose in the air just as much as she did hers, and as much as she pretended not to see me, so I did the same. I told myself that one day Virginia would wish with all her heart that I was her friend, and when that time came, I would look her up and down and pinch my nose and say . . . and say . . . well, I couldn't exactly work out what I would say. But it gave me a deal of satisfaction to think on it.

9

A day or two later the river waters were calmed down enough for us to cross. Ninety wagons, three hundred people, and a great head of cattle to get across a hundred yards or so of deep, fast-flowing water.

Captain Russell set about organizing us. One group of men were set to cutting down trees, and another to fix them together to make a great floating platform, big enough to set a wagon on. Long ropes were attached to front and back, and then a half dozen hearty fellows took the ropes and half-waded and half-swam themselves over to the other side. We cheered them on their way with shouts of encouragement, some screams as well, when one of the men lost his footing and seemed set to be swept away before our eyes.

They scrambled out of the water, and made the ropes fast, hitching them round tree trunks, and the men on this side of the river did the same.

A band of brave souls volunteered to be the first to try out the ferry. Mr. Keseberg's little group of German folks had been joined by Mr. Burger, traveling with the Donners as a teamster, and he stepped up to be one of the crew. Milt Elliott was another, a tough, skinny little fellow with a lazy eye, one of the Reeds' hired hands.

With them was a big bluff Irishman, Patrick Dolan, who had thick black hair and merry blue eyes. He was journeying with a family called the Breens, who I knew a little.

The men on the far bank heaved on the ropes, and the raft went sailing out into the stream. Mr. Burger shouted, "I christen this ship the *Blue Rover*! May God bless her, and all who sail in her!" and we all laughed and cheered.

Mrs. Keseberg and Ada and I were in one of the first groups to cross over. The women all shivered and shook as the ropes were pulled taut, screeching as the raft shuddered its way out onto the water and saying how it looked fearful deep, and clutching at their children. Not me, though. I stepped pretty eager onto that raft and stood near the edge, looking round me and waving to the folks still standing on the bank. Perhaps I had a pinch of my pa's seafaring blood. I could happily have spent the rest of the day floating back and forth; and if I knew how to do it, I would have jumped in the water and swum about, as well.

Some of the men chivvied the animals into the water and forced them across the river. The first few wagons were taken across, and as they rolled off the raft they were hitched up to one team after another, and pulled clear of the riverbank.

It was a task that could not have been accomplished at all, were it not for the number of strong, hearty men we had with us, and the good-natured cooperation of all. Three days it took, but we were finally all across, proud of ourselves for accomplishing this task, with the men laughing and joking and slapping one another on the back. But as much as there was good cheer and comradeship, there was sadness as well, for while we were crossing the river, Mrs. Reed's mother died.

Mrs. Keyes was elderly and had been ill for some time, but Mrs. Reed was her only family and Mrs. Keyes would not stay behind when her daughter left, but determined to journey with her. And here her journey ended, and she was buried with a stone set to mark her grave, and her name carved on it.

Death at the Big Blue.

How very fitting it was, that this should be where I first encountered Mr. Eddy. He made Mrs. Keyes's coffin and carved her name upon the stone that was set to mark her grave. And this coffin and this gravestone marked the point where my life turned in a direction very different to the one I had imagined.

For it was now that Mr. Reed revealed his Plan. He intended to leave the known trail and the good-natured fellowship of the great train, and strike out on a different route altogether. And he was looking for folks to join him.

Mr. Reed could certainly choose his moment.

After Mrs. Reed had been led away from her mother's burial place, weeping for the loss of something so precious to her, and we had returned to our wagons, Mrs. Keseberg sent me to find her husband, for his dinner was cooked and cooling on its plate.

He was standing with Mr. Burger and Mr. Eddy. They were heads bent over something that Mr. Reed was showing them, and he was speaking to them in an undertone.

Something about their whole demeanor spoke of secrecy, and the way that Mr. Reed stopped speaking upon seeing me approaching, and the careless way that Mr. Keseberg stepped toward me roused my suspicions, though I couldn't say why that was.

But I found out. Later that day our German friends—the Wolfingers, Mr. Spitzer, and Mr. Reinhardt—joined Mr. Hardkoop at the Kesebergs' fireside. Mr. Burger was there, and Mr. Eddy, who had brought with him another young man, Mr. Foster, with his wife, Sara, who I knew a little. I hurried Ada into bed, and then sat myself down in the shadow of the wagon and listened right hard to the conversation.

It concerned a new route to get to California, suggested by a Mr. Landford Hastings. He had written up a pamphlet about it, saying that it would take several weeks off the present route. It was this that Mr. Reed had been showing the other men. He, and the two Mr. Donners, would be heading off on this new route once we reached Independence Rock, a month's journey from now. Mr. Keseberg and Mr. Eddy had decided to join them. And Mr. Wolfinger nodded yes, he thought it a good plan as well.

Mrs. Wolfinger objected straight away, stumbling through her words in a mix of broken English and rapid German. She could not see the advantage of it.

"We get to California good with everyone. Is safe, and easy enough. I do not understand why Mr. Reed want to change, and I do not wish it."

Mr. Reinhardt answered her. "Mr. Reed's eagerness to reach his destination and get started on his new life is easy to understand. He's rich, but impatient to be richer still!"

There was some laughter at this, and the usual jokes regarding the Reeds' traveling arrangements, but when the laughter had died down, Mr. Burger spoke out. Traveling with the Donners, he already knew something of the plan.

"We all know why we are going there. The government will sell land to any person who has the money to buy it, and not so much money, either. I have very little to my name; all I have is in my saddlebags, but it's enough. In California I can be my own man, and not in the employment of others."

Mr. Eddy interrupted him, eager to hear the sound of his own voice.

"But we all want good land, that's the thing! Think how many have set off before us over the last few years. Look how many there are in our company alone! And another five companies ahead of us on this route! By the time we get to California the good land will all be gone. Mrs. Wolfinger, do you wish to arrive last, and be stuck with the land no one else wants? With no water for crops, and no grazing for cattle? I for one do not. I vote we head off on the new route and get ahead of the train, and take our pick of the prime land while we can, and let the rest of this wagon train roll up behind us and take what's left!" He laughed, looking around him to see the effect of his words.

This had to be translated into German for the Wolfingers to understand, and I heard Mrs. Wolfinger's reply, muttered in an undertone, that it seemed an unkind thing to do, and somehow deceitful. This was not translated for the benefit of Mr. Eddy, though Mr. Keseberg heard it, and looked uncomfortable. But he spoke out firm enough.

"I am determined to take the route. I have a young family, and my wife—well—"

He didn't finish his sentence, for even though it was obvious Mrs. Keseberg was expecting a baby, it was not spoken of in so many words. Mrs. Foster made a sympathetic face and the men coughed a little and looked about them some.

Mr. Keseberg cleared his throat. "The journey is hard on us all. It's known to be difficult in places. Look how long it took us just to cross the Big Blue, with so many people to deal with. This route is shorter by many weeks and, Mr. Hastings says, much easier. I think it would be a good thing to get where we are going as quick as possible."

Mr. Eddy spoke up again; oh, he had only mentioned the land as being one of the reasons that folks might want to take the new route; as for him, he had two little children as well, and Mr. Keseberg was quite right, it was not about the land so much as the length of the journey.

Mr. and Mrs. Foster nodded agreement, and said they would go back to their wagons and speak to the rest of their party, and try and persuade them the same.

Will and Sara Foster were traveling with her widowed mother, Mrs. Murphy, and a great band of children. The Murphys were part of a little group of stragglers that had been well behind us in the wagon train, but had caught up at the Big Blue. They were on the raft with us when we crossed the river, and while we waited for the rest of the company to get across, they were our neighbors.

The first evening after we landed on the far side of the river, I had passed Mrs. Murphy standing by her wagon with a pail in her hand.

"Dear, would you be a good girl and fetch me in some water?" she asked, catching hold of me. "I would ask Landrum, but he and the others have gone to collect firewood and left me here with the babies."

I looked at her with my mouth agape. Wasn't it bad enough that I had Mrs. Keseberg ordering me here there and everywhere without some perfect stranger joining in? I snatched the pail from her hand and fetched the water with mighty poor grace, but when I got back to her wagon she was waiting for me with a piece of candy in her hand, and kissed my cheek when she thanked me.

It was a little enough task for me to do, and with the candy in my hand and the kiss on my cheek I felt ashamed of my bad temper. I'd never in my life before been given a reward for anything I might do, and all that day and the next I carried that candy in my pocket, rather than eat it.

Next morning I hung around her wagon with my eyes

open for the chance to help her again and I had a reward of a different kind, for I met her daughter, Meriam.

Meriam had not been attending at the school wagon, and was not part of Virginia's group of friends that teased me so. She was a gentle-natured girl, very devoted to her family, and clever, too.

After my unkindness to Leanna I had tried to curb my tongue and had succeeded somewhat. I still could not entirely resist the barbed comments that came so easy to me, but I never meant them to be cruel. I guess Meiam saw this, and my caustic observations on our fellow travelers made her laugh, for she had a sly sense of humor of her own, that gleamed out here and there when least expected.

One evening, after my chores were finished, Meriam had come across and asked me would I like to come and sit by their fireside and keep her company. This was how I met the Fosters, and the rest of the Murphy family.

Mrs. Murphy had married young, so although she was not much over five and thirty, she had a right big family. Meriam was somewhere in the middle, and she had two older sisters: Sara Foster, married to Will and with a little boy, George; and Hattie, with her husband Bill Pike and two babies, Catherine and Naomi. Mrs. Murphy was widowed, and her sight was poor, so she depended on these two married daughters and their husbands something considerable.

Everyone made me welcome. Sara Foster fetched me a slice of pound cake, and Mrs. Murphy asked me about my schoolwork and my family. The little bit I said about my family was vague, no more than that I had brothers and sisters, and that my pa worked on the Cincinnati wharves. Mrs. Murphy said I must miss them, and that it was brave of me to travel so far away. To my surprise I thought, "Yes, it is a brave thing I am doing, and I would surely like to know that my brothers and sisters are well, that much is true."

Since setting out on our journey, my hair had grown out some, and it was pretty enough, being a lightish brown and with a natural curl. It was still only down as far as my ears, but it meant I could leave off the pink kerchief, though I still wore it tied around my neck. But Mrs. Murphy had very long dark hair that she wore in a neat braid twisted round her head, and I looked at it with envy.

Each night before we went to sleep, Mr. Keseberg led us in a prayer. But while he and Mrs. Keseberg were praying for things like patience and charity and good health for their children, I had mostly closed my eyes and daydreamed about what I would do in California and how I would be rich and drive round in a carriage and wear fine clothes. But after meeting Mrs. Murphy I paid more attention to the praying side. Though what I prayed was that I would wake in the morning to find my hair grown down to my waist, so I could wear my hair the same as hers.

10

After Mrs. Keyes's funeral, we left the banks of the Big Blue heading for Fort Laramie, and Independence Rock after that. All through June we journeyed through the plains, dry, arid land that rolled away to the horizon unbroken by any treeline.

It was several weeks since we had left Independence, and all of us had bade our homes good-bye months before that. We had long since had our fill of novelty, and the early days of oohing and aahing about this thing and that were behind us. Folks wanted nothing more than to sleep in their own beds at night, to have four solid walls about them and their belongings unpacked. Our fresh food was gone, and we were living now on dried goods only, and the women spoke of the gardens they would plant up, and the vegetables they would grow.

The men complained about the heat and the animals and that they could not make repairs to the wagons and could not find the tools they needed, laying the blame on their wives' untidy housekeeping. The women grumbled about their husbands' ill humor, and having to juggle frying pans and coffeepots over a few sulking coals to produce a meal.

Those we had started off with as good friends had shown themselves as irritating or foolish. Mrs. Keseberg had fallen out with the Wolfingers over some trivial thing, so they were less at our wagon than before, and Mrs. Murphy's two married daughters weren't speaking over some imagined slight.

So we were all in need of some diversion and at long last it came. For July rolled around, and on the afternoon of July third we pulled into camp and started our preparations for the next day.

The morning of the Fourth dawned bright and clear, and we all were out of our wagons in an instant, with the little children screeching and running about and getting under everyone's feet, as excited as if it had been Christmas.

All the men gathered together, and on the order given they fired their guns as the sun rose in the sky. I guess it was meant to be a salute, and perhaps the folks arranging it had imagined it to be something grand. But instead of one loud volley of shot, there were so many men and so haphazard were the arrangements that not all the shots went off at the same time; and this gave rise to much merriment and teasing.

All along this part of our journey we had been accompanied by great herds of buffalo; slow-moving, stupid animals that gave plenty meat. Now, some of the men went out after them, ready for the evening feast. And Mr. Reed went with them.

Mr. Reed being so very high and mighty and with such a fine opinion of himself, one way and another he had managed to offend many of our traveling companions from the get-go, and for every person that took him at his own valuation, there seemed to be another that looked at him with suspicion.

Most of the folks that set out to cross the Continent were the sober kind, leaving their homes for good reason. For some it was on account of their religious beliefs, and for others it was the thought of having land of their own and making something of themselves. But whatever their reason, from the minute they set foot on the plains, near enough all the men had come to imagine themselves brave frontiersmen and right heroes, and swaggered about fit to bust, with their thumbs stuck through their belt loops—though the truth was that if they'd been in a knuckle fight in the back streets with my pa, not one of them would have come out alive. Mr. Reed was no different.

Traveling with the wagon train was a band of men that called themselves the Old Grizzlies. They were mountain men, for the most part, squinting at the sun from under the brims of their hats, and spitting chewing tobacco into the dust. They were hunters, and all along our journey they went out after game, often bringing back so much meat that it would be shared out with all.

From the start, Mr. Reed had been dead set on being part of this fine band. But they had no time for the city swaggerers and he was never invited to join them. This aggravated Mr. Reed no end.

So, this morning, the Old Grizzlies set out after buffalo. And Mr. Reed went out after them, even though he wasn't asked. Having the best and fastest horse in the entire company, or so Mr. Reed would have everyone believe, he overtook the Old Grizzlies and rode ahead of them, shooting and killing one buffalo after another. Then, leaving the rest of the men to collect up the carcasses and do the butchery work, he came trotting back into camp on his horse, smiling fit to bust and right proud of himself.

For myself, I had a thought of him careering along on his horse, and firing his gun wildly about him, scared half to death of the great beasts grazing placid enough and minding their own business. I thought he was lucky not to shoot himself or his own horse first of all, and if he did manage to kill some unlucky beast, it was because it had probably thought itself in no danger: "Here is a fool and I have nothing to fear from him!"

Of course, Mr. Reed did not see himself in quite this same light.

All this while the younger children had been out with pails, gathering as many buffalo chips as they could—for with no timber for fuel we had to make do with what we could find, and the buffalo droppings burned fair enough—and the younger fellows set to digging fire pits.

These were heaped with the chips and set alight, and the haunches of buffalo set over. The young fellows settled themselves down for the day to turn those spits, no doubt fueled here and there by a dip or two into the ale barrel.

From time to time Mr. Reed could be seen at one spit side or another, ordering the lads to turn the spit faster or slower, and reminding them that it was thanks to him that we would be feasting so well. That summed him up to be sure. That man just lived on praise and being patted on the back.

Most families had brought a couple of bales of cloth in their possessions. Over the last week the women had looked out any that could be turned into red, white, and blue rosettes. Now, those rosettes were used to decorate a platform of boxes set up in the center of the wagon circle. A couple of the men drove posts into the ground behind it, and fixed up a length of twine between them, and then everyone gathered round to watch the Flag being set in place. When it was done, the company bugler stepped up and played a salute, and everyone clapped.

We had made the Flag over at the school wagon. My stitchery left a great deal to be desired, so instead I had been given the task of cutting out the stars. I felt like I could near enough burst with the pride of seeing them up there; twenty-eight nice neat ones, one for each of the States.

Some of the men set out tables made up from planks laid over trestles. The women had been cooking all morning, and now we all crowded up to set out our plates and dishes. We laughed and chatted, and complimented one another—"My, but that pie looks good, Mrs. Eddy," and, "Mrs. Russell, those popovers look light enough to fly away!" And at the same time each of us in the sure and certain knowledge that our own dish was the best.

Mrs. Keseberg had got up some pickled red cabbage, heaped with raisins and chopped onion, and I had made a molasses pudding, still warm and smelling of sugar and cinnamon. It was so mouthwatering that I longed to pick off a bit of the crust and have a taste. I guess little George Foster thought the same, for his hand reached out while he thought no one was looking. His ma slapped it away. Just as well; if she hadn't, I sure would have.

When George had left off crying, and been consoled with a piece of candy, Sara Foster caught hold of me, and said to come over to the Murphy wagon with her.

Everyone was getting gussied up. As we walked past our wagon, Mrs. Keseberg came out of it. She was all in her best frock and finery, with a silk shawl pinned over to conceal her condition, and her hair up in some fancy arrangement and held in place with a tortoiseshell comb.

Ada was with her, her hair in its usual braids; but lo!—each caught up with a knot of tricolor ribbons, and she as proud as could be. Mr. Keseberg was waiting to escort them, wearing the blue shirt that matched his eyes. As Mrs. Keseberg stepped from the wagon, he fetched her a kiss, making her blush like a girl. Then he swung Ada up into the air, saying she looked a princess and making her laugh. Of course, he paid no mind to me at all.

It was wrong of me to care, I guess, but I felt much cast down. I wished with all my heart that I had something better to wear than the hated yellow dress. But I had no time to dwell on it, for as Sara Foster and I got to the Murphy wagon, Meriam came running over to greet us, and pulled me by the hand.

"Quick, quick! We have a lovely surprise for you, come and see!"

Mrs. Murphy was waiting for me, a parcel in her hand.

"We don't know when your birthday is, my dear, but today is the birthday of our Nation, and we want you to have this as a gift from us—" And I opened the parcel to find the prettiest dress, of a pale green ground patterned all over with little white flowers.

I looked from the dress to Mrs. Murphy and back again, hardly believing my eyes.

"It's only an old one of mine"—Sara Foster's eyes were sparkling—"I hope you don't mind it. I thought it would fit you, as we are about the same size. And look—Mama has embroidered you a new collar, and Meriam has a ribbon for your hair."

I scuttled into their wagon as quick as could be, and put on the dress. I tied my hair back with the ribbon, and came out feeling quite shy in my finery. The dress fit in places that the hated yellow dress didn't, and the crisp white collar, embroidered with a border of daisies, framed a lowered neckline that showed my collarbones and a bit more besides. And it had a stiffened petticoat underneath that made the skirt sway a little as I walked.

Landrum Murphy was over to one side. He looked up as I came out of the wagon. He had pretty much ignored me up until now, but I saw that he gave me a second quick look. I stuck my chest out, put a big smile on my face, and walked past him as if I couldn't see him, making that skirt rustle up some. After a couple steps I looked back over my shoulder. He was staring after me. When he saw me looking, he blushed up something remarkable, and turned away in a great hurry.

All dressed in our finest, we gathered together before the platform, and Colonel Russell climbed up. He started off with a fine speech, that our Nation was made up of the bravest of the brave; those that had first set out to find this New World, and after them, those that had fought for the right to govern themselves and not be beholden to anyone else. Then he said we ourselves should count ourselves part of this proud tradition.

"We might think of ourselves as no more than ordinary folks doing the best for our families," he said, in a ringing voice. "But we are so much more than that! We are voyagers and pilgrims all, going boldly out to discover new lands and new lives, and leading the way for others to follow us!" and his words were greeted with whoops and cheers.

He raised his hand, and called for silence. When we had settled down, he read out the Declaration of Independence in a most solemn voice. Some folks looked up to the sky, and some stood with heads bent; and I saw more than a couple of folks wipe away a tear.

When he got to the closing words, "And for the support of this Declaration, with a firm reliance on the protection of Divine Providence, we mutually pledge to each other our Lives, our Fortunes and our sacred Honor," it seemed as if the words were meant just for us, our little band of brave folks setting out through the wilderness together. We each turned to our neighbor, and hugged them, or shook hands, most heartfelt.

After a deal of shuffling about and whispered direction from Mrs. Donner, the smaller children assembled in front of the platform, with much fidgeting and looking to see if Ma and Pa were watching, and waving at their brothers and sisters. One little lad burst into tears at the sight of everyone staring, and ran away to bury his head in his ma's lap; but the rest of them stayed put. At a signal from Mrs. Donner they started up in the patriotic song that they had been rehearsing over and over again.

After the first few lines, we could not resist but join in, and finished all together at the tops of our voices:

"Oh, say does that star-spangled banner yet wave
O'er the land of the free and the home of the brave?"

Then the solemn part of the day was over and the feast begun. The joints of meat were carved and served out, and we helped ourselves to pickles and corn bread, and sat round in little groups, all chattering and laughing and eating like we were starved.

I made sure to get to my pudding before everyone else, and helped myself to a good big slice of it, and then watched to see who else wanted it. Landrum came up to me, and said, "Is this what you made?" And when I said it was, he asked me, quite the fine gentleman, if he could try it, and would I help him to a slice.

I looked at him like he was an idiot. "You can help yourself, Landrum Murphy—I am not your servant!"

The afternoon wore on, and the sun went down. We cleared away the dishes and the men brought lanterns out of the wagons and lit them. Then someone produced a fiddle, and jumped up on the platform with a loud swoop of his bow across the strings.

A cry went up—"The Cincinnati Reel!"—and everyone cheered. We formed ourselves into two great circles; the women on the outside and the men on the inside, facing them. Meriam seized my right hand and someone else my left, and pulled me into the circle.

In front of me was a fellow with bright red hair and

freckles, grinning like a loon. He bowed to me with an exaggerated flourish that made me laugh, and I bobbed a curtsy to him. Then off we went, women circling one way and men the other, with another fellow up on the platform calling out the changes: "Doh-si-doh and swing your neighbor! Doh-si-doh and swing again!"

I danced every dance, one after another; not knowing at all what I was doing, but with fellows catching hold of me and whirling me one way and then another. My feet seemed to know what they were about, even if my head did not. I danced until I was giddy from the music and the warm feel of one fellow's arm around my waist, or another's hand in mine.

At last I had to stop. Breathless and hot, I crept away a little from the dancing, and found a quiet spot to sit on a wagon step, fanning myself with my hand and wishing I had a cool drink. My wish was granted. Up beside me came the lanky red-haired fellow I had danced with at the start. In his hand he held a cup, and offered it to me.

"Lemonade. Thought you might appreciate it. Thirsty work, this dancing!"

We all had brought lemons in our supplies, wrapped in sacking to preserve them on the long journey, because once we headed out into the territories, trading posts were few and far between, and the chance of buying fresh fruit or vegetables was remote. A slice or two of fresh lemon with a sprinkle of sugar was a treat, and thought to be good for the children.

But this was not just lemons and sugar and water. This had a smooth, dark taste beneath the sweetness. I recognized it at once. Try and fool me he might, but I knew the smell of rum, all right.

I said nothing, and took another mouthful. My head stopped spinning, and instead a warm feeling spread through me. I thought how lovely the evening was, and how lucky I was to be part of it, and how sweet this fellow was, to have thought of me and brought me a drink.

I drained the cup, smiling up into his face. His eyes were bright green, and his hair just the color of a kitten my brothers had brought home once, begging Ma if we could keep it. I wondered what it would feel like if I stroked it.

I guess he thought I was flirting with him some. Maybe I was. He smiled back, pretty pleased with himself.

I moved along on the step, and he squashed himself in beside me. Before I knew it his arm had slid round back of me. I leaned my head on his shoulder, dreamy and content, with the music and folks laughing but a few yards away, and me and this fellow sat here, quiet-like, in the darkness.

He hadn't spoke to me at all. I didn't even know his name. He pulled me in closer to him, his hand creeping more round my waist and then upward, stroking and squeezing. He leaned in to kiss me, and I turned my face up and closed my eyes.

I never had been kissed. I sure wanted to be. And if there was more to it, well, I guess I felt dreamy and happy enough to find out what that was.

There was a thump, and a yell. My eyes flew open to find myself tipped off the step and sprawled on the ground.

I scrambled to my feet to see Mr. Keseberg towering over the red-haired fellow, flat out on the ground with his eyes rolled back in his head and a split lip dripping blood on his shirt.

Mr. Keseberg grabbed me and marched me off back to the wagon without a word or a backward look. And that ended my first dance; and my first kiss, too.

I guess I should have been mortified at the way my evening ended. Meriam and I had been trying to cultivate something we called the Sober Voice of Virtue, in order to make us sound more grown up. In my head it sounded something like Mrs. Donner's voice, calm and quiet. Now, the Voice said that I was no better than I should be; it might be that the red-haired fellow was a scoundrel, but even so Mr. Keseberg was very wrong to have thumped him and any decent person would be ashamed of all three of us. But a voice that spoke louder was a voice that said it was thrilling to have some fellow want to kiss me, and to be saved from a fate worse than death by Mr. Keseberg's heroic action.

Next morning I told Meriam of the night's events, using the Sober Voice of Virtue again. But she gave me such a look that in an instant we were giggling, and vowing to look out for Mr. Red Hair and see if he had a black eye.

11

Next morning, with many of our company no doubt as heavy-headed and sore-footed as I was myself, we set off once more, heading toward Independence Rock, a great gray boulder looming out of the plain. We made camp nearby, and folks went off in little groups here and there to look at where previous travelers had scratched their names on the stone, and to scratch their own.

Meriam and I went with Sara and Hattie and their families, taking a blanket to sit on and some food to have our supper as a picnic. When we had walked round the rock some, and looked at what was there, and Bill Pike and Will Foster had scrambled themselves up onto the top of the rock and halloed! down at us, Hattie sat herself down with her back to the rock to nurse baby Catherine, and Meriam and I set out our picnic.

We had some lemonade—with the memory of how I felt the morning after the dance, I thought I would not drink it, but stick to water—and Mrs. Murphy had sent us off with cold pie and some ham, and fruit preserve sandwiched between slices of corn bread.

All the way along the trail we had eaten breakfast,

dinner, and supper sat on the ground, so why was it different to have our meal sat on the ground here? But it was. Hattie Pike might be married with two babies, but she was only a year older than Meriam and me. Sara Foster was not much older again, and the four of us girls felt free and easy together, not like sensible grown-ups at all.

It was a silly thing, but I liked to feel that I could sprawl on the ground to eat my slice of ham if I chose, instead of sitting prim upright; and Will Foster was on his hands and knees with George riding on his back and pretending to be a cowboy, with one hand holding his pa's hair and the other a slice of pie.

When we were eating, I asked Hattie how she come to be married so young. The minute I said the words I wished them back again, for I caught a sight of two-year-old Naomi, with preserve all around her mouth. It occurred to me that perhaps this was an indelicate question, and Hattie had had no choice in the matter. I guess my give-away face said all, but Hattie was good-natured about it.

"Oh, my word, everyone asks me that! But it is a wonderful romantic story, and I like to tell it." She settled herself more comfortably against the rock.

"We all got on board ship, and it was Christmas. We were going from Nauvoo—that's Illinois, where we were living then—and it was right cold. That first night we went to our cabins, and when we woke in the morning the river was froze hard and the boat stuck at the quayside, and we could go nowhere at all!" She let out a peal of laughter.

"Ma was in a fit, but we"—she looked at Sara, and the two of them giggled, flushing up like schoolgirls—"well, we thought it was the best thing that could happen. Because working on that boat were Mr. Foster and Mr. Pike, and we fell in love with them and they with us!"

Sara finished off the story.

"Oh, you can't believe how lovely it was. Everything all sparkling white with frost—the rigging on the ships and the trees on the bank—and the blue sky, and the sun shining. Three days we spent on the boat and then we just got off and went to the church together, and had a wedding there and then!"

I just couldn't help myself, I had to ask.

"But Hattie—how old were you? You can't have been more than fourteen! Didn't your ma mind?"

She looked surprised.

"No—why should she? Ma wasn't much older when she got married. And when you are in love, you know it. What should you wait for? And it's not like Bill is some silly lad who is still tied to his ma's apron strings. He can provide for us. I think I am right lucky!"

It was true: Bill Pike was near enough the same age as his mother-in-law, and Mr. Foster the same, but it seemed not to bother any of them. He was a nice man, and so was Will Foster. They had been friends since they were lads, and gone off together to work on the boats going up and down the Mississippi River.

Hattie's story of the frozen Mississippi reminded me of something, and quite without thinking, I said, "One year, the Ohio froze over, just the same, with all the boats and ships stuck fast out on the water. One morning there was a great to-do, with folks yelling, and I went to see what it was about."

Everyone was listening to me. Mr. Foster took George off his back and sat down next to his wife. I began to wish I had not started the story, for they were all listening to me with smiles on their faces, thinking it would be something amusing. And I was going to disappoint them, and spoil the fun we were having.

But I could not stop, and carried on. "It was a woman. It looked like she had set off from the other side, and she was carrying a baby. And behind her came two men. And they caught this woman and took her back across the river with them."

It wasn't quite the dramatic ending they had expected, and they looked a bit puzzled by it.

I couldn't tell them the truth. For of course the woman was a black slave, making a desperate bid to get to the north bank of the Ohio River and free herself and her child, and the men were Kentucky slave-catchers, intent on dragging her back to the South if they could catch her, or making an example of her if they couldn't.

The men were too far away to catch her. She had but a couple of hundred yards to go and she would be free. All along our riverbank and hanging over the sides of the ships were folks screaming and yelling at her—"Run! Run!"

But the men had dogs with them. They let them loose, snarling and barking, to come racing across the ice. The woman cast one desperate look behind her, and screamed, and turned back toward us with an expression of the most ghastly horror on her face.

Next minute the dogs were on her. The baby fell, and went skidding across the ice, covered in its mother's blood.

The men stepped up, quite casual, and called the dogs off. One of them snapped them back onto their leashes, and the other strolled over and collected up the baby and tied its ankles together, and slung it over his shoulder. Then they walked back across the river, chatting and laughing together and leaving the woman's body where it had fell.

I wished I hadn't told it. I had dreamed about it for weeks afterward, where I thought I could see the woman grabbing at me and begging for help, and I could do nothing to save her.

My story seemed to have brought our fun to an end. Mr. Foster picked the remains of George's supper out of his hair, and Meriam and Sara and I folded up the blanket.

Just as we were done, Colonel and Mrs. Russell came past. They were going to the rock to carve their names, and we joined them.

Colonel Russell took out his pocketknife and carved something official-looking, with the date the train had set off from Independence, and where we were aimed for, California; and Will Foster carved out a sweetheart, and put his initials in it with those of his wife. Hattie Pike, not to be outdone by her sister, said to her own husband, "Put the children's names! For who knows, one day they might come here, and see them, and know that we did it!" So Bill Pike set out, "Catherine Pike, age four months" and "Naomi Pike, age two years" and the date, July 11, 1846.

Those children never did go back to see their names carved into the rock. They never heard how their parents were there that hot day, laughing and telling jokes, and George riding on his pa's back.

Perhaps their names are still there. Or perhaps they are worn away to nothing, with the wind and the rain beating on them year after year.

The morning after our picnic, tragedy struck. I was washing out some clothing down at the creek, when I heard a shot, followed by a terrible scream. I dropped what I was doing and ran back to the camp.

Mr. Foster had been cleaning his gun and had shot Bill Pike dead, right through the heart.

The scene before me was one of horror. Hattie Pike was screaming over her husband's lifeless body, and Mrs. Murphy with her arms thrown around Will Foster, he staring wild-eyed around him, quite as if he knew not where he was or what he was about. It was the first violent death of our journey. But it would not be the last.

12

A few days later we reached another landmark, perhaps the most important of them all—the Great Continental Divide.

So far, all the rivers and streams we had passed flowed eastward, back toward the places we had come from and on into the Atlantic Ocean. But after we crossed the Divide we would come to the Sandy River, flowing west and pointing our footsteps to the end of our journey, California and the Pacific Ocean.

I expected the Divide to be something like a line drawn in the ground, maybe marked with a row of flags, or a signpost—one arm pointing one way saying "East," and the other, "West." I thought to be able to jump from side to side—"Now I am in the East! Now I am in the West!" and I was not the only one to imagine it so. And as we passed into the foothills of the Rocky Mountains, traveling through hills that were enough to make us puff and pant as we climbed steadily upward, we all grew more and more excited at the thought of reaching this magical place.

We broke camp on the morning of July eighteenth—

Continental Divide Day, as we had come to call it—and at noontime we stopped at the banks of a shallow stream. Mr. Reed came past us, all puffed up, and called folks together. He said he had studied the geography of the area right well, and that we should be at the precise spot in an hour or two. Some folks cheered, and others clapped. But Mr. Keseberg laughed, and said, "Mr. Reed, you are sadly mistaken. We have crossed the Divide quite without knowing it. Look, the water in this stream is already flowing west!"

A great shout went up from those around us. Folks crowded to the water's edge and said, "Yes, it is true," and "Oh! Mr. Reed, you have deceived us!" There was some gentle booing—good-humored enough, I guess, though we were all something disappointed—and making him the butt of some jokes.

Mr. Reed did not like that one bit. He blustered about and said that Mr. Keseberg was wrong, and did not know what he was saying. Mr. Keseberg replied quite calmly to him, "No, here is the water and you can see with your own eyes where it is headed," and someone shouted out, "Give it up, man! Admit you are wrong!"

Mr. Reed glared at Mr. Keseberg. He sure did not like being made to look so foolish. I said to myself, "Mr. Keseberg has made an enemy here."

And it made me think of the choice that lay before us. For within a few days, those heading off on the new route would leave the great train as it continued north, and turn south toward Jim Bridger's Fort. This train was to be under the direction of Mr. Reed. Mr. Reed, who could not tell the difference between a river flowing westward and one flowing to the East, and who would rather make an enemy than admit he was wrong.

When the plan to take the new route was first spoke of, I had taken it for granted that I would travel on with the Kesebergs.

The weeks since leaving the Big Blue had been the happiest of my life. I had found myself enjoying my schooling. I discovered that I learned real quick and hardly had to be told a thing twice. Mrs. Donner had told me one time that I was a joy to teach—words that might have come easy to her, but were mighty precious to me. As well, she had asked me if I had thought of being a schoolteacher myself. It would mean I would be free to earn my own wage and spend it how I wanted, and do no man's bidding unless I chose it. I could go where I pleased and live how I liked—and I thought that yes, I truly would like to do so.

The Donners were heading off on the new route, so unless I took the new route myself I would have to abandon my schooling. It would mean leaving the friends that had come to mean so much to me—including Elitha and Leanna—for I had finally found the courage to seek them out and apologize to them, and now we spent a deal of time together. And it meant leaving the Murphys, my very dearest friend, Meriam, and her mother, who had taken me into the heart of her family, and treated me as if I was her own.

I had thought that with the loss of Mr. Pike, Mrs. Murphy might think to take her family and continue with the main train. If she had, I would have been tempted to set off with them. But, if anything, the tragedy had made her more determined to get the journey over as quick as possible. Mr. Foster had never come back to himself after his friend's terrible death. He hardly spoke. He hardly ate. And when the camp was still and quiet in the night, he could be heard screaming out in his sleep. The whole family suffered along with him and I suffered along with them. How could I leave them? The very thought of it was too terrible to contemplate.

But the worst thing of all was the thought of leaving Mr. Keseberg. And it was this thought that led to another: perhaps I should.

Mr. Keseberg and I spent very little time in each other's company. What words we spoke were stilted and awkward, and sometimes it seemed to me that a different conversation entirely lay beneath the one we were having. From time to time I felt him looking at me—how that was I could not say—and that awful blush would rise up and engulf me, so I hardly knew where to put my eyes. But when I gathered my self-possession and turned, he would be engaged in conversation with Mr. Hardkoop or with his wife, or busy with some matter, and I would tell myself it was nothing more than my imagination. He had never, by word or deed, been anything other than honorable, and true to his wife. It seemed that my curiosity about him had turned into something else, and I thought I was a fool and should be ashamed of myself.

I stopped watching him from the corner of my eye. I did not try and listen to his conversation round the fireside with his friends. With every scrap of my will I turned my thoughts away from him. But it seemed that as soon as I decided to put Mr. Keseberg out of my heart, so he determined to put himself more into it.

The day after leaving the Divide, we broke camp later than usual, and did not stop for our dinner until well into the afternoon. We had another five miles to go before we would stop for the night, and when we set off again, Mrs. Keseberg said she was going to lie down in the wagon, and told me to take Ada to walk along with her pa.

I walked along in silence, lost in thoughts of my own and taking hardly no notice of Ada's childish prattle. The sun had already set, leaving the sky a soft shade of violet color, and the first few stars beginning to twinkle above. I suddenly saw one of these stars go flashing across the sky, and whirled round to point at it, crying out, "Look, oh, look! Oh, I wish I knew what made it fly like that!"

Mr. Keseberg's face lit up, and words come bursting out of him in a torrent.

He told me that the stars in the sky were suns, the same as our sun that gives us light, but so very far away that their light was no more to us than a pinprick in the sky. Each star had a name, and a group of stars together was a constellation, and all were named for gods and goddesses and other folk of ancient times. He showed me Orion the Hunter, and the big bear and the little. And he told me of the Christmas star, and how the wise men had followed it to find the baby Jesus.

He described the countries they traveled from, distant lands of silks and spices where they lived in palaces with gardens and fountains. Countries where they worshipped cats, or cows, and where kings and queens wore silken gowns, with tiny dogs carried in their sleeves.

I was astonished to find him so talkative, and I think he was surprised to find in me such a willing audience, for I pestered him with one question after another.

Just in an instant—one hour's conversation, no more—my desire to hear his words overcome my resolve to avoid his company.

I did not wish to leave Mrs. Donner. I would not leave the Murphys. And I could not leave Mr. Keseberg.

My decision was made. I would carry on, and take the shortcut with them all.

13

One rainy day at the beginning of March, I receive bad news about the McGillivray family. Mrs. McGillivray births her baby, a little girl that she names Rose, but has a hard time of it, or so I hear. And one Monday morning when the children arrive for school, the McGillivray boys are not there. The other children inform me that the McGillivray baby has died and the boys are at home and trying the best they can to care for their ma, who is in a bad way.

After school I send Meggie home in charge of her little sisters, carrying with her instructions to Martha to stay another hour or so until my return, and I set off to visit Mrs. McGillivray to see if there is any assistance I can offer.

The way out to the McGillivray home is very poor, and my skirts are sadly muddy by the time I arrive at the ramshackle little homestead. It is no more than a tumbledown cabin over by the town pond. Someone has tried to dig over the rough patch of ground to one side, and there are some seedlings showing through the dirt, more weeds than anything else. A rusted ax sits on the chopping block, and there are some rough logs lying tumbled this way and that; not enough firewood to last more than a day or so, I reckon.

The cabin belongs to Mr. Peabody and he is letting it to Mrs. McGillivray for a good price. I say good price, I mean it is a good price for him. Myself, I resolve to have a word with Preacher Holden and see if he can remind Mr. Peabody of the concept of Christian charity.

The poor woman is lying in bed, weeping miserably into her pillow. A sulky fire smolders in the hearth, and the two older boys are trying to make supper out of some sad remnants of food, which seems to be all they have in their store cupboard.

Their little brother, his face smeary with dirt, is sitting on the floor sucking on a piece of rag, and a big yellow dog lying across the threshold of the cabin looks as mournful and hungry as the rest of them.

I visit for a while with Mrs. McGillivray, who sits up when she sees me and pushes at her tangled hair. After I have made some conversation with her about her children's progress at school, I am a bit lost about what to say next.

It may sound heartless for me to have visited with her and not to have cried along with her about the loss of her child, but there is nothing I can say that will help her deal with her grief; this is one of the hard lessons I have learned in my life. But if I can assist her in a practical way, why, that is something I would like to do. The poor woman needs some help, that I can see, but how I can be of use to her I cannot imagine.

As I get up to go, I spy a pile of sewing on a table in the corner. Her boys come to school in clothes that are worn and mended and mended again every which way. It strikes me that Mrs. McGillivray is good with her needle. If she could earn some coin with it, that might be of more help to her than any amount of soft words. So I ask if she would be interested in helping me some. I can sew a straight enough seam for quilting, which I enjoy, but other than that I am a poor seamstress. Martha's sewing, too, leaves a lot to be desired, and I have a pile of mending sitting neglected in my work basket.

Mrs. McGillivray sits up quite straight at that. Yes, indeed, she would be pleased to do it. She had been in service as a lady's maid in Boston before she was married, and was known for her fine stitchery.

"Oh," she says, "Mrs. Klein, have you ever visited Boston? It is such a very elegant place! My family—the family I was in service with, I mean—had a great house, right in the very center of the town. And my young lady, Miss Lottie—out at balls and the theater, night after night! And her clothes! The finest silks, and Brussels lace—you cannot imagine!

"She cried to see me leave, and indeed—that is—when Mr. McGillivray and I married—" She stops, and gives a half laugh.

"Oh dear. Forgive me. What you must think of me, carrying on so!"

What she means, of course, is that she did not wish to leave her employment, but had no say in the matter. A married woman could not carry on in service. A married woman's place was at her husband's fireside, caring for him, and what an insult it would be, to suggest that a man's wife should undertake paid employment, as if he could not provide for his own family.

I make no reply, though I wonder, suddenly, if Jacob has that same sense of aggravation about him with regards to my own employment, and if the fellows at the lumberyard tease him over it.

I try not to look about me at the poor state Mrs. McGillivray is come to by her husband's care of her. Instead, I rise to my feet, pretty brisk, and command the eldest boy, Matty, to come along home with me.

I sit him down with a slice of plum cake while I look out a pile of Jacob's work shirts that need mending. Jacob is something careless with his clothes and is forever catching his sleeve or pulling off a button or two. And when I send the boy home, I add in the rabbit pie I had set aside for our supper, and a dish of sweet potatoes and onions to go with it. My own family eats eggs and toasted bread, and I say a prayer of such heartfelt thanks over this scratch meal that I suspect they are too cowed to make any comment about the loss of the rabbit pie and the rest.

The shirts come back two days later, mended much better than I could ever have hoped to. I straight away engage Mrs. McGillivray to come into the schoolhouse twice a week and teach the children knitting and stitching.

A good job she makes of it, too, setting the little ones to make cross-stitch potholders for their mothers and the older girls on the intricacies of seams and darts, with the promise of dressmaking once they can sew neat enough.

The older boys are set onto knitting socks. There is some talk round town at this, and a couple of the boys pull faces at the idea. I take no heed of it. I tell them that the Navy men are taught to knit, and if it is good enough for the brave sailors then it is good enough for them. And in any case, the more domestic chores they can do for themselves, the less call they will have to consider their wives as glorified servants, when they come to marry.

14

On the morning of July twentieth, when the wagons began to pull out of camp, we did not, but stayed where we were; me folding quilts and blankets in back of our wagon and Mrs. Keseberg brushing Ada's hair and tying it into its little braids. Mr. Keseberg was harnessing up the animals at the second wagon and speaking in a low voice with Mr. Hardkoop, who was sat on the wagon steps, pipe in his mouth as always, untangling some knot in a coil of rope.

As they passed us, various folks shouted a good-bye, and wished us luck, but one or two asked us, "Are you sure you wish to do this? For it seems a foolish plan to me." Mr. and Mrs. Keseberg made a joke of it, saying that when the others arrived in California, the Kesebergs would be waiting there with a cup of coffee to welcome them.

When all the wagons were finally pulled out, and the last of them could be seen far in the distance, we looked around to see who would be traveling on with us to Jim Bridger's Fort, the first stop on our new journey. Mr.

Reed had been very confident that there were many folks intent on joining this expedition, so I thought to see sixty wagons or more, but we weren't close to even a third of that number. It seemed that many of those who had planned to join us had thought better of it, and departed with the rest.

Here were the Donners and our friend Mr. Burger; Mr. Dolan, the big bluff Irishman who'd crossed the Big Blue on the raft with him; and Mr. Dolan's traveling companions, the Breens.

John Breen was perhaps a year younger than me, and his brother Edward a mite younger still; quiet, studious boys that I knew from the school wagon. They had a mighty annoying little brother, Paddy, who seemed to spend his whole life tumbling out of trees or being fished out of streams. Then there was a whole parcel of little ones, right down to a baby just learning to walk.

Mr. Breen was something of an invalid, traveling to California for his health, and I guess his wife and children had to bear the brunt of the chores, but other than the screams that invariably accompanied Paddy Breen's latest adventure, they never seemed anything other than cheerful.

Our German friends were to continue on with us, and then, of course, there were the Eddys.

Mrs. Eddy had become the very best of friends with Mrs. Keseberg. The whole family had become something of a fixture in our lives. Mrs. Keseberg and Mrs. Eddy spent a great deal of time together, walking along the trail arm in arm in the mornings, and Mrs. Eddy might sit up in the wagon with Mrs. Keseberg in the afternoons, keeping her company while Mrs. Keseberg rested. And when we made camp, with the wagons drawn close and the cooking fires blazing up, with biscuits baking in the Dutch ovens and folks visiting with each other and talking over the events of the day, the Eddys would often visit with us and I would mind the children, Ada, and little James and Margaret.

Margaret was a stocky, rosy-cheeked child, with blue eyes and curly blond hair. She was as unlike my whining little sisters as could be, with a cheerful, sunny disposition and easy to manage. To my surprise she took a great liking to me. She would take my hand, or fling her arms around my waist, or bid me bend down so she could kiss me. I felt foolish at first, to take such pleasure in it, but soon I came to relish the feel of her small fingers clutching my own or her lips against my cheek.

I had never played any of the childish games that the little girls engaged in, and at first I did not understand what they were at. The first time Margaret handed me her doll, and commanded me to play, I sat there helplessly with it in my outstretched hand. All I could see was a stick of wood with a rounded end and some smears of black and red painted on, wrapped in a rag or two. But after a while I could make out that the black and red was a face, made to resemble eyes and lips and cheeks, and that the rags were intended to be clothes, a dress and bonnet, with a piece of frayed knitting wrapped round all, to be a shawl.

The girls were playing with Ada's tea set: some miniature cups and saucers, and a teapot and milk jug. Margaret held out a tiny plate with some crumbs of biscuit on it, and I took a pinch between my fingers, and did as they did, holding it to the little painted mouth and making sounds of "Mm, mm," as if eating something delicious. Ada poured water into a cup, and held it with her finger stuck out, as if she was a grand lady, and sipped it most delicate. She passed the cup to me and I did the same. Then I said, in a high-pitched, squeaky voice, "Oh, how delightful, your Ladyship, such delicious water!" Ada let out a squeal of laughter, and Margaret joined in, lying on the ground and kicking her legs into the air. And I laughed, too.

Although I came to love Margaret dearly, and liked her mother well enough, I began to be most wary of Mr. Eddy.

Mr. Eddy was a strutting little bantam-cock of a man, hardly higher than his wife, and she was a small enough woman to be sure. What he lacked in inches he made up with his tall tales of bravery. He was good company, I suppose, and his tales were entertaining enough. But he stitched them with all the colors he could find, and soon enough folks came to see that he wasn't overly bothered about the exact truth of a matter. His tales came to be taken with a whole peck of salt, and some good-humored eye-rolling.

After some evenings spent listening to him as I carried out my chores, it struck me that although his stories made me laugh, they were amusing at other folks' expense. Somehow there was a sour taste in my mouth when the laughter had died away. No one was safe from his malice, even those he hailed as friends.

It was Mr. and Mrs. Eddy and Mrs. Keseberg who enjoyed one another's company. Although Mr. Keseberg welcomed them to his fire and chatted with them polite enough, often he would take himself away from their company and go off to smoke his pipe with Mr. Hardkoop and Mr. Burger, over at the Wolfingers' wagon.

Sometimes he would spend the evening reading stories to the children by the light of a lantern. I would find some excuse to sit and listen, too; and he would hand the book to me, and let me practice my reading, leaning back with his eyes shut, and a smile on his lips, no doubt amused at my poor efforts.

By the time we arrived at Jim Bridger's Fort, we had been joined by a few folks more. These were Mr. Stanton, a single fellow up on his horse, riding alongside the wagon of his friends Mr. and Mrs. McCutcheon, who had a little girl, Harriet. And there was a spotty-faced French-Canadian lad named Jean-Pierre Trudeau, my age almost to the day. The final family to join us was the Graveses.

Mrs. Graves was a tall, hatchet-faced woman of most decided opinions, and it was clear from the get-go that she expected all, including her husband, a quiet, gentle fellow, to jump when she said so. They were a right big family, eight children plus a married daughter and her husband. There was a tall, spindly sort of son, William, who at nigh eighteen was all bones, with ears that stuck out to each side of his head, and two daughters about my age.

Mary and Eleanor Graves were the silliest girls I ever saw. They spent their time making eyes at all the boys and giggling nonstop at the slightest thing. Every night they put their hair up in rags, parading round the next morning right proud of their pretty curls, though both girls were just as hatchet-faced as their ma, so I can't say that the curls sat right well.

My little group of friends spent some time with them at first, but it was hard work. Mary and Eleanor talked about the clothes they'd like to wear, and the men they would marry and how they would have their houses done up. They thought us dull company for sure, having no time for the childish games we played to entertain the younger children. Instead, they struck up a half-hearted friendship with Virginia Reed, for the girls Virginia had been such good friends with had departed with the rest of the main train and left her to her own devices. The Graves girls spent as much time in squabbling as they did in gossiping and I caught a sight of Virginia once or twice, looking very straight-faced and miserable in their company. I felt something sorry for her. Not sorry enough to do anything about it, though.

We left Jim Bridger's Fort on the last day of July. Mr. Reed gathered us all together, and sitting up on his horse he gave us our orders—that we should all set off along the route he pointed out, and he would ride ahead himself and catch up with Mr. Hastings—the writer of the very pamphlet that had caused us to change our plans—and who was, or so Mr. Reed told us, not more than a few days ahead of us, escorting another group of emigrants. Mr. Reed said he would find Mr. Hastings and ascertain the route, and be back with us in a day or two. With that, he wheeled his horse about, and galloped off. And we did as we were bid, and whipped up our beeves and set off to follow him.

I wonder, now, at the thinking that led these foolish men, Mr. Breen and the Donners and the rest, to follow Mr. Reed and elect to take the shortcut. What was it that spurred them on and blinded them to the dangers we would face? Some set out for California for one reason, and some for another. Some kept mighty quiet about the lives they'd led previous and some—like me—had great good reason to want to leave their past behind.

But as for the others, the family men who led us to our fate, they'd left happy lives behind them in the thought of providing better for their families at the end of the day. I am certain sure that the happiness of their loved ones was to the front of their minds at the start. But it seemed that this was soon enough forgotten. Their hunger for land and their desire for fortune took them over, so that they thought only of worldly success, and how they would look in other men's eyes.

I have come to think that there are no shortcuts in life. It is too easy to choose to do the selfish thing, and to head off in pursuit of your own happiness and your own ambition, and lose sight of what really matters in this world. The slow road, the plain road, and the road that seems dull and much-traveled by others has plenty to recommend it. Men think themselves heroes if they take risks; but to take a risk with the happiness of those who love you and depend upon you cannot be heroic.

To my mind, the man who fears the path of love as being one of dull duty, but sets along it nevertheless, is the real hero at the end.

15

When we first left Jim Bridger's Fort, our route was so easy that the men were slapping one another on the back for their cleverness. The weather was fine, and there was game for the taking, coneys and deer. The route seemed to be everything Mr. Hastings had promised, and we thought the folks who had stayed with the big wagon train to be fools for not coming with us.

On the third day Mr. Reed rejoined us. He told us good cheer! He had spoken to Mr. Hastings, who was but a day or so ahead of us. If we hurried we might catch him, but if not, he had gone over the map again and pointed out the route, and Mr. Reed was confident of the way. So we hitched up our wagons once more, and followed Mr. Reed into the shadow of the Wasatch Mountains.

Our route gradually began to rise upward. There would be a climb up a hill and a gentle descent into a pleasant valley, and then the same again. Each time the climb would be a little steeper, until we got to the point where it was no longer possible for the beeves to pull the wagons directly up the slope. Here, we devised a system of switchback, where the wagons went to the left, always moving slightly up the hill, and then to the right the same. We did something similar to get them down the next side, with the men roping the wagons and pulling on them to slow their descent.

These hills and valleys were all covered with lush grass, and small streams trickling down through rocky outcrops and giving out into pretty pools here and there. Those of us not involved in driving the beeves or steadying the wagons as they lurched their way along, took off our boots to sink our tired feet into the cool grass, for the heat was something fierce. And we splashed our faces in the streams, and enjoyed the shade from the few trees that were dotted here and there.

After a day or two of this, we were tasked with a much steeper hill than before. One team of beeves was not enough to pull each of our wagons up the slope, but we had a spare yoke walking along at the back. We hitched them all up to the one wagon and got that up the hill, and then the same again with the second.

We thought, when we came to the end of that last steep slope, that the worst of our journey was over. But we had a right hard shock when we crested what we thought to be the final rise.

We expected to see the same journey again down the other side, a series of gentle grass-covered slopes. But what lay ahead of us was a great valley, with a terrifying steep slope straight down into it. Slope and valley floor alike were all utterly overgrown with every type of thick shrub and thorny bush. Beyond that rose a steeper, rocky slope again, and another, higher still, behind it.

We looked at one another in great dismay. This was not what we had been led to believe at all. Mrs. Keseberg clutched at her swollen belly with one hand, and her husband's arm with the other.

"Louis! Louis, I cannot do it!—I cannot climb down

through this wilderness! We must turn back, and rejoin the main train—they cannot be so far in advance of us!"

Mr. Keseberg looked at his wife, and looked at his wagon, and set his jaw. "We have to do it. It will take us a week or more just to return to Bridger's Fort. By the time we get back on the original trail the others will be too far ahead and we will never catch them! It's not so bad, my dear. It will take us some time to blaze through a path for the wagons, and in the meantime they will be left here so you can stay and rest in the shade. When the route is cleared and we take the wagons down, you can follow behind, real slow."

It was poor comfort. Mrs. Keseberg's lips trembled. I was scared myself at the sight before us, and felt right sorry for her. I crossed over to her and took her hand.

"Mr. Keseberg is quite right. You need do no more than walk down behind the wagons. I will look out for Ada, and help you all I can."

The look she turned on me was pure fury; her husband could not see her face.

"Of course you would agree with him!" she hissed. "He can do no wrong in your eyes—do not think I cannot see what you are about, right beneath my nose!"

I dropped her hand, and jumped back, startled. I had spoken to her in the spirit of pure fellowship, with no thought of anything other than to comfort her. I disliked her, it was true. But throughout our journey, no matter what the provocation, I had tried my best to bite back the words that jumped into my mouth, keeping my own counsel about the way she spoke to me and about me, and her treatment of her husband. As for my feelings for Mr. Keseberg, I knew not exactly what they were. Unformed, unexamined, I had kept them to myself as well. I had been nothing but loyal. To discover that she had such thoughts of me—deceitful and underhanded—was a shock, and a bad one, too.

I looked across at Mr. Keseberg. He was in conversation with Mr. Hardkoop, and had seen nothing of this exchange. And I was mighty glad of it.

To get down that hill meant slashing our way through with axes and scythes. It took every one of us to do it—every man, every woman, every child old enough to carry a blade. We hacked our way through brambles that tore at our skirts, and stumbled through vines that wrapped themselves round our ankles, sending us crashing to the ground, with the threat of a broken bone to show for it. Whippy branches lashed our faces and arms, and choking clouds of buzzing midges rose up around us, filling our mouths and noses, making us cough and spit.

There were stones of every size, which the smaller children were set to pick into pails and tip aside. We older girls and the women heaved away the bigger rocks, and then there were boulders so enormous that they were higher than a man's head. To move them out of our way the men roped up the beeves, or set themselves to them and pulled, like animals in harness, or set up levers, with four or five of them bearing down, and the rest of us pushing and rocking the stones from side to side, until they finally went careering down the hill, crashing their way through the undergrowth.

Here and there were stands of trees. The men sawed them through, and hauled them aside, and dug out the roots, and we filled the holes where the roots had been with the stones and rocks we'd moved earlier. In this way we made a path that the wagons could travel over.

Once the path was cleared the men roped each wagon and manhandled it down the slope. We all held our breaths, fearing each minute to see a wagon break free and go careering down the hillside to smash itself to smithereens at the bottom—or worse, to take off and drag the men along with it. And the hundred or more head of cattle that were traveling with us had to be harnessed up over and over again in teams of four, and the men pull at them from behind to slow their progress down the hill; we did not want them to break free with the chance of them falling and breaking their necks in their headlong rush.

By the time we had fought our way down that slope to the valley below, we felt like we could die from the efforts we had made. Two days it took us, working from dawn until dusk. Even then we were not done. The last task of the day was to bring Mrs. Keseberg and Ada, and the other little children she had been minding, down to the valley floor to join the rest of us.

That final journey up the hill again near enough finished me. My legs trembled, and every muscle in my arms and back was a fiery throb of agony. As I caught hold of tree roots and rocks to pull myself upward, the blisters on my hands burst open, stinging and oozing pus, and sweat streamed down my face and into my eyes, blinding me.

We got the children, and Mr. Keseberg his wife, and set off for the last time down the hill. I had Ada by the hand, and picked my way down the slope with her, my heart jumping in my chest every time my feet slipped some, or a loose stone went tumbling away down the hill below me.

Some ways behind me I could hear Mr. Keseberg with his wife, he encouraging her, step by step, and she fussing and weeping her way along and accusing him of cruelty in bringing her here and saying she regretted it and wished they had stayed with the main train, and how it was all his fault.

Why was it that even in the direst of circumstance I could still find myself paying attention to a conversation that did not concern me? Being so intent on listening to Mrs. Keseberg's complaining I missed my footing altogether. Next thing I was gone sliding away on my backside, screaming for someone to help me, thinking that I would catch on some rocks and be tipped into the air to go bouncing down the rest of the slope, smashing myself to bits as I fell.

There was a ripping noise, and I lurched to a halt. Without a second's thought I reached out and grabbed on to the person next to me—Landrum Murphy, carrying one of his little brothers pig-a-back. It was Landrum who had grabbed my skirt as I went skidding past. I lay on my back for a moment, half-sobbing and half-laughing, clutching his hand for dear life.

Landrum helped me to my feet. I could hardly stand, I was trembling so, and he put his arm around me and I leaned on his shoulder. After a moment I pulled away from him, and brushed down my dress some; why, I could not imagine, for we all of us were covered in dust and dirt from head to foot.

When we got down to the bottom of the hill Mrs. Keseberg disappeared into our wagon without a word to any. With my hands shaking from tiredness and fright, I made up the fire and got the coffeepot set over, with corn bread baking in the Dutch oven, and I made some salt pork and applesauce with raisins.

No meal could have been more welcome. Mr. Keseberg and Mr. Hardkoop and I ate in silence, so exhausted we could hardly lift fork to mouth. Mrs. Keseberg did not join us, and when I had eaten I took a dish of food into the wagon for her. She took it from me with poor grace, and turned her face away, dabbing at her eyes with the hem of her skirt.

I went across to the Donners, pulled up a hundred yards away. Elitha and Leanna had a length of wool that they were twisting between their fingers in a cat's cradle, and showed me how to play.

The two Mr. Donners were deep in conversation with a couple of the other men.

"I do not understand this route. I have looked once

more at Mr. Hastings's instructions and it says nothing of crossing these mountains—that is, it shows a pass through them. This cannot be it." Mr. George Donner spoke in a low voice.

Walter Herron—one of the teamsters—spoke up.

"Mr. Reed says he spoke to Mr. Hastings and this is the route that was pointed out to him."

There was a silence. I guess everyone was thinking as I was—remembering how confident Mr. Reed was at locating the Great Divide, and how we missed it. Our thoughts were given voice by Mr. Jacob Donner.

"Once we left Fort Bridger I expected we would follow the route of the party ahead of us, the one being led by Mr. Hastings. I'd have thought to see their wagon ruts, at least. There's been nothing—not the remains of a fire, not a dropped horseshoe. Did anyone else see anything, I wonder?"

Mr. Graves was sitting with them, and he shook his head, no; Mr. Herron the same, with a mighty sober look upon his face.

After a moment or two, Mr. Jacob Donner said, "Well, we can't turn back. Say nothing to the rest. Once we are through these mountains I will call a meeting, and perhaps Mr. Reed can explain the route to us in more detail."

Nothing more was said. I bade good night to my friends, and took myself off to sleep.

No bed, no matter how thick with feathers the mattress might have been, could have been more comfortable that night than the ground beneath the wagon, where I slept wrapped in a quilt. I guess we all felt the same. Something woke me in the night—some raised voices maybe—but it was nothing more than a moment and then I was as deep asleep as before.

The next morning dawned gray and humid. I made the coffee and the breakfast, and got Ada ready for the day. Mrs. Keseberg was nowhere to be seen and Mr. Keseberg—grim-faced—told me that she was gone across to the Eddys' wagon to keep company with Mrs. Eddy.

I guess they had fallen out, but that was nothing new. And she was at our fireside that evening, the same as ever.

That day was just as hard as the previous. We fought our way across the valley floor, and the day after that we climbed up the other side, double-teaming the beeves to pull up the wagons, with the men pushing from the back, and the women setting rocks behind the wagon wheels at every turn, to stop them rolling backward. Down the next slope, and up the next hill, and on and on the same.

We had thought to travel twenty or so miles a day. Crossing those mountains, we didn't get more than a couple of miles a day at most. One day it took from dawn until dusk to travel a hundred yards.

It seemed that every time we reached the crest of what we thought must surely be the last great climb, another came into view before us. Hour by hour our hearts grew heavier, and our spirits sank lower. Our thoughts of arriving in California early in September vanished. July turned into August and we were still battling our way onward, hardly any distance from where we had split off from the original train, and nowhere near the end of our journey.

All were concerned about their livestock. Despite our best efforts, beasts fell and broke their legs and had to be shot, and the milk cows dried up from fear, as they were roped and swung down the mountainside, and their calves died. The Graveses had a crate of chickens with them. The crate fell from their wagon and smashed, and the chickens scattered, clucking and squawking as they fled. And the beeves, double-teamed over and over again to pull the heavy wagons up the steep hillsides, began to groan and pant at the slightest thing, exhausted from their efforts.

When we crested the last rise of the last mountain, and finally made our slow and weary way down to the flat valley floor beyond, it was with a sense of great relief. It was very late in the evening, and full dark; cloudy and with no moon. We could hardly make out what lay ahead of us, although we could see that the land spread before us flat to the horizon and we thanked God for it.

After supper was done, Mr. and Mrs. Keseberg, she still something quiet, and Mr. Hardkoop and me—for I had begun to think I had as much right as anyone to know what was going on—crossed over to the center of the camp circle where a fire had been lit for the evening's meeting.

Mr. Jacob Donner stepped up, and said that he had some questions to ask Mr. Reed about the route, but that Mr. Reed wanted to make an announcement first.

Mr. Reed stepped forward, and cleared his throat.

"It has come to my attention that there is someone among us who had behaved right badly. As leader of the company—"

Someone behind me muttered that they had no recollection of a vote being taken to appoint Mr. Reed as leader. Mr. Reed ignored this, other than to speak louder.

"—as leader of the company, I am responsible for administering justice, and I will do so."

There was a shocked silence, and we all looked round to try and find a guilty face. I caught a sight of Mr. and Mrs. Eddy, looking nowhere but straight in front of them. My heart sank, wondering what mischief they had been up to.

Mr. Reed continued that he had been told previous of this person's bad character, and that he had already caused an upset along our journey, at the July Fourth dance when he had beat up on a fellow half his size and half his age, who was doing no harm.

My mouth dropped open. I had no idea that anyone knew of the ruckus at the dance, it seemed to be over so very quick, and felt like it was so very long ago. I looked at Meriam, and she looked a bit red at me, and whispered, "Sorry"—for she had told her sister, Sara Foster, and perhaps Sara had told her husband. Mr. Foster and Mr. Eddy were friends, so I could see how Mr. Eddy had got hold of this juicy little nugget of gossip, and how much he would have enjoyed the taste of it, and want to share it with others—Mr. Reed, evidently.

Then Mr. Reed said, "The person—I cannot call him a man—the person that I speak of has a wife in a particular condition. He is known to have beat her. We might be in the wilderness, but we are civilized folks, and this behavior cannot be tolerated!" Mr. Reed had talked himself up into a right passion, and banged one fist into the other.

"Mr. Keseberg! I call upon you, to come out front of this company and explain to us all what reason you can have for your intolerable behavior, and why we should maintain you in this company with us! I vow, if I had my way, I would send you out of this train this very instant!"

There was a shocked intake of breath. All heads turned to stare at us. And I turned mine to stare at Mrs. Keseberg.

Into my head flashed a picture of her, sat in our wagon with the dish of food untouched on the floor in front of her. I knew in an instant what had happened, and what it was that had woke me in the night.

In my own dealings with Mrs. Keseberg, I had learned that she never came right out and said if a thing had displeased her. She would sit with her face turned away and her mouth turned down, giving out a little sigh from time to time, until she was asked, "What is the matter?"

And then she would give a pretty laugh, and say, "Oh, nothing! Nothing is the matter at all, don't worry about me. I'm just being silly."

To begin with I took her at her word, and let her alone. But then the sighs would grow more, and if I let those sighs alone, too, why, she would start to talk in a high, fast voice, trembling on the edge of tears, about something I had quite forgot, that had happened maybe a week or so previous. She would rouse herself more and more until I hardly knew how to speak or what to say, and would continue in this vein until in the end she would burst out crying.

Once she'd had her cry out, all around would have to pet her and stroke her and fetch and carry for her, until she was quite calm again. Then she'd give out a little trembling smile and say what a silly thing she was, and we would have to smile, too, and say no, no, not at all, and pet her all over again.

She was sharp as a lemon one minute and sweet as lemonade the next; a most wearing sort of woman. I would be glad enough, when our journey ended, to see the last of her.

At the end of an hour's weeping and carrying on about some trifling matter, a look I was supposed to have given her or a dish that I hadn't cleaned well enough, my fist trembled to give her a slap across the head and bring the conversation to an end. And now it occurred to me that, weary to death from the struggle down the mountainside, too late to turn back and frightened of what he had brought his family to; desperate for a night's sleep but faced instead with the prospect of hour after hour of this same carry-on, Mr. Keseberg had come to the same conclusion as me. It seemed his hand had said what his mouth could not.

Mr. Keseberg rose to his feet, his face still but his eyes blazing. He looked first at his wife, who had the grace to blush and look away. He glanced at me, my mouth agape and looking as astonished as he felt, I am sure. He turned his gaze on Mr. Reed, looking him up and down like Mr. Reed had been nothing to him. Then he turned his back and walked off to our wagon without a word.

Mr. Reed could sure make a rousing speech. It did him a favor, too. In the hubbub of conversation that followed Mr. Keseberg's departure, the awkward questions about our route and Mr. Reed's meeting with Mr. Hastings were quite forgot.

I guess Mr. Reed had got wind of the mutterings in that regard, and he tackled them full-on with his closing words.

"We have some hard travel behind us. There is some hard travel ahead of us still—for tomorrow we will be journeying through arid desert land. But that will be one day, no more. Then it will be the easy life for us! I say Ho! for California!—just a few weeks away!" And everyone cheered.

"Ho! For California!" How we were deceived by that thought! For when the sun come up next morning, it was to show us that what lay ahead was worse by far than what had gone before. For now we entered into the Great Salt Desert.

16

A day to cross the Great Salt Desert; just a day. What a lie that was.

Five days it took us to cross that wasteland in the high heat of late August. No shade. No water. Nothing to see but bone-colored earth to the horizon, every way we looked, and our black shadows stretched out before us in the mornings and behind us in the evenings. We traveled with the flat blue sky pressing down on us and the boiling white ball of the sun beating on us, hour after endless hour. A hot wind whipped the dust into the air and filled our mouths and noses, and our eyes and lips stung and blistered with the salt. And all the time the fear grew in us that there would be no end to it. The desert we thought to cross in a matter of hours seemed to stretch on and on, and we began to think we would perish there.

Until now we had traveled close together. By the end of the first hour of this torment, our comradeship was gone. Desperate to get out of the sun, it became every fellow for himself. Our companions pulled ahead or fell behind, we cared not how they fared. They were but distant dots on the landscape, one minute seeming near and the next, vanished altogether, for the desert played cruel tricks with our eyes. We saw pools of delicious water that were not there at all, and stands of shady trees that did not exist. And over all the wind moaned, bringing with it the powerful belief that in the distance a voice was calling your name, begging for help or crying out for loneliness.

It was a thought that was like to drive you mad if you let it, but what else was there to listen to? Just the endless creak of the wagon wheels, the desperate snort of the beeves staggering wearily onward, and the last rattling breaths of those animals that had given up and been left to die alongside the trail.

On the afternoon of the fourth day we caught up with the Reeds' family wagon. Being such a monstrous big affair, near twice the size of ours, the weight of it had broken through the crusted soil so it was axle deep in the sour gray mud beneath.

Their beeves were heads down, grunting with their desperate efforts, sinking to their knees and being whipped to their feet by Mrs. Reed, screaming at them all the while. But it was no use. The wheels would not turn and the animals were doing no more than dragging the great wagon along. The Reeds' cook, Eliza Williams, and her brother Baylis, who was as hard in muscle as he was soft in the head, were behind the wagon, pushing with all their might to help the poor beasts in their endeavors. All four of the Reed children, even the two smallest, were doing their best to help.

Their other two wagons had been unhitched, and it looked as if they were to be abandoned. As we came up to them, Mr. Keseberg called to Mrs. Reed.

"Where are your other beeves?" he asked. "Are you leaving your wagons?"

She stared ahead, pretending not to hear him. I stole a look at Virginia, expecting her to behave the same. So

I was most surprised when she came over to join us, and gave Mr. Keseberg an answer.

"We must leave the wagons, because the beeves are so nearly dead from the thirst that they can't pull more. Father and the hired hands have taken them ahead in the hope of finding water."

There was a moment's silence, and then she burst out, "I am so sorry for the poor animals! And we are all so thirsty as well! I can hardly bear it!"

At that, Mrs. Reed called her back, sharpish-like. Virginia hung her head some and wouldn't look at us again.

Our thirst was beyond endurance. All the same we took but one dipperful of water between us at a time—a sip or two, only. We needed the water for the animals; the beeves were our only hope of getting through this wasteland and reaching salvation, and we were doing everything in our power to save them.

Mr. Hardkoop had left the driving seat and was leading the team instead, and he and Mr. Keseberg were carrying what provisions they could to lighten the load. Little Ada stumbled alongside us on her chubby legs. And for all that Mrs. Keseberg's time was due and past, she walked along with us as well, leaning on her husband's arm. I walked along at the back, with a sack of oatmeal over my shoulder and another in my arms.

Mr. Keseberg looked to where Mr. Hardkoop was walking with the second wagon, and waved his hand to him to stop.

"We'll leave the second wagon here. Give those animals some water, Mr. Hardkoop, and we'll leave them to rest up. When the Reeds come back with water for their team and to get their other wagons, we can do the same."

Mr. Keseberg hesitated a moment, then as if every word was forced out against his will, he asked Mrs. Reed if she would like some water.

"We could spare a half barrel," he said.

"Oh—Ma!" said Virginia, and got a look for it. Mrs. Reed turned back to Mr. Keseberg with a cold face.

"No," she said. "We want nothing from you."

Another full day we walked, making camp under the wagon when the sun went down. The nights in the desert were bitter cold, and with the sinking of the sun that moaning wind grew louder, and the voices in it grew more lonesome, like souls in torment so that you could not bear to hear them. Even though we were near to fainting with tiredness by sundown, when night came rolling in we none of us slept hardly at all.

We rose that last morning in the full dark. With only a few sticks of firewood left, we could do no more than warm up the last of our coffee—a mouthful each, and a crust of hard bread dipped in to be our breakfast.

Even by just that meager light, I could see that Mr. Hardkoop's feet were swelled and covered in blisters the size of dollar coins, and that he could not put on his boots. He saw me looking. I opened my mouth to say something, but he shook his head at me, quick-like, and then turned away, tying his bootstrings together and slinging his boots round his neck, so that when we set off, he was in his bare feet.

As the sky began to lighten I saw that his feet left little spots of red blood in the white dust. How he would manage when the sun came full up and the ground turned to fiery coals I could not say. And Ada cried and threw herself on the ground, refusing to walk further.

Mr. Keseberg was burdened with all that he could carry, bent nearly double with the weight, but even so he took her up in his arms. His eyes fixed on the little spots of blood ahead of us, he calmed her tears by telling her the story of Hansel and Gretel, his voice hoarse and gasping with the effort. How they laid a trail of crumbs and stones to find their way home when they were left alone in the forest, and how their journey ended at a magic house made all of gingerbread and other good things to eat.

I listened greedily, just as much a child as Ada, interrupting every sentence to ask, "But what does gingerbread taste like? What are candy canes?" For I had hardly heard of such things. Lulled by the story, Ada fell asleep, her arms round her father's neck.

Finally the sun appeared over the horizon. And thank God!—before us was a long pool of water lying beneath some low trees, with the beginnings of hills behind. We saw some of the other wagons drawn up there. And at long last we came into camp, and left the desert behind.

When we had pulled our wagon to a halt, and let the beeves loose to drink their fill, and gulped down cup after cup of water ourselves, we set the campfire to blaze up, anticipating coffee and some bacon and grits.

Mr. Reed came over to us in a right taking and asked if we had seen his wife and children. We told him yes, that we had left them behind with their wagon stuck in the mud. Mr. Reed flew into a frenzy. He would not listen to another word, but berated Mr. Keseberg for abandoning them, saying that it was akin to murder to have left them so, and only what could be expected from such a man!

Mr. Keseberg retorted, "Yes, it is true, they have been abandoned and left to make their own way, but you are the one who did it, Mr. Reed, not I! As you see, I have kept my own family close by my side!"

An hour later we spied the Donners pulling into camp, and Mrs. Reed walking with them. And we heard the story of why Mr. Reed had not gone back into the desert for his wife.

He had been first to arrive at the camp, his horse dead beat and lame. A full day he had waited for his teamsters to arrive with the beeves, but they never came and they never came. The teamsters had let the animals loose, thinking they'd head for the scent of water, but the beeves had no more brains than the teamsters did, and as soon as they were set free they'd gone thundering off this way and that, never to be seen again. With no horse to ride and no beeves to take back into the desert with him, Mr. Reed was frantic to think how to go and rescue his family.

After we left them, no sign of her husband come to rescue her and their last drop of water gone, Mrs. Reed had abandoned her wagon and set out with her children and servants on foot. That walk would have been a death march to them, and it was something like a miracle that the Donners found them.

Once their own animals were rested and watered, Mr. George Donner lent Mr. Reed a horse and a mule, and Mr. Graves lent two yoke of beeves. Mr. Reed went back and retrieved his family wagon, though the beeves that had been pulling it were dead. When that one remaining wagon was finally pulled into camp, piled high with all it could carry from the wagons left behind, Mr. Reed flat refused to go back into the desert again to fetch in the others. Mrs. Reed was fit to be tied, and was left to reconcile herself to the loss of nearly all the fancy possessions that she had been so mighty proud of.

Mrs. Reed had a tea service painted all with roses, that had come from one of the big emporiums in New York City, and which she never failed to mention whenever the subject of a hot drink arose. And she had a bolt of silk patterned with fire-breathing dragons, that had been brought all the way from the distant China lands. I longed to see it made up into a gown and Mrs. Reed wearing it, for I could think of no garment that would suit her better.

But now it all was lost; fancy cups of fancy tea with fancy talk to match, and fancy silk gowns. All gone, along with her harmonium and her stitching machine, the chairs that had come to her from her grandmother and the rest.

It was a tragedy for the family, to lose their wagons, I knew that well enough. Truth be told, though, I felt it served them right out. And a mean little smile twitched in my mouth.

To make up for the humiliation, the Reeds threw their weight around instead. For the three days that we stayed in that camp at Pilot Peak, Mr. Reed ordered his teamsters and the other hired hands, whether they were his hands or not, to go and look for his missing beeves. It was plain to see that the beeves would never be found, no matter how many miles folks walked in search of them, wore out by the heat and dazzled by the sun, but they all did what the Reeds told them, and went where the Reeds bid them, like a heap of donkeys. I could not understand it; we were not the only ones who disliked the Reeds' boastful ways.

Our own beeves were near to collapse, needing to be well rested if we had any chance of continuing with our journey. They could not be taken back into the desert to pull in our second wagon. And Mr. Keseberg asked, like Mr. Reed, would anyone lend us a couple beeves or a mule or two.

Our German friends had no animals to spare, and could not help us. And the rest would not, for Mr. Reed had dripped such poison into their ears with his pretty speech concerning Mr. Keseberg's character.

After Mr. Reed had stood up and accused Mr. Keseberg, Mrs. Murphy had took me to one side. She asked if he treated me poor as well, and would I like to travel with them instead.

I told her the truth of the matter. Mr. Keseberg had slapped his wife's face to bring her to her senses when she had worked herself into a frenzy. I did not say that I thought he had done nothing wrong. I did not say that my pa beat my ma so that there were days she could not rise to her feet for it, and my brothers and sisters and me had been at the end of his belt buckle, too—but no one took my pa to task for it, or treated him different because of it.

And I did not say that I thought Mr. Reed had such a very strong dislike of Mr. Keseberg that there was more to his actions than his so-called desire for justice. I only said that Mr. Keseberg had not wished to stand up in front of the company and humiliate his wife by defending himself, and I thought it gentlemanly of him.

Mrs. Murphy said she understood, and what a good girl I was for being so loyal. I seemed to have caused Mr. Keseberg more harm still. I felt worse at that than I could say.

And now Mr. Reed's accusations came to bear on us pretty harsh. For all turned their heads away from Mr. Keseberg's request for help, exclaiming instead in loud voices over the Reeds' kindness. For when their galumphing great wagon was finally heaved into camp, the Reeds made a great show of distributing their provisions among the others, in the spirit of Christian charity. Myself, I thought it was just a low way of getting other folks to carry their goods for them, and that they would be just as quick to ask for their return at some point in the future.

With no help from anyone, our wagon was left behind in the desert, with the mules still hitched up and the spare team of beeves at back. Round our campfire that night, Mr. Keseberg raged about the mean spirit of his fellows, the loss of his wagon and all it contained, and the fate of the animals.

I had learned long ago that crying for myself earned me nothing but a box to the ears. I had never cried for any person since. But I could have wept for those poor animals, dying slowly out there in the desert, knowing only that they served us as best they could and that we abandoned them at the last.

It must have hurt Mr. Keseberg something terrible to see how his good reputation was lost in this way. But after that one night he acted like he had no knowledge of what was said of him. He treated everyone the same as he had before: polite and quiet and offering help where he could. And he continued to smile pleasant enough at Mr. Reed, and nod his head at Mr. Reed's words and then ignore them as he pleased. It was clear that this aggravated Mr. Reed something dreadful, and I thought, "Ha! I hope it makes him mad as hell!"

Eventually Mr. Reed meddled in something he shouldn't have, and found himself at Mr. Keseberg's mercy, and I guess he came to regret his high-handed ways something bitter.

17

We stayed in camp for several days, animals and people alike too exhausted to carry on. At last, well into September, we set out again. And now the Reeds found themselves well behind the rest, going mighty slow, with their mismatched animals plodding along pulling the heavy great wagon as best they could.

Our desperate, every-man-for-himself trek across the Salt Desert had set a pattern. Those with lighter wagons pulled ahead, determined to be first in camp and get the best grass and water for their beasts, leaving those with heavier wagons to trail along at the back. We broke the unbreakable rule of the wagon trains, that all should stick close together and look to one another for assistance. And when we entered into Indian country, we found the real proof of this sensible advice.

We had seen Indians here and there along the way already: traders, with blankets and baskets for sale in Independence, and their children pestering us for treats, and running off with smiles on their faces and a handful of beads or some such. But these were not the same sort of Indians at all. These were warriors.

One afternoon, too tired and too hot for conversation, we were making our slow way through some low hills. Ahead of us, I caught a last glimpse of the little McCutcheon wagon disappearing into the distance. An hour earlier we had passed the Murphys, settling themselves down to eat their dinners. I had waved to Meriam, putting out the plates, and she had waved back with a dishtowel in her hand. But for now, we were alone in the landscape, the silence broken only by the harsh croaking cry of a couple of buzzards, flapping their great ragged wings in a slow circle above our heads.

I felt, rather than heard, a rumble of sound deep in the earth below my feet. I looked over to Mr. Keseberg, a question on my lips—and saw a hundred or more copper-skinned men, half-naked and with their long black hair flying out behind them, come thundering over the hill toward us on their tough little brown-and-white ponies, brandishing bows and spears, a great cloud of dust whirling around them.

I stood openmouthed, completely without thought of the danger I was in, at this astonishing sight. But Mrs. Keseberg screamed, and fled for the safety of the wagon, not looking where she was going and running slap into Mr. Keseberg. He caught her by the shoulders, and shook her, and told her to stop screaming. He shouted that they harried the wagon trains and set out to make our lives impossible, "—but they are not killers!" He had to yell to make himself heard over the noise of the thundering hooves. "I promise you, they will not hurt us!"

And he was right. The Indians rode round our wagon, hollering and whooping, laughing and jeering at the sight of our pale, frightened faces. They did not shoot at us; instead, two of our beeves sank to their knees, blood streaming from the arrows in their necks. Then the Indians wheeled their horses away, and galloped off as fast as they had come. As they passed, I saw they were leading some horses. I recognized Landrum Murphy's gray pony, and a chestnut mare I thought belonged to the Graveses.

"It is amusement on their part!" said Mr. Keseberg, as we watched them vanish away over the hills. I guess he was right. For we unhitched the dead beeves and left them by the wayside and the Indians did nothing with them, but left them to rot.

If those Indians have gone to their Happy Hunting Grounds, I wonder, now, if they are punished; for their sport was to cause us all the greatest of suffering.

It was the custom to put two or three yoke of beeves to pull, and a yoke or two to walk behind the wagon resting. In this way, turn and turnabout, we had gone slow but steady enough on our journey so far. But everyone had lost animals along the way, on the mountains and in the desert, and now everyone lost more to the Indians. And the time soon came when we did not have enough cattle to keep traveling on in this fashion.

Beeves are strong beasts for pulling, better, you would think, than horses. But they are not so hardy as folks might expect. They need so much to keep going: plenty of rest, plenty of grass, and plenty of water. The loss of so many meant stopping to rest those remaining more often, and the lack of good grass made them weak and slow. And although we were now but a couple of hundred miles from the end of our journey at Sutter's Fort, it seemed that the closer we got, the slower our journey became.

We counted out the days on our fingers, and counted out, too, our sacks of coffee and flour and sugar; there was not enough food to see us through. So Mr. Stanton volunteered to ride ahead and return with supplies.

Being one of the single men, riding light with just his pack and his bedroll on his horse, it made sense for Mr. Stanton to head out. But he needed some companion to travel with him, and Mr. McCutcheon stepped up to the task. It meant leaving behind his wife and daughter, and seemed a most unlikely thing to do. This gave rise to no end of speculation among the gossipmongers, and as usual, Mrs. Keseberg and her friends the Eddys were chief among them.

The evening before Mr. McCutcheon and Mr. Stanton were to leave the camp, the Eddys and Mrs. Keseberg talked the McCutcheons up and down. They came to the conclusion that there was trouble in their marriage, and that Mrs. McCutcheon, a young, pretty woman with a cascade of silvery curls, was involved in a flirtation with someone. What started as lighthearted conversation turned into one of speculation, with Mr. Eddy suggesting one name and another for the guilty man, even so much as saying it must be Mr. Stanton, and that Mr. McCutcheon intended to have it out with him when they were away from the camp and shoot him dead.

Mr. Keseberg sat through the first part of the conversation, making an attempt once or twice to turn the talk to another topic, but they would not be gainsaid. After the two women had dismissed Mr. Eddy's idea of vengeful murder with a great deal of laughter, the conversation turned back to speculation once more and lighted on Charlie Burger, the Donners' teamster.

Mr. Burger had an eye for the girls, it must be said. He wasn't right tall, but he was blue-eyed and bronzed from being in the outdoors all day, and his hair bleached quite white with the sun. In the big wagon train he had left more than one girl in a snit with another over him, but he was hardworking and right nice.

Mr. Keseberg finally lost patience to hear his friend being slandered in this way. He told his wife in round terms that she should be ashamed to cast such accusations at a defenseless woman who had done her no harm and to blacken a man's character so.

He could not say it direct to Mr. and Mrs. Eddy, but they got the hint right enough. They removed themselves from our fireside pretty sharp, no doubt to go and remind anyone who would listen how unkind Mr. Keseberg was to his wife, and what an unpleasant sort of man he was, altogether.

I was not part of the conversation, and happy not to be. I thought that there was probably no more reason for Mr. McCutcheon's actions than that Mr. Stanton and Mr. McCutcheon were good friends and had traveled together from the start. Maybe Mr. McCutcheon felt that the slow, dawdling pace of the journey, and the constant chatter of the older children and whining of the younger, the crying of the babies and the women's gossip, was unbearable. Or perhaps it was no more than that he longed to be free, and dash off on his horse, and feel as though he was doing something brave and exciting for a little while.

If that was the case, I could sympathize with him. As one slow day followed another, I had come to feel the same, and longed for our journey to be over.

Whatever his reason, he set off next morning with Mr. Stanton, with our good wishes riding along with them, and for a few hours we were all content and went to our beds with hearts that were glad enough.

This gladness did not last long.

18

That night Mrs. Keseberg's pains began. Helping to birth a baby was nothing new to me. From the age of eight years I had helped Ma so, one after another, year after year. It had frightened me greatly, that first time, with Ma screaming and yelling, and only me to care for her; but this was very different.

Much to my surprise Mrs. Keseberg was quiet and determined in her labor. I fetched water for her to drink, and wrung out a cold cloth to put across her head, and held her hands at the end when the pains got real bad. Even then she made hardly no noise—I guess I yelled louder than she did, for she had a real hard grip on her, and my hands were bruised for days afterward. She clenched her teeth on the wooden birthing stick, and breathed as slow and deep as she could; and the baby slipped out easy enough, just before dawn.

Mr. Keseberg had taken Ada across to stay with the Eddys, and returned to take up his place on the wagon step, and had sat there all the night through. Now I called him into the wagon, and placed his new little son in his arms. He looked at his wife, and then at the baby, with such tenderness in his face that I could hardly bear to see it.

I left them alone and went to the creek, to fetch water for the coffeepot and rinse out the sheets Mrs. Keseberg had been laid on.

I was coming back, pail in hand and the wet sheets folded over my arm, when I saw Mrs. Eddy on the other side of the camp, unloading her cooking pots. She hailed me to ask after Mrs. Keseberg, and I called across that all was well, a little boy arrived safe and sound and to be called Louis after his pa.

I went to carry on my way, but then Mrs. Eddy paused, looking beyond me, as if something had caught her eye. She was joined by one of the teamsters, who called across to Mr. Breen. I crossed the clearing to them, wanting to see what they were about.

As folks began to stir, a few more came to join us. We stood in the half-light, squinting at the distant blue hills where they merged into the dark sky and, beyond them again, the jagged outline of the Sierra Nevada—the Snowy Mountain. Once we were across the mountain, once we had made our way through the pass that wound between its high peaks, we would be in California, the Land of Milk and Honey. And ever since it had come into view, we had fixed our gaze on it, night and morning.

I asked Mrs. Eddy what she had seen. She said she didn't rightly know. Just that something looked different, but she couldn't lay her finger on what.

The sun rose up behind us. The wisps of early morning cloud melted away. Then, like God's finger pointing, a full ray of light reached across the sky and touched the tip of the mountain. The snow gleamed forth, as pearly pink and gold as the Gates of Heaven.

It was a beautiful thing to see; but as one, we uttered a great groan of despair.

It was vital that we got through that final pass before

the winter set in. We were slow on our travels, and late on our journey, but all the same we'd thought to have plenty of time before the snows fell in November. But here it was, not even October. The snow was vastly early.

Mrs. Eddy clapped her hands across her mouth in horror. Mr. Breen dropped his head, and raised his hand, as if to shield his eyes. But the sight of the snow was altogether too much for Mrs. Graves. She let out a piercing scream that roused all the rest of the folks and brought them running from their wagons, her husband included.

For all his meek demeanor, it appeared that Mr. Graves had an iron streak somewhere in him and he had stood up to his wife and had his own way regarding the route they were to take to California, and now he came to regret it with a vengeance.

Mrs. Graves turned on him in a fury. "I only agreed this route upon your word that there was a great number of folks coming along this way and led by Mr. Hastings, who knew the cutoff right well! I never expected to find myself traveling with nothing more than a handful of wagons, and be put to such lengths as we have, to make our way along the trail!" She added, "My mother told me you were a weakling. I should have listened to her, for you always were a fool!"

As one, the other wives joined in, whipping themselves up into a fury and berating their menfolk for their stupidity.

Worn-out from fighting our way through that first set of mountains, and then again by our trek across the Salt Desert, and with our cattle faring so ill, we had long abandoned all hope of beating our fellows to the pass and arriving in California before them. Instead, we had settled for a steady, plodding pace, resting the animals as much as possible, and ourselves as well. But now the men declared that we must make great haste. We must travel fast, and stop to rest the animals as little as we could. And this meant taking everything we did not truly need from the wagons, in order to lighten their load.

The wagons were somewhere to shelter the babies from the glaring sun or the night frosts, and to rest the little ones who could scarce walk. They carried everything that was needed to start new lives in the West, clothes and furniture, tools for woodworking and pots for cooking. But most important of all, they carried everything we had of food and water. And as we relied on the wagons to carry our goods, so we relied upon the beeves to pull them.

The beeves were everything. Our very survival depended on them. We wished them stronger, for they had been short of grass and water almost from the beginning of our journey and were near done in. And we wished them faster—for with this first dreadful sight of the snow, rank black fear came snapping at our heels.

The whole camp turned into a ferment, with folks screaming and running back and forth, with as little idea of what they were doing as ants have when you pour boiling water to destroy their nests.

The Donners' school wagon was to be left behind, with only a few things taken from it and put into their other wagons; and more and more things were discarded from their other wagons as well—trunks of clothes, and chairs, and cooking pots and knives and forks. I was horrified to see Mrs. Donner's folder of flower drawings thrown careless on the ground. I gathered it up and ran across to Mr. Keseberg, and begged him, might I put this in our wagon?

The Kesebergs had traveled light from the start, and there was nothing to be unloaded from our wagon. All that was in there was the provisions, for the household goods had been left behind in the desert. Surely one folder of papers could weigh but very little? Mr. Keseberg said no without a second thought, and turned back to what he was doing.

I was mad as hell. To have my wish ignored so easy, especially when I thought how I had labored all night helping his wife, and had no sleep myself! It was unfair that I should have nothing, for I had brought nothing with me at all! In the past I would have shouted or stamped about in a rage. But this time I just made up my mind. When he was not looking, I crept into the wagon and hid those drawings behind the farthest sacks of food.

"When our journey is ended," I said to myself, "I will produce them, and hand them back to Mrs. Donner with a great flourish!" And I imagined her face, and how pleased she would be.

The bolts of cloth that were to be traded with the Mexicos were left behind to rot, and most of the children's playthings; games and dolls and the rest. I saw a child's red wagon with yellow-painted wheels thrown to one side, and one of the little boys with his fists in his eyes, sobbing bitterly for its loss. Things that the women had packed with such care back East, thinking to see them in their proud new homes in the West, teakettles and chamber pots and brushes and brooms, were heaved careless out of the wagons by the men, and thrown higgle-piggle onto the ground.

The women screeched at every box that was heaved out. As fast as they were unloaded by the men, they were loaded back in by the women, crying and carrying on and turning their eyes at their neighbors.

Mrs. Graves shouted, "Why, if Mrs. Breen can take her copper kettle, then I shall take mine!"

And Mrs. Eddy yelled, "If Mrs. Donner can take a box of books, then I can take my mother's tea set that was given to me on my marriage!"

These neat and proper goodwives in their aprons and bonnets had been as unlike my mother as could be. But now, here they were, screaming at their men like slum strumpets.

An hour after the snow was first sighted, we pulled out of camp. Other than Mrs. Keseberg, asleep on a bed of blankets with the baby asleep beside her, we were all walking. Mr. Hardkoop was leading the wagon, Mr. Keseberg carrying Ada, and me, so tired I could hardly put one foot in front of the other, carrying as many provisions as I was able.

We wanted to run, run just as fast as we were able and get to safety while we could, but we had no choice other than to creep along as slow as snails, our footsteps fixed to those of the smallest child that could walk and our eyes on that tiny shining line of snow, so very far in the distance. And we asked ourselves constantly, is it greater than it was before, or less?

Mr. Hardkoop told only the tiniest of lies, but his punishment was death. At the beginning of our journey, in good weather and good health, with his hat on and the sun behind him, Mr. Hardkoop could pass for fifty. I guess he deceived Mr. Keseberg into thinking him so, when Mr. Keseberg agreed to take him along the trail in return for his help with the driving. But by the time we left the Salt Desert, Mr. Hardkoop's eyes were sunk in, with great loose pouches of skin below. Beneath the weather-beaten color of his face and hands, his skin was kind of gray, and I'd give him a long way past sixty. How he'd expected to work his way along the trail without being found out, I don't know. Maybe, like so many of us, he'd thought the journey to be an easy one of some leisure, to be passed sitting high on the wagon seat, holding the reins of the beeves as they plodded slowly on, and admiring the view. It came down hard on all of us, but especially Mr. Hardkoop, when it proved not to be so.

His feet had mended some after we left the desert, but even though every night he bathed them in a mix of water and vinegar, it was clear that he found it increasingly difficult to walk any distance.

One afternoon, we were walking through some arid stony land, dotted with patches of scrub grass. We were toward the head of our party, with only the Donners in front of us. The Breens were a long way back in the distance, and the rest of our companions behind them again.

Mrs. Keseberg was walking, her arm linked through that of her husband as he guided the beeves. I had Baby tied to my back with a shawl and I was leading Ada by the hand, my eyes fixed on the ground, looking out for any patch of lush grass that I could snatch up for our animals, or any little pool of good water.

Alongside me was Mr. Hardkoop. He was limping, and leaning heavily on a stick. For the last hour he had been catching his breath at every step. I stole a glance at him from time to time, seeing how the sweat rolled down his face. Twice I asked him would he like some water or to lean on me, but he said, no, no, and waved away my offer. I think he was afraid to show that he could not manage.

He walked slower and slower. Eventually he came to a halt altogether, and sank to his knees.

Mr. Keseberg came over to see what was amiss. Mr. Hardkoop let out a wrenching sob. "*Ach,* dear *Gott!* Is over for me—I cannot walk no more!" And he flung his arms around Mr. Keseberg's legs, begging to be allowed to ride in the wagon. But Mr. Keseberg said no.

He didn't do it easy, and tears stood in his eyes, but he held firm to his resolve. "We cannot take you in the wagon. Our beeves are already close to finished, and if I burden the poor animals more it will be the death of them. Look, even my wife is walking and Baby is being carried in the full sun, when he should be resting in the shade!

"We are at the front of the party. There are others behind us with better animals. One of them will allow you to ride along of them for a while, or one of the single men riding at the rear will take you up on his horse."

Mr. Hardkoop was never much of a talker, and apart from a few words here and there we had little conversation. Mrs. Keseberg disliked him, and made little secret of the fact. But he was kind to me. Ada loved him, and he cared for her as if she was his own little granddaughter. And whether we talked or not, or got on together or not, we were bound together on our journey, something like a little family; and Mr. Keseberg's decision to leave him was not as heartless as might be thought.

It happened often. Those in one company, unable to continue with their journey, might rest for a while, and move on again with the next company along. Individuals at the front of a train of several hundred wagons, too weary to travel onward, might wait a day or two, and then join with the wagons at the rear.

The same had happened to us already. At the start of our journey the Donners had taken up Mr. Halloran. Too ill to travel on with his own companions, he had been left by the side of the trail to regain his strength, in the assurance that the companionship of the wagon train would mean that someone would bring him along later. So it had proved. And it would be the same now, or so Mr. Keseberg thought.

Our wagon passed along, leaving Mr. Hardkoop sitting forlorn behind us at the wayside. When we had gone on some, I turned back to look. I saw him holding up his hands to Mr. Breen, leading his horse, which had three of his smaller children seated up on it. Mr. Breen refused him. And then I could see Mr. Hardkoop no more.

It was a hard thing when all came in that night and we discovered that not one of our companions had taken pity on the poor old man. He had been left behind to die, alone and afraid, at the side of the road. Every person in our party had refused him aid.

To my mind, his fate was determined by the very last person in our train, who passed him by and left him there, the right opposite of the Good Samaritan. But it was Mr. Keseberg who was taken to be no more than a murderer, for leaving him so.

19

In the first week of October we finally left the so-called shortcut, which should have saved us so much time, but had cost us so much more, and came round the end of the Ruby Mountains to join the Mary River. We would have landed here weeks before, if we had stayed with our original company.

This wide, shallow river ran through a canyon that spread out with rich pasture to each side; and the canyon cliffs rose high above us, so that much of the time we traveled in the welcome coolness of their shadow. We rejoiced, thinking our fortunes had turned at last, and now we could make good time. But again, as in so many things that befell us along our path, we were too happy, too soon.

After a few days of passing along the Mary River, the river narrowed and deepened and began to run faster and lower down in its banks, and the high sides of the canyon pressed in, closer and closer, until the day came when the trail ran out altogether. We had to leave the canyon and head up into the hills to carry on our way, and this meant double-teaming the wagons up a steep sandy hill at a place called Pauta Pass. The Donners went first and got their wagons safely up, but then they were away, leaving the rest of us to manage as best we could.

On the trail there was a kind of unspoken rule about moving along in the train, and Mr. Stanton had explained it to me.

When we left Missouri and our first great wagon train split into smaller companies, ours under the captainship of Colonel Russell, another was led by a Mr. Boggs. Mr. Stanton and his friends, the McCutcheons, had started their journey as part of this company.

One evening, the Boggs company had made camp close by the Sweetwater River and thought to stay for a day or two and let the animals rest up awhile. Later that same evening another company showed up, and the two parties joined together and spent a merry night together. But in the morning when the Boggs folks woke, they were furious to find that their companions had departed camp before dawn, leaving them well behind.

I couldn't see why that would lead to bad feeling, but Mr. Stanton explained that the second company had a great head of cattle traveling with them. It was feared that these cattle would take all the good grazing ahead, leaving none for the Boggs company's animals.

I thought it a stupid thing to get upset about. Weren't the Boggs's cows and beeves already eating themselves silly where they were camped? And how could the Boggs folks be annoyed at a company that chose to get up early and head out, when they'd already elected to stay where they were and rest a few days?

I thought it just typical of men to bluster about feeling themselves hard-done-by. It was the self-same thing that had led us to leave our companions; the menfolk having the mean spirit of a race upon them and thinking to get one over on the rest of the company.

Getting up that hill at Pauta Pass brought all of that

mean spirit right to the fore, and yet again Mr. Reed's great opinion of himself caused trouble.

The suspicions surrounding Mr. Reed's leadership of us through the Wasatch Mountains had never completely died away. The more we traveled onward, the less folks had turned to Mr. Reed for guidance. Mr. Reed felt it keenly that somehow Mr. George Donner had come to be consulted on each issue, and his words to carry weight in a way that Mr. Reed's did not.

That vague sense of annoyance against Mr. Reed had gone underground, and surfaced again as ill-humored muttering that everyone had to work twice as hard as needs be to clear the trail wide enough for the Reeds' lumbering great cart. Now the Reeds' wagon was away at the rear of the party, needing three teams of beeves to get it up the hill.

No one stepped forward to offer him any help. He was reduced to going from one person to another to ask for assistance and it set him stewing, to be beholden to others. Mrs. Reed as well; she was casting dark looks at all and making comment—in a loud voice, and to no one in particular—about selfishness and ingratitude. And now Mr. Reed took it as an insult to his face that the Donners had gone up the hill before him.

He got more heated still that the Graveses should think to get one over on him by going next, but what got him boiling was that the Graveses should take back the animals they had lent him, to get them up the hill, and order Mr. Reed's teamster, Milt Elliott, to help.

When Mr. Graves finally gave ho-hup! to his team and the beeves leaned into the shafts to pull, Mr. Reed lost his temper. I did not see it, but there was shouting and yelling and then Mrs. Reed let out a great scream. We all left what we were about and run to see what had happened.

Mr. Reed was standing still as stone, with his face as white as his shirt linen, and a bloodied knife in his hand.

And John Snyder, the Graveses' teamster, was lying on the ground, dead.

Mr. Reed looked from his knife to the body and back again. And with a great groan he threw the knife from him and sank to his knees.

There wasn't a whisper of sound except for the rush of the water tumbling away below us, and Mr. Reed's choking sobs, his head laid on John Snyder's chest, saying over and over that he was sorry, and begging for his forgiveness. I do not know which was worse, the sight of the blood or the sight of Mr. Reed's horror at his deed.

Nothing could be done but to bury Mr. Snyder and get on with our journey. Mr. Reed was helped to his feet, and Mr. Breen offered to lend him a team. And then Mr. Breen had no choice but to approach Mr. Graves and ask him to return the animals he had taken from the Reeds in the first place. It was fuel on the fire for Mrs. Graves, and she said no, most decided—"Mr. Reed can stay at the bottom of that damned hill and die there himself!" she said—but somehow Mr. Breen persuaded them, with the promise that when we all got into camp that night the matter would be resolved.

20

When we came into camp that night there was a meeting. Not the Donners; they had a long start on the rest of us and were nowhere to be seen.

The broiling heat that had made August and September so unendurable was passed; and now, although the days were warm and sunny enough, the nights were growing colder. There was a touch of frost on the ground, and Mr. Breen got a big fire lit in the center of the clearing. After we'd eaten our supper, Mrs. Keseberg told me to stay where I was and mind the children, and she and Mr. Keseberg went across and joined the rest of our companions round the fire. I cleared up the dishes and got the children settled for the night, and then poked up the embers of our cooking fire, and put on some more sticks to make it blaze a little. Then I settled myself down to watch, wrapped up in a quilt and leaning against one of the wagon wheels.

The discussion started off calm enough. Mr. Breen held up his hand for silence, and made a little speech. He said that with folks' agreement, he would lead the meeting; George and Jacob Donner were not here, and Mr. Reed and Mr. Graves both had a part in the trouble. Mr. Breen was an Irish, and a Catholic at that, but no one seemed to hold that against him particularly, and his announcement was greeted with nods of the head. He said that we'd hear Mr. Graves's story about what had happened, and then Mr. Reed could speak. Anyone who wanted to say something after that was welcome to do so.

Mr. Graves went first. He said that Milt Elliott, Mr. Reed's teamster, had words with John Snyder about the way he was whipping up the team. Mr. and Mrs. Reed came up to them. Mrs. Reed provoked a great argument, and got herself in such a fury that she went to slap John Snyder across the face. He dodged out of the way, but in his hand he still held his driving whip, and caught her a blow with it, accidental-like. Then Mr. Reed up and stabbed John Snyder.

Mr. Breen asked him a few questions at this. Where did Mr. Reed get the knife? Did he bring it with him? Mr. Graves said he did, and then that he wasn't sure, and maybe it was Milt Elliott's knife.

Milt Elliott was called up to the fire. Mr. Breen asked him, was it your knife?

He answered, yes it was. He'd thought one of the beeves looked to have lost a shoe and was something lame, and he wanted to look at its hoof and maybe dig out a stone, so the knife was in his hand.

Then Mr. Breen asked him, did Mr. Snyder aim his blow at Mrs. Reed deliberate-like? I couldn't say, said Milt, and was told to sit down again.

Mr. Graves answered the question instead. "John Snyder did it without thinking and it wasn't no more than the force a body would use to swat a fly. He would never have raised his hand to a woman, for John was a good man.

"I considered him almost my son, and we expected that when we reached the end of our journey and arrived safe in California, he would marry our Mary."

At that, all turned their heads and looked at Mary Graves, who hid her face in her kerchief.

At this, Mrs. Reed couldn't contain herself. She jumped to her feet in a fury, shouting out that none of what he was saying was true at all! John Snyder aimed his blow at her deliberate and knocked her to the ground with the force of it, and John Snyder was a jealous sort of fellow and Mary Graves was known to look under her lashes at any man who passed the time of day with her! It was she deserved a slap, for she had been making eyes at Milt Elliott!

I gave a little snort of disbelief; I couldn't help myself. Mary Graves was a flirt, sure enough, but even she wouldn't have give squinty-eyed Milt Elliott a second look.

Mrs. Graves screeched at Mrs. Reed's words, and would have flown at her if not restrained. Mr. Graves yelled out that Mr. Reed should control his wife, and if he had been John Snyder he'd have landed her one himself. Mr. Reed retorted that this was rich words from a man who had never said nay to his own wife in his life, and was too much of a coward to do so, now!

This was the signal for nigh everyone in our party who had a grievance against the Reeds, to let loose. There was a right outcry of voices. Over them all was Mr. Graves again, who shouted out that the fact of the matter was that if we were back East Mr. Reed would be hanged as a murderer, and he should be now! Mr. Reed pointed at the folks sitting round the fire, shouting back that he wouldn't accept justice from this raggle-taggle crew, and they had no right to pass judgment on him!

Mr. Keseberg had been sat with his back to me, and I couldn't see his face. I was surprised he had sat there so far in silence. But I guess this last was too much for him. He leapt up, and yelled that Mr. Reed was a fine one to talk about justice and passing judgment, that from the very start he had considered himself better than anyone else and if Mr. Graves wanted Mr. Reed hanged, why, he would provide the rope for it! In a fury he snatched up a rope from the nearest wagon and brandished it in the air.

Even before the words were full out of Mr. Keseberg's mouth, Mr. Graves and his son, William, had Mr. Reed by the arms and were dragging him across the sandy ground to the nearest tree, Mr. Keseberg hot on their heels.

The women all screamed, and I did, too. Mrs. Keseberg ran after her husband, beating on his back and shouting at him to desist. Then Mr. Breen took his gun and fired a shot into the air, startling everyone into silence: and waking up Baby, who wailed.

I scrambled to my feet and climbed into the wagon, hushing Baby as best I could and with an ear turned to events outside, straining to catch what was being said. In the end I grabbed Baby, wrapped him in a shawl, and stuck my head out of the back of the wagon, just in time to see Mr. Reed pull himself free from his captors, and step into the firelight.

I guess fear had quietened him down. He suddenly seemed right calm, though he could not look anyone in the face. Instead, staring at the fire, he said, "I will never forgive myself for what I have done."

At this, his voice cracked, and he wiped his hand across his eyes. "I will go out—if that is what you wish. I will leave the company and ride ahead, for I can see it is hard on Mary Graves, to look at me and see me alive, and know—and know—" At this, he was overcome and could not speak for several minutes. At last he pulled himself together.

"It would be too hard for Mary Graves to look on me, and know that her sweetheart is dead by my hand."

Again there was a buzz of voices, and again Mr. Breen raised his voice to be heard. He said he was not willing to pass judgment on Mr. Reed and he, for one, would not condemn him to death. But that if Mr. Reed wished to leave, then perhaps that was for the best.

"We are a Democracy in our Country," he said, "and I say we put it to a vote. We will go round and each stand up and cast his vote, stay or leave. And I say that the married women have a vote as well."

This was a novel idea. The women all looked something startled to have such responsibility thrust upon their shoulders. Hattie Pike burst into tears, and Mrs. Murphy put her arm round her shoulders to comfort her.

He started with Mr. Graves, who voted for Mr. Reed to leave, and then Mrs. Graves the same. So it went round the circle. Mr. and Mrs. Eddy said he should stay, and so did Mrs. McCutcheon. Several of the women said they would not vote at all.

By the time the last vote was called for, it was split even. The last to vote was Mr. Keseberg. He looked straight at Mr. Reed, and Mr. Reed looked at him. And he knew that his fate was decided, for of course Mr. Keseberg voted yes.

So it was agreed. He would be sent on his way, and was given one hour to make his good-byes.

He was to set out on his journey alone, for no one from our companions would volunteer to go with him, and his family could not, for their wagon was still being pulled by the beeves lent to them by the Graveses.

Mrs. Graves spoke up again, and demanded their return. Mr. Breen tried to reason with her.

"You are the only family left with spare beeves to lend out. You cannot mean to deprive Mr. Reed's family of any means of travel, surely? In the name of God, you could not be so cruel!" He was right heated, not like himself at all.

Mrs. Graves was adamant. She said that she and her family had got stuck with us all, thanks to her husband—and she gave him such a look—stuck with us all, much against her better judgment, and as far as she was concerned, this business with Mr. Reed put the lid on it.

"My family comes first," she said, "and I owe nothing to anyone here. Mrs. Reed is as much to blame for this business as her husband is, and why I should assist her is beyond my comprehension!

"I will do so—in the spirit, as you say, Mr. Breen, of Christian charity—for the sake of her children. But they are my beeves, and they stay within my sight!"

I guess the same thought crossed all minds. Mr. Reed might travel away, but Mrs. Reed and her children would be left behind to take his punishment.

The Reeds' servant, Baylis Williams, who had started off the journey a big, solid sort of fellow, was reduced by hard work and short rations to near enough skin and bone, and had turned right sickly over the past week or two, so he was not fit to go out. Milt Elliott stepped up to go, but Mr. Reed refused to allow him, saying that he was needed to care for the animals. He got a solemn promise from him that he would take good care of his family.

Milt Elliott cried like a baby at this, vowing, "On my life, Mr. Reed, I will do everything for Miz Reed and those poor childer."

Once it was determined that Mr. Reed should go, another vote was taken, as to whether he should take his gun and some provisions. To send a man out with no food and no means of hunting any, and all defenseless against the Indians, was just the same as killing him. I thought it a right shameful thing to do, more cruel than hanging him there and then, and my first thought was that no one would agree to it. But I was wrong.

When Mr. Reed had first spoke up, I had been so affected by his tears and his remorse that I never would have voted to send him out. But now I suddenly thought, "How is it that Mr. Reed has made it seem like he is doing us a kindness in leaving us? That he is doing it to spare Mary Graves? If it was not for his actions in killing a man, Mary Graves would not need to be spared!

"He is a murderer! Yet here I am feeling right sorry for him! His punishment is to be nothing more than to ride off on his horse and get to the end of his journey a sight quicker than the rest of us. While we are all still struggling onward, he will be sat in Sutter's Fort with his pipe in his mouth and his feet up on the fender.

"Let him go out with no gun and no food," I said to myself, "and take his chances! He is lucky to be alive. Let it be in God's hands if he stays so!"

I guess I was not the only one to have discovered that same sense of aggravation. This time round everyone voted and the vote was pretty nigh unanimous. Only Mrs. McCutcheon voted against it. All in all, it seemed that the women in our company had got the taste for power.

21

The river had given up its tumbling drop through the narrow canyons and now the Marysink spread out before us, the place where, at the end of summer, the river vanished away into the ground. It was a long, low valley, with steep sides. In the spring when the rain washed down the mountains and the river was in full flood, this was a great lake. Now, though, the water was slowed to a sluggy trickle and the land about was marshy, filled with pools of water that lay milk-white and stinking in the sun. It was poor water, and we lost yet more cattle from the drinking of it.

We trudged along with Indians riding along the ridges above our heads, then wheeling their horses away. We knew that they were there, hidden from our sight but watching us all the while, and we hastened along as best we could, thinking that we were like fish in a barrel waiting to be shot.

One night we made camp on a sort of grassy island that stuck up out of the mire, and the next morning Mr. Eddy come swaggering along, one of his tales ready for the telling. His desire to set around himself a lurid story and be seen as the hero of the hour was eventually to cause the most evil misery; but at the beginning, his love of a good tale merely got the better of his common sense. So it was now.

He told us that during the night Mr. Breen's mare had gotten loose and stuck herself up to her flanks in the mud. Mr. Breen had applied to him for a hand to get her out, but Mr. Eddy had refused.

"I paid him back in good coin for not riding to the aid of Mr. Hardkoop!" This was said with an easy laugh, and it was obvious that he expected us to look admiring of his high-mindedness.

I stared at him in astonishment, thinking it showed him simple-witted. He had refused Mr. Hardkoop just as much as the rest, and why would we, having the blame finger of Mr. Hardkoop's death pointed at us more than any, find his tale amusing?

Soon came another death in our party. And like the sorry tale of Mr. Hardkoop, the story of Mr. Wolfinger's murder would come to haunt Mr. Keseberg.

Mr. Wolfinger had the best of everything, including a fine rifle, though he admitted himself that he was a poor shot. A day or so after we entered into the Marysink, we came to a place where there was a stretch of good water, with great flocks of birds upon it: geese and ducks and many others that we had never seen before. Mr. Wolfinger took but one look at all this good food before him, and offered his rifle to his friend Mr. Keseberg, for a share of whatever he shot with it.

Mr. Keseberg took the rifle and set off, his eyes fixed on the birds and his finger on the trigger. Not looking where he was going, he missed his step, and plunged down the creekside, catching his foot on some sharp bits of broke willow that dotted the edge of the water. The wood went right through his shoe and his foot and out the other side, and it made me faint to see it. He limped back to our wagon, and the rifle was put down, and forgot, I suppose, while Mrs. Keseberg put salve on the injury and bandaged it up. It never healed right from that day on, and pained Mr. Keseberg something dreadful at times; after that he walked always with a limp.

Over the next few days the ground improved, and one night we made camp in a fine place, with plenty grass for the cattle. We drew the wagons round tight, and set to sleeping, with some of the teamsters put to guard the beeves and the rest of the animals. Our night was peaceful, and in the morning the campfires were blazed up and the coffeepots set on, and bacon put to fry. One by one the men who had been guarding the cattle came wandering in, drawn by the smell. It did not occur to any that those crafty Indians that had been tracking us all this while knew us better than we knew ourselves. The very instant the men took their first mouthfuls of good hot coffee or helped themselves to a slice of bacon off the griddle, the Indians came swooping down, laughing fit to bust I am sure. They killed as many cattle as they could fire their arrows into, and made off with as many horses as they could grab on their flight.

It was with heavy hearts that we looked at the lifeless bodies of the animals scattered about where they had fallen. All had lost something. We reckoned up that from the time we set out, to here, we had lost more than two-thirds of our animals: beeves, in particular. And now some of our number had no animals left to pull their wagons. The Wolfingers were such, and Mrs. Reed another.

The Breens and the Donners took as much as they could carry from the abandoned wagons, and set off with the Reeds and Mrs. Wolfinger walking alongside them—Mrs. Wolfinger crying most bitterly.

Of all our German party, we were now the only ones who had any animals remaining. We took what was left of the Wolfingers' provisions with us, and pulled out, leaving Mr. Spitzer and Mr. Reinhardt to stay and help Mr. Wolfinger cache his wagon.

A great number of travelers were forced to cache their wagons, if they lost their team or an axle break and no one to fix it. The iron struts that held up the canvas to cover the wagon would be pulled out of their fixings, and the wheels took off, so that what was left was just the wagon bed, loaded up with goods. A great hole would be dug in the ground and the wagon bed lowered in, and then the struts and the wheels flat on the top and the canvas over all. Once that was all done the earth would be shoveled back in, and a marker put in the ground. The idea was that once the owner got safe to California, he could return the next year in the good weather with as many teams as he liked, and dig up the wagon and put it back together and fetch the goods home.

Mr. Wolfinger was never to return for his wagon, though. When we made camp that night he did not come in. The next morning he did not come in neither; but Mr. Spitzer and Mr. Reinhardt did, saying that Mr. Wolfinger was murdered by the Indians in the night.

At this, a great stir went round the camp.

The friendship between our German folks wasn't taken much note of in the original train of close on a thousand folks, nor in the large company led by Colonel Russell. But in our little company of fewer than forty adults, mistrust and suspicion had clouded the air from the start. There were those among us who were as pleasant as all get-out to one another's faces, but speaking right malicious about them behind their backs. And to have six or seven of the company sitting together night after night and talking in their own language and laughing among themselves was taken something amiss.

Now, all the bad feeling against the Germans, that had caused our party to leave Cincinnati in the first place, came bubbling back to the surface. I heard all kinds of whispers to the effect that the Germans had killed one of their own for his money, for Mr. Wolfinger was thought to have been carrying a great deal of gold concealed somewhere in his wagon.

It must have been clear to all that we had no part in this. We were in camp with the rest when Mr. Spitzer and Mr. Reinhardt came in with the news. But it didn't stop folks from saying that Mr. Keseberg had killed one person already who was a nuisance to him, Mr. Hardkoop; and got rid of Mr. Reed, another; that he was known to be a violent man, and that Mr. Spitzer and Mr. Reinhardt might have committed the murder, but Mr. Keseberg had planned it.

In this way Mr. Keseberg's character was blackened still further, for no reason other than his choice of friends, and his manner of speech. And I had no doubt that Mr. Eddy had held a long spoon in his hand to stir up this particular pot of gossip.

A few days after Mr. Wolfinger's death, yet another raiding party of Indians came down the hills behind us. The Eddys were to the back of the train, and it was they who suffered the most.

They came into camp that evening and settled down at our fire, and this was when we heard the tale of their suffering. Mr. Eddy told us how his beeves were slaughtered, and he and his wife had to abandon their wagon and run for their lives, barefoot, carrying Margaret and little James, and with nothing to sustain them but a bit of lump sugar that Mr. Eddy had in his pocket.

He told this tale with tears standing in his eyes, and a choke in his voice at the telling. It was a terrible story, to be sure, and our hearts went out to him; but on reflection it proved, like everything else he said, to be as full of holes as a bad-knitted sock.

The Indians' crime was to kill his beeves, not steal his boots. Even at the telling of the story he had his boots on his feet. Two of the Breen boys were walking along of him, and they had managed to load themselves up with provisions, sacks and barrels and boxes of goods. Of course, Mr. Eddy had done the same, for I saw him with my own eyes with his goods strung about his neck.

He said they'd walked for the rest of the day carrying the children, crying from thirst. They'd caught up with the Breens, and Mr. Eddy had applied to them for water, for his children if not for himself. Mr. Breen had refused him, or so Mr. Eddy said, saying that he had scarce enough water for his own family; and Mr. Eddy had replied that he had helped them fetch water the very day before, so he knew that this was a lie, and had threatened to shoot Mr. Breen if he did not hand the water over.

On the next telling of the tale I heard that he had also applied to Mrs. Graves and Mrs. Breen both, for a handful of food, and again been refused.

I would believe it of Mrs. Graves.

From the moment she had joined us, why, a harder and more selfish woman I never did see. In our mad rush to leave Pilot Peak, folks had thrown out or lost items that they then discovered they needed. Not a day went past but there was a hunt for someone to lend out a shovel or for the use of a good sharp knife. But Mrs. Graves turned a deaf ear to such requests, with a stony countenance and the words, "Never a borrower nor a lender be," and that was the end of it.

So yes, I could believe it of the Graveses. Family first and second, and that was the end of it. But I could not believe it of Mr. and Mrs. Breen. Mrs. Breen was known to be the very soul of kindness. And Mr. Breen would no more refuse water to a thirsty child than sprout wings and swoop about in the air above our heads.

It was several days later when I heard the end to this story. It was told me by, of all people, Virginia Reed.

With the loss of her wagons, all her possessions, and

finally her husband, Mrs. Reed had come down from her high place with an almighty crash. She had no choice but to depend on other folks' charity. I guess it had been a hard lesson, and she had gentled somewhat as a result; and Virginia the same. Perhaps she was lonely.

The Graves girls were not much company, for they spent as much time squabbling as they did gossiping. More than once I had seen Virginia cast a longing look in the direction of my little band of friends, swelled now by the addition of Landrum and Lemuel Murphy and the two older Breen boys. Whatever the reason, Virginia had made some efforts to be nicer toward me: a smile here and there at least. I did not think we ever would be close friends, for the hurt of her actions still twitched within me if I let it, but I bore no grudge toward her.

One afternoon, a little while after Mr. Eddy had sat by our fireside and told us his dreadful tale, Virginia and I found ourselves walking close together, she with her little sister and me with Ada. The two little girls had their heads together over their dolls and Virginia came beside me, and told me the end of Mr. Eddy's tale.

He gave out to Mrs. Reed that he had gone hunting and killed so many geese that he could hardly walk for the weight of them. Mr. Eddy said that he had given some to the Breens and some to the Graveses and some to us, though I never saw beak nor feather.

Virginia was right aggravated by this tale and needed someone to hear her thoughts. She said just what I thought myself. Why tell this smiling tale of such generosity to a woman who had nothing of her own, and hungry children to feed? And it would take more Christian forgiveness than I could imagine, to give food to those who had refused it to a hungry child. If any part of his story was true, it made Mr. Breen look a villain and Mr. Eddy a saint. I did not believe a word of it.

Mr. Eddy and his stories! Oh, he was a gifted teller of

tall tales all right, and later still he told a story of killing a bear that made me laugh aloud at the telling.

Even now when I think of it, I have to laugh again. I clap my hand over my mouth with the shame of it. I do not want to think kind thoughts of Mr. Eddy. For I do have charitable moments, when, despite myself, I think that perhaps he was not evil. Perhaps he was nothing worse than a fool, and should be pitied and not condemned for it. He came to suffer along with the rest of us, as time wore on and we became more and more wretched and frightened, with death our constant companion. He loved his family right well, and his wife and children loved him back. And it was true that his tales made folks laugh a little here and there, when we were all glad to think of things other than death, and the ever-present cry, "Oh! when will rescue come?"

22

The mild, rainy days of March give way to an unseasonably warm April, so that by the middle of the month most of the farmers have completed their planting, and the children can be let go to return to school. The weather continues so good that by the beginning of June my early tomatoes have ripened and are already close to falling off the vine and I can see bushels of green ones coming up behind them.

Martha and I cook them every which way we know, until the children groan at the sight of them on their plates, and even Jacob begs me to desist.

We have another new arrival in town, an Indian gentleman called Mr. Sahid. Not an Indian such as we know, but arrived from the country of India, far away across the ocean. Next thing we know we have a new store open up, much to the clear disapproval of Mr. Peabody.

A little after Mr. Sahid sets up, I go in to visit, taking Meggie with me. Mr. Sahid has a whole area of books to one side, and some chairs, and he encourages folks to sit and read right there in the store, which is a novelty to all.

His aim is to set up a lending library. For the payment of a dime, I can take home a book, and when I bring it back in good condition I'll get a half dime returned to me. He has novels published in England, and some of our own American authors as well, and books for cookery, educational books, and books about explorers who have traveled to far distant lands.

I came late to reading, but now it is one of my greatest pleasures. I am like a greedy child, pulling one book after another from the shelves and reading pages at random, until I settle on a book called Jane Eyre, *written by a Mr. Bell, and another which is a memoir by a lady who has traveled in the country of Africa, as a missionary to teach the Christian faith to the natives there.*

This lending library is a most clever idea, for I can see that each time someone comes into the store to return a book, they will be tempted to purchase goods as well. Mr. Sahid has a whole selection of embroidery silks, the finest I have ever seen, in the most beautiful of colors, and skeins of colored wools for knitting. Draped over the counter are some shawls, soft and rich to the touch, and there are bales of patterned cottons, brighter by far than the earth-colored homespuns that Mr. Peabody stocks in the mercantile. Meggie takes but one look at them and turns to me with a face of such yearning that I cannot refuse her.

Meggie is already turning into a beauty. We seem to have more than the usual number of slouching boys walking out our way in the evenings, and Meggie is often to be found down at the gate, laughing with them.

On those occasions Jacob has taken to sitting out on the porch to smoke his pipe, which seems to make him cough much more, and much more loudly, than previously. Perhaps I should be concerned at the extent of the coughing, but I am not. I take him out a cup of coffee to drink while he admires the view, and ask him in a concerned voice if he needs a linctus for his throat, or should

I prepare a liniment for his chest; and he has the good grace to laugh along with me.

Meggie longs to be out of pinafores and spends a deal of time in front of the looking-glass trying ways of pinning up her hair. I cannot agree to the pinned-up hair nor yet the loss of the pinafore, but perhaps a new dress will serve as a compromise for us both, on her promise to make it up herself and ask Mrs. McGillivray for help when she needs it.

After much deliberation, we choose a design of posies of tiny blue and purple flowers on a paler blue ground, just the color to set off her eyes. My own eyes are a shade of green which I guess is pretty enough, and Jacob, like so many of German stock, has fair skin and eyes the pale blue of a winter sky. But Meggie's eyes are the deep color of heart's-ease, or the evening summer sky when the first stars begin to shine.

Jacob often remarks that she is the very likeness of his sister at the same age, back home in the Old Country. This cannot be true—as much as anything because Jacob has not seen his sister for these thirty years or more and she was but a baby when he left, so he can have no idea of how she looked at Meggie's age. But it is a nice thing to say, and Meggie likes to hear his stories of his childhood, his mother and father and his little brothers and sisters so very far away.

I buy a length of fabric for myself, as well. The pattern is a teardrop shape with a little twist, something like a leaf, in white and black and orange, set on a gray ground. Mr. Sahid tells me it is a traditional pattern back in his native land, and is named after a fruit called an ambi. *He does not know the name of the fruit in English, and I cannot understand his description, so it remains a mystery.*

I think it will make me a fine gown to wear for the town celebrations to mark California Day in September—though my earlier suspicions about my condition are realized, and Mrs. McGillivray will need to cut the pattern something more generous than usual. Once the patterns have been cut, there will be good scraps left over. Of course, most of those I shall keep to use myself, but I attend the ladies' quilting bee, where we trade scraps and ideas for quilt patterns. It gives me a deal of satisfaction to imagine the envious look in my friends' eyes when I produce my colorful pieces.

The thing that most attracts my attention, though, is the smell of the store. It has such a fragrance, of something that catches at the back of my nose, musty and spicy, and I ask Mr. Sahid about it. He points to the jars that he is setting out on shelves behind him. These are filled with powders, dark yellows and reddish-browns, and little seeds and roots and dried leaves. They are spices, he says. Not just cinnamon sticks and nutmeg, which I have seen before, and chilies and the other sorts of peppers that the Mexicos use to flavor their foods, but cumin and cardamom, cloves, curry leaf, and a whole host of others.

He takes down one jar after another, and lets me sniff at the different fragrances. Some make my eyes water, and some make me sneeze. I quiz him about how they are used. Are they for medicine, perhaps, or are they for preserving food?

"Preserving, yes, most certainly," he says, "but mostly they are flavorings, and will make your dull food as exciting as you can ever imagine!"

My mind flies to my tomatoes. I ask him, does he have any suggestions what I might do with them? He takes a spoonful of one thing and a pinch of something else, and hands them to me wrapped up in little twists of paper.

"Fry over some onion in good butter, until very soft," he tells me, "and then stir in all these spices I have given you, and cook until you have a smooth paste. Add your tomatoes and mush down, and you can add some other vegetables, if you have any, or fruit."

"Will apples do?"

When Meggie was born, Jacob planted an apple tree for her, and it produces in abundance. I have more than I know what to do with, put by in sacking, and the trees are already showing signs of a substantial crop again this year.

"Yes, apples are good. Then pack into jars, and you have a delicious sauce, what you can call a chutney. It will go with anything, yes, indeed, meat or fish or cheese, and will keep for several months."

Meggie rushes me home, determined to get on with her dressmaking, and I take no persuading. I wish to get into my kitchen and get out my preserving pan, and set to on those unappreciated tomatoes that are falling off the vine.

What with my chutney-making, and the dressmaking, and Martha getting herself betrothed, with her wedding planned for next spring, my journal is put aside for a while.

Right glad I am of it, too. The further along my journey I travel in my mind, the closer I come to writing of such sadness and misery that I can hardly bear to think of it.

At first I wished I had not started writing my story at all. Then I thought to stop, but even my most determined efforts are denied.

My pen has come to have such power over me that I have no choice but to bow before it. The evenings when Jacob is traveled away on business and the children are in bed, I sit in the parlor with a novel from Mr. Sahid's lending library to one side of me. I have my work basket, with the little soft knitting I am engaged upon—the new baby will be with us come Christmas—and perhaps some socks that need darning.

But I cannot settle to anything. The minutes tick by, and I take up my book and put it down again, and find I am sitting staring at nothing, with my darning abandoned in my lap.

Eventually—reluctantly—I fetch my journal and set it

open on the table in front of me. Then the time flies away, and I write until the first few drowsy notes of birdsong start up to mark the dawn.

My eyes blur with weariness, and my hand cramps. But my mind will not be still. It pours out memory like a never-ending stream of water that cannot be contained.

My respite from my journal-writing does not last long. Toward the end of the month something happens that makes my fingers yearn for the pen once more.

Minnie calls by one afternoon to bring some periodicals that were sent to her some weeks previous by her sister. Minnie's family is from Philadelphia, and she has three brothers there; but her sister married into a big Southern family, and lives down in Virginia.

Minnie has read these periodicals already and passed them round our little circle of acquaintance. News from back East is rare and precious and we devour every little scrap of it that comes our way. By the time she brings them back to me once more, they have been read so much that I am surprised the print hasn't faded to nothing, and they are marked with fingerprints and folded-down corners of pages.

She has brought them as a gift for the children. My three girls are following the last fashion for scrapbooking, but Minnie has four giant boys who follow the fashion for punching one another at any opportunity, and rolling around together on the floor like dogs.

There is a copy of Godey's Lady's Magazine. *I have already read it cover to cover, and copied down a recipe or two and some ideas for my garden, but over a cup of coffee Minnie and I marvel again at the fashion plates. There are skirts three times as wide as those we wear here, with fantastical trimmings of fringes and frills. These are not held out by layer upon layer of petticoats but are set over a new invention called a crinoline, a great hoop of wire with a stiffened petticoat of tarlatan set over it.*

Minnie and I each choose an outfit from the illustration. Mine is a color given as chartreuse, which I have to look up in the dictionary—it is a shade of yellow-green—and is trimmed every which way with flounces and puffs in wine-color. Minnie picks out a gown described as being ashes of roses, which we think sounds a most romantic shade. It has a mass of lilac-colored embroidery over the bodice and little pearl buttons all down the front. We imagine ourselves sashaying down Main Street together, and the envious looks we would get from our neighbors.

There is also a fashion plate of something called a Bloomers Suit. This is a set of ankle-length pantalettes and a short gown over, reaching just to the knees. All in white, it is trimmed with frills at wrist and ankle.

We shriek with laughter at the sight of it, and its description, "A convenient costume for practical wear," sets us off again.

Those folks in the cities back East haven't any idea of what practical wear means. Why, we have women here who think nothing of wearing men's pants to go out after cattle. New arrivals might raise their eyebrows, but they pretty soon come to realize that fancy gowns are all very well if you have a lady's maid for the three or four hours a day spent mending and pressing and starching; and if you spend exhausting mornings visiting in order to show off your gown, and exhausted afternoons languishing on a daybed with a dime novel in your hand.

We women here all spend our days about the same: brushing floors and cleaning dishes and washing clothes, making jellies and preserving fruit or putting up vegetables for pickling to see our families through the winter, and baking bread and pies. We feed chickens and tend to goats and cows, feeding and milking them and making butter or cheese. Our evenings are spent in knitting or stitching, until our eyes give out. Then we go to bed, up again at daybreak for another day of the same, most every day of the week and every week of the year.

Of course, we do this with children to look after, babies teething and crying, and older ones squabbling and fighting, and the fourteen- and fifteen-year-olds arguing with us and slamming out of the house in a sulky fit.

The men work from daybreak until sundown, in farming or cattle, or woodcutting or boatbuilding or whatever labor it is that they undertake to earn enough coin to put bread and meat on the table for their families. If a new barn needs building, the men do it. If a gate or fence needs mending, the men do that, too. In the evenings they dig over the yard ready for planting, and chop wood for the fires. And when it comes dark, yes, sometimes they sleep in their chairs before the fire.

But sometimes they, too, wake in the night to hush a crying child, or sit in the barn until daybreak with a birthing animal, and take the children fishing on a Sunday afternoon to give their mothers a rest.

In short, life here is mostly hard labor. Women and men work from sunrise to sunset side by side. No one thinks overmuch of whose right it is to do one thing, and whose obligation it is to do another. We are practical folks, we Pioneers, and rightly proud of ourselves, or so I think.

There is a great movement afoot back East, arguing for women's rights, saying that women should have as much freedom as men to have an education and earn a living, and vote in political matters and be considered equal to men in all ways. I can't help but feel that the women who advocate this the most are those with the luxury of time on their hands: women with servants and maids, and living on the money provided by their husbands and fathers. I wonder if they see the joke of it.

I agree with the idea somewhat. I believe in fairness, as any right-minded person would. But even so, I get riled up by having folks back East, who know nothing of my life here, telling me what I should think and how I should behave.

And the thought of a woman wearing a practical Bloomers Suit to do it, makes me laugh despite myself.

When Minnie is gone, and the dinner is on the stove, an experiment using the Indian spices which Mr. Sahid says is called a curry, or a type of chili, which I hope Jacob will like, for he enjoys spicy foods; and the children are set up at the table with their paste pots and their scrapbooks and scissors, and are arguing already about who should have what, I settle in the chair by the kitchen window. I take up another of Minnie's periodicals that I haven't seen before, the Sonoma Illustrated News, *and settle down to read it.*

And of course, there it is. A True Account of the Desperate Tribulations of the Donner Party by a Survivor . . .

I tear out the page, and thrust it into the kitchen stove.

Stories and lies, stories and lies. They never end.

23

At the end of October, the way began to steepen as we finally reached the foothills of that last great mountain. We followed the path of a shallow creek that came tumbling down the hillside, collecting into deep pools here and there before overflowing and sending water cascading over the rocks beneath. The way wound up through dense forests of pine, the air cold and sharp-smelling, a welcome relief after the exhausting heat of the plains and canyons we'd left behind. Occasionally the trees opened out onto areas of stony grassland, and here we pulled the wagons over to rest awhile, and the animals grazed a little and drank their fill.

Beautiful though this place was, now the vast range of the Sierra Nevada rose above us, black and forbidding against the gray clouded sky. I could not imagine how we could travel through it, with the little children and the beeves and our wagons.

Mr. Keseberg told me not to fear. "We have crossed plenty other mountains on our way, and we have joined the known route now. Wagons cross this mountain with ease, month in and out!"

He said it with a smile, but I could not smile back. The wagons that crossed the mountain did so in the late summer, but we were weeks delayed on our journey, and from the minute we had first seen the snow shining ahead of us, the thought of it had haunted us all. Were we too late to get through the pass? Even as Mr. Keseberg spoke, little dots of snow swirled past us in the chill breeze, and we left footprints behind us as we walked.

But the snow was a pretty sight. The little ones ran about and tried to catch the snow as it fell, and the bigger boys started throwing it at one another, and wrestling one another to the ground in it. Virginia was there and Meriam, who the boys chased, threatening to put snow in her hair, so there was a deal of shrieking; Leanna and Elitha, trying to catch the snow on their tongues, and even the Graves girls larking about with the rest of us.

Something went sailing past my head, and I turned to see a lump of snow splat against a tree trunk behind me. Just at that moment Landrum Murphy ran up to me. He shoved some snow down the back of my dress, making me scream, and then he spun me round and fetched me a kiss. He ran off back to the other boys, laughing and punching his fist into the air, with them all clapping and whooping like he was a hero.

Before I knew it I had caught up a big handful of the snow and made it into a ball, and I threw it right at him, harder than I knew. It hit him square between the eyes and he sat down sudden-like, backward in the snow, looking as surprised and foolish as could be.

There was a moment's shocked silence, then in a second everyone was laughing. We laughed so hard that tears came into our eyes, and we gurgled and snorted for breath; as soon as one of us calmed down enough to stop, we only had to catch the eye of another and off we went again. The boys came across and slapped me on the back, and said what a great throw it was and that I should be a pitcher for their next game of ball. And the girls cheered me and said it served out Landrum, who had tried to steal a kiss from more than one of them.

When we were making camp that night, there was a shout in the distance, "Hollo!" Coming toward us on his horse was Mr. Stanton, waving his hat in the air and a great smile on his face. He brought with him a whole line of mules loaded up with sacks of flour and dried beef and sugar and all manner of good things besides; and riding at the head of the mules were two Mexicos, Luis and Salvatore, come to show us the way through the pass. We cheered the Mexicos, and we cheered Mr. Stanton, but most of all we cheered the news that the pass was still open, and that within a very few days we would be through, and safe and well in California.

We pressed Mr. Stanton for news of our companions. When we'd eventually caught up with the Donners, a couple of days ahead of us on the trail, they'd told us that Mr. Reed had stayed with them one night, and set off again accompanied by Walter Herron: but Mr. Stanton knew nothing of what had befallen them after that. Mr. McCutcheon had been left at Sutter's Fort, too ill to make his way back to join his wife and child, and of course the Eddys were once more to be seen at one fireside and another, with poor Mrs. McCutcheon yet again the source of scandal and gossip.

After weeks of being careful with our food it was a fine thing to sit in the wagon and eat a big dish of Mrs. Keseberg's good beef stew, with doughballs and corn bread besides. Mr. Keseberg was merry, and sang a song to us in German, and Mrs. Keseberg's eyes sparkled, and she told me it was a song that was sung at their wedding.

Mrs. Keseberg was from a family who had one faith, and Mr. Keseberg's family another, and both families were against the match, she said, but they were in love and they would not be gainsaid; then she joined in with the chorus, and he clasped her round the waist and she leaned on his shoulder and they swayed back and forth. I could not help but clap along, and even little Ada banged time with her spoon. Baby slept through it all.

The next morning the Kesebergs and I set off just after dawn. We had hardly gone an hour when we spied wagons halted ahead of us, and we pulled over to discover what was amiss. Mr. George Donner's wagon had broken an axle, and in trying to free some bolt or other he had driven a knife clean through the palm of his hand. Mrs. Donner had the salve out and a bandage and was hard at work dressing her husband's wound, while the men stood round scratching their heads and debating what to do.

A goodly part of our journey was taken up with making repairs to the wagons. Mostly this was mending the wheels. The wooden wheels shrank in the dry heat, and the iron bands round the rim swelled up, so they were constantly coming loose and having to be heated up and hammered back into shape, an afternoon's work. But replacing an axle was a heavy, long-winded job that would take a day at the very least. At last, it was decided that a couple of the teamsters would stay and help, and Mr. Jacob Donner pulled his wagon round to assist his brother. The little bits of Mrs. Reed's goods being in his wagon, she had no choice but to stay as well, and the same with Mrs. Wolfinger. But the rest of us were to carry on, eager to complete our journey now the end was so near. It was a sad day to see our party divide, and to know that our journey together was come to an end.

Virginia and I might not have been the best of friends, but we kissed each other good-bye all the same. As for Leanna and Elitha, why, after our long months traveling together they felt more like sisters to me than my real sisters ever had, and we hugged one another right fierce.

Mr. Keseberg whipped up the beeves. They leaned

into the shafts, grunting with the effort of getting the wagon in motion, and I set my steps to the trail, looking back once or twice to wave to my friends. After a couple of hundred yards, I spied Leanna running to catch up with me. Into my hand she put a lock of her hair, tied up with a little snip of pink thread, and she threw her arms round me, crying most bitterly to see me leaving.

"Leanna, do not cry so! For in just a few days' time we shall meet again in California, and then we shall be merry together!" and I laughed, and she did, too.

How could we know that it would be months before we would meet again? And that when we did, it would be in circumstances as far removed from merriment as could possibly be imagined.

I lay down my pen, and close my journal. It is full dark with no moon, and the night air is thick with the summer heat. A moth flutters around the little pool of light where I sit with my candle. I pick up my journal, and make my way through the house to our bedroom.

I reach in under our bed. Here are the winter blankets, stored in canvas bags with cedar chips to keep away the moths. I move them to one side, and open up my hidey-hole—a loose floorboard. This is where I keep my journal. Perhaps it is a foolish hiding place in the house of a master carpenter, but Jacob would never concern himself with looking under the bed.

I take out what lies there already, and hold it to my face for a moment. A square of ragged cloth, no hint of the pretty pink color it once was. Wrapped in it are five silver dollars; a much worn and folded scrap of paper—what might once have been a drawing of bluebells; and a faded lock of hair, tied up with a snip of faded pink thread.

24

At sunset, we reached the great lake that was to be our final camp before we crossed the pass. After I had made up the campfire, and mixed up a batter with the last of the dried fruit to make johnnycakes and set the Dutch oven to heat, I walked down to the water.

In every direction was forest, row on row of dark pines stretching to the horizon and crowding down to the shoreline; though where I stood was grassy ground and then stones, with reeds and rushes along the water's margin and to each side of the narrow banks of the creek heading back the way we had come. The sky was pretty as could be, a pale color of blue with streaks of pink and orange where the sun was setting behind airy puffs of gold-edged cloud. In the far distance the hills were crimson and lavender-color, and all was reflected in the smooth dark water, as clear as a looking glass. And now, for the first time in all my journey, I let my mind turn to thoughts of my ma.

I had wondered, from time to time, how my brothers fared after I left, and thought on my little sisters some. I could not have forgotten my pa, much as I might have wished it. But I had been resolute in not letting my thoughts linger on my family back in Cincinnati, for the more I heard of the happy lives the other folks in our party had left behind, the more I had been ashamed of mine, and my mother in particular.

I had left home a slattern, I guess. I knew no different. My mother had not brushed and braided my hair for me and tied it in ribbons. She had never made me a pretty dress from dimity cloth or stitched a pattern of daisies onto a white collar for me to wear for best, or sent me to school with a kiss and a smile. She was a drunk, and a whore, with her hair tumbled in her eyes and bruises on her neck and sores around her mouth; as different as could be from Mrs. Murphy and Mrs. Donner and the other women, neat in their simple homespun gowns, with their clean aprons over.

To start with I had hated them for it, mothers and children both, and my own mother most of all. But now I was reminded of better times, that I guess had been pushed to the back of my mind and lost, over the years.

When Pa was a young man, and courting my mother, who still lived at home with her folks, he was something of an adventurer. He had joined a ship plying the West Indies route, and gone off sailing round the whole of the world. One time he brought Ma some sugar candies, all the way from Paris, France, and even when the candies were long gone, she still kept the box. When I was very small, before all the rest of the children started coming along year in, year out, Ma would take down this box, sometimes, and show it to me.

It was painted over with the picture of a beautiful garden. There were archways of stone, and greenery cut into fancy shapes, and a swing with flowers twisted up the ropes. And there were some beautiful ladies walking through that garden, with white hair piled up high with feathers and jewels in, and wearing fine dresses.

The inside of the box was lined with yellow silk, and

here Ma kept her little treasures. She would let me pick over them, and tell me the story of each thing.

There was a tiny silver cross on a chain, given to her by her grandmamma, she said, and a piece of blue fabric patterned with flowers from her mama's wedding dress. A lock of hair, from her sister who had died as a baby; and a piece of horn patterned all over with strange pictures of sailing ships and patterns of knots.

This was from my pa, as well, carved on one of his long journeys on the whalers, for he had lost his employment with the West Indies merchant ships on account of his liking for the drink. Then it was only the whalers that would take him on, a dangerous trade though it was good money enough. But even that didn't last long. He broke his leg and it never mended right, and so it was that he ended up fit for nothing but the wharves, and sodden nights in the alehouse.

I had spent so long fearing my pa and hating my ma that I had quite forgot that there had once been happier times. Now it occurred to me that my mother would not have chosen such a life, and must have expected something very different. I suddenly longed to see her; with every bit of my heart I wished her with me, to eat a good helping of my johnnycakes, and breathe in the cold, green smell of the leaves and the water, and to see the view of the lake that was just as pretty as the picture on the candy box.

"When I get to California," I thought, "I will write a letter home, to let her know that I am safe and well. And I will save up every penny that I earn, however that may be, and send it to her, and beg her to bring the children and join me in my new life."

That night when we went to our beds, it was with the glad thought that the next time we laid our heads to rest, it would be on the other side of the mountain, in California.

The night air was chill, for we were very high in the hills now, and the Kesebergs and I crammed into our wagon to sleep, bundled up in quilts and wearing all our clothes. I lay half awake, thinking about crossing the pass in the morning, and my first sight of California, and what would happen to me when we got there.

It was said that the sun shone every day, that a stick planted in the good soil would bring forth fruit within weeks, and that there were plenty of men looking for wives, so that no matter how plain a body might be, she would find a home and someone to care for her.

I wouldn't ever be pretty. I was too tall for a girl and even with all the good food I had along the way, I was never going to be more than stick thin. But my hair had grown out nice enough, and I guess I had filled out enough in the right places. Enough, at least, to make Landrum Murphy look twice, and want to kiss me; and enough for the red-haired fellow at the dance to put his arms about me. I turned those thoughts over and over in my mind, smiling to myself in the darkness as I did so. I thought of how I would have my schoolhouse set out, and imagined seeing my ma again, and how startled she would be to find me so changed. And with that, I finally fell asleep.

I was woke in the full dark by raised voices. Mrs. Keseberg started up, calling out to her husband, and Baby set up wailing. I scrambled out of the wagon to find that the chill night air had given way to more snow. Two inches or more lay about us, crisp underfoot, and more falling, faster and faster, from the sky. Mr. Keseberg and the other men were whipping the animals back into their halters, and he shouted at me, "Quick! Get the others out of the wagon!"

There was no time for coffee or breakfast. Not even time enough for me to splash water onto my face or run a comb through my hair. Within minutes we were away.

The snow fell more gently as we left the camp, and as

the night faded to a gray dawn it stopped altogether. Daybreak gave us a lowering white sky, with a bitter wind blowing in our faces and no sight of the sun; but by now we were within sight of the pass, a gentle dip between two peaks. We were rejoicing in our good fortune when the storm set in.

The snow fell like feathers shaken from a torn pillow, choking and blinding us. The trail fell away at one side into a deep canyon, but the snow whirled so mad in the air that we could hardly make out where the road ended and the canyon began, and every step we took might be our last. The path rose up ahead of us, a steep sheet of ice beneath the slippery covering of the snow; the animals could not find their feet. Mr. Keseberg yelled at the beeves, "Hup! Hup!" He staggered his way forward to grab at the leader's head, and guide him up the slope, but the animal fell, pulling another with it, and I heard the crack of a bone breaking.

Those ahead abandoned their wagons and fled away past us, scrambling their way back down the mountain and screaming at us to do the same. In blind terror we joined them. Sliding and falling, we went helter-skelter back the way we had come.

25

By the time we got back to the lake, Mrs. Murphy had set up a fire in the shelter of a tall rock and brewed up coffee for all; and we stood round in sober little groups, drinking our coffee, and talking over what we should do.

Mr. Breen thought that the only course of action was to wait out the storm. It was well known that the bad weather did not settle in until after Thanksgiving, and that was three weeks yet. Within a day or two, he said, the weather would change, and we could resume our journey, and we thought he was right.

With everything we owned left up on the mountain, we had to beg for shelter. There was a tumbledown cabin near the shore, that looked like it had been used by trappers, and the Breens moved in there and let us sleep in their wagon along with Mr. Dolan. We were within sight of the Murphys' two wagons, drawn up by the big rock a few hundred yards away, but the Graveses got back in their wagon and took themselves as far away from us as they could manage. Being such a big family, they were not in need of company, I guess, and they never had been sociable. They were still sore about John Snyder's death, and above all I reckon Mrs. Graves disliked the thought of an Irishman being deferred to, and his advice taken.

With our delay, we thought to see the Donners, and those who had been traveling with them, catch up with us at the lake camp, but they did not. So the next afternoon, Mr. Stanton and the Mexicos set out with a couple of the mules and headed back to Alder Creek; returning a couple of days later with Mrs. Reed and her family and servants.

Mr. George Donner's injury hadn't healed well, and he was abed with a fever, too ill to be moved. He had sent a note by way of Mr. Stanton, authorizing the purchase of more beeves and provisions. The plan was that once we got through the pass, we would send back such supplies, and in a week or two the Donners and the rest would follow us. The plan seemed sound, for next day it began to rain in torrents, washing away the few inches of snow that surrounded us in the camp, and it was decided to resume our journey.

The last steep climb up to the pass was a difficult one and would need double-teaming to get the wagons up, but the few remaining beeves were skin and bone, and exhausted to the point of death. It made more sense for those with no wagons and no animals to complete the journey on foot and follow Mr. Donner's idea, to send back provisions and animals to enable the rest of the families, and our wagons, to be brought safe home.

Those who decided to set off with us were Mr. Breen, leaving his family behind to wait for his return; Mr. and Mrs. Eddy and their two little ones; and Mr. Stanton and the Mexicos, to show us the way. Mrs. Reed's party was to come with us; and Mrs. McCutcheon and her little girl, Harriet. Mrs. McCutcheon's wagon was left up on the mountain, with her team hitched up, so she thought to walk up with us, and either continue with us through the pass, or else claim her wagon and bring it back down to the camp.

Mr. Dolan offered to come along with her, to help her either way; and of course, Mrs. Keseberg nodded her head to Mrs. Eddy at this news, for it seemed to prove the truth of their rumor-mongering.

It was decided that we should start out as early as possible the next morning. So, at first light, we started up to load the animals ready for our journey. Mr. Stanton had made a rule about loading up the animals and it was this: that each person could bring what supplies of food they had, and a few necessities for when they reached the other side. He meant light things like a bag of coins, or a change of clothing, but everyone had a different idea of what they should take.

As well as the last of her provisions, Mrs. Reed had brought a bale of calico and some books back from the Donners' camp, and now she pitched up with them, saying that she would need them to trade when we reached Sutter's Fort. Mr. Dolan was wanting to pack his tobacco box, though he had no tobacco left in it, and Milt Elliott his rifle, though he was a right poor shot and in any case had no ammunition. Poor Mr. Stanton was everyone's enemy, saying no, no, to each and every silly thing.

"Necessities only! Just what is needed for a few days!" was his cry, but he was ignored altogether.

We were to carry the babies and toddlers, with the rest of the little children up on the mules. We thought to take two or three of the stronger beeves to carry our goods, but not being pack animals, they bucked and fought our efforts to load them. It meant that we did not start until the early afternoon, with bad feeling already in the air.

In our first tumble back down the mountain, Mr. Keseberg had injured his bad foot even further, and now he was unable to walk any distance at all. He was put up on a mule, with his foot in a kind of sling. He had Baby tied in a blanket on his back, and took the smaller children up in front of him in turns, to give the women a rest, and Mrs. Keseberg and I took it in turns to carry Ada.

So once again we set off on our journey up the mountain.

The rain that had fallen so hard in the camp hadn't reached here, and to our dismay the way was still deep in snow, but it was froze pretty hard and we could walk on it without sinking too far in. Even so, every step was hard labor, and before long we were hot from the labor and cold from the snow at the same time. But we plodded on, and by the time darkness came, we were only a mile or so from the pass.

All of us were shaking with fatigue and the children fractious and crying, so it was decided to stop and eat something before carrying on. We'd come up to where the abandoned wagons still stood, a sorry sight with the canvases caved in from the amount of snow that had settled on them. Mr. Keseberg dismounted from his mule, and he and the other men went and unhitched the teams. The animal that had broke its leg, and its companion that had fallen with it, were dead. And as soon as they were set free of their halters, the remaining animals ran away down the mountain, despite our best efforts to catch them.

Our resting place was a shallow depression in the snow, with some young pine trees dotted here and there. Virginia and I stirred ourselves enough to collect cones, and when we had an apron-full we set them round the base of one of the small trees, and Mr. Dolan got out his tinderbox and set them alight. They caught up something beautiful. It was a fine sight, to see those comforting little flames, for it was freezing hard by now. After a few minutes the tree itself caught alight and blazed up, casting a welcome warmth upon us all.

Some food was got out and we all ate something, and then we sat for a while gazing at the fire and complaining how tired we all were, and how much our legs ached with the trudge through the snow. Someone said how nice it would be to stay here in front of the fire, and someone else said that it would make sense to put off the rest of the journey until the morning, when we would be fresh and make good time. One by one we wrapped ourselves warmer in our shawls and the blankets and quilts we had brought with us, and nodded our heads in the heat of the fire. Some of the little children lay down with their heads on their mothers' laps, and fell fast asleep.

I was brought to by my arm being shaken, and a pinch, and a voice in my ear. I had shut my eyes but for a moment, I thought, but now a hazy moon stood full above me, and Mr. Keseberg was calling me, "Wake up, wake up!" He was shaking Mrs. Keseberg, too, and raising his voice for all to hear.

"Don't stop! If we stop, we will never get through! Wake up, wake up!"—at the top of his voice—"we must carry on as long as we can, no matter what!"

"It is easy for you to say that," come the drowsy reply from Mr. Eddy, "for you are riding on a mule and the rest of us walking and you do not know how tired we are!"

At that, Mr. Stanton joined his voice to Mr. Keseberg's. "Look, we can be through the pass in an hour or two. When we get through it the journey on the other side is easier, and then we can rest, but we must carry on and get through the pass while we can."

He got the same reply—"You are up on your horse and it is not the same hardship for you."

I wonder at our slowness to act and get across the pass come what may.

At the start of our journey, when Mr. Reed was persuading all to take the short route, he and the two Mr. Donners and the other men had read through Mr. Hastings's guide time and again. In there, it said beyond doubt that the winter snows did not set in until well after Thanksgiving. This was a pure fact, known to everyone who set out on the journey, and even though we could see the snow with our own eyes, it was another pure fact that Mr. Stanton and the Mexicos had returned from California and assured us that the pass was still open.

So, even though we had experienced the storm on the mountain previous, and even though we were walking through snow that was far deeper than we had anticipated, most of us seemed unable to truly comprehend the danger we were in. It was as if everyone's hearts and minds were still in the safety of their homes back East, where the weather was just something to be grumbled at, because it made the sidewalks slippery or a few chickens perish in the frost. Not one of us took it serious; not one of us understood that the weather does not go by Man's calendar.

The snow did not think to itself, "I have come too early and will depart with my head down in shame." It did not say, "I will wait until after Thanksgiving, for that is when I am expected." Like an unwelcome guest, it arrived too early and stayed too long, and never cared what we thought of it.

So we all lay ourselves back down in the snow, willful ignorant of the danger we were in, and fell asleep.

And it snowed.

I opened my eyes to whiteness; nothing more. It took me a moment to understand that I was beneath the snow; jerking upright I found nothing around me but a desolate, deserted landscape. Had all departed in the night, leaving me to perish alone on the mountain? I cried out at the thought.

Beside me the snow heaved. Mr. Keseberg's head came up and he gave a great shout himself, jumping up and brushing the snow from where it had hidden him. One by one the others followed suit. We were like souls rising from their graves on the Day of Judgment. And our doom was plain to see.

For the animals had been left untethered overnight and had run away and vanished, taking our scant provisions with them. The snow was so deep that we could scarce move one foot ahead of the other, and now the way across the pass was barred to us all.

We arrived back at the lake for a second time with our heads bowed under the shame of our failure. Those folks who still had wagons took shelter in them, and those of us with none crowded into the Breens' cabin, or took shelter in their wagon once more. But we had sixty souls to find shelter for, and wagons are not made to be houses; they did not keep out the bitter cold, and we could not sleep night after night crammed in together like pickles in a jar. So it was decided that we would set to and construct cabins; as many as could be made with the materials to hand.

We had tools, and the wagons were constructed so that they could be taken to pieces and the boards and canvases put to good use. But we had so very few of them. Of the twenty or more wagons we had started out with, all that remained was the two that the Murphys had managed to get through, two belonging to the Breens, and two belonging to the Graveses.

There were pine trees about us, too many to count, and they could be felled and used—if we had men strong and fit enough to undertake the labor. But we had lost so many of our number, through death or departure. Of those left, half perhaps were sick or injured, or too elderly to be much use. Ten men fit enough for the work was all we had. And as for the rest of us, what were we? Five or six hearty women, no more; a half dozen of us older children. A couple of nursing mothers, with babies and toddlers. And a whole army of little children, looking to us for their every need.

26

Once we accepted that we had to make camp for the winter, and that our journey was over for a while, we were, in some strange way, content. After so long traveling, we were heartily sick of it; I for one, for it was close on ten months since I had set off from Cincinnati. We had no real reason to fear what would become of us—the interruption to our journey was an inconvenience, but we thought ourselves well enough provided for. The snow around us in the camp was but little; we had food enough to last—if we were careful—for a few weeks until the snow stopped and the pass was open again. Before us, the lake stretched away into the far distance, filled with fish, no doubt. Surrounding us was mile after mile of tree-covered valleys and hills reaching to the horizon; a vast forest filled with game. And at every dawn and dusk, long skeins of ducks and geese went arrowing across the great empty skies above our heads.

So on that first morning we began the work of constructing our cabins with something like eagerness in our hearts.

The day started sunny and blowy. After breakfast was

done, a couple of the men set to felling the trees. The older boys trimmed off the branches, and then the mules were hitched up to haul the trunks across to the building site. Here, a couple of the women notched the ends so they would fit together, and the remainder of the men lifted them into place.

The smaller children were set to collect stones to make the hearths and chimneys. And under the direction of Mr. Eddy, the rest of us started to dismantle the Graveses' wagons, to use the planks and canvases for their cabin floor and the roof.

At first, it seemed a simple enough task. We got on quite quick; and we were merry enough, thinking that we would be provided with cabins for all in just a matter of a few days.

Of course, it did not work like this at all. As with near enough everything we did, and even in the most compelling of circumstance, it seemed we could not undertake one task without disputes and fallings-out; and although the first cabin we set to work upon was that of the Graves family, it was the Graveses who caused the first falling-out.

Mary and Eleanor Graves had been left to tend the campfire and keep coffee on the go, and make the dinner. As the morning went along the sky clouded over. A bitter wind got up, and snow started drifting in the air once more. The two girls disappeared into the shelter of one of the Breens' wagons where they primped up their curls and gossiped, paying no mind to their task.

The fire went out, and when we stopped at midday there was no hot coffee or food prepared. There was a great argument about whose fault it was, with the two girls blaming each other and the rest of us furious.

After we had sat a little over what we could find to eat, leftover corn bread and cold beans, we returned to our task. But the good feeling of working hand in hand was gone. And now the months and months of relentless hard labor that had been our lot came to bear on all of us something terrible. The tree fellers stopped to rest more and more, and worked slower and slower, until in the middle of the afternoon they came to a halt altogether. Mrs. Breen called them into her cabin, and brewed up some hot tea, and made them grits and peas.

Mrs. Eddy and Mrs. McCutcheon gave up their work and got a fire going again, and brewed coffee and made biscuits for the rest of us, for by then all of us were near weeping with cold and hunger. After we'd eaten something, and a little warmed, we went back to our task. By now the daylight was fading fast. The women with nursing babies had to feed them, and the mothers of the little children needed to give them their suppers and to get them to bed. But the rest of us battled on.

Me and Virginia and Meriam, along with Landrum and Lemuel, went back over to the tree felling. There were a dozen or so felled trees, with the tops chopped off and left in a great heap to one side, branches and cones and needles all tangled together and the trunks hauled out into a clearing, waiting to be trimmed. So we picked up the axes and saws ourselves and began trimming these away as best we could; as each one was finished, we hitched up the mules to haul it over to the building site, where William Graves and his father rolled the trunks away.

The Graveses having elected to set themselves up such a distance from the rest of us meant that they were a long way from the tree felling. Back and forth we went until all the trunks were shifted, our feet frozen, our fingers blistered and bleeding from splinters and nicks, and our hands red raw with the cold. I swear we walked a couple of miles or more in that way, which we need never have done, had the Graveses had more of a neighbor spirit in them, or if we had less.

After a while Mr. Keseberg and Mr. Stanton appeared and set up the sawhorses, and then the rest of the men gradually came out to join them. Between them they got the trunks sawn to size, and the ends notched, and lifted them into place.

Once the walls of the cabin were up, a couple of planks were laid across the top, and the canvases nailed on to make a roof, and the rest of the wagon planks carried in and laid to make the floor.

At this, the rest of the Graves children came swarming round and carried in all the rest of the articles that had been stored in the wagon. And the very minute their last bit of possessions were in, Mrs. Graves called all her family inside, and the door banged shut behind them. They lighted their fire, and put their coffeepot on it, and set to cook themselves a dinner. And all this with not a word of thanks or the offer of a cup of coffee to all the folks that had helped them so willing.

That first night the Kesebergs, Mr. Dolan, Mr. Burger and me bundled ourselves back into the Breens' wagon, mad as hell with the Graveses. But at least, we reasoned, next day they would be there to help us at our end of the camp.

Next morning we clambered out of the wagon at dawn to discover Mr. Stanton and the Mexicos already hard at work, yet again hauling logs over to the Graveses' cabin. They were nowhere to be seen, but then one of the Mexicos fetched up his hammer and started banging, and next thing Mrs. Graves come flying out and laid into him good and proper.

It made good sense to build a second cabin onto the back of the first, for it was as if one wall was already constructed, but it infuriated Mrs. Graves to discover that she was to have neighbors, and even more when she discovered that her neighbors were to be not only the Mexicos and Mr. Stanton, but also Mrs. Reed's family.

When the walls were up, there were no planks to make a roof. Mr. Graves poked his head out of doors to hand over a spare canvas, which was nailed roughly into place. The men said after, that they heard his wife give him a tongue lashing for this small act of kindness. I was not surprised to hear it.

The rest of us started on building a second cabin against the tall rock where we had gathered to drink coffee after our first flight down the mountain after the storm. Mr. Graves came out to help, and William, too. But to no one's very great surprise Mrs. Graves and the girls stayed put in their cabin and never showed their noses out of doors for the whole of the day.

By midafternoon the cabin walls were up. There were gaps aplenty where the logs didn't fit right well, so the wind whistled through some, but it was a good-size cabin and sound enough. Mr. Eddy took some of the wagon planks, and made a partition at the back of the cabin, saying that for the time being, at least, this little room would serve as a shelter for his own small family; and then the rest of the wagon planks were laid over to make the roof. With no planks left, the cabin was made do with a packed-earth floor.

By now we all were like to die from tiredness. Worst hit were the men. Mr. Eddy collapsed and had to be carried inside and laid down on a blanket, where he slept the clock round, and Milt Elliott was glassy-eyed, and staggered when he walked like he had spent his afternoon in the alehouse. Most of the men were like enough the same, and could not have built another cabin, that day or the next, whether they had wanted to or no.

With all the wagons gone, the Kesebergs and Mr. Burger and I were left with nowhere to shelter for the night. So, once the walls on the Murphy cabin were up, we left the others to finish off, and set to build something for ourselves, round back of the Breens' cabin.

At first we had some help here and there, as one task after another was completed and the workers came across to give us a hand. But when the Murphy cabin was complete, and the fire was lit, the good smell of cooking began to drift on the air, and the same from the Breen cabin as well. One by one our fellows laid down their tools, and went down to the lake and washed their hands and faces, glad enough to see the end of labor, and have a hot meal, and shelter for the night.

But we labored on, as the afternoon wore into evening, and the sun sank down behind the mountain.

We had got some of the trunks that had been felled earlier, and spare planks given us by the Breens, and they gave us a couple of canvases, too. After he'd eaten his supper, Mr. Dolan came out to help Mr. Keseberg and Mr. Burger. Along of him came John Breen and his brother, Edward. God bless those boys, for they were as tired as any and still willing to help us. To my mind they put the older men, safe indoors with a hot meal inside them while we were out working in the snow, to shame.

Meriam and Landrum came too. We crossed over to the great pile of discarded branches and treetops, and tried to salvage as many of those as we could, but it was a horrible task. The branches were covered with prickly needles that scratched our arms and hands and legs, and caught in our hair and clothing. Every cut we made released some horrible sticky sap so our hair and faces and hands were thick with it, and bugs flew out at us.

The first time a great moth fluttered into my face, I screamed and clutched at Meriam, and she screamed back and clutched at me, and the boys laughed and made fun of us. But it was halfhearted sport, and after that one time we were too exhausted to indulge in such childish carry-on.

After we'd carried the branches over to the Breens' cabin, the others gave up the task and went indoors. But I carried on, going where I was told, and holding what I was given. It was like being in a dream—past hunger, past speech, past thought altogether.

I don't know why we did it. I don't know why we didn't bang on the door of the Breen cabin and beg shelter for one more night. It was as if none of us could put one clear thought after another, and all that drove us on was the instinct to have shelter of our own and the determination to get the task finished.

We managed to construct a kind of little shanty, butting up against the far wall of the Breen cabin. What we built was a poor enough thing, not much more than a few slender trunks fixed to the roof of the Breen cabin, and sloping away to the ground. We laid branches across, tied into place with ropes, and nailed a canvas over these, with another across the entrance as a kind of doorway. It was shelter of a sort, something more spacious than the wagon we'd been sleeping in, at least, and we thought it would do, until such time as we regained our strength, and could build something better.

Everyone else was finished by now, and the rest of the camp was quiet and dark, all asleep. All that was left awake was our little band, Mr. Burger and Mr. and Mrs. Keseberg, the children and me, sick at heart and trembling from head to foot with tiredness, the lack of food, and the bitter cold. Mrs. Keseberg and the rest went inside, but I stood for a minute, too tired even to take the three steps that would have brought me into the shelter.

I would have given everything in my whole world, then, to be back in Cincinnati, even with my pa shouting and my ma screaming with the thud of his fist landing on her. I wanted, more than I have ever wanted anything in my life, to be huddled in my bed with a couple of my sisters, with the rain dripping through the roof, and the singing in the streets outside as the alehouses let out.

I drew in a ragged breath, and went into our shelter, wondering how long it was to be my home.

Mr. Burger had lain down at the far end of the lean-to and was asleep already. Mr. Keseberg was sat with his back against the wooden wall of the cabin, with his eyes closed. Ada was fast asleep. I covered her with another shawl, and helped Mrs. Keseberg to spread out the blankets and quilts. When that was done, she gathered the children to her, and lay down with them, weeping softly.

"Louis." Her voice was not above a whisper. "Do you think it is true, that we will be here but a month or so? I wish I could believe it. Oh, my dear, I am sore afraid."

And with that, she fell asleep.

It reminded me of something and I asked Mr. Keseberg, what is it? He answered me in a low voice, with his eyes still closed for tiredness, it is the Christmas story, how the shepherds were looking out for their sheep; and he said, "The angel of the Lord came down upon them, and the Glory of the Lord shone round about them, and they were sore afraid."

I ventured my head out of the shelter. The sky stretched high above us, not angel wings but black crow feathers spread out across heaven. The moon over the mountain was a cold white eye, staring straight at me, and I was sore afraid, as well.

I curled myself into the littlest ball I could, and lay there all that long night, shaking with cold and fear.

27

It seemed that Mrs. Keseberg's fear was well-founded. Thanksgiving came and went but the snow stayed, and more came to join it. And we were still in the camp, with no thought of being able to leave.

One afternoon, I was in the Murphy cabin with Mrs. Eddy and Mrs. Keseberg and a couple of the other women. We all had stitching or knitting to hand. The cold was something hard to bear, and most folks had set off with only a change or two of light clothing, so we were using what scraps we could find to make hats and scarves for the children. Ada and Margaret and the other children were at our feet, engaged in some game with their dolls, and the men out chopping firewood.

I was knitting squares in a plain stitch. It was pretty much all I could do, but when they were finished they could be sewn up one side and across the top to be mittens. They would not win a prize for their beauty at any country fair, that much was certain, but they served a purpose. I thought the same was probably true of me.

The cabin was warm enough, with a good fire blazing

up. Mrs. Murphy put the kettle over, and when it boiled she made us some tea. There was no milk or sugar, and it was not much more than a flavor in hot water, but it was welcome enough.

"I wonder that Mr. McCutcheon has not returned." This was Mrs. Eddy. Mrs. Keseberg opened her mouth to speak, then cast a look at Mrs. McCutcheon, head bent over her work, and thought the better of it. But Mrs. Eddy was not speaking with any malice; she bit the end of her thread, and held up the cap she had just finished to examine the stitching. She went on, "At Sutter's Fort—there must be folks wondering what has become of us, surely? Mr. Sutter himself—the mules that he lent to Mr. Stanton—he must be looking for their return."

Mrs. McCutcheon spoke next. "I hope my husband is well, but I fear he is not. I cannot imagine what has become of him." She dashed at her eyes with the hem of the jacket that she was stitching. "But you are right, Mrs. Eddy, to wonder why we are left in this way. Colonel Russell would have expected to find us there when he arrived. What of Mr. Hastings? Didn't he think us to be close behind him on the trail? And Mr. Reed and Walter Herron must have got through, surely. Where are they?"

It was the first time we had put into words what we had begun to dread: that maybe no help was coming for us. The thought was too terrible to contemplate.

"But—we cannot manage! Look, look!" Mrs. Murphy stood up, and her knitting dropped to the floor, unheeded. She half-ran across to the corner where her provisions were stored. "I have a half sack of flour and the same of oatmeal, and some rice—it's not enough! It's not enough!"

It was a sad little array of goods, to be sure—a few sacks, half-empty, and a couple of boxes and casks, and a side of salt bacon hanging from the ceiling, not much left on it at all.

"If no one comes for us—what will we do? Oh, dear God, what will we do?" Mrs. Murphy gave a choking sob, and bent her head and began to weep. Meriam jumped to her feet, and ran across to fling her arms round her mother, and looked at me and I looked back at her, with the same fear in our eyes, I am sure.

Day by day we grew more despondent. Folks turned upon one another, women blaming their husbands and the men blaming the weather, and all of us blaming Mr. Reed most of all. Our spirit was near gone; and our provisions, too.

Mr. Breen called a meeting to see what could be done. There were too many folks to fit into one cabin, so this meeting—like the meeting that was held to decide Mr. Reed's fate—was held out in the open. The snow had let up, and it was a bright sunny day with a blue sky. We collected together a great deal of wood, and lit a fire, and stood round, and Mr. Breen started, as he had before, by making a little speech.

He said that whether we liked it or no, we were all here together and looked to be staying put for the time being and that ill-feeling, if there was any such—and he looked over our heads as he spoke, so that he would not catch anyone's eye—if there was any ill-feeling we should put it to one side, and that we should work together for the good of all. Everyone nodded their heads virtuously at this fine sentiment.

Then he asked Mr. Eddy to step forward, and tell us how he had fared in his hunting.

Mr. Eddy had gone out a few days before, telling us how he would return with deer aplenty, and that there would be fresh meat for all. He was out all day, but returned at sunset with nothing. Now, he told us that the reason was that the harsh winter weather had driven all the game out of the mountains and that in his opinion—and he kind of laughed, and looked round at all—his *humble* opinion—and he lowered his eyes to look modest—there was little point in wasting time and effort in trying to hunt further and we should think of other ways of finding food.

Mr. Eddy had spent so long telling everyone what a great hunter he was, that folks had come to believe him. Now, there was a general muttering round the circle, with the other men saying, well, if he can't catch anything, no one can.

Their spirit might be broke; they might be content to give up without a fight, but I was not. I thought that they could defer to Mr. Eddy and believe him all they liked, but I thought it more that Mr. Eddy felt a fool for coming home with nothing after his boastings.

I spoke up in a loud voice.

"That cannot possibly be true! The animals can't have run away all in one go! And even if the deers have, there must still be some little animals, rabbits and such!

"There are traps left in your cabin, Mr. Breen, I have seen them with my own eyes, and it must be worth setting them out at least!"

All looked something startled at hearing me speak out. The married women could have their say, and the older boys might venture an opinion or two but we girls were not supposed to.

Mr. Breen raised his eyebrows at me, and Mrs. Keseberg snapped at me, "Be quiet!" and apologized to Mr. Eddy for my rudeness. I might have been talking to the snow itself, for all that anyone took notice of what my opinion might be.

My pa said it was impossible for a girl to think and understand the ways of the world, and it was a man's job to do so, and brought the lesson home with his belt when I asked why this, and why not that. So I shut my mouth tight, glowering at Mrs. Keseberg, and keeping my thoughts to myself, though it didn't prevent me from turning them over and over in my head in a silent fury.

Beside us was a great lake full of fish. Even as we spoke they could be seen snapping at the last few insects that were foolish enough to alight on the water. Now one of the men stepped up to recount how he had spent a morning fishing, but was forced to give it up after an hour or so of standing shivering in the water. Another nodded his agreement. "Yes, that's true, I tried, too, but there are no fish to be had."

A few days previous I had watched these men at their halfhearted work, and I had been determined it could be done. I made Meriam and a couple of the boys come with me and we went out to have a go ourselves. We hadn't any fishing line, but we tried picking threads from our clothes and knotting those together, and Lemuel Murphy spent a long hour unraveling a length of rope to make a fine string. We had no fishing hooks but we had hairpins, and bent those into shape and baited them with bits of corn bread.

Despite all our efforts, the fish just swam past, taking as little notice of our precious scraps of food as they would a fallen leaf or a bit of twig floating on the surface. Great fat things they were, as well.

Meriam remembered the bugs in the woodpile. Maybe those would be more tempting as bait, so we all trooped off there to see if we could find more, but that was no good, either; they'd flown themselves back into the forest or something else had come along and eaten them. So I guess I was a little more forgiving of this story than I was of Mr. Eddy's.

Mr. Breen then said, "Well, if there is no game to be had and we cannot catch the fish, what else can we do? For there are some among us who have more than sufficient for their needs, but many of our friends here are reduced to nothing. My suggestion is that everyone brings their food into my cabin and we count it up, and then divide it out so that everyone has a fair share."

There was a moment's shocked silence.

No one wanted to say it was a good idea, because it made sense that the person who said it first would be the person who wanted it most. To be right truthful, I guess that person would have been Mrs. Reed, who had nothing to her name whatsoever and a goodly number of folks to provide for; but I reckon it would have took more courage than she possessed to say so and sound a beggar.

When we came down off the mountain the second time, Mr. Keseberg and I had gone into our abandoned wagon and brought back into camp all that we could carry. So we had some dried goods: peas and pumpkin and onion, a sack of oatmeal and one of cornmeal, and a bit of rice, and some other odds and ends. But I guess neither Mr. nor Mrs. Keseberg wanted to say what we had got, for fear it should be taken and handed out to others. The rest clearly felt the same. Finally Mrs. McCutcheon stepped forward and said just that; that she had only enough for herself and her child. She understood that there were others not as fortunate, and she was right sorry for it. She might have nothing to share, but then again she wanted nothing either, and that was her view on the matter.

Mr. Breen nodded, yes, he understood that, and then Mrs. Breen spoke up. "We have sufficient for our family, too," she said. "We are lucky in that we brought our wagons safely along the trail. But we can live frugal enough and find a little to spare for others if they need it."

This was kindly meant, but it had the opposite effect to what she intended and stung Mrs. Graves into speech. "Well!" she started, and this single word was enough to make her feelings pretty clear.

"I have no need of charity from you, Peggy Breen, I

thank you kindly! And if you wish to see your children half-starved because of other folks' foolishness"—and she fixed Mrs. Reed with a stare—"then you go right ahead. But I have been careful all along, and I have twelve bodies to provide for. If anyone thinks I am going to help them and see my family suffer as a result, why then they are very much mistaken, and I think you will find that there are others here who would agree with me.

"There has been some talk about our cabin, and why we choose to live a distance from the rest of you. I can tell you why that is. I do not want folks knocking my door to ask for charity. Charity begins at home, as the saying goes, and I will not see my family go without for the sake of folks I hardly know.

"Mrs. Murphy, you have a large family to provide for; do you have so much that you can give half of it away to strangers?"

There was an uncomfortable stir at this. To be described as strangers when we had traveled so far together and worked shoulder to shoulder was unexpected, and unpleasant as well.

Mr. Breen stepped forward with his last suggestion. He said we should slaughter all the remaining animals. With no feed, and snow covering what grass there was, it was plain that they would perish in any event, so it would be as well to slaughter them now. And how did folks feel about sharing the meat, at least?

At this, finally, Mrs. Reed found her voice.

"I do not wish for charity," she said, drawing herself up and looking about her. "But my provisions are all gone, and I have no animals neither, so what am I to do? How am I to care for my children and my servants?"

She reminded us how she and Mr. Reed had shared their stores with those less fortunate, when they came out of the desert, and said that surely the folks that had benefitted then should have some care for her now.

There was an uncomfortable shuffling of feet here and there, but no one stepped up in reply.

Then she said, "My husband will be waiting for me in California, and I will buy some beeves, if anyone is willing to wait for payment until we reach our destination."

The Eddys were in the same fix—no animals and scarcely no provisions—and had kept quiet throughout, but now Mr. Eddy said the same, that he would like to purchase beeves, and had the money for them there and then. He unbuttoned a pocket on the inside of his jacket, and pulled out a handful of gold coin, to show his good intention.

Mrs. Graves looked at the gold and looked at him. "Very well, Mr. Eddy. We will sell you two beeves for fifty dollars." Everyone gasped. It was all the money he held in his hand, and a good healthy animal could be bought for ten dollars at the start of our journey. These animals were nothing but bones and skin, and it was touch-and-go which got them first—starvation or the butcher's knife.

Mr. Eddy had no choice but to agree. Mrs. Graves turned to Mrs. Reed. "There is no guarantee that we will be paid. For myself, I doubt that your husband ever reached California at all."

I thought I spoke blunt, but this was cruel. I caught a sight of Virginia's white face. Virginia was very close to her pa, and I guess she had comforted herself with the thought that he was safe and waiting for them and it was a shock to be reminded that it might not be so.

"But I wish to be charitable. I will sell you two beeves at sixty dollars, Mrs. Reed, on your note of promise. And the same for the ones you have already had from us and lost."

When all this bargaining was concluded, and with much discord and bad feeling in the air, the men began to slaughter the animals. As soon as the first sank to its knees, the blood pouring from its throat, the rest knew that death was come for them. They raised their great heads to the skies and bellowed, and kicked at their traces and tried to escape; and those that were but loosely tethered pulled themselves free and ran away. And in the middle of all this the wind got up, howling round our ears, and it began to snow again.

One morning, Mrs. Eddy and Margaret arrived at our shelter and came in to visit with us for a while. For a little it was like old times back on the trail.

When we had taken our provisions out of the wagon, I had tucked the little cups and saucers of Ada's tea set into my pocket. Now, I set them down in a corner for the girls to play, and turned away to look out some crumbs to be the dolls' food. I heard Ada give a shout of anger, and then the sound of a tussle. When I turned back it was to see Ada crying, and Margaret with a red face, close to tears herself. She had taken the dolls' food, and crammed it into her mouth.

I swung Margaret up into the air, hoping to make her laugh and stop the children's squabble. She flew up in my arms as light as a little bird, not at all what I was anticipating. I hugged her to me, and with something of a shock I realized that beneath her layers of clothing she was wasted away to nothing. I looked more closely at Mrs. Eddy. She had been a plump enough soul at the start of our journey, but now her fingers were like claws, and where her sleeves had ridden up I could see that her arms were thin as twigs, and covered with a fine coat of hair, like to an animal.

Most casual, I asked Mrs. Keseberg if she would like me to put some coffee on to heat. She cast a quick look at Mrs. Eddy's face, humiliated and despairing at the same time, and said, "Yes, we will have some coffee, and I don't know about you, Mrs. Eddy, but I am quite peckish and could fancy a morsel of corn bread. Oh, and you would be doing me a kindness if you and Margaret would help me finish up this jar of preserves, for it will spoil if not used today."

But it was the first and last time that we made a pretense that all was well, and that nothing was amiss. After that day we had nothing to spare for anyone else, and all in camp were the same.

What is it like, to know such hunger that you are like to die from it? I cannot speak for the rest, but I am sure their experience was no different from my own.

I dreamed of food, all night long. Vivid dreams, so real that for the first second or two of waking I believed them to be true. I could smell the food cooking. My mouth watered at the thought of what was waiting for me: a heaping dish of oatmeal with hot milk poured over it and a big spoonful of molasses, to be followed by bacon and biscuits, hot from the griddle and dripping with butter. Cup after cup of coffee, milky and sweet. But that thought fled away as I came full awake, and I could have cried with the disappointment of it.

Breakfast was flour mixed with water and baked into a cracker, no bigger than the palm of my hand. Our noontime might be a spoonful of rice, nothing more. As the day wore on, my stomach hurt with the hunger, so that I was near crippled with the pain of it; but all that would be there on my plate at the end of the day was a spoonful of stew, mostly water, a few grains of rice, and another cracker, smaller than the one I had eaten for my breakfast.

Oh! It is easy to be kind, and thoughtful, and concerned for others, when you have a full belly and more food in the store cupboard. It is a luxury to relish hunger after a day's labor, knowing that the reward for that labor is to sit over a great plate of good things to eat.

But to spend your every waking moment wishing for just a mouthful of food; to see a child staring at your plate with desperate longing in their eyes; to eat that food in front of them, caring more for the food than for the child—that makes you feel something less than human.

Hunger is an evil thing, and brings with it the worst of human nature; it is an agony of the flesh, but it is an agony of the spirit as well.

28

Every alternate Saturday afternoon, I attend the Ladies' Quilting Bee. There are a dozen or so of us ladies and we take it in turns to meet in one another's houses.

The first Saturday in June our meeting is at Mrs. Gerald's boardinghouse. We assemble at her house in a most daring frame of mind. It is an entirely respectable establishment, or so we all assure ourselves, but rumor has it that her past is something questionable.

When Jacob fetched me here, there weren't above fifty souls in the district. The only businesses were Peabody's Mercantile, the blacksmithery, and the lumberyard. Now there are near forty families in town, with more folks arriving by the month. And what was once a muddy lane where the cattle were driven down to the stockyards has turned into Main Street.

Good boarded sidewalks have been built. New businesses have opened. And only last year a Dining Rooms opened up, with a room set aside for ladies only, where we can sit with a cup of coffee and a slice of pie, if we wish. Though it overlooks the not-so-respectable saloon where the roustabouts come in on a Friday night to spend their wages.

The country families come in once a week to do their marketing, and travelers pass through on their way to the towns on the coast. There are so many babies born, that there are plans for next year to build another room onto the school, and I can see that we shall need another after that. How respectable we all sound!

But the truth is that California is the land of brave souls who adventured here, and lost souls who washed up here. Many have fetched up in our little town having encountered hardship along the way, and many folk would rather not dwell on their past lives. We generally try to keep ourselves to ourselves, far as we are able, and carry with us the words of the Bible about casting the first stone and judging not.

So, although we all know that old Peabody's son drank and gambled away the fortune in gold he dug out of the hills in '49, we do not say it aloud. And if rumor has it that Mrs. Gerald bought her boardinghouse with the proceeds of her time as a riverboat gal, well, we do not say that aloud, either; though Minnie and I stick pretty close together as the maid shows us into Mrs. Gerald's parlor.

Mrs. Gerald's parlor is the first thing in fashion. The walls are covered from ceiling to floor in a pale paper with green vines twisting through a brown trellis work pattern. On the mantel she has two green glass lamps with some fancy gold trim to them; a great gilded mirror behind; and there is a rich Turkey carpet on the floor, with button-back chairs in crimson velvet to match.

It is exceedingly sumptuous, and Mrs. Gerald steps across to greet us, dressed just as sumptuous herself in blue-and-white-striped silk.

Minnie murmurs to me below her breath, "If only we had our Godey's gowns to wear!"

I whisper back, "Oh, my word, yes! I would surely like

to be dressed in those wine-colored puffs instead of my let-out brown homespun! But can't you just imagine, if we had turned up in the Practical Bloomers!"

Minnie laughs so hard at this that she has to go outside to recover her composure.

I cannot think why Mrs. Gerald would want to engage in so simple and homely a task as quilt-making, but I daresay that no matter how fancy-dressed she might be, and no matter what she has come from before, she is the same as the rest of us underneath, wanting some friendship and lively conversation as we all do. And there certainly is enough lively conversation in our bee to keep anyone content.

We are engaged in sewing squares for the pieced quilt we will present to Betsey Mueller for her Hope Chest. Preacher Holden finally plucked up the courage to ask for her, and they are to be married at Christmas. Betsey is a right sensible girl, practical and hardworking and able to keep a confidence. I reckon she will make a good preacher's wife.

We have been engaged upon this quilt for some weeks now. To begin with there was some heated discussion over its design, for this year we have a great occasion to celebrate.

September marks California's ten-year anniversary of statehood. It is something we are all pretty proud of. We are to have a parade and a dance, and there is to be a baking contest for the best peach pie.

Some of the ladies thought that the quilt should mark this momentous occasion—the day, that is, not the winning pie. However, hot on the heels of California Day comes the presidential election in November. And here in California the two things are tied together in such a knot that we cannot pick them apart.

California was the thirty-first state to join the Union. Declaring itself a free state, it tipped the uneasy balance of power between the fifteen free states in the North, and the fifteen slaver states in the South. Two more free states, including our neighbor, Oregon, have since joined the Union, and it seems to me that we three will decide the outcome of an election based on the dreadful issue of slavery. But just declaring ourselves as a free state does not mean every person would vote for Mr. Lincoln. In our own little town there are as many folks here from the South, or with family in the South, as from the North.

Feelings on this run so very high that even something as humdrum as our little quilt has turned into something political, for a quilt to mark our anniversary would be a quilt to mark the election as well. I am not alone in thinking that sending a new-married couple to sleep under a Political Statement is not the best start to their future. And after a deal of to-and-fro, the matter has been decided in favor of making squares to represent our own lives in our small town in this year 1860; and the presidential election is left to take care of itself.

My square is a representation of my garden. A row of orange carrots round the outside, and an inner row of purple beets, all with green tops, and a pink rose in the center. Some of the ladies look at my handiwork a bit doubtful, feeling that the colors are something bold and not altogether pleasing to the eye, but I pay no heed to their helpful suggestions and stitch away, perfectly happy in my work. Minnie is making a square that shows her four boys fishing. And Mrs. McGillivray is copying a poster that she found in the pocket of Matty McGillivray's pants, before he ran away from home; an advertisement for the Pony Express.

This is mostly in embroidery, for she has a marvelous touch with a needle. It shows a fellow galloping away on his horse, and underneath,

WANTED—YOUNG, SKINNY, WIRY FELLOWS not above eighteen, expert riders, willing to risk death daily. Orphans preferred. Wages $25 per week.

Seeing his ma working all hours to provide for the family, teaching in the schoolhouse and dressmaking, too, no doubt Matty thought it a brave thing to go off to earn a living in this way. I can surely see how thrilling it would sound to a young lad. Twenty-five dollars for a week of horse riding? What riches!

I reckon his ma has different thoughts on it entirely. The Pony Express riders race across the country, a hundred miles or more in a day at full gallop, alone against the wilderness and the Indians and any rotten fellow along the way who thinks little of murdering the rider for the sake of whatever he might carry in the mail pouches. Maybe it makes it easier for Mrs. McGillivray to bear, if she stitches her heartache into a patch.

As I say, along with our sewing, we engage in conversation—more conversation than sewing, most of the time.

Today the conversation begins straightforward enough. But every topic seems to lead to bad feeling, and we end up hopping from one thing to the next like to a frog on hot stones.

We start off by talking about California Day. The anniversary itself falls on a Sunday and there is to be a special service at church. But there has been a great debate about the rest of the celebration—the parade and the dance. Some folks are adamant that dancing and parading could not be countenanced on a Sunday, and others equally adamant that to have them on any other day would be to miss the point entirely. In the end it was left to Preacher Holden to decide. The parade and the dance are to be held on Saturday, and after the service on Sunday we are to have a potluck luncheon.

Even though it was decided weeks ago, not all are entirely happy with the solution, and our conversation about it gets a little heated.

I sure would like to add my thoughts on the matter into the mix. It reminds me of the way the German folks in Cincinnati were drove out of their homes because of their love of entertainments on a Sunday, and I wouldn't like to see our small town to go the same way. But it is second nature to me to avoid speaking of anything that will lead back to my past, so I turn the conversation to the peach-pie contest instead.

Some of the ladies say we should all use the same recipe and be judged on our baking skills alone. At that, a whole chorus strikes up, that it would be pretty dull to have all the pies the same and we should be allowed to make whatever we choose! So our conversation on this matter gets pretty heated as well.

Mrs. Jackson asks me, very casual, what I think on the matter, and what sort of pie I might be making. She is a light hand at pastry and fancies her chances. I guess she is going to make her mother's recipe for a pie with a crumble top. I have eaten it before and it is pretty good. But although I may be poor at stitching, I reckon myself a dab hand at baking, and I am dead set on winning that peach-pie bake-off. I have in mind a recipe that uses sour cream and a pinch of spice to give extra flavor. This recipe is my secret and, try as she might, Mrs. Jackson is not going to catch me out.

Rather than answer her, I turn to Mrs. McGillivray and ask her what she thinks about the coming-up election for the new president. Here the conversation gets itself so boiled up that it knocks the arguments about pies and parades into a cocked hat, and I wish I had thought of something else to say.

We start off with talking about Mr. Lincoln, and that goes along pretty much all right for a few minutes. But of course, that leads onto the issue of slavery, Mr. Lincoln being so set against it. And one of the women makes a comment to the effect that she thinks it a terrible fuss about nothing much.

"Mr. Davies"—Isobel Davies blushes scarlet, for she is very new married—"I mean—that is, my husband—he says, here are folks with food on the table and homes provided for them for the price of a day's labor. And I agree with him, and can't see the wrong in it."

She is very young, not more than eighteen, and newly arrived from North Carolina. Her head bent over her work, she carries on, "Why, Father says our blacks at home are perfectly happy, and I think it must be true. We treat them fine, just precisely the same as white servants. I surely don't see that the color of their skin makes any difference."

There is a moment's silence at her remark, broken by Mrs. Gerald. Her voice is surprisingly gentle. "But, my dear, we are not talking about servants. We are speaking of people who were forced from their homes and set to a life they never chose and can never escape, are we not?"

I cast a quick glance at her, thinking to myself, here is a woman who speaks from the heart. Perhaps her life has not always been as pleasant as it is now.

Mrs. Davies lifts her eyes from her work, and looks from one horrified face to another in innocent surprise. "But they were pagan savages living in the jungle, before! How can that be better than living in civilization?"

Mrs. McGillivray comes up pretty sharp. "If all you can say is something so silly then you'd best be quiet!"

I guess like me, she had been biting her lip over what she should and shouldn't say, and at last it was impossible for her to keep her mouth shut.

"You know nothing about it! There were slave owners up in the mining camps. Men who arrived with ten or fifteen of them, thinking to sit themselves back in comfort and let their slaves do all the labor for no money and punished if they paused even for a moment. I've seen a slave

whipped, for no more than helping himself to a drink of water without permission, so that the skin on his back peeled off like the skin of an orange, leaving the bone open to the sky!"

"Oh my!" This was Mrs. Holden. "Mrs. McGillivray, I am sure we all—"

But Mrs. McGillivray would not be still. "If those mine owners had any conscience, they'd have paid for honest labor. Working alongside those black men were white men who had families to provide for! Some of them would have been very glad for a day's pay for a day's work.

"Why should the slave owners come into the camps and think to make an easy dollar at the expense of the black men's lives and the white men's families? Tell me that!"

Mrs. Holden very much dislikes being interrupted in this way, and makes a sharp reply herself, about what ruffians the miners are altogether. Mrs. McGillivray answers back, that Mrs. Holden being so proud of California's statehood, she should be grateful to those ruffians—for if it wasn't for them there would be no statehood at all!

The words might not have been to Mrs. Holden's liking, but Mrs. McGillivray is right.

The year after I arrived here, gold was discovered on Mr. Sutter's land, and folks flooded into California in search of it.

Some of the early arrivals found gold lying there for the taking, more or less. They moved on pretty quick away to the coast, buying themselves land and constructing great houses, and some of them poured money into setting up businesses and building schools and churches. But they were followed by another wave of folks and another after that, until the land along the foothills of the Sierra Nevada was a seething mass of prospectors.

And they were desperate folks, to be sure. I guess they arrived thinking that, like in their towns back East, there would be trading posts and provision stores, but of course this was not so.

The folks that had settled in the region already—the homesteaders and the religious folks who wanted to live a quiet life away from any sort of persecution—found their little settlements overrun with the mining men, looking for food to purchase. There was none, for what folks grew or farmed was pretty much only enough to sustain their families. And so the mining men turned to thievery. Folks woke in the mornings to find their cattle stolen, their chickens gone, and the crops vanished from the fields; their vegetable gardens smashed and trampled and no food left to feed their families.

We were lucky here; we are too far away from the gold fields to have had much trouble, but we have all heard the tales.

The good side of the bad, though, was that between one year and the next, our population went from seven thousand folks to seventy thousand. Of course, we did not know this at the time, but I suppose the government kept count. Once the population reached sixty thousand, a vote could be held to see if folks wanted California to apply for statehood, and of course everyone did.

I guess the respectable folks who take such relish in our admission to the Union try to ignore the bitter taste that comes from knowing that it is owed to the ruffians up at the mining camps, even though these same ruffians felt so strongly about slavery that in some places they would not countenance it in their midst and drove the slave owners out of the diggings.

Everyone has an opinion on one thing or another. What starts off as a lively discussion turns into a fierce argument, with even the most ladylike among us yelling at the top of her voice and shouting down her neighbor. In the end Mrs. McGillivray gets herself into such a fluster that she drops her sewing, and bursts into tears.

We all look at one another something shamefaced to

have made the poor woman cry. In our enthusiasm for the subject, we have just completely forgot that her husband and her two older sons are themselves those very ruffians; and poor little Isobel Davies, who has done nothing more than repeat what her father and husband have told her, is already weeping into her handkerchief in the corner of the room.

Mrs. Gerald says, "Oh my Lord, if I'd known you quilting bee ladies to be such a lively crowd I'd have joined you all a great deal earlier!"

Then she says she has just the thing for the hysterics, and rings for the maid to bring in a bottle of brandy and some glasses. She pours herself a generous measure and drinks it off, and then one for each of the rest of us.

We all look askance at the idea of drinking spirits, let alone in the middle of the day! But she says, "Oh, it is purely medicinal, for I think all of us are something upset"—and pours herself another.

Preacher Holden runs a temperance household. Mrs. Holden takes up her glass with much hesitation, looking around at us and saying how she is so very upset that she is close to the palpitations, and her son would allow that a drop of brandy is known to be good for the heart, would he not?

At that, she swallows it down in one, albeit with a ladylike wrinkle of her nose, and much genteel coughing, then says, "Why, I declare I do feel something restored. I'll take a drop more, Mrs. Gerald, if you would be so kind."

29

In the middle of December, Baylis Williams died. He was a simple-witted fellow, but there was no harm in him, and he was real devoted to his sister Eliza, the Reeds' cook. He had arrived in camp in a poor state of health and had been laid abed ever since, but his death was a shock to all, for he was the first of us to die from simple cold and hunger, and according to his sister, it was a right cruel and painful way to go.

We could not believe it. Even when his body was carried out from Mrs. Reed's cabin, with his sister weeping over it; even when it was buried in the snow, we could not believe it.

Belief and lie; they go along hand in hand, for it is belief in a lie that gives the lie its power, and the lies we tell ourselves are the ones we believe the most. We could not believe in the snow on the mountain, even as we floundered our way through it. We believed we would be rescued, when there was no sign of it. And we had not believed we might die; but here was the proof of it.

Mr. Eddy's carpentering skills were called upon once

more to fashion a coffin. When it was done, he and Milt Elliott carried it into Mrs. Reed's cabin. After a while, Mr. Eddy come to the door and called in Mr. Stanton and Mr. Dolan. Then the four men fetched out the coffin with Baylis Williams laid inside.

We had all come to escort him to his burial place. The men took off their hats as the coffin came out of the cabin and one or two of the women wept.

We set off in silence, but Eliza stopped in her tracks, and said, "Baylis couldn't sleep at night when he was a little lad—he was too afeard of the dark—and I used to sing to him. Oh, poor boy, he will be frightened now!" Her voice gave out on a choke, and Mrs. Reed put her arm round her shoulders for comfort.

Ada's hand crept into mine, and I squeezed it hard, thinking of poor Baylis Williams as a little boy being scared of the dark, and in his coffin now. Walking beside me with her arm tucked into mine was Mrs. Murphy. I guess she felt the same as me, for she lifted up her voice and started to sing. It was a song I had heard many times along our journey:

> *Lead, kindly Light, amid the encircling gloom,*
> *Lead thou me on,*
> *The night is dark, and I am far from home;*
> *Lead thou me on.*
> *Keep thou my feet; I do not ask to see*
> *The distant scene: one step enough for me.*

All joined in, and we sung our way through the trees to the grave place, our voices thin and little in the silent, snowy landscape.

When we got back to camp, Mr. Graves went off in a huddle with Mr. Eddy. And the next morning he called a meeting.

"I grew up in Vermont; for those of you who do not

know it, Vermont is about as far in the Northeast as it is possible to go.

"There, it snows hard through the winter, and the Indians have a type of shoe that makes it possible for them to walk across the surface of the snow. Mr. Eddy thinks he will be able to make such shoes under my direction, and I propose that we make up a party, to attempt to cross the mountain.

"We have waited for the snow to go, and it has not. We have waited for help to come, and it has not. Now we must find our own salvation, or we shall all go the way of our poor friend Baylis Williams.

"I shall set out. Mr. Eddy has agreed to come with me. My daughter Mary and my married daughter Sarah and her husband have agreed to attempt the journey, too.

"Mr. Stanton will come with us, and the two Mexican fellows as guides. Who else is willing to venture forth with us? I propose it should be those that are the strongest among us, and those that have the means in California to purchase food and animals to send back for those left behind. And someone should go back to our friends at Alder Creek, and see if any there wish to come along, or if they have provisions enough to spare to aid us."

So next morning, Milt Elliott and a couple of others set off for Alder Creek. And the rest of us set to work on the snowshoes.

Mr. Eddy took the wooden oxbows that were left of the wagons, and cut each one in half, and then sawed them crosswise, giving curved strips of wood. Holes were drilled through at intervals, and as each pair of curved sides was completed it was given over to the women. We unraveled lengths of heavy rope and rebraided them into strings, then threaded them through the holes in the wooden sides until we had something like a net suspended in a wooden frame, about three times the size of a foot.

There were sixteen pairs of these snowshoes made in all, and I wished more than anything that I was to be of the party.

I wanted to try out the snowshoes, and go gliding across the snow like a wild animal, or an Indian. I imagined returning from California like Mr. Stanton had, riding back into camp on a mule with everyone cheering me for my bravery, and handing out food to all. But most of all I wanted to prove that I could get the better of the mountain.

It loomed above our heads, a mighty fortress keeping us out of California, or the wall of a great prison, keeping us in camp. It was our enemy, a brooding giant, waiting to catch us and grind our bones for his bread. Twice it had defeated me, once with snow and once with sleep. I felt its power over me increasing every day, and sometimes I caught myself staring at it, willing it to let us pass. But I could not go. I had no rich friends to help me in California; no notes of promise to exchange for animals and food. My duty lay with the Kesebergs, and my heart with little Margaret Eddy; but last of all I could not bear to leave Meriam, and Mrs. Murphy, for Hattie Pike, Sara Foster, and Sara's husband, Will, were to join the Snowshoes party.

I was horrified to hear of their leaving. Mrs. Murphy's eyesight was failing, worse by the day, and she depended on her grown daughters and her son-in-law for nearly everything. They were woeful short of food, and I could not comprehend how Hattie and Sara could leave their own little ones, for Naomi and George were too small to walk and too heavy to be carried and were to be left with their grandmamma.

I went across to the Murphy cabin to make my farewell to them, and Sara took me to one side.

"I cannot bear to stay and hear the children begging for food; and Hattie is so starved that she cannot feed the baby anymore. Will won't go without me, and he must; he cannot stay here."

I agreed with the last. You would not know Will Foster for the cheerful fellow he had been at the start of our journey. From the instant he had shot his friend Bill Pike he had become a changed man, more withdrawn and miserable by the day. His temper was such that he was near deranged at times, and his screams of rage could be heard from one end of the camp to another. One morning I had come across little George Foster weeping round the back of the cabin, a great bruise on his face, and had my own suspicions about how this had come about.

"Lemuel is coming with us, but Landrum and Meriam are to stay and help Mama. We will be at Sutter's Fort in a few days only. Then help will come and take the rest of you out. Promise me that you will look after Mama for me, and the children—oh, swear to me that you will care for my little boy!"

I said I would. "With all my heart, I swear it. I will look out for Mrs. Murphy, who has been more of a mother to me than my own mother ever was. And on my life I will care for little George."

Sara Foster hugged me close, and thanked me, wiping the tears from her eyes.

With no news back from Alder Creek, the snowshoes finished and all eager to get started, there was still one place remaining, and Charlie Burger said he would go out—though I begged him not to.

For the past few nights, Mr. Burger had lain in our shelter coughing all the livelong night. He winked at me when I quizzed him about it, and said, "Not to worry, sweetheart, I am strong enough to march through the Mountain and get to Sutter's Fort. By the time the new year comes around I shall be back, and I'll bring you a green hair ribbon to match those pretty eyes, and some pumpernickel bread!"

He might be able to make a joke of it, but I could not. And I was right to be concerned, for within an hour or two of setting off, Mr. Burger returned, much distressed, and took refuge once more in our lean-to, coughing and shivering and too ill to be moved.

30

The afternoon was drawing in and the light fading on Christmas Eve when Milt Elliott finally returned from Alder Creek. Real pleased we were to see him, and crowded about him, asking for news of our friends. It was cruel news, to be sure.

He told us that the journey there and back was one of great difficulty, for the way was very poor. Conditions at the Donners' camp were even worse than ours.

The Donners had brought tents with them for the older children to camp out on the trail. They'd begun by putting them up in the shelter of some big trees, and started to dismantle the wagons, thinking to build walls round these tents and a roof over. But a great storm had come upon them, right sudden and fierce, and they had been forced to abandon their work, managing only to make a rough lean-to over the tents to keep off the worst of the snow. By the time the snow had let up enough for them to try and construct something better, all the boards and such were buried under such snow that they could not be found.

Mr. Jacob Donner had died, leaving his sick wife and

their seven small children to fend for themselves, and Mr. George Donner was raving with fever. Mrs. Wolfinger was ill abed as well, and not likely to last many more days. They were woeful short of food; and Mrs. Tamsen Donner was left to care for all—near on a dozen children and three invalids, with help just from the lad who'd joined us at Bridger's Fort, Jean Trudeau, and Leanna and Elitha. Everyone else—the teamsters who had stayed to help them—was dead, along with them our good friend Mr. Reinhardt.

It was desperate news and we could hardly comprehend it. So many to die, and in so short a space of time!

We wished with all our hearts that those few remaining would come up to the camp with us, and at least be in company. Mr. Elliott said he had suggested it to them, but it was impossible. With no animals and no wagons, they could not get the tiny children through the snow and anyway, Mr. George Donner could not leave his bed, and Mrs. Tamsen Donner would not leave him.

It was ill news, to be sure, and we were mighty sober about our business for the rest of the afternoon.

The weather was just as miserable: sleeting needles of ice mixed in with pelting rain that wet us through the second we stepped out of doors, and left everything in the cabins as sodden as we were ourselves.

At the beginning of our imprisonment in the camp we had welcomed the rain, for each time we thought that it might signal a thaw. We would go to sleep thinking to wake at last to the sight of the good earth, with the snow washed away and escape possible. Each time our hopes were come to nothing. The rain turned always to snow, and each day we would open our eyes to find ourselves buried deeper and deeper, and more trapped than the day before. But this night we thought that maybe our luck would change; maybe a miracle would happen.

We were invited into the Breens' cabin to celebrate

the holiday. Mrs. Keseberg and I tucked up Ada and Baby and saw them asleep, then we walked the few steps that took us into the Breens' cabin. Mr. Keseberg stood back and ushered us through the door, quite as if we were grand folks going into a ball and he bowed to us, "My ladies!" making us laugh.

Even though so many of the adults had left with the Snowshoes, it was still crowded. Folks who had seen one another but an hour since were laughing and chattering as if they were but newly met. Over to one side was Meriam, and Mrs. Murphy. I could not help but look at Landrum. To my confusion, he was looking right at me, and he winked. I blushed, and quickly turned my head away.

Such foolishness lasted but a moment, for Mr. Breen called for quiet, and suggested we start with a prayer. So we bent our heads, hoping for forgiveness for our sins with the most sincere of hearts, and asking God for aid as He saw fit.

Meriam and Virginia and I had collected rushes from the banks of the lake, and set them to soak for a few days in a little bit of melted grease to be candles. Now they were lit in the corners of the cabin, one for every member of our party who had set out with us and was no longer here.

We thought of them as we said our prayers. First, for those who had set out to obtain help for us—Mr. McCutcheon and Mr. Reed and Mr. Herron first of all, and then our friends who had left with the Snowshoes. We asked God's mercy on those in our party who had died, either in camp or back along the trail—Baylis Williams and John Snyder—those dead at Alder Creek, and Mr. Hardkoop and Mr. Wolfinger. We said a prayer for Bill Pike. And below my breath I added in another prayer, this time for Will Foster, suffering such agonies of guilt over his friend's death. We remembered Mr. Halloran, who had died of the consumption no more than a few days into our journey, and Virginia's grandmamma, laid to rest on the banks of the Big Blue.

It was a sad thing to look at so many tiny flames quivering in the draft and threatening to blow out at any minute, and a sober one, too, as we all thought of how our own lives could be blown out in an instant, by one gust of a chill wind.

We said a special prayer for the safety of the Donners, away at Alder Creek. And I thought of them, keeping company with their dead, sitting there on this Christmas Night in the black darkness, snow as far as the eye could see in every direction, and no sound but that of the wind ghosting through the treetops.

When our prayers were finished and we lifted our heads, we all seemed filled with God's Grace; and when Mr. Breen finished speaking we hugged one another and wished each other a Merry Christmas. For that little space, bad words were forgotten and animosities put aside.

Mr. Keseberg cried, "Next Christmas we will be safe and merry in California!" and there was laughter and kind words spoken.

All had found a tiny helping of food to bring with them, a handful of flour for some biscuits or a spoonful of molasses, some grits or beans. Even Mrs. Graves stepped up with some coffee and a bit of sugar, but the highlight of our feast was contributed by Mrs. Eddy: meat, come from a bear that Mr. Eddy had killed some days before he left. And this was when I heard the tale of Mr. Eddy and the bear.

Despite his avowal that there was no game left in the mountains, one day Mr. Eddy had gone hunting and found the trail of a bear. He began tracking it, gun cocked and ready for the kill. But the bear was just as cunning as Mr. Eddy and somehow snuck round the back of him. It started out with Mr. Eddy tracking the bear and thinking what a fine dinner he would have, and ended with the bear chasing Mr. Eddy and thinking the same.

Off they went, Mr. Eddy running for his life and the bear lumbering behind, growling and showing his teeth. They came to a great tree, and Mr. Eddy ran round the tree and the bear ran after him. Faster and faster they ran, until in the end Mr. Eddy ran round so fast that he caught up with the bear and shot him in the back.

I think I never laughed so much. We all cheered Mr. Eddy, and wished him luck in crossing the mountain, and thought kindly of him. With all his high tales of his bravery and great deeds, it was a story that made fun of him that made us like and admire him the most.

When the merriment was over and we were making ready to depart, Mr. Breen suggested that we make one last prayer to give thanks for our survival so far. It was a hard prayer to make, and I was not the only one to feel so.

He finished with these words. "Jesus said, 'Suffer the little children to come unto me.' He did not mean that they should suffer, as our children are suffering now. He meant that they should be allowed to turn to Him, for comfort and protection; and I say to all, remember that God's Grace shines upon us, even in our darkest hour."

It seemed that these words in particular sat heavy on Mrs. Murphy's mind. When we crossed into the Murphy cabin next morning it was to find Mrs. Murphy taken to her bed, much distressed. Landrum told me she had repeated Mr. Breen's words over and over when they got back into their cabin, and she repeated them many times again throughout the course of that Christmas Day.

For our Christmas meal, the children had bones, boiled and then roasted, to gnaw on. The water they were boiled in was what we had, nothing but a thin broth with a few scraps of meat from a beeve's tail floating in it.

To give the children some amusement, and to divert ourselves from the hunger that beset our every waking minute, it was decided that each person should tell a story. Mrs. Eddy told the story of Jesus born in a stable, and Mr. Keseberg one about a lady who lived in the sea, with a fish tail instead of legs, and how she longed to live on the land and marry a prince. Landrum told a tale of when he was a little boy. He tried to stay awake all night to see Santa Claus, but fell asleep and dreamed about having his face washed, and woke up to find that his Christmas gift was a puppy licking his ear. The children all laughed at this, and then it was my turn.

I wished most heartily that it wasn't. I knew no stories at all, and my memories of Christmas were mostly about drunkenness and thievery and the rest, and not fit to share with anyone. I usually spent the day walking the streets of the town, pressing my face against the shop windows to see the counters piled high with fine things and wishing I had them. But I had to say something, and so this was the story I told.

"Back home in Cincinnati," I said, "in the big house where I used to live, with my brothers and sisters and Papa and Mama, in every room there would be a big fire blazing in the hearth, the flames leaping and crackling, so hot you can hardly get near it.

"After breakfast we would put on our warm coats, and Papa would take all us children out to the common ground by the town pond, to watch the folks skating on the ice. A man would be roasting chestnuts over hot coals nearby, and the air would smell like burnt wood and something sweet, too. And my papa would put his hand in his pocket and bring out enough money to buy a great bag of these chestnuts, and we would peel them and eat them while we listened to the German band.

"Afterward, we would go home, where Mama had been cooking for days beforehand, and there would be too many pies to count. Every which sort of pie," I said, "with a butter crust and a filling all of sugar and nuts, or apples with a twist of lemon rind dipped in sugar sat on the top.

"For our dinner we'd have a great goose with onions round, and potatoes roasted in butter and dripping fat. For pudding we'd have sugarplums and marzipan and little cookies made with sugar and spices; and oranges, that Papa would bring us off the boats, for he worked as a hauler down on the quayside and could lay his hands on near enough anything."

The children looked at me wide-eyed. Some of them had never seen an orange. "It's a fruit," I said, "round like a ball and the same color as a pumpkin."

I told them how it was ate: cut in half with a lump of white sugar put on the top and the flesh dug out with a spoon. And I tell them it's sweet, sweeter than molasses, sweeter than honey, sweeter than anything you have ever eaten in your life before.

"So sweet it makes your eyes water!" I said, screwing up my face to make them laugh.

Margaret Eddy had been sat on my lap through this story, leaning against me with her doll hugged to her, and half-asleep. But now she sat up straight and put her hands to each side of my face, gazing intently into my eyes. "Can I have one?" she asked, patting my cheeks. "Can I have one? One of the sugar cookies?"

"Oh, sweetheart, I don't have any to give you!"

Margaret burst out crying. "I want one!" she sobbed. "I want an orange, and one of those sugar cookies!" and scrambled down from my lap and ran over to her mother.

Mrs. Eddy took me to task. She said, "Oh, how can you torment the children so, with this tale of sugarplums and oranges and great fires?" But I knew no other story I could tell, for I was right ashamed of the truth of it. Our Christmas was spent with Ma asleep and snoring drunk and Pa still in the alehouse, drunk as well, and no great fires or a table heaped with good things.

The ice skating part was something true. I'd take my brothers with me, and they'd lurk somewhere out of the way, while I went and asked folks if they'd like me to watch their belongings for a dime while they were off on the ice. There was always some fellow wanting to leave a heavy coat so that he could show off his fine figure with some swoops and leaps.

As soon as this fellow had got well out onto the ice, and was too busy admiring himself to notice what we were up to, my brothers would head off with the coat in one direction, and I'd head off with my dime in the other.

A dime would buy a good big bagful of those hot chestnuts. I bought them with the proceeds of thievery and lying, but I'd cared nothing for that. They were the whole extent of my Christmas dinner; and right good they'd tasted, too.

I guess Mr. Keseberg could see that my story was a long way from the truth, for when I had pitched up at his wagon I must have been looking very far from well-fed and well cared for. He looked at me very sober, and when no one was paying us much mind, he reached out and squeezed my hand.

Mrs. Murphy lay quiet in her bed most of the day, and it was clear that the remembering of happy Christmases past, and the thought of her children out there on the mountain and alive or dead we did not know, weighed her down something terrible. At suppertime, when there was nothing to eat but a few grains of rice boiled in water, she turned her face to the wall, and sobbed quietly to herself.

William Murphy took down the Bible and read aloud and that quieted her somewhat. But I think that was the point when her heart broke; and she never came back full to herself again. For from that day she hardly stirred, lying silent most of the day, rousing herself only to feed little Catherine.

How that poor baby survived I cannot say. She was

fed on no more than a few tiny spoonsful of flour and water. To see her sucking feebly on this thin paste and to know that there was not a drop of nourishment in it, and that once it was gone there was no more, was a terrible sight to see. Mrs. Murphy's heart was broke with the misery of Christmas, and fear for her children; but as the weeks wore on I think it was the sight of Catherine's baby face, once so rosy bright but now withering away like a little winter apple, and to see her lying listless in her cradle, too weak even to cry, that broke Mrs. Murphy's spirit.

Christmas marked the point when all fortunes turned bad. A day or so afterward we woke one morning to find Mr. Burger sweating with a fever, muttering to himself in a hoarse, gasping voice, and breaking into little snatches of song.

It was plain to see that he was ready to die. Mr. Keseberg sat next to him and took his hand, speaking to him right soft. He told him that he would never forget him, and said a prayer over him, and I think this comforted Mr. Burger somewhat, and he quietened down.

After a few minutes, he turned to me and said, clear as anything, "I haven't forgot that green ribbon, sweetheart." Then he turned his head away, and muttered something in German that I did not understand, and died. Mr. Keseberg bent and kissed his friend on the forehead, with tears streaming down his face.

Mr. Keseberg said that Mr. Burger had wanted him to have all his possessions, and he vowed to treasure them all his days. But the next day, when we were at the Murphys' cabin, Mr. Spitzer went into the lean-to and helped himself to Mr. Burger's good overcoat and his waistcoat, too.

Mr. Keseberg was as angry as I have ever seen him, and took his fist to Mr. Spitzer and knocked him clean to the ground.

Mr. Keseberg didn't spread the story of why he hit Mr. Spitzer, but of course folks asked where he got the black eye; and Mr. Spitzer told a tale to all. He said that he went into our lean-to on purpose to look for evidence regarding Mr. Wolfinger's death, and he was right to do so, for he had found Mr. Wolfinger's rifle. This proved, or so he would have it, that he, Mr. Spitzer, had been falsely accused and was innocent of all wrongdoing. And he said that when he challenged Mr. Keseberg about it, Mr. Keseberg had hit him.

Yet again the cabins buzzed with gossip about Mr. Keseberg. In all our misery and despair, I wonder yet that Mr. Spitzer wanted to thieve and lie, and that the rest wanted to think about murder. Surely there was death enough for all, without raking up more.

31

Help did not come; help did not come. When the Snowshoes left, we calculated that we had enough food to last until a rescue party arrived. We calculated two weeks—three at the most. But those three weeks had come and gone long since.

Folks were driven to desperate measures. Mrs. Reed was no exception, and she arrived at our door one morning asking for our help. She was setting out to cross the mountain, on foot, in her light summer clothes, with no provisions of any kind—this was her plan. Virginia was going with her, but she wanted us to look after her smaller children, for even she could see that the little ones would not get through.

We agreed to take five-year-old James, and his little brother Tom. It was the only thing we could do to help, though of course we begged her not to go. We thought her demented—perhaps she was—for a more foolish plan there could not have been.

Milt Elliott was going, and now, lanky William Graves surprised us all, just like his father had done previous with his help regarding the snowshoes. He told us that, following John Snyder's death, Mr. Graves had made a pledge to Mr. Reed, to look out for Mrs. Reed and the children. This was a great mystery. Perhaps on reflection Mr. Graves had felt that there was fault on both sides: that John Snyder had tormented Mr. Reed, or that his blow to Mrs. Reed had been something deliberate. However it had come about, I would hazard that Mrs. Graves had nothing to do with this pledge, and once Mr. Graves left with the Snowshoes, I think she decided that the promise had gone with him, for she tormented Mrs. Reed at every opportunity she could get. But now, William Graves said that he would honor his father's pledge to look out for the Reeds, and if Mrs. Reed insisted on leaving, then he would keep her company on her journey.

Eliza Williams set off with them, though with great reluctance, and she was back near as quick as she started, saying that the journey was pure foolishness. Sure enough, a few days later they all returned, ill and shaking with the cold, and the two men carrying Virginia between them, for so bad froze were her feet that she could hardly stand.

When they returned, they were worse off than when they started. For, the minute they left the camp, before they were even out of sight, Mrs. Graves took her canvas off Mrs. Reed's roof. Mrs. Graves also took the few hides that Mrs. Reed had saved from the slaughtered cattle, and that she had attempted to use to make her roof more watertight.

The rain and the snow blew in and destroyed what little bedding and clothing were left. With nothing much to hold them together, the walls tumbled down as well. When the Reeds finally stumbled back into camp, it was to complete destitution. And Mrs. Reed came to our door again.

We spent so much of our time at the Murphy cabin that maybe Mrs. Reed thought our lean-to was abandoned, and reckoned to take it over, but it was not the case. We still had our small bits of belongings stored in there, what we had managed to salvage from the wagon, and we still slept in there at night. So Mrs. Reed applied to the Breens instead; and although their cabin was filled to bursting, those good souls took the Reed family in with them.

For several days there was much going back and forth between the Breens' cabin and that of the Graveses as Mr. Breen tried to persuade Mrs. Graves to return the canvas and the hides. But Mrs. Graves refused him in round terms, thinking, I suppose, that having the hides here and now was worth more than promises of gold in California. And for the first and only time, I heard that good man, Mr. Breen, rail against another in our party, despairing of the cruelty and hardness of the woman.

It was as well that Mrs. Reed and Virginia did not move into the lean-to. One night, something woke me. Not the wind gusting about us—it was a still, silent night. I lay for a moment, wondering what it could be. Not Baby, not Ada—both asleep next to their ma, and Mr. Keseberg asleep, too, lying with his head on his arm. The quilt that covered him had slipped down some, and I reached out to pull it over him more, when the noise come again. I flew up out of my covers, and crouched there, my heart pounding in my chest.

My fear was the wolves. For the last few nights we had heard them howling somewhere in the distance and we thought it only a matter of time before they came right into the camp.

I imagined poking my head round the canvas that formed the door of our lean-to and seeing those yellow eyes gleaming at me. Mr. Keseberg's tales of wolves that dressed themselves up in grandmother's clothes suddenly didn't seem near so amusing. But it wasn't a wolf that had woke me up. The noise came again, a long, creaking groan. Something brushed past my face, and I looked up, just in time to see the canvas above me rip apart. A torrent of snow began cascading through our roof.

I screamed, "Wake up! Wake up!" I grabbed at Mr. Keseberg, shaking and shaking him. Even as he woke and jumped to his feet, there was a thunderous crack. The timbers that formed the wall of our lean-to broke across. Timbers, canvas, snow, and all came tumbling down around us.

I grabbed the children and Mr. Keseberg grabbed his wife. We scrambled out of the way just in time, as the whole construction came crashing to the ground.

In the front of our lean-to the snow had been packed hard where we'd walked in and out so many times, and the same with pathways through the camp to one cabin or another. But flying out, we discovered that this little area was quite disappeared. Instead there was snow higher than our heads, and we had to claw and fight our way up to the surface. The moon was up, and it shone on entirely flat land. Where the cabins used to be was nothing. And where the lake met the land could not be told.

We were right next to the Breens, we knew for a fact. We must have been stood right aside their door, but there was nothing of them to be seen. Next moment, we heard some muffled conversation, what seemed to be coming from below us, and then we could make out a shape in the snow that proved to be the top of their chimney. Mrs. Keseberg left the two of us holding the children, and stepped across and shouted down the chimney.

"Mrs. Breen! Mrs. Breen! You are all covered in snow so deep we cannot see you! And we are out here with our lean-to collapsed and the children like to freeze to death!"

Mr. Keseberg called to her, "Tell them to poke up a broom or such to show us where their door is!" A moment later a stick with a kerchief tied to the end came heaving up out of the snow.

I grabbed the canvas from the ruin of our lean-to, and as many blankets as I could recover, and wrapped the children up tight and pulled the canvas over them. Then Mr. and Mrs. Keseberg and I used our hands to scoop away at the snow where the Breens' door should have been.

After a few minutes, we could see a little strip of light, and then Mr. Breen's face looking up at us in astonishment, where he was stood in his doorway holding a lantern. He passed us up a couple of shovels, and we passed him down the children; and then we dug away, making a set of steps to lead down into their cabin. After an hour or so hard work, we finally fell through their front door, hands and feet froze with the cold so that we couldn't hardly feel them at all. Mrs. Breen set the kettle to boil, and had some last scraping of chocolate powder that she used to make us a drink. I thought I had never tasted anything so delicious in my life.

When the sun was up, Mr. Breen and Mr. Keseberg went and dug out the Murphys, and the Breen boys and I went and dug out the Graveses, making some only half-joking remarks that it would serve them out if they were left to scramble out of their cabin as best they could, with no help from us. Then the Kesebergs and I moved what last of our belongings we could find in with the Murphys.

32

Next morning we awoke to no food at all. Not a spoonful of rice remained in the sack, not a mouthful of beans. Mr. Keseberg sent William Murphy out to fetch the last of the hides from the ruin of our lean-to. This is what we were reduced to eating.

These hides were the skins of the dead animals, and had been used to cover over the cabin roofs. Where they had got wet in the snow and rain, and then warmed when we had some feeble sunshine, they had begun to rot, and the smell of them was hardly to be endured.

We cut them into strips, and put them in the cooking pot with a bit of water and boiled them up all the day. The stench of them was beyond belief, and the look of them no better. They melted into a thick glue that we choked down, like to vomit from the feel of it in our throats.

We ate everything and anything we could. The smallest mouse that ventured across the floor of the cabin in search of a crumb was seized upon and thrown, tail and whiskers and all, into the cooking pot. The very laces of the men's boots, made as they were from leather strips, were roasted on the fire until they crisped up, and the children sucked on them. And we found one of the Graves children in tears, one day, for he had enjoyed his dinner, eating heartily for once, only to ask afterward where his dog was, and to find that his dog and his dinner were the same thing.

William went out with a long face, not liking to be told what to do. He was a long time coming back, and it turned out that he had spent part of the day with his particular friend Paddy Breen. He'd had his dinner there, and told us that they still had some bits of meat left.

He was angry, and blustered about, saying that if we were not in the cabin all the livelong day there would have been meat enough for his family, too, and telling Mr. Keseberg that he was not his father and that he could not order him what to do and where to go, and shouting at Landrum that he was the man of the family and to get up out of his bed and order us out of the cabin.

For poor Landrum was taken to his bed, very ill indeed.

When we had very first started out on our journey he fancied himself a real fellow with the girls. He was always swaggering back and forth with tales of what girl was sweet on him; how this one had given him a smile and how that one had looked particular at him as he passed by.

It might have been true, and had I thought myself a pretty girl and was given to flirtatiousness, I guess I would have given him such a look myself. His hair was a mass of black curls, and he had sparkling green eyes and long eyelashes that a girl would envy.

When Landrum had chased me and stolen that kiss, back on the first snowy day, and I had thrown the snowball, I had laughed myself silly at his startled face, along with all the rest. But sometimes at night when I was falling asleep, I had remembered Landrum's face on the night of the dance, when I came out of the Murphy wagon in my pretty green dress, and how he had stumbled over his words when he asked me for a slice of my pie. And I imagined that kiss again, and wanted somehow to cry, that I had made him look so foolish for it.

Now, though, thoughts of kisses and snowballs seemed very far behind me. I could hardly remember the girl I was then. And it was a most sorry sight to see him lying there, staring at the ceiling and muttering to himself all the livelong day.

He was worried about a pony that his pa had given him when he was just a little boy, and kept asking after it, in a thin, thready voice.

"The Indians took him. The Indians took him. Poor old boy. Pa, I lost him, I'm sorry, Pa. Poor old boy. Poor old boy."

He would pick away with his withered fingers at the blanket that was laid over him, and push it from him.

"So hot. Too hot. Water. Water. The Indians took him. Poor old boy."

Next morning Mrs. Murphy roused herself, the first time in a long while, and set out to the Breens to ask them to spare some meat. They gave her a tiny piece, mostly bones, but enough to make some soup, thickened just a little by a handful of flour. There was a spoonful for each of us, and the rest went to Landrum, though it wasn't enough to stop him crying and begging for more.

How Landrum kept alive I do not know, but the next day Mrs. Murphy went back to the Breens once more, and again they gave her some small amount, and a few bits of dried onion and some herbs. The rich smell of it cooking made our stomachs churn and our mouths water, but there was no more than a mouthful or two, and we told her to give it all to Landrum. But it was too late.

Mrs. Murphy was inconsolable. She said that it was her fault, for when she was coming back from the Breens she had eaten some of the meat herself, raw though it was, and that if she had cooked all yet Landrum might have been saved. In vain we told her that it would have made no difference, and that she needed to eat something herself, for the woman was nothing more than a living skeleton. Many times I had seen her pretend to eat and then slip that mouthful to one of the children; I doubted a morsel had passed her lips for days before. But the guilt of it overwhelmed her. She returned to her bed, clutching Catherine so close that the baby whimpered, and ignoring all else.

I could see that the baby would not live, and it was a miracle that she had kept alive so long. And I dreaded to think what would happen with Mrs. Murphy when the baby was finally taken from her.

During the night it snowed more, and we woke to a blizzard, such that we could not put a face outdoors. Our wood was gone and there was no means of getting more. So we had no fire, and it was cold, the likes of which you could not imagine; so cold that our bones ached with it, fingers so frozen that we dropped what we picked up, and our toes so numb that we stumbled when we walked.

You would not think the weather could get worse. But as the day wore on the wind grew more, howling around us so that we could not hear ourselves speak; and then it grew stronger still. At some point there was a shuddering crash that made the earth under our feet shake. It was a great tree in the forest, being torn out by its roots; it was followed by another, and another after that.

Occasionally there was a lull, when the wind shifted direction; a few moments of calm. And then the wolves could be heard, a chorus of unearthly howling in the far distance, answered by the same blood-chilling lament closer to hand.

The wind died away as dawn broke the next day. The snow still fell so that you could not see your hand in front of your face. And to our horror we found that Baby had died in the night.

Mrs. Keseberg screamed, and ran about the cabin, Baby clasped to her breast. Then she fell to the ground, crying as though her heart would break.

The blizzard did not let up. We could not leave the cabin. And Mrs. Keseberg sat in a corner for hour upon hour, holding Baby and rocking him, and crooning a lullaby. Sometimes she jumped to her feet, thrusting Baby at us and begging us all, could we not see that he was still breathing? Did we not think that there was still some life in him? It was a horror to us all to look at that tiny body wrapped up in its quilt, with Baby's face showing all blue-white and his sightless eyes and his downy gold hair all dull and strawy now, but it was terrifying for the little children.

Little Naomi Pike put her thumb in her mouth and rocked to and fro, keening. Harriet McCutcheon crawled across to me and pulled herself upright, and clung, her head buried in my lap, so that I could not stir from my seat. Through it all, Mrs. Murphy listened for the wolves, and howled when she heard them as if she was one herself.

After some time, Mr. Keseberg caught his wife, and wrestled the baby from her arms. Mrs. Keseberg clawed at him, calling him a murderer, and then fell to her knees, clutching at his clothing and begging him not to put Baby out in the cold for the wolves to steal him; and swearing that if he did, she would never forgive him, and would never speak to him again.

But he set his face against her. He wrapped up Baby

in his quilt to be his little shroud. And he opened the door of the cabin to reveal a solid wall of snow, and dug a hole in it, like something a little animal would creep into for shelter, and slid the poor little mite inside. Then he closed the cabin door, and took to his bed, pulling the blanket over his head, and lay in silence for the rest of the day.

Harriet McCutcheon died next. She had never spoke a word since Mrs. McCutcheon left, but now she called out in a hoarse, rasping voice, begging for her mama. And the next to die was my own poor darling girl, little Margaret Eddy.

The year turns round, and the boiling days and humid nights of late summer are full upon us. We sleep with all the windows open and nothing but a sheet to cover us.

Jacob snores beside me. I hear the mournful cry of an owl swooping through the woods, and the cut-short anguished squeal of some tiny creature snatched up in its claws.

Eventually I rise from my bed. I walk through the house and into my kitchen, with the big table that Martha scrubs clean each day with salt and sand, and the chairs that Jacob made with his own hands, a new one each time a baby came along and each carved with a little animal—a cat for Meggie and a rabbit for Hannah, and for Clara a family of bears.

I stand at the kitchen window. From here I can see the shape of the mountain in the far distance, black against the starry indigo sky. Even in this heat I shiver, thinking of twenty feet of snow up at the pass, and more falling. I turn away.

So far I have made my way through the house in the dark. I do not need a light to know where to place my steps in my own home. But now I light a candle and take it with me.

Beyond the kitchen is another little room, with a stone floor to keep it cool, cedar shelves to keep away the insects, and no windows to let in the vermin. This is where our food is stored. A slab of good butter melting away to nothing in a dish with a lid over it, another of sweating cheese, and a side of cold beef. German sausages hang on hooks from the ceiling, and bunches of herbs, and plaited strings of onions left to dry. There are apples wrapped in sacking; eggs in a china dish; and row upon row of the bottled preserves that I make through the summer and into the fall, from the currants and string beans that I grow in the garden. Packages of coffee, and tea, and chocolate powder.

And there are sacks of flour and sugar, and bags of dried goods, oatmeal and grits, beans and peas and rice. More, by far, than we could ever need.

I count them, checking to make sure I have not missed anything, and then count them again to make sure.

I imagine how many days they will last for. And I think how Mrs. Reed, so rich and so proud when we started off, fell to her knees before Mrs. Graves, begging for a handful of rice to feed her children, and how Mrs. Graves looked across at her own children, and refused her.

I have my own children now; another on the way. I put my hand to my belly, thinking of the babies and little children who died in my care: Catherine Pike, Harriet McCutcheon, Margaret Eddy and her little brother James. And Mr. Keseberg's tiny son, Louis, and George Foster. I would not say it to another living soul, but the truth is, if I was Mrs. Graves, I would have done the same.

I would refuse all and any, no matter who they be or what my heart tells me, to save the life of one of my children. And I can hardly live with the shame of having such plenty before me.

33

So. Margaret died; that sweet and lovely child.

Mrs. Eddy was close to death herself by now, lying in her bed in the little room that Mr. Eddy had constructed for his family. She begged us to leave Margaret safe in her arms, so we took little James Eddy in with us, and carried Margaret in to lie with her mother.

For the three days it took Mrs. Eddy to die, I sat with her. I pulled the blanket over her when she pushed it off in her fever, and sponged her face with cold water. Mrs. Eddy did not know me. She called me by her sister's name, asking me did I remember this thing and that? Stories of when she was a girl. And she asked for her mother, and wept that she did not come.

Toward the end her sight failed, and she begged me over and over to light the candle, saying that she was afraid of the dark—though lit it was, and the light shining full upon her face. Eventually she fell silent. I held her hand, and sang, some silly little song or another, just so she would know she was not alone. And I stroked Margaret's little face, and put my lips to her cheek and kissed her good-bye.

When the wind died away and the snow stopped, the Breen boys came across and dug out our steps for us again.

Meriam and I sped out of the cabin as fast as could be, right thankful to get out into the clean-smelling air. We went across to the Breens and called in for Virginia. Paddy Breen came, too, and we all walked a little way into the forest, collecting cones and bits of fallen wood.

All around us, trees lay uprooted. If we had saws and axes and some men to help us, we could have got ourselves plenty logs. But it needed more strength than we had alone. After we had collected what we could, we sat down. There was some weak sun filtering through the trees, and it was lovely to feel it warm on our faces, and we sat there for a while on one of the fallen tree trunks, with our faces tipped to the blue sky.

When Meriam spoke, her voice was very low. "Do you think anyone will come for us? Or will we all die here, do you think?"

John Breen answered that his family prayed for help every night before they went to sleep, and he was sure that help would come very soon, and we should all be saved.

We sat in silence for a while more.

"Have you ever seen the ocean?" Meriam asked me.

"No," I replied. "I have seen the Ohio River, though. That's plenty big. And there are paddle steamers on it and all kinds of other boats. Ships going right across the ocean, as well, and bringing back all manner of things. I once saw a man with a monkey on his shoulder, and it snatched a cracker right out of my hand!"

Paddy Breen stared at me, his mouth agape. "That's grand! A monkey, you say? I'd sure like to see a monkey take a cracker out of MY hand!"

John cuffed him round the head. "If you had a cracker

in your hand, Paddy Breen, it wouldn't be a monkey that would snatch it from you!"

We kind of laughed at that, but soon enough we were sober again.

Meriam smiled a little.

"When we started out, all I wanted was to get to California and see the ocean. And after that to be married in a lace gown with a long train behind and a garland of pink and white flowers on my head, and for there to be a party for all my friends with a great wedding cake." She added, softly, "I don't suppose I ever shall, now."

John Breen flushed up bright red at that, and jumped to his feet and made a great show of collecting up his wood. I reckoned he was set sweet on Meriam, and it would have been sport to have teased them about it, but I didn't.

Meriam had been the prettiest girl in our little band of travelers when we set off, with great gray eyes and thick black eyelashes and shiny dark hair right down to her waist, that she wore tied back with a ribbon. But now, her eyes were sunk deep into her face, with dirty-looking shadows round, and her lovely hair all dull and as sparse as my own, which came out in handfuls.

Meriam and Virginia and I walked back to the Breens' cabin with the boys, and went in to visit for a while. Their cabin was much neater and tidier than ours, for it had a proper wooden floor and a table to sit up at, and even a couple of benches that the previous inhabitant had left behind. Mrs. Breen gave us a morsel of bread and a cup of hot water with some little bit of sugar in it to share, and asked us our news. I told the Breens about all the deaths in our cabin, and they told us theirs. Mr. Spitzer had staggered into their cabin in the height of the storm, demented by the hunger, and had died begging for even a morsel of meat to taste before he died, but they had none for him.

The other little bit of news was that in his delirium he had spoke of Mr. Wolfinger; and had begged mercy from God, for it was he had killed him.

Mrs. Breen told me this last in a quiet voice, and said that she would like Mr. Keseberg to know that she was sorry to have doubted him, and would tell him to his face, when next she saw him.

With Mr. Spitzer's death, that left only three men in the camp. Milt Elliott was in the Breens' cabin along with Mrs. Reed and her children, but he was on the point of death himself and of no use to anyone. The others were Mr. Breen, ill in bed, and Mr. Keseberg, who could hardly stand. So now there was no one but the two older Breen boys, Virginia and Meriam and me, to bury the dead.

Baylis Williams had been buried with a song, and prayers said over his grave, and a wooden cross with his name on driven into the ground to mark his resting place. But those days were long behind us, and now we could do no more than lay the bodies on the ground at the edge of the camp, and shovel snow over them.

The steps that the boys had cut for us to get from our cabin up to the surface were hardly wide enough for one person to walk up. John carried little Harriet out of the cabin and up the steps easy enough, and Edward carried Margaret. But taking Mrs. Eddy from the cabin was a terrible thing.

Her body was set rigid, and it took four of us to wrestle her to the surface. The boys went ahead, carrying her feet, and Mr. Keseberg and I held her arms. But Mr. Keseberg had not the strength to get up the steps with her, and there was not room for us to walk side by side.

In the end the only way to get her out was for the boys to take her ankles, and haul her from the top. Her dress and ragged apron dragged down over her head, so her stained rags of undergarments were on show to the boys and all of us. Meriam wept; and I turned my face away, with the horror and shame of it.

Sometimes in my dreams I see Mrs. Eddy's waxy white face, with her head banging on each step to raise a little flurry of snow as they heave her up. In my dreams she opens her eyes and looks straight at me, smiling, and I jerk awake.

I tell myself that all is well, that the sounds I hear are only Jacob breathing steady beside me, and the big clock in the hall ticking out the seconds. But its chimes are like to those of a bell tolling for the dead, and I am afraid to close my eyes again.

34

Well into February, four long months since we had first arrived in camp, we finally beheld what we had dreamed of and prayed for: six strangers, stout and hearty men come to be our salvation. They stared about them in astonishment as more and more of us emerged from the snowy depths, falling upon them with screams of delight.

We looked behind them, expecting to see a great train of mules and carts loaded with supplies. But our joy was short-lived. The snow was as deep on the mountain as ever before, and animals and wagons could not get through.

They had come on the word of Mr. Reed, who had arrived safe at Sutter's Fort with Mr. Herron. Virginia clutched hold of her ma at this news, and they whirled each other round in delight to know he was safe. But it was a mixed blessing, for when Mr. Reed had left us we had been well provided for with animals aplenty and most folks still in possession of their wagons. So these men had come merely to act as our guides, and help us through the pass, and were horrified to find us in such dire need.

We quizzed them: but hadn't the Snowshoes party arrived safe? And hadn't they told of our terrible suffering? They knew nothing of it. They knew only that the Snowshoes had got through the mountain, arriving at the homestead of a Mr. Johnson, some distance from Sutter's Fort. Word had been sent to the fort, but only an account of the Snowshoe survivors—that eight of their number had perished on the crossing—eight! Our hearts failed us to hear it—and that there were more of us left behind needing assistance. There had been no word as to the truth of how very ill and wretched we were, and the men had brought no food or clothing with them at all.

Some of the men set off for Alder Creek. Upon their return, bringing back as many as they could, the party would leave again, with those they thought could manage the journey through the mountain. But they also told us that Mr. Reed was busy recruiting more men, and a second rescue was close behind, no doubt better equipped than this one.

Those who had gone on to Alder Creek arrived back the next day with grim faces, bringing with them a raggle-taggle band of children: what remained of Mr. Jacob Donner's poor orphaned family. They seemed to be in a much better way than we up at the lake, with some color to their lips and cheeks that we had not.

With them came Elitha and Leanna. Meriam and I ran to meet them. They hardly recognized us at first, and hugged us, laughing and crying at the same time.

They said that upon hearing that their pa and stepmamma were not to travel with them, the girls had refused to leave as well, but Mrs. Donner had bade them go. She made them promise upon their lives to never say a word to anyone in California about what had befallen them and how they had lived. I thought this was sound advice. The rescue men were scarce able to look any one of us in the eye. Pity and disgust were close neighbors indeed.

"If I get through the mountain," I thought, "never will I speak of what I have seen to another living soul"—a resolve I have kept to this day.

With Elitha and Leanna came their cousins George and William. It was a dreadful sight to see these little boys, nine-year-old George and twelve-year-old William, acting as manful as they could and declaring that they would look after the girls and get them through the mountain. To see them so small and starved against the great men come to rescue them filled me with a fierce anger against the foolish old men of our party, the Donners and the Reeds and the rest, who had brought us all to this dreadful state, and left these boys to do men's work.

Also leaving were the Breen boys, some of the older Graves children, and last of all, Mrs. Reed's party. And I was to go, too, and take Ada with me.

I had no possessions to collect together. Everything I owned was in my skirt pocket, where they had been all this time: Leanna's little twist of hair, and my pink kerchief, so badly faded from the sun that it was near impossible to tell the color. Folded up small was the drawing of bluebells that Mrs. Donner had given me, and with it the little heap of silver dollars, my fee for the journey that Mr. Keseberg never had taken from me.

Now I held the money out to him, but he took my hand in his, and folded my fingers back over the coins. "I hardly feel that I have merited payment for bringing you to this dreadful place. You will have need of this in California, much more than I can have use of it here."

He left his hand folded over mine. I could not help myself, but burst out, "Oh! I wish you were coming with me! I shall miss you most dreadfully!"

I meant it. I would miss him. For the first time in my whole life I had met someone who talked to me as an equal, who opened my eyes to the world and showed me what it was to have dreams and ambitions. I had watched him with his children, and wished my own pa had been as kind; and watched him with his wife, and wished I would have a husband as caring. And I had seen him as a friend, weeping over Mr. Burger when he died in his arms, and wished him such a friend to me.

As for Mrs. Keseberg, these months in the camp had changed me, more than I knew. The childish resentment I had felt toward her was long since vanished away, and I felt sorry for her, more than I could think possible, at the loss of her child. I crossed over to where she was folding up Ada's clothes into a bundle, and spoke most sincere to her. "I thank you, Mrs. Keseberg, with all my heart. You have taken good care of me, and now I can repay you, for I shall take such very good care of Ada. Come what may, I will get her safely through the mountain, and wait for you in California, I promise you most faithfully!"

Mrs. Keseberg stopped in her work. She stared at me with her eyes narrowed.

"Ada? You need have no care for Ada. You may do as you see fit, my dear! And you, Louis, live or die I care not. You brought us to this wretched place and now I have lost everything!

"I am not staying one more day in this hellhole! There may be another rescue and there may not. But I am not waiting to find out."

I stared at her in amazement. Just as Mrs. Donner had refused to leave her sick husband, so I had taken it for granted that Mrs. Keseberg would not leave hers.

"If I were married to—to anyone," I thought, "I would not go out and leave him here alone." But I buried that thought most hastily, and my telltale face with it, and went out to join the others.

We had our little belongings tied on our backs, and blankets and quilts huddled around us, poor protection from the weather. I stood with my friends, Meriam and Virginia, Leanna and Elitha, John and Edward Breen. I was so glad to be with them and to feel that I was not setting out all alone. But it was hard to see upon their faces the same mix of fear and hope that I am certain showed upon my own.

Mr. and Mrs. Keseberg stood at a distance to say their good-byes, and I could not help myself but look. I saw him go to put his arms around her, and I saw her pull away. I saw him go to kiss Ada, only for Ada to be snatched from him.

Mr. Keseberg was a great tall man, and Mrs. Keseberg a tiny slip of a thing, scarce reaching his shoulder. But he broke under her will. He turned away, brushing his hand across his eyes as he did so.

I turned my face away, and caught sight of Mrs. Murphy. Mr. Keseberg had brought her out of the cabin to say good-bye to Meriam and her grandchild, Naomi, who was going out tied on the back of one of the rescue men in a blanket.

Mrs. Murphy had Catherine in her arms, peering shortsightedly about her and muttering to herself. The three little boys staying behind, George Foster, James Eddy, and Simon Murphy, were clustered around her, clutching hold of her skirts and watching us with desolate faces.

With every step that took me farther away from the camp and toward freedom, I thought of Mr. Keseberg and Mrs. Murphy struggling to look after those four children all alone. Mr. Keseberg could hardly walk, and Mrs. Murphy could hardly see; and the words I had spoke to Sara Foster haunted me.

"With all my heart, I swear it: I will care for Mrs. Murphy, and on my life I will care for George."

Slower and slower grew my steps. I looked around me at my little group of companions. I thought of us making our slow way onward, plodding mile after wearisome mile across the mountain's great, cold face; soft fingers of snow poised ready to brush us away, as easily as one would flick aside a few bothersome ants on a hot summer's day.

I would die on the mountain. I knew it. My last remains would be swept away by the wind and the rain. There would be no stone to mark my place; I would be forgotten.

I turned on my heel, ignoring the shouts of my friends, and fled back the way I had come. Mr. Keseberg was standing there, watching us. I ran to him, and he caught me, and held me close. I knew that I would never see my friends again.

35

My birthday falls at the end of August, and Jacob springs a great surprise on me. I have known something was afoot, for I caught him once or twice in the kitchen talking to Martha in an undertone, a conversation that stopped the second I stepped into the room. If Jacob was any other man, or Martha any other sort of girl, I might look upon this whispering with a degree of suspicion, but I do not.

First thing in the morning on the day before my birthday, I am astonished to see a smart buggy pulled by two horses draw up on the road in front of the house. Jacob jumps down from the driving seat, and the girls and I go running out to greet him.

"My lady!" Jacob sweeps a great bow to me. "Your carriage awaits!"

"What—I mean—what is this? Jacob, what is going on here?"

Meggie turns to me, her face lit up with the thrill of the surprise.

"Pa has arranged to take you away for a treat for your

birthday, and I have known for a whole week and said nothing! Isn't it the best surprise ever?"

Not to be outdone, Hannah chips in. "Martha is going to stay here and look after us, and we have promised to be good and not cause mischief."

Clara scowls, and stamps her foot on the ground. "No one told me!"

Meggie replies, "That's because you are a baby and cannot keep a secret!" and Clara bursts into tears.

I send Clara indoors to fetch an apple for each of the horses, and she is all sunshine again and runs off quite happy, and Jacob explains my treat.

He has some business over near the coast, and he has arranged it to tie in with the Sonoma County Fair. We are to go and visit the fair for two days, and stay in a proper hotel, and eat our dinners in the dining room each night. After that, we will spend a day at the coast so that Jacob can attend to his business, before heading back home. What with the stops along the way, we will be gone altogether for a week, and Martha has agreed to sleep in the house and take care of the girls.

It turns out that Mrs. McGillivray is in on the secret as well. When I go to pack my valise, I discover a parcel on the bed, and here is my new gown finished, ready for those fancy dinners.

The hotel is very grand, with white steps leading up to the front door, which has pillars on each side, and the hallway is laid with fancy colored tiles and oriental-looking rugs over. There are some little side tables, each with an arrangement of flowers, and several large, gloomy-looking paintings in heavy gilt frames on the wall.

A young lad in a uniform takes my valise and shows us upstairs, and as we pass I catch a sight of the dining room where we will be eating our dinners, and think to myself that I am very glad of my new gown.

That evening, as we are about to step out of our room, Jacob produces another surprise. A gray silk shawl, with a border of heavy fringing. I shake it out, marveling at how beautiful it is. I go to put it on, but Jacob takes it from my hands, and arranges it round my shoulders himself.

"My dear, you look beautiful. Just the same as you did when I first laid eyes upon you, and knew in an instant that I wanted you for my own."

Jacob is the least sentimental of men. In all the years that we have been married, he has never once spoken of love, or drawn my attention to the beauty of the night skies or bid me listen to a bird singing in the treetops.

There have been times when I have wished with all my heart that he would do so. Times, too, when I have maybe thought my life to be little more than a comfortable-enough arrangement; and might have felt some regret at it, if the truth be told. But now he speaks these words so heartfelt that I blush, and know not where to look, feeling almost that this man is a stranger to me.

Next morning we set off to the fair. There are tents everywhere, with banners and flags flying over, and such a crowd of folks that I cling onto Jacob's arm, in fear that I will lose him.

There is a display of farm machinery, and something that catches Jacob's eye: a man demonstrating steam power, with a whole array of miniature devices powered so. Jacob quizzes him, would it be possible to drive a sawmill in this way, and how could it be designed? The two men set their heads together and I guess they would stay on this fascinating subject for an hour or more if left to it, but Jacob tears himself away and we walk on.

There are pens of animals, each the best in its breed: sheep, horses, cows, chickens, everything you can think of. And there is a display of beehives. I think I would like one for my garden, how lovely it would be to have honey for the taking; though I am not so sure of the costume that the beekeeper is wearing, gloves and a veil and a hat and all, to avoid being stung. Hannah has a morbid fear of bees, having been stung by one when she was little, and I think of her quivering in the house, too afraid to venture outside, and abandon that particular idea.

Jacob and I spend some time in the Ladies' Tent, which has display upon display of needlework and watercolor paintings and other handicrafts.

On one stand is a large glass dome. Within is a display of wax flowers, made by a Mrs. Bradley, so lifelike that folks are crowded round, marveling at them. I dislike them intensely. They look so real, and yet are not, and to see them so stiff and still, imprisoned in their glass case, makes me shudder. I am reminded of the story of Snow White, eating a poisoned apple and falling asleep, and her body kept in a glass coffin. I imagine her awake, and knowing of her fate, but unable to break free.

Poor Jacob. He makes a gallant effort to display an interest, escorting me from one display to another, but his heart is hardly in it. Eventually I say to him, "Go and look at the steam machinery, I know that is what you would prefer. You can leave me here and I will be perfectly happy. I see a display of quilts at the far end of the tent and I would surely like to spend some time looking at them."

We agree a place to meet for our luncheon—there is a coffee stall a little way along—and he goes off, and I over to the quilting display.

When I get to the coffee stall, Jacob is nowhere to be seen. I sit for a little while and rest at one of the tables, but I am in the full sun and after a few minutes I think I must get into the shade. Next to the coffee stall is a fruits and vegetables tent, and I step in for a minute or two.

The first thing I see is a stand comprised of rows of barrels stacked up one on top of another, and an arrangement of glasses and bottles. Behind them is a great banner reading BUENA VISTA VINEYARD, NATIVE WINES AND BRANDIES, *and here is a most elegant-looking gentleman with a set of fine moustaches, engaged in conversation with a small group of folks.*

I cannot help myself. I stare at the gentleman, and the barrels stacked up, and the banner, and listen as hard as I might to the conversation—I have thought at times that eavesdropping on what other folks might be saying is a poor trait in my character, but I am sorry to say it is one I cannot eradicate. He is telling them about the wine, urging them to sniff at it, and then to sip it; that it tastes of chocolate and spice, and how it is kept in specially made oak barrels that have been shipped all the way from France.

Eventually these folks depart, and he nods at me and asks me if I would care to sample something. He holds up a bottle with a label that reads, "Vin de la Montagne." I smile at him.

"I will not, thank you all the same. But can you tell me something of your vineyard? How did you plant it, and where have the grapes come from, and tell me, how do they grow, for I have never seen a grapevine in my life. And I have heard, as well, that folks dance on the grapes to get the juice, can this be true?"

The poor gentleman looks quite taken aback at this outburst. He answers me with great good humor, only to be met with another stream of questions directed at him once more.

He tells me that his vineyard is set on a hill, which is a novelty and not the perceived method at all. To his mind, vines growing on the slope get more sunshine and more rain, and their roots are not set in standing water, which he believes to be harmful to the plant.

He has dug into this hill and made tunnels lined with bricks in which to store the barrels—casks, he calls them—and here they stay cool. And no, in his vineyard folks do not dance upon the grapes, for he has a great press that extracts the juices. But it is true that in the Old

World, where even the smallest of farms might grow a quarter-acre of vines, the local folks do get together and produce the wine in this way.

At last, with great reluctance, I must make my goodbye, for over this gentleman's shoulder I can see Jacob, casting about this way and that, looking for me.

The gentleman—"Colonel Haraszthy at your service, ma'am," he introduces himself, with a military click of his heels—says to me, "Why is it you are so interested, if I might ask?" And I answer him, that I was once acquainted with someone who had dreamed of such a venture himself, but I thought that his dreams had come to nothing, in the end.

Colonel Haraszthy answers me, "Well, that is a pity. California will be a great wine country, if I know anything about it."

He asks me where I live. When I tell him, he says that he believes that part of the country would grow fine grapes, and, smiling, perhaps I should think of starting a vineyard of my own. It is clear that this remark is no more than gallantry. I thought he considered me a sensible woman asking sensible questions, and not some featherheaded girl acting foolish. I draw myself up, feeling insulted.

I guess he sees the change in my face, and he quickly adds, "Forgive me—I do not mean to cause offense. Some ladies of my acquaintance are setting out on such a venture, and I admire them exceedingly for it. Please allow me to give you my card. I would be happy to furnish you an introduction to them."

He hands me his card with a flourish. I tuck it away in my reticule, and join my husband.

I am pretty quiet for the rest of the afternoon and Jacob looks at me something anxious once or twice. In the end I say that the sun is so hot and the crowds so great, would he mind if we returned to the hotel.

I try so very hard to be content with my life. I look to the future and try not to think of the past; but it was a hard thing to see this man so successful and delighted with his life, and be reminded of Mr. Keseberg, sitting by the light of the campfire with Mr. Wolfinger and Mr. Burger and poor Mr. Hardkoop, he speaking with such eagerness of his plans, and they of theirs, all to come to nothing.

And I wish above all that it had not reminded me of my own lost dreams of adventuring onward, sailing away with the wind in my hair, going where I chose and doing as I pleased, seeing the world and achieving something splendid.

What are dreams? Smaller than dust, lighter than air. You cannot see them with your eyes; you cannot weigh them in your hand. But they are powerful strong, and you cannot kill them, no matter how much you might try. They creep into your mind and torment you, be it the darkest hour of the night or the brightest hour of the day.

And thanks to my wretched dreams, Jacob's treat is spoiled, when he has made such an effort to please me.

I hate myself for it. But I keep that card.

36

It was as well that I stayed. Not more than an hour after the rescue started off, the Reeds' two boys were brought into our cabin, too little and too weak to manage the journey. And Mrs. Murphy soon became very ill indeed.

With the brilliance of the snow outside and the darkness of our cabin her sight had become worse and worse. She could hardly see to put her hand to the fire and was become a danger to herself and all. As the days had passed she had become increasingly withdrawn and silent. Her older daughters had left her; Landrum had died; she heard the news that Lemuel had perished. Each time she became more scattered in her wits. But the worst was still to come. For the day after the rescuers left, Catherine died. And I carried the tiny body, no more than the size of one of the little girls' dolls and as light as a feather, out of the cabin and put it into the snow beside the rest.

Next morning I woke to find Mrs. Murphy walking round and round the cabin, searching for something.

"Where is it? I had it in my hand, and now I cannot

find it. You, girl!"—pointing at me—"Help me look. Where is it? I had it in my hand, and now I cannot find it."

I led her back to her bed, and sat her down with the quilt wrapped around her, and made up the fire and put water to heat.

Mrs. Murphy would not be still. Again, she got to her feet, and crossed the room, lifting up blankets and peering into corners.

"I cannot find it! Where is it? I had it in my hand, and now I cannot find it!" She began to weep. Again, I led her to the bed, and sat her down, imploring her to stay still, but she would not cease her quest. Round and round she went once more, and again after that.

The kettle came to the boil, and I sat her down once more, and fetched her a cup of hot water to drink.

"What is this?" She flung it straight at my head, accompanied by a stream of language filthier than anything I had ever heard in the back streets of Cincinnati. I reeled back, my head cut open and blood dripping down my face, and my clothing soaked.

I screamed at her, "Be still! Be still!" and in that instant she came back to herself.

"Oh, my dear—why, whatever has happened to your poor face?" and she looked at me full of love, and took my hand, and kissed it.

I was ashamed of myself, and buried my face in her shoulder, saying, "Oh, I am sorry to have shouted at you so!" Mrs. Murphy patted me on the back and said, "Sweetheart, let me find something to dress that cut." Then she stood up and crossed the room, saying to herself, "Now, where is the . . . where is it? I had it in my hand, and now I cannot find it. I had it in my hand, and now I cannot find it."

As time had gone on the wolves had drawn closer to the camp. Now they were among us night after night. We heard them, growling low in their throats as they circled the cabins. Flakes of snow would fall from the roof as the animals padded back and forth above our heads, and we lay rigid in our beds, listening to every footfall. They howled, and their fellows howled in return.

Mrs. Murphy became obsessed by them. If we managed to fall to sleep, it would be for a few moments at most; for when they howled, Mrs. Murphy would howl, too, and bang on the roof with a stick.

In vain I begged her to stop. I remembered how our lean-to tumbled down around our ears. The cabin roof was hardly any stronger, and I imagined it giving way as well, a great gray wolf come crashing down in our midst, twisting and slavering, teeth and claws at the ready as he fell.

It was March when the second rescue party arrived with Mr. Reed leading the way. These men were better supplied than the first, though again they were all on foot; they still could not get animals through the snow, which they told us to be twenty foot or more, up at the pass. Some of the men continued down to Alder Creek, and the rest made camp near us.

Mr. Reed came down into our cabin, overjoyed to find his boys safe. He told us that as he left Sutter's Fort, he had seen the men from the first rescue, Mrs. Reed and Virginia in their company, heading in. I could imagine how he felt to see his wife and daughter safe and well.

Mr. Reed was kindness itself. He gave us some good food, and brought in wood for our fire, and set water to heat, all the while telling us of his adventures between leaving the train—what seemed so very long ago to us now—and arriving at Sutter's Fort.

He and Mr. Herron had made good time to start with, until Mr. Reed's horse went lame. Mr. Herron shot it, and they butchered it and took the meat with them, and as well they did, for game was scarce. They were not bothered overmuch by Indians on their way, but the journey was longer than they expected. Once through the pass it was another three days' journey down the other side of the mountain, and then they'd had no food at all.

Mr. Reed told us that he arrived in California to find there was a war on, so it was impossible to send back any help, for all the fit men were off fighting the Mexicos. Those who said they would bring us help were nothing but roustabouts and broken-down fellows; Mr. Reed didn't trust them not to take the food and animals he purchased and never be seen again. But he thought it no great matter if we waited for help to come, and it was not until he met up with the poor remnants of the Snow-shoe party that he finally heard the truth of our situation. Our story was taken up by the newspapers, and at long last folks stepped up to assist him.

All this was said with a right choke in his voice, and when he heard the story of how his wife and children had suffered, how some had taken against them to the last, and how we had helped them, he was so moved that he wept, and embraced Mr. Keseberg, and called him his dearest friend.

After a few days, Mr. Reed's rescue made ready to depart. Mrs. Graves and the rest of her family were to leave, though it must have been a hard task for Mr. Reed to assist them, knowing how cruel they had treated his family. And all the rest of the Breens were to go with him, and sorry I was to hear it.

My life had become a lonely one, strange to think it, when I was surrounded by people at every minute of the day and night. But those I had grown to love had deserted me—my darling Margaret Eddy, Meriam and Landrum and all the rest of my friends, Mrs. Murphy, worst of all. She had been like my mother, and now she was become my worrisome child. Mr. Keseberg had turned away from me. His conversation, laced with that dry sense of humor so akin to my own, and which meant so very much to me, had stilled, and he lay silent and morose all the livelong day.

I cared for all, and no one cared for me. All but Mrs. Breen. Once in a while I left the cabin and went across to visit with her—when I thought I could not stay one more minute in the same room with Mrs. Murphy without screaming, or when the children wept and begged for food that I did not possess and had no way of obtaining. Now even that small comfort was to be denied me.

I wished with all my heart that I could leave with Mr. Reed's rescue, and be out of this misery. But I could not. Yet again there were more children needing rescue than there were rescuers to do it. George Foster and James Eddy were to stay behind. Simon Murphy was ailing, and could not be moved. Mrs. Murphy was not fit to go out; Mr. Keseberg could not walk. There was no one else to care for them. They must stay in the camp. So I was doomed to stay in it, as well.

The three men who had gone to Alder Creek did not return. Instead, the French lad, Jean Trudeau, arrived. He brought a message from Mrs. Donner. As if by some miracle Mr. George Donner kept alive, but it could not be for much longer. She would see the poor man into his grave, and then she and these men would bring the rest of the children, and join us at the lake.

Mr. Reed left us with food enough for ten days, and promised that he would send supplies again. In this way we could manage until such time as the weather improved—not more than a few weeks, surely—and then mules could be brought through the mountain to take us all to safety.

The day after Mr. Reed's departure, I was making a meal of beans and rice when I thought I heard my name being called. I looked up, startled—for we were the only folks left in the camp now. It came again. I left the fire, and ran up the steps to the outside.

Abandoned in the snow were three little girls. These were Mrs. Donner's children, six-year-old Frances, and her baby sisters Georgia and Eliza, all wailing fit to burst. Heading away were two of the men who had stayed at Alder Creek, loaded up with packs so heavy they could hardly stand. I screamed after them, "Come back! Come back!"

Of course, they did not.

Frances told me that her mama had given them gold and jewelry and every last piece of her good clothing, including a silk gown, for them to carry the girls across the mountain to safety in California. When they got to our camp, the men had set the children down out in the open, told Frances to shout my name, and then marched off without a backward glance. I could not comprehend greater villainy.

And yet again our cabin was filled with other people's children, with hardly any means of providing for them.

37

With some good meals inside him, Mr. Keseberg regained his strength somewhat. At long last it seemed the snow had stopped, and we had blue skies and sun. Mr. Keseberg was able to get out and fetch us firewood; and with the good food and the fresh air he came back to something like his old self, sitting on a stool by the fireside and telling stories to keep the children amused. And we began our conversations again, and I heard once more of his plans for his vineyard. With the promise of Mr. Reed's final rescue, food sent for us, and mules to take us out, it seemed that at long last we would get to the end of our journey, and our lives would be set back on the path we had envisaged.

But this was all an illusion. For with three more mouths to feed, the food that should have lasted us two weeks was gone in less than one; and the blue skies and sun were accompanied by a biting wind, so if anything it continued colder. And little George Foster died.

So many died, that you might think the death of one more child to be of little consequence, other than to those who loved him. But it was his death that settled Mr. Keseberg's fate, and, as it turned out, my own.

So, George Foster's death. I will write down the circumstances of his death in full, for much was said at the time and since, and all of it lies from start to finish. I turn my head away from the tales that are told of our time in the camp and keep my own counsel, but I will say this. What is true and what is believed are two vastly different things. And those who believe in the tales that are told of poor little George Foster's death should be ashamed to be so deceived.

When we had set to and constructed the Murphy cabin, there had already been some small mattresses in the wagons for the children to sleep on overnight. A half dozen beds—some of them stacked one atop another, in the way that the cattle roustabouts slept in their shanties—were fashioned from the wagon planks, under the direction of Mr. Eddy.

At one end of the cabin was the little room divided off where Mr. Eddy and his wife and two children had slept. At the other end was the chimney hearth, with the cooking pots set over the fire, and a couple of small stools to sit on.

There was no window. But for the first weeks in the camp there was light enough, for the sun shone in around the doorframe, and through the gaps in the wall where the logs didn't fit well together, and some days were fine so that we could leave the door open to air the cabin through. In the evenings, or the miserable days when the weather was poor, it was comfortable, for we had a lantern and a few candles and the firelight to see by. With neighbors visiting from time to time, and we stepping out to go visit with them, life in the Murphy cabin was not as bad as it could have been. But those days were long gone.

Within a day of the food running out, Mr. Keseberg

and I began to weaken once more. Collecting wood became an impossible task. There were axes and saws, but Mr. Keseberg was too weak to use them and we could not go out together, for Mrs. Murphy could not be left for a second unattended. Mr. Keseberg could do no more than gather what he could carry from the few sticks and branches that had fallen to the ground. Our fires became as little and feeble as we ourselves, and we trembled uncontrollably from the cold.

We took the planks that had formed the Eddys' bed and some of the other beds, too, to mend our fires; and when they were consumed, debated whether to take the planks from the remaining beds as well. But the little warmth we still maintained in the cabin meant that the snow that surrounded us melted through the chinks in the walls and beneath the door, and the earth beneath our feet was mud, soaking into our clothes and bedding. If we burnt the last few beds, the mud would be all we had to sleep upon.

I wished we could move into the Breens' cabin, for it was in better condition than ours by far. But although Mr. Keseberg and I could have got across to it, Mrs. Murphy could not, and the little boys could not, and we could not have carried them.

On the night that George Foster died, I had gone round the cabin to settle the children to sleep.

My legs were so swollen it was painful to walk more than a few steps, and I was so weak that I had to sit down at every bed as I moved along. The Donner girls were tucked into one bed, top to tail like fishes in a basket. James Eddy and George Foster were in another. Both boys were fevered and restless. It was clear that it was only a matter of time before one or both of them would die.

I would never have thought to be so very matter-of-fact about the death of a child; to acknowledge that it would happen, and to merely wait for the event. But I guess I was hardened to it, by then.

I pulled the quilt better over them, where George had kicked it off in his dreams, and then climbed into bed next to Mrs. Murphy, and lay there for a while, listening to the drip, drip of water from the ceiling.

Those nights when I had lain awake planning my future in California, or thinking of a conversation I had that day with Mr. Keseberg, or blushing in the dark as I remembered Landrum's look when I stepped out of the Murphy wagon in my new dress, and, later, his kiss, were long past. I had given up praying at night for rescue, or telling myself that in the morning a miracle would happen—the snow would be gone overnight, or I would remember a store of food I had hid and quite forgot about. I simply lay in dull silence, staring at the ceiling, knowing that closing my eyes for sleep meant opening them at waking, to endure another day of privation and misery that seemed unending.

In the night, George woke, crying for his mother. His sobs roused me, enough to see Mr. Keseberg cross the room to him.

George could not stop his tears, and held out his arms to be picked up. Mr. Keseberg took him back to his own bed that he shared with Simon Murphy, who was sound asleep and did not stir. Mr. Keseberg laid George down beside him, pulling the blankets close over them both, and he began to sing to him quietly in German. It was a lullaby he used to sing to Ada, and I fell back to sleep myself, listening to his voice, so gentle and soft in the darkness.

It seemed but minutes that I was asleep and then I woke with a start. Mr. Keseberg was standing over me, pinching my arm.

The room was lit red by the dying embers of the fire. Black shadows scurried across the wall as Mr. Keseberg's candle shook in his hand. I could see George, open-eyed and waxen pale in the next bed.

"'Wake up!" Mr. Keseberg spoke in a whisper. "That poor child has died. We must take him out of the cabin before Mrs. Murphy sees him!"

I sat up, but my movement disturbed her. She jerked upright, saying, "Catherine! Catherine!"

For days now, Mrs. Murphy had hardly stirred from her bed. She would lie staring at the ceiling and muttering to herself, counting up on her fingers the names of those who had died around us. "Landrum," she said, "Harriet, Margaret. Eleanor Eddy. And the babies, Louis and Catherine." But now she gave out a bloodcurdling banshee wail, and fair flew across the room to snatch up her little grandson in her arms.

She ran back to her own bed with him. Here she crouched, panting, over the body, staring about her through the matted tangle of her hair, which over the weeks and months of our imprisonment had turned quite white.

The little girls had been frightened of her from the start, whispering that she was a witch. They tumbled out of bed and ran screaming to the far end of the cabin. Here they fell to the floor, holding on to each other and weeping in fear. I staggered across to them, falling to my knees and crawling the last yard or two. They hid behind me, and we shrank back against the wall.

James lay still in his bed, too close to death himself to take notice. Simon curled into a ball, pulling a blanket over his head. And Mr. Keseberg crossed to Mrs. Murphy's bed, intending to take George from her; but at the sight of him she set to screaming dreadful things in her broken voice, accusations of murder and cannibalism and I don't know what. He staggered backward to the nearest bed and sat down, with his head sunk into his hands.

We stayed that way for an age, too afraid to move. Eventually the poor woman quieted down, still holding George close to her, and muttering beneath her breath.

I gathered the little girls together and persuaded them back into their bed, and then I crossed over to Mrs. Murphy. I sat down beside her with my arm around her shoulder, and stroked her hair with my hand. Eventually she went limp, and leaned against me, tears streaming down her face, and at last she consented to let the child go.

Mr. Keseberg lifted him from her arms, so very gentle. "My dear, let me take him. He is safe now, and nothing can harm him more. I will take good care of him, upon my word I will."

"Yes, take him." Mrs. Murphy took Mr. Keseberg's hand, and looked full into his eyes. "But I beg you, do not put him out in the snow for the wolves to get him. Promise me, oh, promise me you will not."

He kissed her cheek, and said, "I swear."

I brought James out of his bed and put him in with the little girls, hoping that their warmth would revive him somewhat. Mr. Keseberg carried George's sad little corpse across the room and laid it in the empty bed and pulled the blanket across it. And I blew up the ashes a little and put on the few sticks of firewood we had remaining, and set some water to heat. I dropped the last little bits of hides into the cooking pot. It was the last of our firewood, and the very last of our food. When these scraps were gone, there was nothing left at all.

I left the fire, and opened the cabin door to look out, hoping that this endless night would be over and it would be daylight at last. The moon was gone, and the thousand distant stars that had shone so steady above us throughout our journey had departed with it. Just a handful remained, glimmering fitfully in the clear sky and winking out, one by one, as the sun came up.

On one of those afternoons when we were walking together—such a very long time ago, or so it seemed now, and more like something I had dreamed, only—Mr. Keseberg had told me a story. It was the story of Pandora, left in charge of a box of treasures. She was told not to open it, but she did. All the miseries of the world came flying out; but one thing remained in the box, and that was Hope.

He had told it as a good thing, how that last little bit of Hope will never desert us. But now I saw the story in a different light. It seemed to me that Hope was another name for the cruelest torment of all—an empty, deceitful promise of help that would never come.

I wished Hope gone with all my heart. It would be a comfort to finally accept that there would be no miracle for me. I would welcome death as my escape from this torment. I longed for it, more than I had ever longed for anything.

I stood in the doorway, with my face to the sunrise, and thought it would be a kindness to all if I were to turn and seize a knife, and sink it into each of us, myself at the last.

But Hope would not let me.

All that day, Mrs. Murphy could not let George alone. No matter how much I besought her to leave him be, she would rise from her bed and take the blanket from the poor child's face, and take him in her arms, singing to him and crooning over him. And at last, Mr. Keseberg put the poor child out of harm's way.

Decency and shame had been let go long since. When we got to the stage where we could hardly get out of the cabin and up the snow steps to the surface to see to our natural needs, necessity had forced us to turn the little room that the Eddys had occupied into our privy. We kept a pail in here for our mess, scattering ashes from the fire over it. Mr. Keseberg took it outside when he had the strength, or I did, but those days were getting fewer and fewer. Mostly the pail was overflowing, and no doubt the stench of it overwhelming, though we had become something accustomed to it, I guess.

Now, Mr. Keseberg carried George into this vile room, and when he came back, he said to me in an undertone that he had hung him up by his clothes on a nail that Mr. Eddy had driven into the wall to put his coat on, for there was no bed to lay him on, and the floor was a quagmire.

Poor little boy. I remembered him on the day of our picnic at Independence Rock, rolling on the grass with jam in his hair. And later, cowering in front of his father, with a great bruise darkening his face.

In order to distract the children from Mr. Keseberg's grisly task, I had looked out Ada's little tea set, and set the girls to play tea party. I sat beside Simon, recounting one of Mr. Keseberg's stories about a boy who climbed up a beanstalk and found a goose that laid eggs of gold. But my ruse didn't work. When Mr. Keseberg reentered the room, Frances paused in her game of pouring water from the little teapot. Instead, she smiled and clapped her hands and said, "Hurrah, today we shall have a fine dinner!"

This was the secret of how these children had come to us with such rosy lips and round cheeks! They had been kept alive by the eating of their dead fellows.

There had been talk before, of doing such a thing. In her first mad days after Catherine's death, Mrs. Murphy had spoke of it, somehow it had become fixed in her mind and taken root there, but we had never needed to do it. We had the hides, foul though they were, and at the very worst point of hunger the first rescue had come to our aid, and then again Mr. Reed's party.

I did not know how the folks in the other cabins had fared. I had not asked. All I knew for certain was that we had not resorted to such foul measures. Perhaps we should have, and saved poor little George Foster. Perhaps we must, to save the rest.

We all would die within a day or two if something did not happen to save us. Someone had to make the decision, and there was only me and Mr. Keseberg to do it. But even as the thought formed in my head, I knew in my heart that the decision was made. If no help was with us in the morning, I would do it. And I prayed to God with all my being, to forgive me, and to help me.

God answered my prayer, though not as I expected. Next morning Mr. Clarke arrived from Alder Creek. He was the last man who had stayed behind from Mr. Reed's rescue, a good, kind man, unlike his terrible thieving companions. He brought with him a great slab of meat from a bear he had killed, and it was just in time, too.

My decision to use the only food that was left to us was made too late. Whether we had wanted to do it or not, it was impossible, for neither Mr. Keseberg nor I could rise from our bed.

I can only imagine Mr. Clarke's thoughts at the sight that met him as he descended the steps into our cabin and opened the door. The cabin lit by one flickering candle. No fire, and grave-cold. The smell that greeted him, and the filth; and when he stepped farther into the cabin and lit the lantern that he carried with him, the sight of George, hanging from the nail.

James Eddy had died in the night. Now little Georgia and Eliza were playing with his body like a large doll, combing James's hair and making pretend that he was asleep, and shouting in his ear to wake him. Mrs. Murphy was sitting in her bed in all her mess, for she had so lost her senses that she would not stir from her bed even to use the pail. She was doing her counting, and singing to herself in a thin, high voice.

I could not share a bed with her, and I lay huddled next to Mr. Keseberg, both of us shaking with cold and unable to stand.

The only lively bodies were ten-year-old Simon and six-year-old Frances, who were trying to make up the fire with some last ends of twigs and pinecones, and the little girls, engaged in their horrid game.

Mr. Clarke made up the fire. He put water to heat, and dropped the bear meat into the pot; all this in terrible silence. Then he took Simon and the little girls away, and left us to our fate.

38

The next day another rescue party arrived with Mr. Eddy and Mr. Foster in the forefront, hastening to save their little boys; but they arrived too late. I was never so sorry for anyone as I was then for Mr. Eddy. The look of joyous expectation upon his face when he came into our cabin looking for his son was something terrible to behold.

Mrs. Murphy greeted the men's arrival with an ear-splitting scream, and fell upon her son-in-law, clawing at him and crying out that Mr. Keseberg was a monster, killing the children one after another for the delight of feasting on their flesh, and begging him to save her.

Mr. Foster recoiled from her with an ashen face, and I shouted her down, "Mrs. Murphy! Be silent, I beg you, for the love of God!"

Mr. Eddy lifted his son most tenderly, with tears streaming down his face, and held him close, and carried him out of the cabin. But Mr. Foster looked at George and staggered outside to vomit in the snow; and it was left to Mr. Eddy to return and take the poor little boy away.

Will Foster and Henry Eddy. We had traveled so far together, and suffered together, and our lives were bound together. I wanted to say a prayer with them over these children's graves. And to say to them how their children had died, and that I was sorrier than I could ever say for their loss. But I was slow climbing up the steps behind them, and when I reached the top I had to sit to catch my breath; and Mr. Eddy had taken the two boys some distance away, and I could not get there.

I watched as he dug the two graves, and laid the children in, and covered them over with the snow. Throughout, Mr. Foster stood by, staring into the distance with a still face and seeming hardly to know what Mr. Eddy was about. When Mr. Eddy had finished, he took Mr. Foster by the arm, and they crossed over to the Breen cabin and went inside and shut the door.

I made my slow way across the snow, intending to go in and explain to Mr. Foster what had happened, and give my solemn vow that I had honored my promise to his wife; I had done my best for his family and could have done no more.

When I got to the door, I could hear Mr. Eddy speaking. He spoke pretty low, but his voice carried clearer than he knew, and I heard every word he said.

". . . known as a cruel, vicious man," he was saying. "All were agreed on that score! He got rid of old Hardkoop, if you remember, when he became a nuisance to him. He beat his wife. When good Mr. Reed called him to account, why, Mr. Keseberg tried to get the man hanged, and when that failed, he turned all against him, and had him sent away from his family!

"And as for the murder of Mr. Wolfinger—why, we never did get to the bottom of that. I swear I would have killed him with my bare hands, rather than discover that he was left in charge of my son!"

Mr. Foster made no reply.

Mr. Eddy continued, "My wife—my daughter—all my family, dead in his care!" He gave out a muffled sob. "He made out he could not walk. He has said he could not leave the camp for it. But why should we believe anything he says? I think the truth of it is that he chooses to stay behind, to be free to indulge his depraved appetites to the full!"

As if this wasn't bad enough, next I heard my name, and I pressed my ear to the door. I did not catch what was said. I heard Mr. Eddy give a low, sneering laugh, and then there was silence.

I hardly knew whether to laugh or cry. To hear Mr. Eddy's voice, so choked with grief, and yet his manner just the same as I remembered him night after night round our fire, cooking up a story that was a dizzying mix of lies and guesswork, with just a pinch of the truth sprinkled over to give flavor.

I could not face him. I stumbled back to our cabin, and went in. And I crossed over to Mr. Keseberg and told him what Mr. Eddy had said. He bowed his head and wept.

In all these weeks that we had been together, all boundaries had been broke down between us. We spoke of our lives—our childhoods, his father who beat him and his mother who died when he was a lad; and I of mine, in the backstreets of the city. I told him of my dreams for Landrum, that I had never admitted fully even to myself. He spoke of his wife, and how he feared she had never loved him truly, but had married him to escape her parents, stricter even than his own. We shared all, though neither of us uttered a word that suggested we had come to care for each other as anything more than friends.

But now all I could think was, that if any man ever

needed the comfort of a woman's arms around him, this was the man.

We did not see Mr. Foster again. Next morning Mr. Eddy came alone into our cabin, telling us that he had news from Alder Creek. All that was left there was Mrs. Donner and her husband, still hanging on to life by the very thinnest of threads.

Mr. Eddy said that she had sent us a message. It was the same as before. As soon as she was able—by which she meant, when her husband finally died—she would leave Alder Creek and come to find us. But he added that the rescue party could not wait. They would be departing later that day and we must decide what we would do.

"If you wish to stay and wait for Mrs. Donner," he said, "then we will leave as much food as we can spare, enough for two weeks at least. The snow is melting on the mountain. If you are truly unable to walk, Mr. Keseberg"—and he looked away, unable to meet our gaze—"if you cannot walk out, then you might decide to wait here until we can send some mules through to fetch you out. Or if you can walk, after all, then you can come with us now.

"I will step in again in an hour, and see what you have both decided."

Mr. Keseberg and I turned it over and over between us.

He said I should go. The men would help me, and there would be food enough to sustain me. But he would stay. He was nothing close to able to get through the mountain, he thought. And what of Mrs. Donner? How could he leave, knowing that she would arrive in the camp and find herself abandoned and alone?

When Mr. Eddy came back into our cabin, I asked him what was to become of Mrs. Murphy.

"Surely Mr. Foster would want to stay and care for

her? Mr. Eddy, you promise food for two weeks more, and rescue at the end of it. So there is no reason for Mr. Foster to leave, and the poor woman is beyond help. She has been in despair with the loss of her family, and it would be such a comfort to her to at least die with him holding her hand!"

Mr. Eddy just could not help himself. He cast a quick glance over his shoulder, as if thinking someone might be listening and then turned back, leaning toward us with the avid, gossiping expression I knew so well.

"Poor man! I think him deranged! I hardly understand myself why he chose to return here, for even on our journey through with the Snowshoes he was close to breaking. But there was no stopping him, he was determined to come back.

"Think of what he must be feeling now—his child dead! And poor Mrs. Murphy—well—we can see how she is, and come to this while he and his wife have been feasting in the California sunshine; for he has been living the high life, I can assure you!

"Do you remember him, in the days after he killed his brother-in-law, Mr. Pike? That was nothing as to his behavior now! He has not spoke a word since we arrived here, and I think he would do violence if he stayed."

I discounted half of what Mr. Eddy said, and ignored half of what was left, but this much was true: I did remember Mr. Foster in the days after he had killed Mr. Pike. He had beat George, when he had never laid a hand to him before, and raged at his wife and insulted Mrs. Murphy to her face at every mild word she spoke to him.

I wondered what Mr. Foster would say to his wife, when he got back. Would he want me telling my friend Sara Foster the truth? That her mother had been raving, on her deathbed and mortal terrified, and he had left her so?

If anyone had a reason to wish me lost upon the mountain, it was Mr. Foster. I was afraid of him, as much as I was afraid of the mountain. And I would not leave Mrs. Murphy. Will Foster might not respect the promise he had made to his wife. But I would respect mine.

So I did not go with them.

39

In October our dedicated band of quilters assembles once more. Our squares have all been stitched together into one large piece and set upon their backing, and now we are at Minnie's house for the quilting, for the Arbuthnot barn is the only place big enough to hold the quilting frame.

In the main the quilting stitch is only straight back-and-forth, but in reminder of where it is being quilted, it has been decided that the stitch along the plain border should be a design of apples. They are everywhere, piled up along one wall in crates and half barrels. The barn smells delicious.

The Arbuthnot land is planted with acre upon acre of these trees. For the past few years nothing much has happened except the trees get a little taller and have a few leaves more. But this spring for the first time all the trees came full into blossom, and what a beautiful sight it was, too, a great mass of pink and white flowers and the blue sky behind.

Minnie invited us for a picnic. The girls ran about collecting the blossoms that had fallen to the ground, and

John Arbuthnot gave Jacob a tour of the orchard. I tagged along, asking questions all the while.

Now the apples are gathered in, and I can tell which are which and what they are to be used for. In one crate is some most unappealing-looking fruit, speckled and brownish and squat. This is a variety called Ashmead's Kernel, and the trees were shipped over from England. It is renowned for its delicious flavor. Another variety is Winesap, which I know already. It is a lovely red color and a good keeper, either in sacking for a few weeks, or cut into rings and dried in the sun to keep right through the winter. It makes excellent pies. The last is Northern Spy, which I think an odd name. It comes from New York State, and is so juicy that it is nigh on useless. It dries away to nothing, and would bake away to nothing as well, giving soggy pie crust and not much else.

But this juiciness is the whole point of it. With some help from Jacob, John has spent the summer constructing a cider press and now, while we are quilting, John and his eldest, John Junior, and a couple of other boys I know from the school are heaving the crates onto the mule cart to be carried away to the press, and the barrels filled with apple juice brought back, to be left to ferment.

When the quilting is finished for the day, and our friends have departed, Minnie takes my arm and asks me to stroll along with her a little. Minnie has been pretty quiet all afternoon, and I can tell something is worrying at her. We take a turn or two up and down, and I ask her about her plans for the next spring.

Our picnic being such a success, Minnie is thinking of inviting other folks to come and see the apple blossoms for a little fee. They could picnic under the trees if they wished, and maybe they would like to walk over to the cider press and purchase some of John's cider.

My brain flies away with me, and next thing I have turned Minnie's little idea into a whole Apple Blossom

Festival. I make one suggestion after another as to what could be done, most of them pretty silly, I guess: fire-eaters and jugglers and all sorts.

Minnie seems hardly to be listening, and suddenly she says, "You know it is John Junior's birthday in a week or so—well, when my sister in Virginia sent me the last lot of periodicals, she sent me a bank note for ten dollars."

"That's a deal of money!" I say, not knowing quite where the conversation is headed.

"Oh—no, it was for all the boys' birthdays, not just John Junior, and to buy them Christmas gifts as well," she says, absently. "But the thing is—it is drawn on a Virginia bank. John went to cash it at the Wells Fargo. They took it, but the teller said to him, quiet-like, for John is in and out of there and the fellow knows him, that if he had any more notes drawn on a Southern bank, to cash them quick, for Virginia money—all the paper money in the South—is going to be worthless after the election. Can this be true? What does it mean?"

We are back at the house now, and she stops walking, and turns to face me.

"I know that the South is threatening to withdraw from the Union if Mr. Lincoln becomes president. But surely—I never thought it meant there would be a war!"

Minnie and I go into her kitchen. I lift a pair of muddy boots off a chair and put them over by the back door, and collect up Minnie's knitting off the table from where it sits in a muddle of plates and crumbs, and put it into her work basket. Minnie sets the kettle to boil. Then we sit down together at her kitchen table and continue our conversation over the teacups.

It is unthinkable that our Nation should be so divided against itself that North goes against South into battle. Being so very far away on the other side of the country I guess we would not be caught up in the fighting—I pray to God we would not—but near enough everyone here has family back East. Minnie's family is in the North, and she has three brothers there, but her sister's husband is from the South. Will brother fight brother-in-law, hand to hand on the battlefield? How should it be avoided?

Our conversation leads round to the election again, and we return to a topic of conversation our quilting bee had been discussing earlier in the afternoon: a woman's right to vote. This had arisen due to an article that was in Minnie's latest edition of Godey's Magazine*—the very one that came with the ten-dollar bank note.*

Being something hampered by my size, for the new baby will be here in only a few weeks, I was not working at the quilting frame but sitting to one side, putting the finishing touches to a cover for the new baby's crib. The pattern is called Little Red Schoolhouse, except that my schoolhouses are not red at all, but each a different color.

After a while I grew bored with it, and Godey's Magazine *being at my side, I thought to read something aloud.*

I chanced upon an article written by a learned professor of medicine at a college back East, printed in reply to another article concerning the movement for women's suffrage. This professor was adamantly opposed to the idea.

He said that a woman's brain is proved by science to be less developed than that of a man, and does not have the same capacity for logical deduction. Moreover, it is a known fact that the workings of a woman's body each month weaken the mind. Experiments are being conducted to see if this is related to lunacy—lunar meaning moon, and lunacy describing the way in which the inmates of the Bedlam asylums experience delusions once a month when the moon is full.

In short, it concludes, women are incapable of rational thought, prone to madness and delusion, and therefore incapable of managing their own affairs. Under no circumstances should they be given the power to vote; rather, they should be thankful to be married, and grateful to their husbands for so cheerfully shouldering the great burden of their care, and making such decisions for them.

The article is greeted with a mixture of reactions. Some with derision—Mrs. Gerald for one, not married and running her own business perfectly well; and some with nodding agreement—Isobel Davies, who seems to have hardly set a foot outside her father's house before her marriage, and appears incapable of formulating a thought without seeking her husband's approval on the matter.

Of all folks to get fired up about this, I would have thought the least likely to be Mrs. O'Donoghue, a quiet woman and head of the Ladies' Church Committee, but now she speaks out pretty plain.

"Am I deluded," she asks, "in thinking that the drapes in my parlor reek something horrible so that they have to be taken down and aired out on the washing line? Or am I correct in logically deducing that it is because my husband has smoked a cigar in my parlor after I have taken myself off to bed, when I have expressly forbid it?"

This is obviously a sore point with her. She is very proud of her house and keeps it shiny as a new pin. All the same it is greeted with a gale of laughter.

I reply, "Is it a sign of madness brought about by your woman's condition, that upon this discovery you would like to hit your husband over the head with the frying pan? Or is it the perfectly justifiable action of a sane, but furious, woman?"

We are laughing so much that at first we don't notice John and the boys come into the barn; when we do, we laugh even more. The poor fellows scramble themselves back out into the open air as fast as they are able and I say, "Well, I guess as far as they are concerned that proves the point!"

It was all so very lighthearted; but now, sitting in Minnie's homely kitchen, she worrying about her family, and me thinking of Jacob's two grown sons from his first marriage, that are away in Washington serving with the Navy, with wives and children to provide for, I think that perhaps having the vote is a fearsome responsibility and that our frivolity is something misguided.

If I was asked whether it is fair, that men can vote on issues that affect their lives and those of their families, but women cannot, I would say no, most decided. I don't believe for one moment that women are deluded and irrational. But we have soft hearts, that much is true.

If we voted, perhaps we would be guided by our hearts, to keep our own menfolk safe, when our conscience tells us to choose the hard path, and vote another way entirely. Would we vote for our men in particular, or mankind in general? Would a woman in Connecticut think her son's life a fair exchange for that of an unknown black slave, eight hundred miles away in Georgia?

I cannot help but be reminded of Mr. Reed: our little band of folks sitting round the fire and voting to send him away into the wilderness.

If being given a vote means I must decide whether to send a man to his death, I do not think I want it at all.

40

Next morning we awoke but Mrs. Murphy did not; she had been blessed with a peaceful death in the night. The camp, once so filled with people it was almost a little town, was deserted. Our cabin, so crammed with bodies at times there was hardly space to move or sit, was silent and empty. Of the sixty folks or more who had been here once, now there was just Mr. Keseberg and me.

I set water to heat, and then I took Mrs. Murphy's filthy clothes from her, and Mr. Keseberg stripped away all her bedding and took it, and her soiled clothing, out of the cabin and burned it.

I took a cloth and washed her, looking with great pity at her wasted limbs and treating her as gentle as I would a child. I washed her hair and combed it out for her as it dried, and then I braided it and twisted it round her head in the way that she had liked. I relished the task, sad though it was. I had felt so very helpless in the face of Mrs. Murphy's suffering. Soft words and handholding were all I'd had to offer her, and much of the time I had screamed and raged at her, suffering agonies of self-loathing as a result. But now I could do her some real kindness, small though it was, and restore her to some dignity.

When Mr. Keseberg came back in, we lifted her body, as light and frail as one of the children's, and wrapped her in a quilt, and laid her on one of the beds. We would not bury her in the snow. She had such a fear of the wolves that it seemed more of a kindness to leave her safe indoors.

She lay peaceful at long last, in that quiet room, with her little bits of possessions around her. Her spoons and forks washed clean and laid out on a cloth on the hearth; her own tin cups hanging from nails in a neat row nearby. Her knitting had been laid aside when her sight grew too poor for it, a pair of socks in blue worsted yarn, one complete and one with the heel waiting to be turned. Now I found her work basket and laid it by the fireside, so it looked like she had just stepped away from it for a spell, and would be back at any minute to finish what she was about.

When this was done, and the cabin was as tidy as I could make it, Mr. Keseberg and I took what food remained, and left that grim place for the last time. He shut the door behind us, and we climbed to the surface of the snow.

How silent and empty the landscape was. An unbroken blue sky arched over us; the great lake slumbered beneath its virginal blanket of snow. We could have been the only two people left alive in all the world. And the sun shone on us, pitiless, and showed us what we were.

Mr. Keseberg was a stooped and limping echo of what he had been before. He was not much over thirty, but looked twice that age: the once-gold hair silvered, the once-bronzed skin mottled white. Even his very eyes seemed to have faded to a washed-out gray, set deep in their sockets, with pouches of skin beneath. But still I saw him the way he was the first time I laid my eyes upon him, a broad-shouldered, swaggering fellow, with thick fair hair curling onto his collar, and his eyes the color of violets when they met mine.

As for me, I had been a skinny, ragged wretch of a girl when I met him. A starved, bedraggled drab of a woman was what I was become. But I didn't care. I took his hand, and went into his arms; and I kissed him.

Maybe I had dreamed of starlight and sweet music; childish, girlish fancies. Those days were long behind me. I thought we would die here, that was the truth. I did not believe help would ever come. And I did not wish to die alone.

His arm around me, my hand in his, we walked together to the Breens' cabin, so clean and neat compared to where we had spent so many long days. We gathered in firewood and built up a great fire, and heated water on it and washed ourselves. And there we stayed, sleeping at night in each other's arms. No one to see us. And no one to judge.

A week passed, and another. Mrs. Donner never came to join us and the rescue, promised so very faithfully with Mr. Eddy's handshake given on it, never came either. I took a grim pleasure in knowing that I had been right to mistrust him. Every hour we looked again to the horizon in the hope of seeing some rescue. Every night I counted up our dwindling supplies of food. And then one day—yet again—it was all gone.

I reproached myself most bitterly, and Mr. Keseberg, too.

"We should not have lingered here! What were we thinking? We should have left when we could. Better to have died on the mountain than face the only choice that is left to us. Die, or commit the last, unforgiveable sin!"

I had thought of it before, when the little Donner girls came to us. I had thought of it again, when George Foster died. But that was to save others. This was to save myself, and I could not do it.

The cabin door was open. I could see the sky, a vast, high arc of the palest blue, cloudless. The weak sunlight shining on the snow made it glitter and sparkle. It was too pretty a day to speak of such dark things.

Eat human flesh? I couldn't even say the words aloud.

"I have made my choice." My voice shook. I was as frightened as ever I had been. "I would rather die than eat such food. But—but—I beg you. Give me an easy death. Don't let me suffer." I turned and looked Mr. Keseberg full in the eyes. His face was grave, and still. "It is all I will ever ask of you."

But he would not.

"We have traveled so far together, and fought for our lives, and the lives of those we loved. I will not give up! I will not give in! Others made the choice. You know it, however much you might pretend you do not! They did it. So can we. I am going to live, whatever it takes, and you are, too!"

He took up a knife, and an ax, and led me outside.

The snow was melting faster each day. As it did, the bodies that had been buried had begun to appear; an arm sticking up from the surface one day, a foot, another. But the first body that had come full to the surface was that of Landrum Murphy.

His eyes were closed, and he simply looked to be asleep, although he was as white as the snow that had covered him. It was a terror to look at his still face.

"I cannot do it! I cannot! We must not do this thing!"

"We will! We must! His spirit is gone. What remains is nothing. Meat, that's all—no more than a deer, or a bear. If you cannot help me, then turn away; but I am determined.

"We will eat as heartily as we can this day. And tomorrow we will obtain more meat, and take it with us and leave. Mrs. Donner is not coming. I think she must be dead. If we are going to cross the mountain, we must do it while we still have the last remaining strength to do so. And we will cross the mountain, and arrive in California, and start our lives again." He took my hand in his. "Together, if you will have me."

I turned away from him. I took a deep breath, trying not to think how Landrum had pulled my hair and teased me, and the feel of his lips on mine.

Then I turned back. I would not make Mr. Keseberg undertake this dreadful deed alone.

Landrum was no more than a skeleton with skin covering the bones. There was no flesh on his limbs. The meat was on the inside—liver and lights, kidneys and brains and the marrowfat in the bones. To find it meant searching for it.

Mr. Keseberg lifted the ax above his head. Down it came with a splintering crunch, and Landrum's head fell apart in two pieces. Mr. Keseberg laid the ax aside. Reaching in with his hands, he pulled the brain free.

I drove my knife into the wasted, shriveled skin of Landrum's stomach. I sliced it across, and then another slice upward, and folded back the flesh to show a great mess of innards, white tubes all crammed together. I dug in with my hands and pulled the innards free, so they snaked across the snow.

Then I cut out Landrum's liver and kidneys, retching and gagging at the sight of them in my hands.

I cooked brain, kidneys, and liver with the marrowbones, using the last withered scraps of onions that remained in the sack, and the last spoonful of oatmeal; a pinch of salt and pepper. All against my will, my nose twitched with the smell of it cooking in the pot. When Mr. Keseberg ladled it out onto my plate, it was rich, with a dark gravy. I ate it. One plateful and then another. I could not help myself.

I lay awake all that night. Nearing dawn, I up and out of the cabin, and vomited into the snow.

Next morning, Mr. Keseberg took a knife and cut up the remains of the cooked, cold brain, and handed the plate to me. I took up a slice in my hand, smiling at him. When he was turned away, I dropped it back into the pot.

"We cannot leave without knowing what has become of Mrs. Donner. And I feel so very much stronger that I shall go to Alder Creek, and if she still lives, I will fetch her back with me.

"Do not come with me. It might be that our paths would cross, and she arrive in our camp, and we in hers. Stay here and rest your foot as much as you can." I took a deep breath. "You were right. About taking as much—meat—as possible, to see us on our way. While I am gone, you can get more.

"I promise you"—and I kissed him—"I give you my solemn vow. I will return."

But this last was a lie.

There was nothing for me in California. No family to welcome me. No home awaiting me. Nothing but to say good-bye to my last friend in the world, and continue on my own once more. For despite what Mr. Keseberg had said, and how, for just those few hours, I had chosen to believe him, I knew he did not mean it. He said it to deceive me, and to save me. For he loved his wife, I had seen it all along. He loved his child, too. And at the last, he would not leave them.

I had eaten that dreadful food once, and to no purpose. Come what may I could not eat it again.

41

I arrived at Alder Creek to find not a sight of Mrs. Donner. There was nothing but the sad remains of their camp: some little tents peeping above the snowline and within, a body wrapped in a sheet. The sun was shining down, and all was silence; not even a bird singing in the trees. A colder and emptier situation you could not imagine.

The minute we are born, Death sets out on his journey to greet us. I had determined to wait for him no more, but to set my steps to find him. But it would not be in this desolate place.

Beside me the creek went tumbling away downhill, swollen with snowmelt, and throwing little cascades of water into the air that glittered in the sun and threw colored rainbows into the air. And I set to follow it. I traced my footsteps back down the trail that we had climbed with such hope all those many months before. I walked all day, though hard going it was, stumbling as I made my way along and needing to rest often. But every slow step lightened my spirit, for here was life starting anew. A bird gave a sudden trilling cry, and was answered by another. Their song was echoed by a third, someplace in the distance. The dense forest gradually gave way to woodland and a soft haze showed where the fresh yellow leaves were unfurling in the sunshine. Here and there I saw green shoots thrusting through the snow, and I knelt down and brushed the snow away so that the brown earth beneath was discovered. A rabbit hopped across my path, taking no heed of me other than to pause for a moment, ears back and nose twitching, before deciding I was of no consequence and continuing his journey. I laughed aloud. The spring was returning at long last.

The sun was hot on my face, and presently I stopped to take a drink from the creek. There were some boulders that were free from the snow, and I sat here and rested. I was trembling from head to foot. I had no food, and no way of getting any. My plan was simple. I would walk onward until I could walk no more, and then I would find somewhere pretty and peaceful and make myself a bed for the night. I knew I would die. But I was ready. Death would be my friend, at the last.

I thought of Mr. Breen's prayer that he had said every day and that he had written down for me. I took the scrap of paper from my pocket and looked at the words, though I knew them pretty much by heart. Now I closed my eyes and said as much of it as I could remember, bowing my head and folding my hands. I said,

"Ever blessed and glorious Joseph, kind and loving father, and helpful friend of all in sorrow! You are the good father and protector of orphans, the defender of the defenseless, the patron of those in need and sorrow. Look kindly on my request. My sins have drawn down on me the just displeasure of my God, and so I am surrounded with unhappiness. To you, loving guardian of the Family of Nazareth, do I go for help and protection.

"Listen then, I beg you, with fatherly concerns, to my prayers and obtain for me the favors I ask."

It was a long prayer, and I said it all, slowly and with great thought over the words, thinking all the time of Heaven. Whether I would be accepted there, and whether the little children who had eaten that food, and the poor mothers who had been driven to give it to them—for the farther I walked away from the camp, the clearer my thoughts became, and I could see that Mr. Keseberg was right; there must have been more among us than I admitted, who had done so—whether those children and those mothers would find a home in Heaven after all their suffering and their dreadful sin. I thought we must. God would not be so cruel as to punish more, those who had suffered so much already. And being so truly sorry for what we were driven to must count in our favor.

"Oh, good Father! I beg you, by all your sufferings, sorrows, and joys, to hear me and obtain for me what I ask."

This was the point where you could ask for your wish to be granted. I had nothing to ask for except to die easy, and so I asked for that.

"Obtain for all those who have asked for my prayers everything that is useful to them in the plan of God. Finally, my dear Patron and Father, be with me, and all who are dear to me, in our last moments, that we may eternally sing the praises of Jesus, Mary, and Joseph."

I opened my eyes. The sun was as shining as ever; the creek still running with water; the trees rustling in the breeze. I climbed to my feet, and set off along the trail for the final time.

I rounded a bend, and there, in the shelter of some small trees, were five or six little tents. Standing in my path was an Indian girl carrying a basket filled with roots. She dropped it with a sharp cry, and two young men squatting at a fire stringing bows jumped to their feet and ran toward me.

I turned to flee, but my feet gave out beneath me. I sank to my knees and covered my eyes with my hands, and thought of St. Joseph answering my prayer.

The Indians did not kill me. They gave me a blanket made of strips of woven rabbit fur to wrap around me, and a mat to sleep on, and led me into one of the tents, and there I stayed, too weak to do more than sleep, and eat, and sleep again.

One afternoon the woven mat that covered the entrance to my tent was removed, and I was summoned forth. I emerged to find the men departed, and all the women standing round, waiting for me. At the front of them was what I thought must be a wisewoman, or some such; very old, with hair that was turned completely white, and hung in long, wispy braids over her shoulders. She wore a great necklace made from feathers and shells, and I remember thinking we must be a ways from the ocean, here, and wondering where the shells had come from, and that I had not seen her before, and wondering if she had been summoned especially to deal with me.

She showed me that I must take off my clothes, out there in the open. I had no shame, or no courage to resist, I know not which, but I did it without a second thought. There were gasps when I stood in front of them entirely naked. I knew what they saw: each rib showing near through my skin, and my belly sunk in.

My clothes were picked up on a stick, and carried to the far end of the clearing, where a fire had been lit, and they were dropped on it.

One of the girls brought a flat paddle of wood, which she used to scoop some grease from a small basket, and approached me with it. I stepped forward to take it, and she jumped back in alarm. It was clear that no one would come near me or touch me. I stood still, raising my hands to show that I meant no harm, and she leaned down and placed it on the ground in front of me, and then backed away, and showed me in gestures that I should rub this all over me, hair and all. It looked to be something like bear grease, and ashes perhaps with some green leaves pounded into it, and smelt about as bad as anything could.

When I had covered myself in it to their satisfaction, I was led to the creek and bidden, by signs, to wash myself. All through this the old woman squatted down at the creek edge, and sang a low song, with her eyes fixed on me all the time. When I was clean once more, and right glad to be so, I was bidden to step out of the water, and given some clothes: a skirt and a tunic, made from animal skin, and shoes made from woven grass and tied to my feet with strips of hide.

Other than the old woman's singing, all this had been conducted in silence, and then I was led back to my tent.

As I improved in health, I slept less. In the evenings I was given a place to sit, near enough to the fire but something away from them all. They shared out their food, each taking what they wished from a communal pot, but my food was set out on a woven platter and put down in front of me. I was with them, but no part of them.

I watched them. I reasoned that they could have killed me but instead had kept me, and fed me, and if they had meant me any harm it would have come earlier than this. All the same I was wary, waiting for trouble. I might not have spoke to them, nor they to me, but all the same I listened as hard as I might, intent on discovering their language and something of how they lived, and to see what was to become of me.

One night around the fire, there was a sudden shout of laughter from a little group of men, absorbed in some story of their own that they were telling over in low voices.

And one of them stepped into the firelight to share it with the rest of the group.

He engaged in playacting of a sort, with cowering and grimacing. Everyone roared with laughter, and then a young boy was pushed to his feet. He made his way into the center of the circle, where he was presented with three white owl feathers, and there was more laughing and pointing. With a shamefaced look and a laugh of his own, he accepted the feathers and stuck them into the braided leather strip that held back his hair, and returned to his seat, where he was clapped on the back by his neighbors.

To my surprise I found that I understood the entire story, not just the playacting part but some odd words here and there as well. He had been frightened by something in the woods and had made a great show of himself, but it was nothing more than an owl swooping out of a tree above his head.

That night, and the nights after, alone in my tent, I went over the words I understood, practicing them below my breath. By and by I came to understand a goodly part of what they said. They were travelers, moving from place to place and living upon what they found. This camp was only a resting place, and they were heading back the way I had come, up to the lake. They were only waiting for me to be rested and strong enough, and then we would move on.

Day by day the sun rose higher in the sky, and soon enough all the snow was gone. Seven weeks after I stumbled into their camp the Indians continued with their journey, and took me with them.

We traveled light, with just our sleeping mats and the rabbit skin blankets we slept in tied on our backs. As well as their bows and arrows, the men and boys carried the makings of our shelters: long poles that they carried between them on their shoulders, woven matting tied in rolls and slung on their backs, and coils of fiber slung over their shoulders. And the women carried baskets that contained our food: dried berries and meat, and flour made from acorns. This was made into flat cakes with the water from the creek, and roasted on hot stones. We ate it with a thick paste that tasted like it was made from onions.

We climbed back up through Alder Creek, and once again I looked upon the sad remnants of the Donners' camp.

Standing so forlorn in the sunshine were those pitiful little tents, still. And now I could see all the things that had been hidden away beneath the snow. There were broken sticks of furniture tumbled this way and that, and a scattered array of cooking pots and knives. Mrs. Donner's books were there, sodden and mashed into the dirt, and there were broken slates, and carpenter tools.

A wild dog growled at us over a pile of bones. I picked up a stone and flung it at him. He yelped, and scurried off into the shelter of the trees, his tail between his legs. Other than that, there was no sound, except for Mrs. Donner's wedding ring quilt, made, she once told me, with all the scraps from the girls' dresses, and now all torn and filthy, flapping in the breeze.

I stepped forward, thinking to fetch it away with me, and my foot crunched on something.

Beside me was a wooden crate broken open, like someone had been searching through it. I had stood on the contents, that were spilled over the ground. I bent down, and pulled back the lid a little. It was full of broken china, painted with pink roses—Mrs. Reed's teacups that had come from the emporium in New York City, and that she had been so mighty proud of, way back at the start of our journey. I thought they had been left behind when she lost her wagon in the desert, but I guess Mr. Reed had known what they meant to her and had rescued them. And then she had been determined to keep them at all costs, and had carried these teacups with her and put them into the Donners' wagon.

I hardly knew whether to laugh or cry at the foolish woman. Without knowing what I was doing, I fetched up one of those broken bits of teacup to my lips, and said, "Oh, what delicious water, your Ladyship!" in a squeaky voice, as if I was playing tea party again with little Ada and Margaret Eddy. Then I clutched that bit of painted china to my heart, and for the first and only time in all our hardships, tears come into my eyes and streamed down my face.

The Indians turned their eyes at me and then at one another. Then they led me away from that dreadful place, and we continued our journey up to the lake.

We made our camp at a place a long way from the cabins where I had spent so many dreadful days.

I stayed here with them for one day and night only. They did not intend to keep me with them, that much was clear. But just that one day and night I spent back at the lake was enough for me. It was just as beautiful as I remembered it. I saw again the hills reflecting in the calm water, and the soft wind sighing through the trees, and the pink and gold and violet of the evening sky. But as well, I could see that there was food in plenty, if we had but known it.

The women dug roots from the plants that grew along the margins of the lake to roast in the embers of the fire, and good eating they made. They gathered great handfuls of peppery-tasting leaves from the shallower reaches of the creek, where the water ran more gentle. Pinecones were picked apart to reveal soft white seeds, and long sections of bark were sliced from the living trees and split apart to reveal a layer of thin white flesh. This they roasted on hot stones around their fire until it was crisp. With that, and the fish the men caught, we ate full well.

I watched the men, marveling at how easy it was. They wove reeds together to make nets, and then one stood in the water to one side of the creek mouth, and another to the other side, and together they walked slowly to the bank. In this way they drove the fish before them, flapping in the water as they were forced back against their will. Someone else reached down with a deep basket and scooped up just enough fish for that night's meal, and the rest were let go, to live or die another day.

Again and again, my mind turned to our party, how we all of us sank into the greatest of despair, when, had we but known it, there was food for the taking, enough so that the babies and children might not have died calling for their mothers, in those long cold nights.

I ventured next morning to the edge of our camp. Here was the tumbledown remains of the lean-to where I had stayed with the Kesebergs, and the Breen cabin, now with the roof caved in.

I wondered whether this was where Mr. Keseberg had ended his days, waiting for my return, or if he had gone searching for me. Did he think to find me in the Murphy cabin at the end?—and was his body in there now with that of Mrs. Murphy's, both of them moldering away together, a dreadful thought.

Perhaps he had given up on waiting for me, and managed somehow to stay alive and get across the mountain in the end, to join his wife and child.

I knew he could not be there still. Even so, I called his name, gently like a whisper, half-dreading and half-hoping that he would walk out into the sunshine and stand before me, his hair all golden in the sun, as it was the very first time I saw him.

But he did not come. And I did not go and look for him.

42

Two of my Indian companions led me through the mountain and down the other side and into California. I had been in such mortal terror of the mountain, and yet now I walked up its steep slopes with no more fear than if I was walking along the street back home.

After a further day's traveling they pointed out a long, low building away in the distance. Then, without a word, they turned and vanished back the way they had come. And this is how I finally arrived at Sutter's Fort. Alone, in the early part of the summer, and in the clothes that those Washoe Indians had give me. My skin weathered and browned by the sun, and my hair darkened with oil and braided down my back.

I approached the place with great apprehension, not knowing what to say when I got there or what welcome would await me; turning over and over in my mind how I might explain myself, and wishing I could say nothing at all.

Sutter's Fort was a big place, a stockade with a great stone wall built round enclosing barns and stables and outhouses. It was a pretty rough place by the look of it, and right busy, with folks coming and going, mostly men, and some Indians here and there, but there was a family or two, as well. Just as I approached the entrance, a couple of carts rolled up, accompanied by a little knot of people and a string of heavily laden mules. I walked along with them, keeping my head down, and passed through the big wooden gates pretty much unnoticed, I guess.

Inside the walls it was something like a small marketplace. There was a blacksmith over in one corner with horses tied up to the hitching rail waiting to be shod, and a pretty bay mare being walked about by a prospective purchaser who was feeling her legs and looking at her teeth. There was a dry goods store, and beside it a wagon drawn up with a woman selling garden produce. Squatting on the ground were a couple of Indians with blankets and baskets set out for trade. They were Washoe, but not folks I had seen before, and I kept my distance from them.

I cast about me, trying to decide what to do or where to go. Near me was a respectable-looking man with his wife and child, all dressed decent and sober enough, saying that they were intending to get their dinners in the servery. Across the yard I saw there was a doorway open with a couple chairs and tables set outside, and I made up my mind that this is what I would do, too. I would take the money that had traveled with me from Cincinnati, and buy myself some dinner, and sit and eat it while I decided what to do next.

Buy myself some dinner! It was a little passing thought that popped itself into my head as if it was nothing, but it grew and grew, blotting out the mutter of conversations around me and the ring of the blacksmith's hammer, and the clop of the horses' hooves.

The blood pounded in my ears. Buy myself some dinner! I could make no sense of it. It seemed easy and impossible, both at once. That thought was followed by another. Here I was in the middle of strangers, none of them hungry and all, seemingly, in the best of health, concerning themselves with such everyday tasks as shoeing horses and purchasing corn. I had money in my pocket and food all around me, just as it was the day I left Cincinnati; and now, just the same as then, no one in the least bit concerned about me, and caring nothing for what had befallen me. These folks went about their business as if I wasn't there at all, stepping around me and looking straight through me. It made me want to shout at them,

"Hey! Don't you know who I am? Don't you want to know where I've been, and what's happened to me?"

It was as if all that time between leaving Cincinnati and being here had never existed at all. For a mad moment I thought perhaps I had dreamed it all. This made me feel so peculiar that I had to find a place to sit down in the shade, and take a few deep breaths.

Eventually, and feeling something more collected, I crossed the courtyard and went in at the servery door. It was a plain room with a half dozen tables and benches to sit at, and a counter at back. Behind the counter was a door, which I guessed led into the kitchen. I sniffed the air for what was cooking, my mouth watering at the thought of what I might eat. Ham and cream gravy with fried potatoes, perhaps, and even a slice or two of apple pie.

But what a disappointment!—there was no food to be had. For Sutter's cook had been killed in a knife fight just the night before, and Mr. Sutter was turning folks away, pretty mad to have to do so, I could see.

I stayed put as the other folks left, and when it was just me and Mr. Sutter, he gave me a quick, angry look.

"You can vamoose as well, girl; go on, git!"

I stared at him. It struck me that I hadn't spoke a word to another living soul for weeks, and I wasn't sure if I could, now.

A crafty look come over Mr. Sutter's face. "You alone, girl?"

I looked quite blank, wondering why he wanted to know and what I should reply. He grabbed my arm, and hustled me over to the counter. He picked up the coffeepot, and poured out a cup of coffee, and then pointed at it, and then at me.

"You pour out the coffee and give folks a piece of pie"—pointing at a pie dish that had some sorry remains of something in it—"and I pay you—look—" He held up a coin and mimed again, coffee, pie, coin. "Understand?"

I nodded, and picked up the coffeepot and poured a cup, and pointed to the pie, acting dumb.

So there I was, with a corner to sleep in, in exchange for pouring coffee and baking pies. I guess if anyone had known the sort of food I'd cooked previous, those pies would have had a different flavor altogether. Just as well that they did not.

I came down off the mountain and into California to discover that the tale of our sufferings was being churned over by every person who came along: the fur trappers and the loggers from the north, and the travelers that arrived from the East; the Mexicos that came up from the south, and the rag, tag, and bobtail of everyone else in the district who stopped in to trade.

They'd arrive at Sutter's and stay a night or two, and sit over their coffee and pie or set themselves down outside with their tobacco, and talk us up a storm.

All had their own opinion of what had taken place, and none had the slightest understanding of what we suffered. Each tale was more cruel and judging than the last, and there were dreadful jests made, too, that stabbed me to the heart upon hearing them.

It never occurred to any that the scowling silent Washoe girl pouring their coffee could be an opinionated

Cincinnati girl come out of the mountains, and even less that I could be part of that very story that was adding such spice to their biscuits and creamed corn and gravy.

I soon came to be right thankful that I had taken note of what Mrs. Donner had told Elitha and Leanna, to keep quiet about their time in the mountain. It seemed I was the only one who had the great good sense to keep my mouth shut. Along with all the rest of the folks that crowded the fort, there were newspaper writers, like to a plague of rats, their eyes darting this way and that and noses twitching for a juicy morsel of gossip.

They were on the lookout for stories of what they called the "Donner Party Angels." I came to understand that a newspaper with a likeness of any of my friends sold hundreds upon hundreds of copies, but if that likeness was of a pretty girl, to make a man feel sentimental, or a poor orphan child, to make a mother's eyes fill with tears, why then those hundreds of newspapers turned into thousands, right across the whole country.

Much as I came to despise these newspaper accounts, nevertheless it is how I found out news of my friends: who survived and who perished in their journey across the mountain.

All I knew of the Snowshoes party was from Mr. Eddy's few words: that many of them had perished, noble Mr. Stanton among them, and of Mr. Foster's behavior. It was a right shock now to read the accounts of their suffering and how they survived.

The Snowshoes, with Mr. Eddy and Mr. Foster leading them, had got lost crossing the mountain. So rather than take a week or so to get to help, as we had all expected, it had taken them more than a month.

The reason they had got lost was very simple: It was that they had abandoned Mr. Stanton, their guide. Mr. Stanton, the best and kindest man who had ever lived, and who had come back through the mountain when he did not need to, in order to bring us food and save us.

But yes, the minute he had faltered they'd turned their backs on him and left him to die, utterly alone, and marched off on their way without a backward glance.

This had left them with the other two guides, the Mexicos, Luis and Salvatore. Did the Snowshoes think, we must look after them at all costs, for they are our salvation? No, indeed. Mr. Foster shot them both dead in cold blood, for the sole purpose of eating their flesh.

Each newspaper account was more bloodthirsty than the last. I know—who better?—that folks will do anything, anything! when it comes down to live or die. To commit cold-blooded murder to do it must surely be the most evil deed of all; but even then it was committed in such extremity that perhaps I could understand it. But to boast of such depravity! To sell such an account to the newspapers and receive coin for speaking of what was done! That is beyond all my comprehension. And who was the person who boasted of these deeds the most, and saw them written in the newspapers, and received coin in his hand for it?

Why, Mr. Eddy of course.

43

How I escaped attention I do not know. I guess the folks at Sutter's, and that included the newspaper folks, considered me just a Washoe girl, and never thought to ask how I came to be there; but I wondered that, in all his accounts, Mr. Eddy did not mention my name.

Perhaps he believed me dead, or wished me so, at least. He knew me to have a sharp and mocking tongue. If the newspapers had found me, I would have called him a liar and made him look a fool, and he wouldn't want to risk that. For Mr. Eddy was the newspapers' darling, telling ludicrous tales of his bravery; and I have no doubt that the tales he told grew mightily in the telling, and that for every account I read, in the few newspapers that I came across, there were a dozen more in others. As time went on, Mr. Eddy's lies and half-truths and exaggerations passed into hard cold fact, and came to be accepted as truth, as far as folks who knew no better were concerned.

About three weeks after I got to Sutter's Fort, Mr. Fallon arrived. He was a great, rough bear of a man, with a heavy black beard, and a right coarse way of speaking. He was hailed as a hero, and made much of, for it turned out that only a few days after I left our camp, Mr. Fallon had arrived in it. He had it that he had set out to rescue Mr. Keseberg and Mrs. Donner, but I did not believe it. I thought it more likely that he and his fellows, a band of ruffians to be sure, had gone over the mountain in order to plunder what was left of the possessions that folks had left behind them. With them had gone, yet again, Mr. Foster.

Mr. Foster! I could not believe it. He was the kindest, most loyal of men when we began our journey, but after the death of Mr. Pike, all feeling for friends and family had turned into the most monstrous cruelty; in the end, to murder and cannibalism. Surely he would be the one person who would want to travel as far away from his crimes as he could? Yet he returned to the scene of his suffering again, and then again, as a rabid dog eats its own filth.

As I write my journal I think I see what drove him to it.

When I arrived at Sutter's Fort and stood in the courtyard and thought, for one mad moment, that no time had passed since leaving Cincinnati, and that I had been asleep and dreamed the rest, I found such comfort in the thought that I held it to me. It was a dream, no more. And it was over. I was awake, and at last I could carry on with a normal, everyday sort of life and never think on it again.

Mrs. Donner had said, "Never speak of what has happened to us."

And I added in words of my own. "Never think of it. Ignore it all. Pretend it never happened."

I turned my mind away from it then, and after, with the absolute power of my will. Yet still I dreamed of it, night after night; I dream of it still. I wake at dawn to find Jacob lying silently beside me, and I choke with terror, thinking him a corpse. Or wake in the dark with a start, and think to see Mrs. Murphy standing in a corner of the room, staring at me. And I weep for the horror of what I might see if I light the candle.

I write my journal knowing my words to be true. But even as I write them I do not believe them. I say to myself, "It cannot possibly have been as cold as I remember it! It cannot have been so desperate, surely?" And I ask myself, "Why did we do this thing, why did we not do that?"

I long to go back, and make it come right in the end. But I cannot turn back the clock, and save those who died, no matter how many times I do so in my imagination.

I am sure that all of us who came out of the mountain have suffered so—all of us close to madness in one way or another. Perhaps different folks deal with it in different ways; I by waking in the small hours, night after night, year after year, to count how many sacks of flour I have and how many of beans.

Perhaps something of this was true for Mr. Foster. Maybe he thought that by traveling back through the snow yet again, and looking once more upon the poor little cabins, the remnants of our cooking fires, and the sad little bits of belongings that were abandoned there, the outcome would somehow be different, and he would find some peace.

Did it help Mr. Eddy to recount it, over and over? And Jean Trudeau, the lad who stayed with Mrs. Donner? For he is the same; one story follows another in the newspapers, and each contradicts the last. Even the children who were too small to remember much at all, why, they too have accounts written up. I wonder, have these children grown up in the shadow of their parents' obsession and grief? Why else would these children bear that same terrible burden on their shoulders?

I stayed as far away from Mr. Fallon as I could, looking at him out of the corner of my eye. I wondered what he knew of me. And I longed to know what had befallen Mr. Keseberg. I was soon to find out.

Next morning when I walked into the servery carrying the coffeepot in one hand and a dish of ham and grits in the other, it was to find a mess of folks talking most excited, waving newspapers round in the air and passing them from hand to hand. Mr. Fallon was in the center of this little group, holding forth to all who would listen. I was sickened to my stomach by what I heard. His words were read from the newspaper and shouted round the room, and as he listened, he nodded. "Aye," he said, "that is true, and that is what I saw."

For set out that day in the *California Star* newspaper was what was said to be his journal, that he wrote up while he was traveling to our camp and when he was there. It could not possibly have been true. Mr. Fallon was an uneducated villain of a man who could not write even his own name, and the thought of him sitting down with pen and paper to write up this account was beyond belief. Yet here were his very words, or so the newspaper would have us believe.

It said that he had arrived in the camp to find Mr. Keseberg sat gloating over a pot full of innards, and swearing up and down, with a ghastly smile of good cheer, that such food was so delicious he would rather eat it a thousand times than any other good meat; and that the meat was taken from the body of Mrs. Donner.

A further account of Mr. Fallon's actions was read out, and to cheers from his fellows and much slapping on the back he agreed with all: that he had tortured Mr. Keseberg.

He threatened to leave him behind to die. Next, that he would kill him there and then. One time he set upon him with his bare hands round his throat. He poured water over his head, while a fellow held him down on the ground so that Mr. Keseberg was close to drowning; and he half-strangled him with a rope at another. Two days passed in this way, with Mr. Keseberg begging for his life, pissing himself for fear, and crying in the most abject misery.

All this was done in order to force Mr. Keseberg to reveal where money was buried and to aid Mr. Fallon in his search for jewels and the rest. Mr. Fallon eventually forced Mr. Keseberg to strip naked, and searched his clothes. Here he had found a good sum of money, and had pocketed it, to bring it back, he said, to the children of those that Mr. Keseberg had robbed.

I knew that this was Mr. Keseberg's own money—the money he had brought with him to purchase his land and set up his vineyard. This man had stolen it, and left Mr. Keseberg destitute. And I did not believe for one moment that it had ever got farther than Mr. Fallon's own pocket.

Every word was greeted with whoops and hollers and shouts of encouragement. For the *California Star* had also published yet another account—this by Mr. Eddy. And Mr. Eddy's account had made out Mr. Keseberg to be such a monster that his torture at Mr. Fallon's hand was felt to be justified.

Mr. Eddy had given an account of his own arrival in our camp with Mr. Foster, the day after the deaths of poor little James and George. Did it tell of our hideous suffering, and the way in which Mr. Foster deserted his kindly mother-in-law and left her to die, alone but for the kindness and mercy of Mr. Keseberg? Did it tell the tale of how the little Donner girls were left in Mr. Keseberg's charge, when the men supposed to rescue them had abandoned them?

It did not. Rather, it said in plain black print that Mr. Keseberg "took a child of about four years of age in bed with him, and devoured the whole before morning; and the next day ate another about the same age before noon."

These words were what Mr. Fallon repeated to the room now. It was evident that he had learned them by heart.

At this, a great roar went up. The call for coffee was forgot, and whisky demanded instead. Someone shouted out that Mr. Keseberg was in charge of Mr. Sutter's riverboat, and would be here himself in just a few days' time, and then they should set upon him once more and get the truth from him! That he should have been hanged for what he did! And if the law wouldn't do it, why, they would do it themselves! And more whisky was drunk, and then more again.

If I had been afraid of discovery before, why, my fears then were nothing to what I imagined now. I thought of Mr. Keseberg arriving, to be set upon by this pack of animals and dragged into the courtyard and murdered in front of me.

One glance between us and I would be discovered. It took no imagination to see how my part in this story would sound; that we bedded together, rutting like animals in the filthy darkness of that cabin alongside the dead bodies of our companions. How we indulged in our gruesome feasting, gnawing on the bones of dead infants and surrounded by the skulls of dead children.

I flew out of the servery, and ran to my bed and crouched there, panting like a cornered animal, thinking to collect my things and run away; but where could I go? How would I live? For I was in trouble, the kind of trouble that could not be concealed from the world for many weeks longer.

My fear gave way to the blackest despair, such that I thought it would be easier to walk myself into the river than live another day in such misery.

44

The very next day, Jacob came in to trade.

If I was writing one of the dime novels that old Peabody sells in the mercantile, and that I sometimes read in the evenings, when the children are asleep and Jacob is in his study scratching away at his accounts (and which I don't precisely hide from my husband, but I don't exactly wave about beneath his nose, neither, for he would tease me for reading such trash), I would write that our eyes met and I fell into a swoon, and that he took but one look at me and was instantly, and hopelessly, in love with me that minute.

It was not at all the case. I noticed him because he was trying to trade with the Indians, half in English and half in German, and making a poor fist of it altogether. Since I spoke something of their language and German, too, it seemed natural for me to lose patience with his stuttering speech and sort out the matter for him.

I don't know who was the more surprised, Mr. Sutter at hearing a silent Indian girl speaking German—and then English, with an unmistakable Cincinnati twang—

or Jacob, when he looked at me proper, with my green eyes and my height, and my hair. I'd left off braiding it with oil, so it wasn't black at all, but just a plainish light brown. Jacob knew me straight out for a white girl, and not Washoe at all. I could have bitten out my tongue for being so foolish. A silent Washoe girl working in the servery was more or less invisible, but now I had made such a mistake that I had put myself in the gravest danger.

I have never ceased to wonder what made me do it, when I had been so very careful and was so very frightened. I can reach only one conclusion. That I knew, the instant I clapped eyes upon him, that I could trust him.

He was a deal older than me, a widower, with two grown sons joined up into the Navy. A short, stout man with graying hair, not well featured at all and not sharp-dressed or flash with his gold. But I could see he was a kind man, and dealt honestly with all, and well respected. We had a few conversations here and there, and even in my misery and terror, we made each other laugh.

Jacob left Sutter's after two days, to travel into the mountains to sort out some business to do with felling the oak trees that grew in great abundance on the western foothills. On his return he stepped in to see me. I heaped his plate with beef stew and greens and a slice or two of corn bread, and brought him a good helping of applesauce with a piece of buttered pound cake, and kept an eye on him as he ate. When he had finished, and sat back in his chair, searching his pockets for his pipe and tobacco, I took across two cups of coffee and sat down with him.

I asked him, straight out, "Sir, will you take me with you as your servant?" I could see that his plate was empty. "Didn't you enjoy your dinner? And was the dessert good?" For again, it was all vanished.

"You can see that I can cook," I said. "I will keep a

good house for you, and be honest in all my dealings, and I ask no more than a room to sleep in and food upon the table."

"No," he said.

My heart sank to my boots. I had talked myself into believing he would take me, and I had not thought beyond this chance.

"I do not need a servant, for my sons are grown and gone. I am alone, and I live in one room at my lumberyard and eat in with the yard hands. But"—and he turned a fine shade of red—"I will build you a fine house and care for you, if you will do me the great honor of becoming my wife."

I did not love him. To marry without love, I thought, was no more than a way of earning my keep on my back, and made me no better than my ma, and the other wharfside whores. What I wanted was honest employment, where I would earn my own money for a day's labor. But I could see that I had no choice, though I thought, even then, that I owed it to him to deal fair with him or not at all. So with a shaking voice and my eyes to the floor, I told him of my trouble.

He reached across and took my hand.

"Yes, my dear, I know of it. I have been married before and have two children of my own, and you are not as good at concealing secrets as you might think. But it makes no difference to me. And another thing"—and here, he looked anywhere but at me, and turned an even darker shade of red, if such a thing were possible—"another thing. I know not what you were doing before you came here, and if you wish to tell me you may. But I will never ask."

I looked him straight in the eye.

"Sir, I cannot say. But I promise you it was nothing deceitful, and caused no harm to any living being." He nodded. My word was enough for him.

And with that my fate was sealed. I promised to care for him and keep him, and honor him. And I swore to myself, that I would do nothing to harm him. For these thirteen years, I have kept that promise. He has been everything I expected: a decent man.

I thought myself grateful to him. There have been times when I have been sad that I cannot look at him and have my heart turn over with the passion and longing I once dreamed of. But even though I did not marry for love, it has grown within me over the years. I love this kind man, who has given me my house and my yard, my little town and my church and my neighbors. And my children, most of all.

But this happiness is itself a kind of misery.

For this is Mr. Eddy's heroic deed. To have assisted in making Mr. Keseberg's name the byword for depravity across our entire Nation. And to leave me in the very greatest of fear, beyond all fear that can be known, that one day my secret will be discovered. And then my husband will look at me with new eyes, and my happy life will be over.

45

This is a book of darkness. It is what lies within my heart, and no one knows of it but me. I carry it with me always, this tale of death and despair.

I clothe it in homespun, darn it into stockings, bake it into apple pies, dig it into my vegetable plot, take it to church with me. The summer sky reminds me of it, and the fall wind that whistles down from the mountains; and the snow, worst of all.

It hardly ever snows here, and I thank God for it.

I draw a neat line beneath these words and put down my pen, and stare into the fire for a moment, thinking; yes, it is a terrible story. A story of such suffering that it haunts me, day and night, and will stay with me until I die.

But in writing my journal I have remembered something else: the happy times we had. To outside eyes our little company might seem to have argued and fought its way across the great Continent of America; and a deal of that is true. But I had not grown up knowing such love and kindness as I did on our terrible journey, and it is a sobering thought.

I pick up my pen again.

At the bottom of the page, I write,

"This is a true account of my journey with the Donner Party."

I sign my name. My real name, the one I was known by on that journey and before I married Jacob; and the date, November 6, 1860.

I rise heavily to my feet, and take my journal into our bedroom. I lock it, for the last time, with the key that hangs around my neck on its silver chain. And I take the chain from around my neck, and place it with the journal, my pink kerchief, my silver dollars, Mrs. Donner's drawing of bluebells, and Leanna's lock of hair, under the floorboard beneath the bed.

November 6, 1860; the day of the presidential election. Today it will be decided: the fate of our Nation.

Although the new Township Hall will not be completed until the spring, elections have already been held for the council members. Jacob is to be the township officer, which is a great honor. As such, he is away all day helping to supervise the ballot, which is being held at the Dining Rooms on Main Street. It should be held at the local courthouse, but we don't possess such a thing in our town. Disputes here are mostly settled by Sheriff Jackson—those that have not already been settled by a fistfight.

It is expected to be exceedingly busy. Jacob tells me that the sheriff will be standing by with a couple of deputies, for there might be some trouble, given what strong opinions folks have.

With a perfectly straight face—but despite himself, a smile in his voice—he adds that it is a good job the mem-

bers of the Ladies' Quilting Bee will not be attending the vote. News of our screeching and screaming and the subsequent imbibing of spirits spread through the town like wildfire, no doubt by Mrs. Gerald's doing.

Jacob and the other officials have a fine dinner planned for after the ballot is closed and the papers locked safely away. I doubt he will be back until well after dark. With no supper to cook for him, and an hour or so before the children arrive home from school, I think to rest for a while.

I lower myself onto the bed, and pull the quilt over me. The new baby kicks inside me. The dust motes swirl in the thin afternoon sunshine. I watch them for a while, my eyes heavy.

The trees have turned color and the leaves begun to drop. It is a blessing to welcome these days of crisp mornings, the nights turning cool at long last. Some things have changed in our town.

Mr. McGillivray, whose children came to school at the beginning of the year in rags and bare feet, struck lucky with his gold claim after all these long years. He came into town looking for land to buy and wishing to build himself a great house to show off his wealth. Jacob accepted the commission to build the house, and I managed to persuade him to sell Mr. McGillivray the land over at the lake.

When the McGillivray house is finished, Jacob will start on ours. I gave in to his dream of a grand house when I realized that four children in one room was an impossibility; but Jacob has agreed for us to stay here, and has purchased the woodland that butts onto our land at the back, so he can add to what we already have. He is thrilled with the notion that at long last he will be getting his beloved wraparound porch and fancy balustrades and the rest.

I am thankful that I will not lose my garden, though my

view across the pasture is something spoiled. The land has been purchased by some farm people. They have fenced it round and ploughed up the violets and poppies and tall grasses, and are hard at work planting rows of orange trees.

As I expected, a new schoolteacher arrived at the start of October, formally appointed by the school board. She is something young and from a smart college back East and full of modern ideas about education for women. Even though school has only been back a few weeks, she has already filled Meggie's head with notions about applying to go away to college herself, when she turns sixteen.

I wish with all my heart that my clever girl should do something wonderful with her life, but the thought of her traveling back East and leaving me behind is almost more than I can bear. Like many things, I keep that thought to myself. Meggie is thrilled at the prospect, and Jacob mighty proud of her, and beginning to put aside the money to pay for it.

I have no need of Martha now, with so much time on my hands. She did not marry her young man, Simon Cooke. He left his employment at the blacksmithery and went off to join the railroad company. There has been some talk these months past of building a railroad that will enable a journey all the way from the East Coast to the West in a matter of days. Nothing is decided, and Jacob says it will be years, perhaps, before this plan comes to anything. But in the meantime the railroad company decided to carry out some work to see if it would be possible to open up a pass through the mountain range. They came recruiting for laborers, and I guess Simon Cooke thought to earn a good wage with them; he needed to provide not only for Martha when they married but also his widowed mother and his two little sisters. But he was killed in an accident when they were blasting with dynamite.

Martha finds herself in a poor fix, now, with a child on the way and no husband. She has stayed living at home with her mother, who makes her life a misery, or so I hear.

Mr. Sahid's lending library has done well, though his store did not. It seems that few folks share my love of exotic foods and spices. So Mr. Sahid cleared out the shop space and turned it into an office, with a desk and a printing press, and now we have a town newspaper.

Folks have been quick to step up with a story or two for print. First of all was an account given by Mr. McGillivray about his years spent working his mine claim, and how it felt to strike it rich at long last. Some folks think of his story as boastful pride in his new money, and I doubt his wife is so pleased to see her name in print, with a description of their privations and how their children suffered. But the story sold a number of newspapers and I guess Mr. Sahid was thrilled with the success of his new venture.

It seems to have given him the idea for a series of articles about leading figures in the town, and he stops me one day when I am passing on my way to the mercantile, saying that he would like to write up something about Jacob. Would I ask him to step into Mr. Sahid's office one day, when it is convenient? Of course, I will not.

I do not use the lending library anymore, and miss it greatly. And I walk a different route to the mercantile now, and avoid speaking to Mr. Sahid if I can.

"Mama?"

I open my eyes.

Meggie is standing beside me, holding Clara by the hand. Hannah is there, too. Meggie, bless the child, has given the little ones their supper. Their hair is neatly braided and their faces scrubbed, ready for bed.

I must have slept a long time. The sun has gone. The

room is shadowed and dim, and the evening air strikes chill. Meggie crosses to the dresser, and lights the oil lamp that stands there. Its gentle light blooms around her and I see how her eyes are the purple-blue of the anemones that grow at the feet of my rosebushes, and her hair corn-color. My lovely girl, slim and tall and as unlike her sisters as can be, for Clara and Hannah are two sweet little dumplings of girls, with their father's mild blue eyes and silvery fair hair that shades to a mousy brown in the winter.

"We want you to read to us, Mama," says Hannah, holding out the Grimms' Book of Fairy Tales *that Jacob's family sent for her birthday. Meggie takes my hand, and helps me to my feet and we set off to their room, with the girls' new little kitten, Bertie, whisking up the stairs ahead of us.*

Clara and Hannah climb into bed and I sit beside them. Bertie jumps up and walks round and round in a circle, kneading the covers until they are to his liking, and Meggie perches herself at the foot of the bed, unwilling to forgo a story at bedtime, no matter how grown up she considers herself.

Clara turns over the pages of the book until she finds the right page, and Meggie sighs.

"Not that one again! Clarrie, I have heard this story more times than I can count!" Clara ignores her, and sticks her thumb in her mouth, a habit I cannot cure, no matter how much bitter aloe juice I paint on it.

I sigh myself, and take a breath, and begin to read. "The story of the twelve dancing princesses. Once upon a time there were—"

"Wait, Mama!" cries Hannah. "We haven't chosen our dresses yet!"

She and Clara turn to the color plate of all twelve princesses in a variety of colorful gowns, and huddle together picking out which they would like to be. Hannah wishes to be the princess in the gold dress, and Clara in red. I am to be in blue, and Meggie in green.

When that is settled, I continue with the story. "Each night their father, the king, locks them in their room in the castle to keep them from harm's way. But each morning the servants find a pair of worn-out dancing shoes at the foot of each bed."

"What a mystery!" I say, widening my eyes at the girls. Clara takes her thumb out of her mouth long enough to giggle.

"So," I continue, "the king offers a reward to any brave man who can solve the mystery. If he does, he can marry one of the princesses. And if he doesn't . . . ?"

"He will have his head chopped off!" cries Clara, gleefully.

Hannah frowns at this. She has a very strong sense of what is fair and what is not, and feels that the punishment is something unjust. "You shouldn't be punished if you do your best but it doesn't work," she says virtuously, and I smile to hear my own words repeated back to me.

"One day," I continue, "a poor, weary soldier passes by the castle. As a young man he set out to see the world, but he has been journeying a long time. Now he thinks he would like to lay down his sword and have a home of his own. He sees one of the princesses and falls in love with her, and decides he must solve the mystery so he can marry her and live happily ever after in the castle.

"Now, he is lucky enough to own a cloak that makes him invisible when he puts it round himself. That night he wraps himself up in his invisibility cloak, thinking it to be a fine thing that will allow him to go where he likes and do as he pleases, and all the while keep him safe from discovery.

"He goes and stands beneath the window of the princesses' room. Just as the clock strikes midnight, he hears

music begin to play in the distance. The window opens and all the princesses climb out down a silken ladder. Then they set off to dance their way through the forest, following the sound of the music.

"The soldier is as enchanted as they are, and can't help his feet from dancing along behind them. They arrive at a magic palace all made of silver and glittering precious stones. The soldier follows them into the ballroom, but a terrible thing happens: As soon as he enters the ballroom the door slams shut behind him and he is trapped.

"He thinks at first to hide, but there is nowhere, for the room is small and crowded, and the music makes him want to dance so he cannot stand still. And now he is very frightened. As he dances the princesses might see his feet peeping out from beneath the cloak; or maybe one of them will dance too close and catch the cloak as she passes and pull it from him and he will be discovered.

"The cloak that he had thought to give him the freedom to do as he likes and go where he pleases and no one catch him, turns into a prison. He cannot take it off, and must spend all his time making sure he stays safe inside it.

"The poor soldier passes the night in great fear, jumping out of the way as the princesses dance round him, and dodging from this side of the room to that, hopping and skipping as he goes but all the time frightened that the princess he loves so much will find him out, and then she will be very angry that he has been so deceitful, and then all his dreams of marrying her will come to nothing."

"And he will still have his head chopped off!" says Clara with satisfaction.

"Yes," I say. "I suppose he will have his head chopped off."

"Poor soldier," says softhearted Hannah. "I expect he wishes he never had that cloak."

"No, indeed," I say. "He thought that hiding under the

cloak would keep him safe, but it put him in worse danger still. I daresay he wishes he had left well alone, and never clapped eyes on that beautiful princess, but just carried on with his soldiering and gone to some other place, far away where no one knew of him. But he didn't.

"When the dawn comes the magic palace vanishes away and those princesses, carrying their dancing shoes that are quite worn-out, go home and go to bed, very tired to be sure. And the soldier tells the king the mystery is solved and he marries the princess, and they all live happily ever after."

No matter how many times I tell this story, Hannah is always outraged at the ending. I suspect she thinks that one day I will tell the story with a different ending, but of course I cannot. Now she sits bolt upright in bed, frowning.

"I don't think they could have been very happy if that princess ever found out that she was married to someone who would be so deceitful and play such a nasty trick on her and her sisters! I think it would be a better story if he was found out and all the princesses shouted at him!"

"And threw stones at him and then pushed him into the lake!" adds Clara for good measure.

I laugh a little at my daughters, looking so angelic and sounding so bloodthirsty, and stoop to kiss them both good night.

Meggie and I make our way back down the stairs and into the parlor, where Meggie sets herself down at the little table and bends her head over her homework.

I plump up the cushions in Jacob's chair, and I sit myself, and gaze into the fire, thinking of the children's story. I wonder if that soldier would one day tell the truth of the matter—how he came there and what he had done.

Would he conclude that the relief of laying down the heavy burden of his secret was worth the risk of losing all? And would he say to that princess, whom he loved so dearly, that he wished for something more; that he needed to make his mark on the world, and if she truly loved him she would set out with him on his journey once more?

I think of Jacob, saying to me, "I will never ask."

I do not have to tell him.

But I think I will.

Author Notes

Mr. Fallon's Account of the Fourth Relief

The following is an account of the Fourth Relief, which headed into the mountains in April 1847, seven months after the settlers first arrived in their final camp.

The chance of finding anyone alive at this point was virtually nil. In reality, the Fourth Relief was a salvage operation, with the members of the party taking a sizeable cut of whatever goods they managed to recover. With no national banking system in operation, emigrants would have taken all their money with them in the shape of gold coin, jewelry, or other valuables, often sewn into clothing or concealed in secret compartments built into the wagon structure. Rumors abounded that those in the Donner Party who had lost their wagons had taken their valuables with them, and buried them at the lake camp.

The leader of the party, William Fallon, was a rough mountain man, and it is highly improbable that he was educated enough to have written what is purported to be a journal of his expedition to the camp. The Fourth Relief Diary also contains a number of factual errors, and was more likely to have been written up by a journalist, so should be read with a very critical eye.

* * *

California Star, June 5, 1847

EXTRACTS from a JOURNAL
Written by a Member of the Party
Latest from the California Mountains

The extracts which we give below are full of thrilling interest. Mr. Fellun the writer, better known as "Capt. Fellun," set out from the settlements in April last with six others, to extend relief to the remaining sufferers of the emigration, still within the mountains, and also to collect and secure the scattered property of both living and dead. He succeeded in reaching the cabins, and with the exceptions of Kiesburg not a soul survived. They returned, bringing with them this man, and large packs of valuable property. Kiesburg was found in truly a lamentable situation: a long subsistence upon the bodies of his deceased comrades had rendered him haggard and ferocious-looking, and the unsatiable appetite of the cannibal displayed itself on frequent occasions, even after animal meat have been placed before him. This fondness for human flesh he had suffered himself to acquire in preference to the beef or horse meat of which he had an abundance. And it is to be feared that his conduct in the mountains was far from justifiable, and a hidden transaction of guilt remains yet to be brought to light.

We commend the diary as being a plain though well written document, and we have published it in the writer's own language, abating nothing from it in point of interest. Mr. Fellun certainly deserves credit for his management of the affair, as it will be seen that he effected the desirable end.

"Left Johnsons on the evening of April 13th, and arrived at the lower end of the Bear River valley on the 15th. Hung our saddles upon the trees, and sent the horses back, to be returned again in ten days, to bring us in again. Started on foot, with provisions for ten days, and traveled to the head of the valley, and encamped for the night; snow from two to three feet deep. Started early in the morning of the 15th, and traveled twenty-three miles; snow ten feet deep.

April 17th. Reached the cabins between 12 and 1 o'clock. Expected to find some of the sufferers alive, Mrs. Donner and Kiesburg in particular. Entered the cabins, and a horrible scene presented itself—human bodies terribly mutilated, legs, arms and sculls scattered in every direction. One body, supposed to be that of Mrs. Eddy, lay near the entrance, the limbs severed off, and a frightful gash in the skull. The flesh was nearly consumed from the bones, and a painful stillness pervaded the place. The supposition was, that all were dead, when a sudden shout revived our hopes and we flew in the direction of the sound. Three Indians, who had been hitherto concealed, started from the ground and fled at our approach, leaving their bows and arrows. We delayed two hours in searching the cabins, during which we were obliged to witness sights from which we would have fain turned away, and which are too dreadful to put on record. We next started for Donners' camp, eight miles distant over the mountains. After traveling about halfway, we came upon a track in the snow which excited our suspicion, and we determined to pursue it. It brought us to the camp of Jacob Donner, where it had evidently left that morning. There we found property of every description, books, calicoes, tea, coffee, shoes, percussion caps, household and kitchen furniture, scattered in every direction, and mostly in the water. At the mouth of the tent stood a large iron kettle, filled with human flesh, cut up. It was from the body of George Donner. The head had been split open, and the brains extracted therefrom, and to the appearance, he had not been long dead—not over three or four days, at the most. Near by the kettle stood a chair, and thereupon three legs of a bullock that had been shot down in the early part of the winter, and snowed upon before it could be dressed. The meat was found sound and good, and with the exception of a small piece out of the shoulder, wholly untouched. We gathered up some property, and camped for the night.

April 18—commenced gathering the most valuable property, suitable for our packs, the greater portion requiring to be dried. We then make them up, and camped for the night.

April 19—this morning, Foster, Rhodes, and J. Foster started, with small packs, for the first cabins, intending from thence to follow the trail of the person that had left the morning previous. The other three remained behind to cache and secure the goods necessarily left there. Knowing the Donners had a considerable sum of money, we searched diligently, but were unsuccessful. The party from the cabins were unable to keep the trail of the mysterious personage, owing to the rapid melting of the snow; they, therefore, went direct to the cabins, and upon entering, discovered Kiesburg lying down amidst the human bones, and beside him a large pan full of fresh liver and lights. They asked him what had become of his companions, whether they were alive, and what had become of Mrs. Donner. He answered them by stating that they were all dead. Mrs. Donner, he said, had, in attempting to cross from one cabin to another, missed the trail, and slept out one night, that she came to his camp the next night, very much fatigued, he made her a cup of coffee, placed her in bed, and rolled her well in the blanket, but the next morning found her dead. He ate her body, and found her flesh the best he had ever tasted. He further stated, that he obtained from her body at least four pounds of fat. No traces of her person could be found, nor the body of Mrs. Murphy, either. When the last company left camp, three weeks previous,

Mrs. Donner was in perfect health, though unwilling to come and leave her husband there, and offered $500 to any person or persons who would come out and bring them in—saying this in the presence of Kiesburg—and that she had plenty of tea and coffee. We suspected that it was she who had taken the piece from the shoulder of beef in the chair before mentioned. In the cabin with Kiesburg were found two kettles of human blood, in all supposed to be over one gallon. Rhodes asked him where he got the blood. He answered, 'There is blood in dead bodies.' They asked him numerous questions, but he appeared embarrassed, and equivocated a great deal, and in reply to their asking him where Mrs. Donner's money was, he evinced confusion, and answered, that he knew nothing about it—that she must have cached it before she died. 'I hav'n't it,' said he, 'nor the money, nor the property, of any person, living or dead!' They then examined his bundle, and found silks and jewelry, which had been taken from the camp of the Donners, amounting in value to about $200. On his person they discovered a brace of pistols, recognized to be those of George Donner, and while taking them from him, discovered something concealed in his waistcoat, which on being opened was found to be $225 in gold.

Before leaving the settlements, the wife of Kiesburg had told us that we would find but little money about him; the men, therefore, said to him, that they knew he was lying to them, and that he was well aware of the place of concealment of the Donners' money. He declared, before Heaven, he knew nothing concerning it, and that he had not the property of any one in his possession. They told him, that to lie to them would effect nothing; that there were others, back at the cabins, who, unless informed of the spot where the treasure was hidden, would not hesitate to hang him upon the first tree. Their threats were of no avail; he still affirmed his ignorance and innocence. Rhodes took him aside and talked to him kindly, telling him, that if he would give the information desired, he should receive from their hands the best of treatment, and be in every way assisted, otherwise the party back at Donners' camp would, upon its arrival, and his refusal to discover to them the place where he had deposited this money, immediately put him to death. It was all to no purpose, however, and they prepared to return to us, leaving him in charge of the packs, and assuring him of their determination to visit him in the morning; and that he must make up his mind during the night. They then started back and joined us at the Donners' camp.

April 20—we all started for Bear River valley, with packs of one hundred pounds each; our provisions being nearly consumed, we were obliged to make haste away. Came within a few hundred yards of the cabin which Kiesburg occupied, and halted to prepare breakfast, after which we proceeded to the cabin. I now asked Kiesburg if he was willing to disclose to me where he had concealed the money. He turned somewhat pale, and again protested his ignorance. I said to him, 'Kiesburg, you know well where Donner's money is, and d—n you, you shall tell me! I am not going to multiply words with you, or say but little about it, bring me that rope!' He then arose from his pot of soup and human flesh and begged me not to harm him; he had not the money nor the goods; the silk clothing and money which were found upon him the previous day, and which he then declared belonged to his wife, he now said were the property of others in California. I then told him I did not wish to hear more from him, unless he at once informed us where he had concealed the money of those orphan children; then producing the rope I approached him. He became frightened, but I bent the rope around his neck and threw him, after a struggle, on the ground, and as I tightened the cord and choked him, he cried out that he would confess all upon release. I then permitted him to arise.

He still seemed inclined to be obstinate, and made much delay in talking; finally, but with evident reluctance, he led the way back to the Donners' camp, about ten miles distant, accompanied by Rhodes and Tucker. While they were absent, we moved all our packs over to the lower end of the lake, and made all ready for a start when they should return. Mr. Foster went down to the cabin of Mrs. Murphy, his mother-in-law, to see if any property remained there worth collecting and securing; he found the body of young Murphy, who had been dead about three months, with the breast and skull cut open, and the brains, liver and lights taken out; and this accounted for the contents of the pan which stood beside Kiesburg, when he was found. It appears that he had left at the other camp the dead bullock and horse, and on visiting this camp and finding the body thawed out, took therefrom the brains, liver and lights.

Tucker and Rhodes came back the next morning, bringing $273 that had been cached by Kiesburg, who after disclosing to them the spot, returned to the cabin. The money had been hidden directly underneath the projecting limb of a large tree, the end of which seemed to point precisely to the treasure buried in the earth. On their return, and passing the cabin, they saw the unfortunate man within, devouring the remaining brains and liver left from his morning repast. They hurried him away, but before leaving, he gathered together the bones and heaped them all in a box he used for the purpose, blessed them and the cabin, and said, 'I hope God will forgive me what I have done, I couldn't help it! And I hope I may get to heaven yet!'

We asked Kiesburg why he did not use the meat of the bullock and horse instead of human flesh. He replied, he had not seen them. We then told him we knew better, and asked him why the meat in the chair had not been consumed. He said, 'Oh, it's too dry eating! The liver and the lights were a great deal better, and the brains made good soup!' We then moved on, and camped on the lake for the night.

April 21—started for Bear River Valley this morning, found the snow from six to eight feet deep, camped on Yuva river for the night. On the 22nd, traveled down Yuva about eighteen miles, and camped at the head of Bear River valley. On the 25th, moved down to the lower end of the valley, met our horses, and came in."

* * *

Although the events depicted in this novel are based on fact, this is a work of fiction. My great regret is that for the sake of clarity I have had to concentrate my efforts on just a handful of the Donner Party members. There were many more than I have mentioned here, all of them equally tragic and equally heroic. I wish I could have given every one of them a voice.

There are some primary source materials, in particular a diary kept in the camp by Patrick Breen, and some not-quite-so-reliable accounts written by survivors from the party. Many of these had been small children at the time and in some cases these accounts were written a considerable time after the event. There is a diary purportedly written as a contemporaneous document by Mr. Reed. However, it would appear that many of the entries were made at some time after the event, probably by Mr. Reed himself and possibly as an attempt to justify his poor leadership.

W. C. McGlashan wrote a long and somewhat florid account of the party's travails based on interviews with these survivors and others, and there are some contemporary newspaper accounts, published over the years, including several contradictory interviews given by Jean-Pierre Trudeau and several more by Mr. Eddy.

None of these accounts wholly explains the sequence

of events or the rationale behind the various decisions that led to this tragedy. Although since then there has been a flood of writing on the Reed-Donner Party, much of this has been little more than a rehash of speculation and misinformation. On that basis, I make no apology for inventing a character who did not exist, and, through her voice, drawing my own conclusions as to what happened, when, and why.

The Thirty Days Prayer

A note about the Thirty Days Prayer mentioned in Patrick Breen's diary. Mr. Breen was a devout Catholic. Although I have been unable to determine precisely which prayer this would have been, the list of Catholic prayers includes only one that specifically mentions thirty days in its title; on that basis and given the very appropriate wording of the Thirty Days Prayer to St. Joseph, I have taken the liberty of assuming this is the prayer to which he was referring. I am indebted to Dr. Kate Wharton from Lambeth Palace (thank you, Kate!), for her advice on this matter.

"Lead, Kindly Light"

I have quoted this lovely song as being sung for Baylis Williams's funeral. The lyrics were written in 1833 by John Henry Newman, an English cardinal. Although I cannot ascertain whether the song was known in America more than ten years later, it seems reasonable to assume it was, so I took the authorial liberty of including it, as it seems so very apt.

Louis Keseberg

Louis Keseberg eventually arrived safely in California and was reunited with his wife, though Ada Keseberg perished on the journey out of the mountains. He fathered several more children but his life proved to be a catalog of misfortune and disaster, as one business venture after another failed. He never recovered from the slurs cast upon his character by the reports of Mr. Eddy and Mr. Foster and the contents of the Fourth Relief diary, and died in penury.

The Washoe Indians

This peaceful nomadic tribe inhabited the foothills of the Sierra Nevada. There is one mention of them in Mr. Breen's diary, when he records meeting a member of the tribe and being given some fibrous root vegetables to eat. In their own (oral) history they recount seeing white settlers trapped in a camp and making some efforts to assist them, by leaving food for them at the edge of the camp. Based on the geography of their travel patterns, it seems more likely than not that the camp referred to was that of the Donners at Alder Creek. It would seem that the food they left was either not discovered, or was not recognized for food as such, and that, upon witnessing the camp inhabitants resort to cannibalism, they were too afraid to make further contact with them.

It was also the Washoe Indians who carried the few survivors of the Snowshoe Party down off the mountain and to the Johnson homestead.

Mr. Eddy's Death

Mr. Eddy's death is recorded as being on Saturday, December 24, 1859, but my narrator could not have read his obituary in the *Sonoma County Journal* on that same day as it was not published until January 1860. Again, I hope my readers will forgive me.

Acknowledgments

Thank you, first of all, to Eric Myers, my agent, and John Scognamiglio and the rest of the team at Kensington Books, for taking a chance on an unknown author, encouraging me, and answering my innumerable questions along the way.

I was greatly helped by the following: Dana Goodyear's article published in *The New Yorker*, April 14, 2006, *Excavating the Donner Party*; Daniel M. Rosen's website, The Donner Party; and Kristin Johnson's website, New Light on the Donner Party. I also made full use of a fantastic photographic record of the trail with accompanying notes compiled by Mr. Ted Davison, which gave me a useful visual guide to the route and the terrain covered by the party. I must also thank Mr. George Webber from the Buena Vista Winery in Sonoma for his advice.

Thanks also to Gillian Slovo and the rest of my friends from the Faber Academy writing course, whose encouragement and constructive criticism helped me get started on the novel (particular thanks to Kate Wharton from Lambeth Palace for her help regarding the "Thirty Days Prayer"). Carrie Plitt, Lizzie Kramer, and David Smith were generous with their advice.

Vicky Hurst and Debby Turner have been unwavering in their belief in me. Heartfelt thanks, last but not least, to my family, who have cheered me on at every step.

A READING GROUP GUIDE

WHEN WINTER COMES

V.A. Shannon

About This Guide

The suggested questions are included to enhance your group's reading of V.A. Shannon's *When Winter Comes*!

DISCUSSION QUESTIONS

1. One of the underlying themes of the novel is that of a woman's role in society at the time. How is this explored, and how does Jacob's gift of a journal, and the accompanying silver chain and key, introduce us to this theme?

2. Throughout the novel there is reference to storytelling in all its various forms. Discuss the significance of the various forms of storytelling that appear in the novel. There are some "hidden" references to fairy tales—can you identify these?

3. We never discover the real identity of our narrator. Is it significant that she finally uses her real name when she signs her account of her journey with the Donner Party—and why is it never revealed to us, the reader?

4. Throughout the novel there is a motif of flowers, gardens, and horticulture in various forms. What does this represent to the narrator, and how does it contribute to the structure of the book in general?

5. How is the theme of motherhood and mother-daughter relationships explored through the novel? What does it contribute to the narrator's relationship with her own mother?

6. How do you think Jacob will react to the disclosure of his wife's secret?

7. Is Mr. Keseberg a sympathetic character?

8. We are first introduced to Mr. Eddy through the medium of the newspaper where he is described as a hero—"the savior of the Donner Party"—on the basis

of his journey through the mountains to get help for those left behind. Mr. Keseberg is likewise presented as a villain. How do you think our narrator would be presented in a newspaper account?

9. Why do you think the novel is structured with the two different time elements? Would it have been as (or more) effective written as a straightforward description of the journey?
10. Why do you think the visit to the Sonoma County Fair is included in the novel?
11. What is the significance of the various discussions about slavery?
12. Jacob Klein, Louis Keseberg, Landrum Murphy—how do these three impact on the narrator's life? In different circumstances, which of these would she have married?